# A Tail for Two

## MARA WELLS

sourcebooks
casablanca

*For my dad, Herman Geerling, who taught
me the three Ps: prayers, perseverance, and
patience. Thank you for a lifetime of love.*

Published by Sourcebooks Casablanca, an imprint of Sourcebooks
P.O. Box 4410, Naperville, Illinois 60567-4410
(630) 961-3900
sourcebooks.com

Printed and bound in Canada.
MBP 10 9 8 7 6 5 4 3 2 1

# CHAPTER 1

*I'LL NEVER SWIPE RIGHT AGAIN.* CARRIE BURNS EYED THE man waving her over to a small table for two wedged between a sickly potted spider plant and the large front window of the newest coffee shop in her neck of Miami Beach. The small neighborhood was, as her ex-husband used to describe it, "just north of the tourist trap" that was South Beach. The space was perhaps too intimate, as evidenced by the number of people Carrie bopped with her oversize shoulder bag when she squeezed by them on her way to lucky date number thirteen.

Not that this was her thirteenth date with him. Oh no. In her limited time in the online dating world, she'd never been on a single second date. But after a dozen first dates, she'd hoped that number thirteen would be the one. Not The One, with wedding bells and coordinated calendars, but at least a second date. So far, though, it wasn't looking good.

For one, the man, a banker named Daniel Merrifield, was significantly older than his profile picture and dating profile suggested. *Late thirties? Yeah, right.* Not that there was anything wrong with aging. She hoped to live to a ripe old age herself, but she was really over older men who only wanted to date younger women.

And it wasn't like she was so young herself. With a failed marriage behind her and a toddler waiting for her at home, Carrie often felt older than her actual thirty years. She hadn't yet found a gray hair amid her brown strands, but with the dual strain of maintaining her business and caring for her active son, she was expecting one any day. She glanced at her phone before sliding into the seat across from Daniel. No panicked messages from the babysitter, a teen girl who lived with her parents in the condo above Carrie's and who both Carrie and her son, Oliver, adored. No, the only one feeling panic was Carrie.

"Hello, Carrie." Daniel half stood, then quickly sat again, smoothing a palm down his paisley tie, and handed her a menu. "Order anything you like. My treat."

Carrie really shouldn't judge him on so few words. And yet. "I prefer separate checks."

Daniel frowned, salt-and-pepper eyebrows slamming together over his prominent nose. "The espresso is quite good."

"You've been here before?" Carrie kept her attention on the menu, scanning the double-sided laminate sheet for her favorite coffees—something with as much sugar as caffeine and preferably topped with about three inches of whipped cream. "Do you live nearby?"

"No, Brickell." Daniel picked at the corner of the menu, shredding the laminate seal. Another strike, him making things worse for a start-up coffee shop in the ultra-competitive Miami market by defacing their new materials. Of course, the owners could've sprung for a more durable menu in anticipation of customers like Daniel, but folks new to owning and operating small businesses weren't always prepared for the idiosyncrasies of the public.

Carrie resisted the urge to take the menu from him with a gentle reprimand about respecting others' property, like she would've done with her son, and instead listened to Daniel as he gamely pushed forward with their date. "The espressos have good Yelp reviews. That's what I'll order, if a waiter ever deigns to give us some attention."

"The Beach is kind of famous for its poor service." Carrie forced a laugh. *What's the point of dating if you don't have a good time?* She would have a good time. *They* would have a good time. She folded her hands on top of her menu and smiled across the table at Daniel's serious face. "The upside is there's never a rush. We'll have plenty of time to get to know each other a bit."

Daniel checked his watch, a combo time keeper and activity tracker-type contraption, clearly not charmed by her smile or her there's-always-a-silver-lining worldview. "I have a meeting in less than an hour."

"Oh." Carrie schooled her features. It was four in the afternoon. Even if they only spent twenty minutes together, factoring in travel time, he should've counted on at least an hour, if not longer, for their date. What kind of banker had after-hours meetings? The kind who lined up multiple dates on the same night was her bet.

Daniel half stood again, scanning the crowded room until he locked onto a server standing by the cashier. Daniel snapped his fingers and pointed at their table before sliding back into his seat with a disgruntled sigh.

Carrie didn't like Daniel's attitude about their server, wherever he or she might be. Carrie'd worked her way through college waiting tables at a diner near her campus. Serving was hard work, work she'd gladly left behind when she graduated, and she found herself bristling at his whole attitude.

In fact, everything about this date was one huge red flag. She should run while she had the chance. Pretend there was a babysitting emergency. Yeah, that was what she'd do.

"What can I get for you?" Their waiter couldn't be any older than Oli's babysitter, a hair shy of sixteen. He was gangly, the kind of tall a man grows into, but he'd need a few more years to look comfortable in his body. A giant Adam's apple bobbed as he recited some drink specials for the day.

Daniel ordered his espresso, but Carrie was swayed by the list of specials.

"May I hear them again?" She smiled at the waiter, and his cheeks flamed.

Daniel sighed like this whole thing tried his patience, which made Carrie want to ask more questions. But that would merely prolong the date, so she selected a salted caramel latte with extra whipped cream and let the waiter escape.

"What do you do again?" Daniel waved a hand, like the answer was a wisp of smoke he couldn't quite grasp.

"I own an interior design firm." She slipped him her brightly colored business card out of habit. Single-mom, single-proprietor businesses required a lot of hustle.

"Right." Daniel fluffed a paper napkin on his lap, leaving the card untouched on the table between them. "Decorating."

"Design." Carrie knew she shouldn't be annoyed. She took a calming breath and fingered the single pearl on the white-gold chain around her neck. "I create the feel of a space using color, shape, pattern."

"Like I said, decorating. I'm sure you're good at it." Daniel's gaze tracked over her face and down into her cleavage. She was always overdressed, but that was her thing. In her line of business, she couldn't afford to be seen with a hair out of place or an outfit not perfectly coordinated. Clients drew conclusions in a blink of an eye, and Carrie liked to think that the world was full of potential clients.

"Thank you." Carrie wasn't sure his comment was a compliment, but she decided to take it as one. It was clearer by the moment that they wouldn't suit romantically, but if she played nice and made a good impression, maybe he'd remember her name if his bank ever decided to redesign their lobby or upgrade their executive offices.

Their drinks arrived, his a tiny cup he downed like a shot, hers overflowing with whipped cream topped with a caramel drizzle. She took a long, hot sip. Her first true smile of the afternoon overtook her face.

"So what do you think of this place?" Daniel swirled his empty cup. "Design-wise, I mean."

Carrie took a moment to soak in the atmosphere, to review her initial impressions, to think about the Coffee Pot Spot as a client.

"First, no dying plants." She used her chin to indicate the failing spider plant behind him. "If you're going to have plants, they've got to be alive and healthy. Anything less is depressing and creates a negative atmosphere. Given they've been open less than a month and that poor spider is already on its last legs, I'd say no live plants for them."

"Aren't fake plants tacky?" Daniel clinked his empty espresso cup on its miniature saucer.

"I don't love fake plants. There are other ways to bring color and life into a room. Some outdoor photography perhaps. I'd have to talk theme with the owner. And also room capacity. Of course, you want to get as many chairs in the room as possible, but not at the expense of safety. Anyone with a bag creates a fire hazard when they set it down." Carrie swept her arm to indicate the book bags, briefcases, and purses as large as hers blocking the aisles from where they hung on the backs of their chairs.

"Why wouldn't their designer have thought of that?"

"My guess? The owners did the design themselves." Carrie took a long sip of her drink. Caffeine and sugar, such a heavenly combination. "It's always tempting for new business owners to try to save money that way."

"It makes sense." Daniel nodded like he was a design expert. "Tables, chairs, hang some stuff on the wall. How hard can it be?"

Carrie let out a long, controlled breath. This was part of her job after all, educating people about why they needed her. "Let me put it to you this way. I've lived in homes my entire life. I'm very familiar with what makes a house: walls, roof, foundations, electrical, plumbing. How hard could it be, right?"

Daniel snorted. "It's not the same thing."

"Isn't it? I can watch videos about how to install a ceiling fan. Why should I hire someone else to do it?"

"I'm getting your point." Daniel drummed impatient fingers on the table. "There's more to it than meets the eye."

"Yes." Carrie nursed her coffee, perversely compelled to drink as slowly as possible in light of his haste. "If I do my job well, the effect should be effortless. I don't want clients to see the design; I want them to feel it."

In her eagerness, Carrie leaned across the tiny table. When she pulled back, the table wobbled. She grabbed the edge to correct it, managing to tip her coffee at exactly the right angle to pour salted caramel latte down the front of her lavender silk tank top and right onto the lap of her favorite pencil skirt.

Daniel stood like he was going to help her. But what could he do?

She shooed him back down with a wiggle of her fingers. "I believe that's my cue to head home to my son."

"Your son?" Daniel looked stunned.

She mentioned being a mother on her dating profile, but she'd found most men didn't do much more than look at pictures before deciding which way to swipe.

"He's two, almost three." She reached into her bag and pulled out Winnie-the-Pooh wipes and a stain-remover pen. "Quite a handful." Using her son to scare off Daniel may have been overkill, but the look on the banker's face was worth it.

"Nice to meet you." He threw down a couple bucks for his espresso and fled the scene. The gangly server showed up with a damp rag and helped her put herself to rights. She left him a generous tip and squeezed her way out of the overcrowded coffee shop. Thirteen was definitely not her lucky number.

---

Lance Donovan pulled his work truck up onto the front lawn of the Dorothy, the decrepit Art Deco building his younger brother, Caleb, had convinced him to renovate. And it had taken some convincing. At eighteen, Lance had left home and never looked back. He'd never wanted anything to do with the Donovan real estate legacy his grandfather built and his father so casually destroyed. One summer interning at the Donovan main office was enough to open his eyes to the truth: his father, Robert Donovan, real estate tycoon and pillar of the Miami community, was a crook. It'd taken another decade and a half before he'd been caught, but Robert was now serving time in federal prison. As far as Lance was concerned, Robert was exactly where he belonged, and Lance'd had no intention of ever getting tangled up in a Donovan scheme again.

Somehow, though, Caleb got through to him. Maybe it was earnestness, Caleb's real desire to make the building a better place for the people who lived there. Maybe it was genetics, as much a part of him as his Donovan blue eyes and blond hair. Maybe it was destiny. Whatever it was, Lance now had one hell of a project on his hands. Step one: Get the Dorothy up to code so she could pass her long over-due forty-year inspection.

While he waited for the diesel engine to cool, he flipped through the city inspector's notes. Roof, electrical, plumbing, elevator. All pretty standard stuff on an old building and easy enough to do in the next few weeks. Once they passed the forty-year inspection, if everything went according to plan, he'd be done with the whole remodel in ten, twelve months tops. What job ever went to plan, though? In fifteen years of construction, he'd learned to expect the unexpected—and padded time estimates accordingly.

Lance swung out of the truck in a practiced move, his steel-toed work boots planting firmly on the Dorothy's scraggly grass. His crew should arrive in the next twenty minutes or so, but he always liked to arrive early on the opening day of a new job. It was corny, he knew, but he liked to spend a few minutes with the building, letting it know they were here to help and asking for its patience while they transformed it.

Inside the old-fashioned lobby with its stained terrazzo floors and fake palm tree in the corner, Lance took a seat on a sketchy rattan chair and closed his eyes.

"Sleeping on the job already?" A deep voice interrupted Lance's private moment with the building.

"That's how I make the big bucks." Lance stood to clap his brother on the shoulder. They were similar in height, though Lance had a few inches and a few pounds of muscle on his little brother. What marked them as brothers were the unmistakable blue eyes they inherited from their Grandpa William and the square jaws that hinted at their stubborn natures. They hadn't grown up together—different mothers, different homes—but in the few weeks he'd been working with Caleb, Lance had learned to respect his younger brother. He was a good guy, much too idealistic to be a true Donovan—a trait that made Lance feel protective of him. Ridiculous, of course. They were both grown men. Still, Lance hadn't been part of a real family since his divorce, and he had to admit that Caleb and his fiancée, Riley, felt like family.

LouLou, Caleb's step-poodle, jumped on Lance's knee and shoved her head into the flat of his palm. Lance scratched her head and grinned at Caleb.

"You ready for all the chaos?" Lance motioned toward the elevator with a dramatic sweep of his arm. It was the first major project, since it was the most urgent in the fifty-five-plus building. Between heart conditions, canes, and walkers, many of the residents would be unable to reach their second-floor apartments if the elevator went out.

"More chaos than wedding planning? Impossible." Caleb tugged on LouLou's leash. "We need to head outside. Little dogs, little bladders."

Lance shook his head, overgrown hair brushing his ears. "You love it all, don't you? The wedding stuff, the poodle."

"I love Riley."

Caleb's face was so serene that Lance had no doubt of his brother's sincerity. He bit his tongue to keep from telling Caleb what marriage was really like—how it starts out all sparkly and sex on every surface of your home but ends in bitter words, resentment, and divorce lawyers.

Caleb pointed at the glass doors. "We'll be at the dog park if you need us."

"Wait!" Riley busted through the stairwell door and into the lobby, wild strawberry-blond hair flying in all directions. "I want to go, too."

"Didn't Grams need you?" Caleb handed the leash to Riley. LouLou spun, managing to tangle her front legs in the nylon lead. Caleb knelt to untangle her.

"Classic Grams exaggeration." Riley rolled her eyes. "What she needed was batteries in her TV remote changed. We're good. Let's go before another crisis arises. I wanted to talk to you about maybe changing venues?"

"That's my cue." Lance strode to the glass front doors and held one side open for his brother and soon-to-be sister-in-law. "No wedding talk in front of the bachelor."

Riley turned wide eyes on Caleb. "You didn't ask him?"

Caleb stood, LouLou's leash free and clear. "When have I had the chance?"

"Now's a good time." Riley nudged him toward his brother. "LouLou and I will be outside. Catch up when you're done."

"Done? I don't like the sound of that." Lance crossed his arms over his chest, narrowing suspicious eyes at Riley.

Caleb ran a hand over his buzzed-short hair "Look, Lance, I know we haven't always been close."

"Like ever." Lance snorted.

"But we are brothers." Caleb plowed on, clearly uncomfortable. He rocked back and forth on his heels. "And I do need a best man for this wedding."

"Me?" Lance rocked back on his heels, too. He'd almost forgotten to invite Caleb to his own wedding. It'd been his ex-wife, Carrie, who'd insisted on inviting his dad's side of the family. He was glad she'd forced the issue, but at the time, he'd been angry at Caleb for doing nothing at his reception except drink by himself in the corner. No brotherly toast? What had he expected, though, from a brother he hadn't talked to in years? Families were complicated, no doubt. "Best man?"

Caleb smiled. "Yeah, you. My big brother. My business partner. Who else?"

"Knox?" Lance named their oldest brother, throwing him under the bus in his panic to get out of anything having to do with weddings.

Caleb's smile widened, the smug bastard. "Yep, Knox, too."

"Well, you can't have two best men."

"Yes, I can. It's my wedding. I make the rules."

"That's not how weddings work."

"It's how our wedding is going to work."

"You really don't want me." Lance didn't want to be the rain cloud on Caleb's sunny day. He decided honesty was his best policy. Or whatever. "I'll curse the whole day."

"It's important to me." Caleb kept that patient smile on his face, reminding Lance of all the times his mother had come to pick him up and Caleb had stood outside the house waving and smiling until their car was out of sight. "It's important to Riley."

Lance sighed. He did like Riley. She'd done something to Caleb, made him less of a Donovan and more himself somehow. He sighed again. He'd known how this conversation would end as soon as it started.

"Fine. I'll be your best man."

Caleb slapped him on the back. "Excellent. Wait 'til you see the cummerbunds."

Lance groaned. Weddings were so not his thing.

# CHAPTER 2

"HOLD ON, YOU LITTLE PISTOL." LANCE TUGGED ON LouLou's leash, once again cursing himself for agreeing to poodle-sit for Caleb and Riley. They hadn't even left on their cruise yet, an extravagant affair they'd arranged for the Dorothy's second-floor residents to get them out of the building while the elevator was being replaced. The two occupied apartments on the first floor hadn't wanted to be left out of the fun, so they got tickets, too. Leave it to his softhearted brother to foot the bill for a vacation. Then again, once the wheels of justice crushed the Dorothy's former management company for embezzling funds from the building, Caleb would be well compensated.

Why was he letting this bossy canine pull him to the dog park again? Oh right. Caleb claimed Lance needed practice. Riley was anxious about leaving LouLou. Apparently, since adopting the small dog, Riley and LouLou had never been apart for more than a day. Riley would feel better, Caleb had explained, if she knew that Lance and LouLou were already pals before the trip.

Lance could empathize. When he and his ex-wife separated, she'd kept their Jack Russell, Beckham, and he'd missed the dog more than he thought he would. He missed the comforting lump of him under the covers, warming his feet in the night. He missed Beckham's excited yip when someone knocked on the door and the crazy jumping for joy when Lance came home. No matter how late it was,

Beckham was always thrilled to see him. His ex? Not so much. She'd roll to the edge of the bed when he climbed in, her back to him, pretending she didn't know he was there.

It hadn't always been that way, of course. In the beginning, they'd burned up that king-size bed in the bedroom she'd decorated in his favorite shades of blue. They'd doted on their puppy, taking long walks around the neighborhood and bringing him to weekend brunches on Lincoln Road. Waiters brought Beckham a bowl of water and a dog treat, and he'd settle under the table, happy to shred a paper napkin while Lance and Carrie shared a pitcher of mimosas. Not that he loved mimosas all that much, but they were Carrie's favorite, so he sipped them and enjoyed how animated she'd get after the second one, waving her hands around and telling stories about work too loudly. Yeah, he'd loved that version of Carrie and, truth be told, missed her, too.

He shook off glum thoughts about his ex. Sure, there were things he'd do differently now, but ultimately, their breakup was for the best. One workaholic was tough on a relationship, but two ruined it. By the end, the only thing they'd had in common was Beckham.

LouLou halted in front of the dog park gate, waiting for Lance to lift the latch. Inside, she wiggled while he unhooked her and opened the second gate. He hung the leash on one of the many hooks mounted on the fence, watching as LouLou sprinted for a large black Lab lounging near one of the newly planted palm trees. The big dog rose to its feet, greeting LouLou with a butt sniff and a nudge on her side. Lance missed how it happened—secret signal? habit?—but the two took off at a run, LouLou weaving figure eights through the lush grass while her dog park buddy chased her.

"Good friends, aren't they?"

Lance had to look down to see who was talking. A small, steel-haired woman grinned up at him, a tissue crumpled in one hand that she used to dab at the perspiration gathering on her hairline. Her tropical-print blouse was louder than the last rock concert he'd attended.

"Eliza." He greeted the woman warmly, kissing both cheeks in Miami fashion. They'd had a few encounters when he'd been doing the planning stages for the renovation. She and her dog didn't live in the Dorothy, but she enjoyed watching the goings-on from her house across the street.

"Is everything okay with Riley?" Eliza's crinkled eyes showed more smile wrinkles, but now they were furrowed with worry. "Why do you have LouLou?"

"Practice for the cruise."

"Ah." Eliza's face relaxed. "Me, I can't stand those things. Long lines. Too many people. Good food, though. I'll give 'em that."

"So I've heard." Lance couldn't remember the last time he'd taken a vacation. Was it? No, it couldn't be. Surely he'd gone somewhere with someone since his and Carrie's long weekend in the Keys right before the wedding. He simply couldn't think of it right now. Tampa maybe? No, that had been for a job. Man, he needed some time off and a plane ticket to somewhere far away. Greece popped to mind, but no, that had been Carrie's dream. The honeymoon they'd postponed and then never taken.

"Ah well." Eliza called Lady to her. "Got some family

coming into town soon, so I'll have a full house. My brother, his kids, his grandkids. Amazing how time flies, isn't it? Blink your eyes and the kids are grown. My oldest grand-nephew just made partner at a law firm, if you can believe that!"

Lance made sounds of agreement, understanding this was the type of conversation that didn't require a response, not unless he also had lawyer-type grandnephews, which he didn't. Though he might soon, the way Caleb and Riley carried on.

"Anything I should worry about here?" Lance pointed out LouLou snuffling in the grass, tail wagging while she gleefully shoveled dirt with her nose. Better to change the subject before he was made captive to a detailed discussion about the life and career choices of all Eliza's extended family. "It's been a while since I had a dog."

"That one can take of herself. Make sure you've got her leash on when you leave. She's a runner. Riley can tell you; once she gets going, she's hard to catch."

"Duly noted." Lance planted his hands on his hips and watched LouLou inspect the base of each weaving pole with her nose.

"Guess we'll be seeing you around." Eliza waved her tissue at him and strolled toward the gate, Lady trotting beside her.

Once both gates were closed, Lance relaxed onto a bone-shaped bench, tilting back his head with a long sigh. The past week had been a whirlwind of construction prep. And by whirlwind, he meant haunting city hall, waiting on permits to clear, and spending hours on the phone tracking deliveries. His nightmare scenario was that the residents would return from their cruise and the elevator wouldn't yet be operational. Elevators weren't his specialty, so he'd brought in an elevator company—one he'd worked with before—to handle the installation, but he was still the contractor and therefore still in charge of the schedule.

A cold nose nudged his hand where it rested on the steel bench. Thinking it was LouLou, he casually petted the dog's head, but instead of the poodle puff, he encountered the coarse coat of a terrier. Lance opened his eyes and found himself staring into the eyes of an adorable Jack Russell. It had the same brown mask as Beckham, with the same white stripe between his eyes and the same white body with one large spot over his left hip.

"You could be Beckham's twin, couldn't you?" He scratched under the dog's chin, exactly the way Beckham liked, and the dog's tail beat wildly. "What do we have here?"

A mutilated tennis ball hung out of the side of the dog's mouth. Lance played a bit of tug-of-war to free it, a game that made the dog's tail beat even faster, and inspected the mangled toy. It was still roughly ball shaped, so he gave it a throw, and the dog tore after it, springing across the dog park as fast as his little legs would take him.

"That's my dog." A muddy hand slapped down on Lance's jean-clad knee. A kid looked up at him with big, blue eyes set in a tiny but sharp face. His dark hair was cut short with a longer bang fighting back against the gel that was supposed to hold it out of the boy's eyes.

"He's a handsome fellow. Reminds me of my old dog." Lance gently pried the child's hand off his leg. He was in work clothes, so the dirt didn't bother him. The kid's parent was probably nearby, though, and he figured they didn't need to find their son cuddled up to a stranger in a park. Didn't they have programs in schools warning kids about stranger danger anymore? But this boy looked too young to be in school yet.

"My old dog," the boy repeated, leaning against Lance's leg.

Lance scooted over on the bench. Really, this kid needed to learn some boundaries. "Yes, I had a Jack Russell just like this one. His name was Beckham. What's your dog's name?"

"Beckham!" The boy clapped his hands together. "Beckham is a good dog."

Lance didn't have a lot of experience with young children, or any children for that matter. "Your dog is also named Beckham?" It seemed incredibly unlikely, but hey, who better to name an athletic, driven dog like the Jack Russell after than the retired footballer who'd inspired a whole generation of American soccer players? He'd certainly thought it was the perfect name when he and Carrie found the dog bouncing off the walls, literally, of his pen at the local animal shelter.

The boy clapped again. "Beckham!" The terrier bounded back, jumping higher than the kid was tall. Lance laughed at the sight. This Beckham was so much like his old dog that Lance's laugh turned brittle. It *was* Beckham, his Beckham. His ex must've given his dog away to complete strangers.

Why? She knew he'd take Beckham back in a heartbeat, so the only reason that made any sense was malice. She'd fought to get ownership of Beckham and then given him away at the first chance, just to spite Lance. He'd never thought she was that cruel, but divorce showed you a lot of things about your mate that you didn't necessarily want to see.

"Oliver! Beckham!" A woman's voice caused both the boy and the terrier to spin toward the gate.

It couldn't be, but of course it was. Dark hair pulled back in a smooth, high bun, coordinated leggings and tank top with green and gold accents, dark running shoes with gold laces. Even dressed for a workout, Carrie still managed to be chic. She held a smoothie in one hand, cell phone in the other. A small knapsack rode low on her back. He had time to take it all in, the very realness of her. Straight back, long neck. Sleek sunglasses that hid the hazel depths of her eyes. Was pineapple-mango still her go-to smoothie choice, or had her tastes changed in the years they'd been apart?

"Carrie." The one word felt awkward on his tongue. Too heavy. Too unused. Even in his head, he usually called her his ex. Carrie felt too intimate. Held too many memories, memories he'd done his best to obliterate. Still, here they were, popped into his mind as fresh as the days they were made, as painful as the conversation where she'd handed him divorce papers. Yeah, Carrie.

"Lance?" She whipped off her sunglasses, and her gaze ping-ponged from where Oliver's hand rested on Lance's knee to Beckham's enthusiastic licking of Lance's work boots. "What're you doing here?"

Her voice was the same, that low timbre that strummed through him, soothing nerves he hadn't known were agitated until they calmed. Perhaps they'd been agitated for years, three years and nine months to be exact, but he pushed that thought away along with the other uncomfortable memories and forced a smile to his face. At least she hadn't given his dog away. There was that to be grateful for at least.

"Caleb owns that building now." He pointed toward the Dorothy with his chin. "Lives there, too. I'm watching his dog. Or rather, practice watching for when he and his fiancée, Riley, take all the old folks on the cruise."

"You're finally talking to Caleb?" Carrie shoved her sunglasses back on and took a visible breath, chest rising and falling, drawing his attention to how the workout wear outlined her breasts. Okay, he could admit he missed Carrie's breasts, their weight in his hands, the way her nipples puckered before he even touched her as if anticipating the pleasure to come. That part of their relationship had never been an issue, and as he felt an ill-timed erection pushing against the fly of his jeans, he was hard pressed to remember exactly what all their issues had been.

"Uh, yeah." His voice came out as awkward as his body felt. "We're partners, actually. With Knox."

"Well, that's something, isn't it?" She stood so still that he knew she was nervous. She'd trained herself to hide all signs of nervousness. Carrie was not a fidgeter. She clamped down on her muscles the same way she did her feelings— total control at all times.

"How've you been?" It should've been his first question. He knew how to schmooze clients, but his small-talk skills scrambled at the glimpse of skin through the mesh cutout that ran diagonally across her leggings. Just as well. She ignored his attempts at polite chitchat.

"Oliver, come here." She held out her hand, and the grubby kid patted Lance's leg and hopped over to Carrie. She stepped so that she was between the child and Lance. "We'll leave you to it then."

"Wait." It'd been so long since he'd seen her that he

wasn't quite ready to watch her walk away. "What're you doing here? Do you live nearby?"

Carrie shook her head, the movement unsettling her bun. It didn't fall, though. It wouldn't dare. "Not exactly. We like to take Beckham on adventures. You remember how he is."

"Our little Jack Russell terrorist." Lance quirked a real smile her way, quoting a Jack Russell blog they used to follow when they first adopted Beckham. He'd been such a handful that they'd needed lots of advice. Luckily, the internet was full of it, and Jack Russell owners loved to talk about their rambunctious pets. Saying *terrorist* instead of *terrier* referred to how the little dogs took over your life and, if not exercised and kept busy enough, could wreak utter destruction in the home. "Still doing the big walk every morning, huh?"

Perhaps sensing the adults weren't going anywhere soon, Oliver plopped onto the ground. Beckham trotted over and climbed into his lap, nudging the boy's hand with his nose for petting. Lance remember that move all too well. How many mornings had Beckham woken him up with demands for attention? Carrie was not a morning person by any stretch of the imagination, so Beckham learned early that Lance was his best bet for an early-morning outing.

Carrie didn't answer his question. "We should be going."

Except Oliver and Beckham were now wrestling and oblivious to Carrie's attempts to get their attention.

"Cute kid." Lance didn't want to ask, but he had to. "Your son?"

Carrie's whole body stiffened. She nodded.

"How old is he?"

"Almost three."

Lance let out a low whistle. "Dang, Carrie, you didn't waste any time remarrying. And I guess husband number two talked you into kids, huh? Well, good for him."

"I did not remarry." Carrie's lips didn't move as she bit out the words.

"Oh." Lance's muscles tensed. He wasn't sure why. Maybe the shock. Carrie, a single mom? From the beginning of their marriage, they'd been in agreement: no kids. They had their careers to focus on, and neither one of them wanted to re-create the disasters to be found on both sides of their family. What happened to not only change her mind but to also make her go for it on her own? He rubbed his temple, trying to imagine a scenario in which she ended up with a baby. He did not like the first option that popped to mind. "Wait a minute. How old is Oliver?"

"I told you. Three." Carrie leaned down to hook Beckham to his leash. He protested by sprinting away, one of his favorite games. Oliver took off after him.

"No, you said 'almost.' Almost three." Lance wasn't the numbers guy his brother Caleb was, but he could handle the basics. Checking account, accounts payable and receivable. Counting forward and backward from nine months. "When's his birthday?"

Carrie mumbled something he couldn't hear.

"Did you say December?"

"Yes, he's a Christmas baby. Is that what you wanted to know? Are you happy now?"

Christmas Day minus nine months equaled a March conception, but he and Carrie split up in February. In fact, he'd sent back the divorce papers on Valentine's Day. Just because. So Oliver wasn't his. He should be relieved, right? He'd never wanted kids, never would. That Carrie changed her mind didn't mean he had to change his. Good for her. Girl power and all that.

"Congratulations." Now he was the one biting out words. Deep down, he could admit he didn't like the idea of Carrie having a baby with someone else. *Tough cookies, Lance.* "He's a good-looking kid. Seems smart, too."

Carrie choked on a swallow of smoothie. "Oh please. Complimenting him is like complimenting yourself."

Lance's eyebrows crashed into each other. "What're you talking about?"

Carrie searched his face, her hazel eyes filled with messages he couldn't read. "You don't remember."

Oliver and Beckham bounded back, the dog sliding to a stop directly in front of Carrie and the boy clinging to her leg.

"Say goodbye to the stranger," Carrie coaxed her son with a stiff jerk of her chin that tipped the bun at an awkward angle. It dangled like it wanted to fall, but Carrie quickly rewound her long, dark hair and secured it with a green band.

Oliver looked up at him, those eyes as blue as Grandpa William's. As Caleb's and Knox's. As his own. But women weren't pregnant for ten months, and besides, Carrie wouldn't have his child without telling him. Sure, they'd been angry at the end, but not so much that she'd keep something like this from him. No, ten months put Oliver in the safety zone of someone else's problem. Lots of people had blue eyes, and in every other way, the kid was the spitting image of his mom, complete with double dimples and her fine, sable hair.

"Bye-bye!" Oliver waved a dirt-streaked hand at him.

Carrie tugged on the leash, and Beckham followed her to the gate. Oliver chased after them, turning his head every few steps to look at Lance and wave again. Lance waved back.

*You don't remember.* Remember what?

And then he did. March. Grandpa William's birthday party. They hadn't told the family yet about the divorce, although Grandpa William knew they were separated. Even so, they'd been given the same bedroom they always shared when staying over, and rather than make a fuss, Lance offered to sleep in the reading chair by the window. But he'd had a few too many at dinner, and after dinner. So had Carrie. He hadn't slept in the chair.

He'd reasoned that one more time wouldn't hurt anything. The ink was barely dry on their divorce papers, and they were both willing. Who knew? Maybe it was the start of a reconciliation. It was hazy, all the details, but one memory stood out crystal clear. Waking up in the morning with an armful of Carrie, her sweet body curled into his. He'd felt peaceful for the first time in months. God, he loved this woman. He had tightened his grip, and she woke up, flipping to rest her head on his chest. She'd twisted her neck to look him in the eye.

"This doesn't change anything. You know that, right?"

Even with her warm body next to him, he'd felt chilled enough to pull a blanket over them. "Of course," he'd said, inching away from her. "Why would it?"

"Old habits." She'd swung her legs over the side, her back to him. "They're hard to break."

He'd wanted to say she was more to him than an old habit, but she'd already shrugged on her bra and was shimmying into her panties. She looked over her shoulder at him. "I'm sure your girlfriend wouldn't like to know about last night. I'll keep my mouth shut if you will."

He nodded, her words a blow to his gut. She knew about Rachelle? How? They'd only been seeing each other for a couple of weeks, since he'd finally flirted back with his client's daughter. After he signed the divorce papers, what did he have to lose? He'd hurried to finish up the Florida room Rachelle's father wanted added to the back of his ranch-style home so there'd be no conflict of interest. As soon as the last screen was in place, he'd asked Rachelle out for drinks. They'd been having fun together, that was all. It wasn't like he'd posted about it on social media or anything. His relationship status was still married, a situation he needed to update but couldn't quite bring himself to do. Not yet.

"Well?" Carrie fussed with the bow on the waistband of her panties. The elastic stretched across her smooth stomach, and he couldn't take his eyes off the freckle that lived an inch south of her bellybutton.

Lance shook his head, trying to get his mind right. "Last night never happened." The words came out as a vow. He'd taken the whole episode and buried it deep in his mind.

"That's the spirit." Carrie had smiled at him and slipped into the emerald sheath dress she'd worn to the party. In their five years of marriage, he'd zipped her up a million times. That morning, she didn't even ask. Her fingers fiddled with the zipper until she'd pulled it all the way up, taking twice as long as if she'd asked for his help. And somehow, that was the moment he really knew it was over. The zipper said it all.

Watching Carrie now as she carefully closed the double

gate and held Oliver's hand while they crossed the street to a small SUV across the street, it hit him harder than a ton of concrete pouring out of a mixer truck: Oliver was his son.

Worse, if he hadn't run into them today, she never would've told him.

Even worse, he didn't chase after them. Because honestly, he had no idea what to do. He sank back onto the bench, and LouLou jumped onto his lap. She licked at his chin, and for once, he didn't push her away.

"I'm a father," he told LouLou. She wagged her tail, and he smiled. "Yeah, it is pretty great, isn't it?"

# CHAPTER 3

SHE SHOULD'VE TOLD HIM. CARRIE CHASTISED HERSELF while she buckled Oliver into his car seat. He was such a good child, full of smiles and easygoing. He watched her out of his Donovan-blue eyes, patient as she fiddled with the complicated straps and buckles. Beckham was less patient, bouncing beside Oliver on the back seat. Once done with her son, she maneuvered Beckham into his red booster seat and strapped him in, too. He immediately pressed his nose to the window, adding more nose smears to the already smudged pane.

Taking her place as the chauffeur, she started up her Chevy Blazer and headed home to their small condo. It was only a few miles from the dog park they'd explored today, but with beach traffic, it'd take them fifteen minutes to get home. Why had she decided to go to Fur Haven? The write-up in the free local paper had described it as a paradise for dogs, and while it was certainly quite nice with all its shiny new equipment and fresh plugs of grass, "paradise" was stretching it a bit. She was always on the lookout for new places to take Beckham. The dog did love novelty. Although she'd seen Caleb Donovan's name attached to the park, she hadn't thought he'd be around, and she surely hadn't thought his brother would be anywhere nearby. Last she'd heard, the brothers hadn't spoken in years.

Now Lance was somehow working with Caleb and Knox? If the brothers were pulling together after their father's terrible trial, more power to them. She'd wanted to call Lance so many times during the media frenzy surrounding his father's conviction and sentencing, but she never had. One, because she had no right to, not anymore, and two, because of Oliver.

Which brought her back to that moment at the park when she'd seen her son standing next to his father and something inside her had flipped over. *Kerplunk.* Maybe it was her stomach that made her so queasy at the thought Lance would find out. Maybe it was her heart that made her eyes tear at the sight of father and son together. Maybe it was her pride that made her march over to them like nothing was amiss and try to brazen her way through the encounter like she hadn't kept a major secret from Lance, a secret she knew he was entitled to know but had rationalized away. He'd never wanted kids, and he'd stopped wanting her. She'd done him a favor, really, not telling him. What would he have done? It would only have led to more ugliness between them, and there'd already been plenty of that.

Besides, she'd intended to tell him. A few months after Grandpa William's birthday party, she'd taken a home pregnancy test. And gone to her gynecologist. And thought long and hard about what she wanted to do. She'd driven to see Lance, who still lived in their old condo on South Beach, to tell him she'd decided to have his baby. She'd planned to reassure him that nothing was expected of him, but she imagined that at some point, the child would want to meet its father, and she hoped Lance would be open to that idea.

She should've texted. Instead, she'd gotten caught up in some ridiculous fantasy where the pregnancy news magically brought her and Lance back together. Months of distance and miscommunication would disappear, and they'd be a family. A reunion like that should be face-to-face. She'd convinced herself surprising him was best. Looking back, she could only blame crazy pregnancy hormones for such delusions.

Rachelle opened the door. Rachelle, with her spiked pixie haircut and heavy eyeliner. Rachelle, who Carrie knew about in a theoretical way but hadn't actually met yet. Rachelle, who'd started dating Carrie's husband the minute the divorce was finalized. No, Rachelle had not been part of her baby-news plans.

"Hi." Carrie had stood on her old welcome mat, a sunburst made of coir fibers harvested from coconut husks, feeling uncharacteristically shabby in her stretchy yoga pants and off-the-shoulder knit top. "Is Lance home?"

Rachelle took her time looking Carrie up and down. Shabby and shabbier. Carrie looked back. It was hard to imagine a woman more different from herself. Rachelle was model-thin in a black tank top and satin shorts that looked like pajamas. It was midafternoon. Perhaps the shorts were a fashion statement of some kind.

"Lance?" Rachelle finally drawled out. "He's still sleeping." Rachelle yawned like Carrie was keeping her from joining him. "I'll tell him you stopped by. What's your name?"

"Sylvia." Carrie gave the name of her best friend from high school. If Rachelle didn't know who she was, Carrie wasn't about to be the ex-wife popping in with some maternity news. No, Lance could ponder who the mysterious Sylvia was for five seconds and then shrug it off. He wouldn't remember that Sylvia had taken a gap year in

Europe, fallen in love with a Parisian, and never returned to the United States.

"Okay." Rachelle leaned against the open door, light from the hallway catching on a ring. A diamond ring. On her left hand.

"Sorry to bother you. Tell him it wasn't important." Carrie lurched away, sure she was going to hurl all over the mother-in-law's tongue plants lined up in a neat row in the courtyard. She hadn't, though. Morning sickness was still a month away. She did, however, drive herself home and cry. She was going to be a single mom, and she was pretty sure it was going to suck.

Now, only a few years later, Carrie couldn't imagine her life without Oliver. She checked on him in the rearview mirror, happily bobbing his head to the song playing on the speakers. She used to love her Justin Timberlake and Taylor Swift, but these days, it was Disney songs and "Itsy Bitsy Spider" blasting from her sound system. Oliver was trying to create the thumb and pinkie finger ladder motion of the spider, but his coordination wasn't quite there yet, and he kept going thumb-thumb, pinkie-pinkie. It was so funny Carrie was tempted to whip out her phone for a video to send her mom, but they were almost home, and she didn't want to take the time to pull over. They'd see her mom, or Gamma as Oliver liked to say, in a few minutes, and Carrie's hectic day would begin.

Pulling into street parking across from her building, Carrie began the detail-oriented process of unpacking Oliver, Beckham, and the assorted child and dog accessories that traveled with them both. Chasing down a runaway chew toy and stuffing it in her purse, Carrie ran down her plan for the day: new-client meeting first thing, then on to the down-town penthouse currently under renovation to check on the aurora-marble and pearl-glass bathroom tiles that were supposed to be installed yesterday but that she suspected were not. This contractor had been nothing but problems—behind schedule every step of the way for no reason she could discern. It made her nervous. If this bathroom went well, she had a feeling the client would hire her to do the rest of the dwelling. If not, as she'd learned in the past, it'd be hard to collect final payment from an unhappy client. Home for a quick snack and snuggle with Oliver, and then off to a cock-tail hour where she hoped to get some new leads on jobs.

Working for herself was a lot of hustle, but it was a lot better than the position at the large design firm she'd had while married to Lance. As her own boss, she was able to make her own schedule, decide with whom and how much she worked, and most importantly, make time for Oliver. Yes, she missed her steady paycheck and premier health benefits, but thankfully, she and Oliver were healthy and doing fine on a low-cost health plan, and by hook or by crook, she was able to pay her bills.

"Here, let me help." Gamma lifted Oliver out of his car seat and propped him on her hip. Carrie's mom had recently turned fifty-two, but she sure didn't look it. Dark hair dyed to silky auburn and cut in an easy-to-care-for short bob with long bangs, she could pass for Oliver's mom herself. "How're you, Oli-Oli-oxen-free?"

Oliver laughed at the familiar nickname and gave his grandma a sloppy kiss on the cheek. "Don't worry about him at all today, Carrie. I know you've got a lot going on. Oli and I will be fine."

"I know." Carrie hefted the bag with Oliver's snacks, board books, and stuffed animals and Beckham's treats, extra leash, collapsible water bowl, and chew toys over her shoulder. The dang thing seemed to get heavier every day. Who needed a gym membership when you had a kid and a dog?

She led the way through the propped-open gate of their condo building, taking the right pathway through the front garden—a landscape of overgrown bougainvillea, lush liriope, and the pièce de résistance: an enormous staghorn fern hanging off a gumbo-limbo tree. Honestly, she'd bought her condo primarily because of that nearly six-foot staghorn fern. It made her happy every time she walked to her front door, and Oliver enjoyed jumping to brush his fingers against the lower curling fronds.

At their door, Gamma fished a key out of the front pocket of her cargo pants, and Carrie relinquished the heavy bag to the bench she'd placed there for exactly that purpose. It also helped create the sense of a foyer in a space that was so small it had no business having a foyer. The condo had originally been a one-bedroom, but she'd worked her contacts to move the kitchen opening to another wall so she could enclose the small dining room, creating a junior bedroom as the real estate agents called it.

"Who wants to wear his red dinosaur shirt today?" Gamma cooed while peeling Oliver out of his muddy dog park shirt. "And how about a bath first?"

"Beckham, too?" Carrie called, hopping down the short hallway to her bedroom on one foot while she took her cross-trainer off the other. She landed sideways on her queen bed, a decorating compromise between the king-size bed she'd wanted and the square footage of her bedroom. She toed off the other shoe. "And can it wait 'til I grab a quick shower? I've got a client meeting in less than an hour." One bathroom meant many such compromises. Her son could be dirty a few minutes longer. Didn't exposure to germs help build immunity?

"Sure, we'll have a little snack, won't we?" Gamma's voice faded as she walked into the kitchen. Carrie heard the refrigerator door open, then the *click-click* of Beckham's toenails on her hardwood floors. He was ever-optimistic about the refrigerator, and with good reason. Even if no one specifically meant to give the dog treats, Oliver's eating habits—namely, his ability to get as much food smeared in his hair and on the floor as he got in his mouth—meant there was always plenty of cleanup duty for the dog.

Carrie was just stepping out of the shower when she heard the soft ping of her phone. She wrapped a towel around her hair and shrugged into her short satin robe.

We need to talk.

Carrie didn't need caller ID to know it was Lance. After her divorce, she'd changed his entry in her address book from Lance Donovan and the picture of him stuffing wedding cake in his mouth to Don't Answer and a picture of the yellow and black circles used to label toxic chemicals. She knew who it was, and she didn't have time for drama right now. She checked the time. Less than half an hour now to put on her business face and meet Dimitri Orlov. If all went well today, she'd be drawing up plans for a redesign of his three restaurants. And if she got the job, she wouldn't have to worry about income for the next year. What a relief it would be to take a break from the constant scramble for new clients. So Lance could wait. It wasn't like Oliver's paternity was some kind of emergency, and the kind of conversation they needed to have couldn't be rushed. She needed this job, for Oli's sake as much as her own. She would deal with Lance once Orlov signed her very detailed contract.

She slicked back her hair—no time for a blow-dry—into a long, low bun and secured it with a jeweled barrette. She'd mastered the five-minute face but took an extra two minutes for eyeliner. After slicking on her favorite MAC Ruby Woo lipstick, she grabbed her portfolio bag, gave Oliver and her mom a quick kiss goodbye, and keys in hand, swung open her front door.

"Lance?" Carrie almost slammed the door in his face. Almost. Her fingers flexed on the brass doorknob, knuckles whitening. "How do you even know where I... Did you follow us from Fur Haven?"

Lance took a step forward like he was going to mosey on in, uninvited. She blocked him with her body, a move that brought them close enough that she could feel the heat of him. Lance's body temperature ran higher than hers, a fact she'd appreciated on cold nights when she could roll them into a blanket burrito and steal all that delicious warmth. She shoved down the snuggle-rich memories and her ill-timed awareness of him and scowled. "Answer my question."

"Public records." He waved his phone at her, a phone that was two generations newer than hers but looked twice as beat up. He'd always been hard on phones, going through LifeProof cases faster than she could order them on Amazon. Too bad their marriage hadn't been LifeProofed; she wouldn't be scrambling now to avoid justifying some pretty unjustifiable behavior on her part.

"Uh-huh." She caught her lower lip between her teeth and tasted her own lipstick. Damn it. Now she'd have to reapply it in the car, never the best idea with such a dark red. If she'd learned anything from watching her parents fight, it was to be on the offensive. "Still creepy. Extra creepy."

"What? That I found your deed in public records? It's not that hard. They are, you know, public." He shoved his phone in his back pocket, and she hated that she couldn't look away from the way the movement tightened his pale-blue T-shirt across his pecs. If anything, Lance looked even more built than when they'd been together. He might own his own company, but he'd never been the kind of manager who could stay off a job site. Looked like he still didn't—the way his T-shirt hugged him tight enough to hint at the hard abs underneath spoke to hundreds of hours of physical labor.

"Comforting." She smacked her lips, hoping the color would even out on its own. Goodness, it was hard not to stare at those abs. "You should've tried my phone instead. I don't have time for you right now."

Lance snorted. "Some things don't change." He leaned a forearm against the doorframe, his body inches from hers, that heat moving over her, through her. "But you owe me an explanation. Big time."

An excellent point. She swam through the dizzying number of hormones clouding her brain, fought past the urge to step into his arms and soak him up. She couldn't let him see how his nearness affected her. No weakness allowed.

"You're right, and I will explain." She pushed her carefully manicured pointer finger into the center of his chest with a *tap-tap* meant to annoy him away from noticing how her breath hitched when she touched him. "But now is not that time. I'm meeting a new client."

"Different year, same song. People really don't change, do they, Carrie?" Lance's head tilted so his temple rested against the frame. His blue eyes bored into her, and it was all she could do to hold his gaze. In the first years of their marriage, she'd loved seeing herself reflected in his deep blues—smart, sexy, sensual. She'd had all the s-words going for her. She still saw s-words in his eyes, but it sure didn't feel the same. Suspicious, skeptical, scornful.

Let him think whatever he wanted about her. If her silly heart bruised, so what? As long as he was mad at her, he wasn't thinking about Oliver.

"You're making me late." She kept pushing with her finger, like drilling through granite, until he took a step back and then another one. "Text me. We'll make an appointment."

"So civilized." His snarl was not.

She removed her finger from his chest and clicked the door shut behind her. "I hope we can be."

He pulled out his phone and messaged her: Now is good for me.

She kept walking toward her SUV, but she returned the text before climbing into her Chevy: *I'll check my calendar and get back to you.*

You have twenty-four hours before I call an attorney.

Carrie's silly, bruised heart pounded hard in her chest. He wouldn't, would he? She couldn't take the chance, not with Oliver at stake. *When you put it like that, you sweet-talker...*

She let the three typing dots bounce for an ominous few seconds before sending the rest. *Coffee? 2 p.m.?*

He sent her a thumbs-up, and she added the first place that came to mind: *The Coffee Pot Spot?*

Her time, her place, her rules. She wouldn't let Lance Donovan bully his way into her son's life. But she did owe him an explanation and an apology. Luckily, she'd had three years to rehearse her speech.

# CHAPTER 4

LANCE WATCHED UNTIL THE FRONT GATE SLAMMED behind Carrie, the scent of her fresh from the shower still in his nostrils. He rubbed his nose with the back of his hand and plunked onto the top of the three stairs that led up to her ground-level condo. What had he thought would happen? Of course she didn't have time for him. Wasn't that always their problem? Two workaholics, one relationship. A bad combo from the beginning. Still, he couldn't quite quell the curiosity he felt about the new client. Who was she working with? Was it a big account? Small? How was her business doing? More importantly, was she able to provide Oliver with the kind of life he deserved?

A line of industrious ants detoured around his booted foot, angling toward the edge of the step and into the lush but overgrown tropical garden. An out-of-control bougainvillea bush covered the back fence, undoubtedly a cheap security measure as anyone trying to climb over the back gate would have to contend with hundreds of spiky thorns. The fuchsia blooms were lovely, as were the bird-of-paradise flowers planted to the right of Carrie's stoop. However, both could use a good pruning.

Carrie's place was comfortable but not fancy, lots of potential without a lot of follow-through. The paint job was a bright yellow with orange accents that had faded over the years to a melted sherbet hue. He was a handyman at heart, and he couldn't help but note that the sidewalk could use a good pressure wash, and the whole place wanted painting. What the property really needed was an influx of cash, and he found himself wondering again what Carrie's financial situation was. Surely, if she'd needed money for Oliver, she would've reached out to him. Knowing her stubborn streak, he couldn't quite let his worries go. He didn't want his son growing up without financial stability.

Of course, Lance knew from firsthand experience that an excess of money did not equal a happy childhood or close family bonds. Money can't buy happiness, but he'd found it easier to be happy when he wasn't worried about having the lights turned off if he didn't make his payment on time. The first few years out of the Donovan nest had been rough. He'd refused any money from his well-meaning mother. If his father had offered to help, Lance wouldn't know. He'd never answered his calls.

Yeah, he'd made some mistakes, but they were his mistakes to make. He'd gotten the power turned back on the one time he'd missed a few too many of Florida Power & Light's deadlines, found new roommates when old ones disappeared in the night owing two months' rent, and learned how to cook ramen and eventually any other kind of noodle that needed boiling before eating. He was proud to be something of a connoisseur of the Publix spaghetti sauce aisle, having different flavors that suited different nights of the week and different moods. He remembered Carrie's favorite had been the Parmesan and Romano marinara. He hadn't eaten it in years, but he suddenly found himself craving it at—he checked the time—nine thirty in the morning.

"Lance?"

The familiar voice made him leap to his feet, inadvertently squashing some ants in the process. "Sherry! Long time, no see, huh?" He immediately felt like an idiot. Of course they hadn't seen each other in years. He was the ex-son-in-law after all. What reason could they possibly have to stay in touch? But when he turned toward her, he saw one very large reason propped on her hip stuffing a handful of soggy Cheerios into his mouth. Oliver.

"She finally told you?" Sherry blew straight up, causing her bangs to bounce over her eyebrows before settling back down. "It's about time. I've been on her since the beginning. You had a right to know."

"Um, yeah." Absentmindedly, he reached down to scratch Beckham behind the ears. The dog melted against his leg, and Lance bent his knees to scoop the dog up.

"Too bad you never returned any of my calls." Sherry covered Oliver's ears like he was the hear-no-evil monkey. "I tried. I really did."

Shit, she was right. She'd called him a bunch of times in that first year of the divorce, but he'd always sent the calls to voicemail. *You need to talk to Carrie.* She'd left a dozen similar messages. *You need to hear what she has to say.* He'd hit Delete and erase the call log so Rachelle wouldn't ask uncomfortable questions about why his ex-mother-in-law was up in his business. He'd thought Sherry took the divorce a bit too hard, harder even than Carrie apparently had, but he'd rationalized that Sherry's emotional state was no longer his concern. If she returned to drinking, well, Carrie could take the blame for that, too. He'd been wrong, though. So wrong. He should've picked up the phone at least once. Maybe then he wouldn't have missed the first few years of his son's life.

He couldn't say all that, not after having brushed her off all those years ago. He settled for a polite and, he hoped, friendly sounding, "Where are you off to on such a fine day?"

It wasn't that fine a day. It was, in fact, overcast and rumbling like rain wasn't too far off, which was sure to upset the tourists who flocked to Miami Beach for high season. But the subtropics did what they did, and no amount of tourist cash could change the weather. Besides, he didn't know how he felt about Sherry taking care of Oliver. He remembered too well her many trips to rehab and Carrie's heartbreak every time her mother went back to the bottle. At least today, Sherry's eyes were clear, her skin creamy and bright. A lot can change in nearly four years, he reminded himself, and looking at Oliver, it struck him that a lot had changed in only one day. A son. His son.

"We're going to take a stroll around the block." Sherry pulled the dangling leash out of her front pocket and clipped it onto Beckham's collar, conveniently at her eye level with Lance holding him. "They just got back from a big walk, but I always like to wear out the both of them before leaving Beckham in the condo while Oli and I run errands."

"I can take him." Lance didn't know where the words came from. Him, watch a kid? Insane.

But Sherry misunderstood him. "Oh, I don't know how Carrie would feel about that," she said as she handed over the leash to Lance. "It would be a blessing, though, wouldn't it? To have only one little terror to look after instead of the two? Oli and I could head to my hairdresser's straight away if you had Beckham. You'll have him back by lunchtime, won't you? Oliver makes quite a mess, as I'm sure you can imagine, and I rely on that hyper dog to help with the cleanup."

"I—uh—sure." Lance looped the leash around his wrist, like he'd done in the old days to keep Beckham from ripping it out of his grip when he took off at a full run after whatever squirrel or tumbleweed of a plastic bag caught his eye.

"Fantastic. He clearly remembers you. It'll be fine." Whether Sherry was reassuring herself or him, Lance wasn't certain. She patted his cheek like he was no older than Oliver. "You two be good. See you in a few hours."

She swished out, much like her daughter, his son on one hip, diaper bag banging on the other. The front gate slammed behind her.

"Well, buddy, what do you want to do today?"

Beckham barked and wagged his tail.

---

Lance watched Mendo wipe muddy dog paws off the rough denim of his work overalls. He knew Mendo was over fifty, but he was afraid to guess how far past the midcentury mark he actually was because if Mendo ever decided to retire, Lance would be out one excellent construction foreman. In the early days, Lance did everything, but once Mendo came along, he'd been happy to give over the day-to-day management duties to someone else so he could better keep his eye on the big picture of the entire project.

"Dogs on-site now, eh, Boss?" Mendo squatted to scrub under Beckham's chin. Behind him, the Dorothy stood in her dilapidated glory. "Reminds me of the old days. This dog looks a lot like your old one. Beckham, wasn't it?"

"This is Beckham."

Mendo kept up a steady two-finger rub, and Beckham's

back leg thumped wildly on the sandy ground. "Naw, that dog was a lot more trouble than this one. Couldn't sit still to save his life."

Lance kicked at a patchy section of weeds. "I guess we all mellow with age."

Mendo barked out a laugh and stood. "True, too true. What're you doing with him? Didn't Carrie get custody in the divorce?"

The downside of working with the same foreman for a decade. He knew too much about everything. "We ran into each other this morning."

"Mmm-hmm, and how was that?" Mendo's face was carefully blank. He'd been against the divorce from the very beginning, calling Lance all kinds of stupid in both English and Spanish. On multiple occasions. "You stole the dog?"

"No, he's on loan. Until lunch." No need to get into the fact that Carrie didn't know he had Beckham. Clearly, Sherry had executive decision-making power when Carrie left for work. That was what he told himself whenever a niggle of doubt crept into his mind. He'd taken good care of Beckham for the first years of his life. She'd have no reason to object to him dog sitting. Except she would, if she knew. So she wouldn't know. Simple solution. It wasn't like she could get mad at *him* for keeping secrets.

"How's it going here?" Lance changed the subject deliberately, tugging the leash until Beckham came over and sat on the toe of his work boot. He'd never quite gotten the hang of the "heel" command. He was more of a "toe" dog.

"Bit of a hiccup. The van taking everyone to the port is late."

Lance looked through the glass front doors of the

Dorothy to see Riley pacing the hallway, cell phone to ear and arms waving wildly. Her hair was in its usual messy ponytail, and her bubble-gum pink T-shirt was bright enough that a lesser man might squint. He bravely looked on, sighing heavily. "Let me go see what's happening. We're supposed to be able to start with the roof today."

"Two weeks is a pretty tight schedule, seeing as they've got a total of three old roofs to rip off before we can lay the new one." Mendo chuckled and pulled out his phone. "Three roofs. What inspector signed off on that brilliant idea?"

"Codes change. Even the newest roof is old enough to vote." Lance gathered his patience and settled it around himself like a cloak. It was a technique he used when dealing with especially fussy clients, but he had a feeling he'd need it for dealing with whatever chaos was brewing through those glass doors.

"I'll let the guys know to take their time coming in this morning." Mendo pulled out his phone, an older model that he kept in meticulous shape. Mendo was nothing if not a stickler for details. "Think we'll be able to start by eleven?"

Lance tried to gauge Riley's level of agitation from a distance. "Let's say noon to be safe." Then he remembered his coffee date, er, coffee appointment with Carrie. "You can handle the afternoon, right, Mendo?"

"Sure, Boss. Expecting to run into a certain someone again?" Mendo grinned at him, his teeth surprisingly white and strong for someone his age. Then again, maybe they were dentures. What did Lance know?

"We're going to talk. Carrie and me," he clarified, in case Mendo thought he meant the dog. Why would he?

The upcoming talk was making him edgy. Only one thing to do when his emotions got the better of him. Bury them in work. "I'm going in." He handed the leash off to Mendo. "Wish me luck."

Mendo laughed. "It's going to take more than luck to get all those folks on their way. Imagine, a whole building going on vacation together? What kind of crazy is that?"

"My brother's kind of crazy." Lance sucked in a big breath and pushed open the doors. "Riley? What's going on? How can my men get to work if you're all still here, milling about?"

In fact, only two people sat on the ratty rattan sofa— Riley's Grams in an oversize floppy straw hat and giant sunglasses next to Mr. Cardoza, a dapper older gentleman Lance met on his initial walk-through of the project. Grams was deep in a story, waving her hands around enough that Mr. Cardoza had to duck a few times to keep from getting whacked inadvertently.

"Grams!" Riley swerved to avoid a story-flailing hand. "Where's GW? I thought he was going to be here by now."

Lance grinned. He loved that Riley called his and Caleb's Grandpa William "GW," mainly because Grandpa William hated nicknames of any kind but for some reason had allowed Riley to make one up for him. Lance had been terrified of ol' GW for most of his childhood, sure that he was being measured, judged, and found wanting at every meeting. Even when married to Carrie, Lance had found holidays and such to be more like command performances than actual family time.

Since Lance and Knox had been roped into Caleb's crazy scheme to rehab the Dorothy, though, Grandpa William was practically jovial—popping in on the construction site without warning to give unsolicited but tolerated advice, insisting his three grandsons join him for outings on his boat on the weekends, even cracking the occasional off-color joke. No doubt about it, Grandpa William had changed. If Lance felt a twinge of loss at the idea that this version of Grandpa William would've made a better grandpa than the one in his childhood memories, well, he shook it off. Lance didn't look back. In fact, his entire business was built on looking forward. Construction was all about improving the future.

"You know my grandfather, Riley. He can't be rushed."

Riley checked the time on her phone and blew out a long breath. "An hour late is definitely not rushing. And where are the rest of them? I swear these residents are turning me gray before my time."

Apparently, Riley's Grams wasn't so busy telling her story to Mr. Cardoza that she couldn't eavesdrop on them, too, because she paused long enough to say, "Pish-posh. You come from a long line of women who never go gray." She patted her own coiffed and clearly colored hair, which was sprayed into a helmet meant to withstand ocean breezes but might possibly stand up to hurricane-force winds.

Riley turned pleading eyes Lance's way. "Save me," she whispered. Out loud, she said, "I'm going to do a second-floor sweep for our stragglers."

As if on cue, the elevator groaned and dinged, disgorging another three people and their rolling suitcases, one man and two women. The gray-haired man was valiantly trying to drive three overloaded bags, but one of them had a broken wheel and kept veering to the left.

"Constantine, let's get these bags off the elevator and

then take them one at a time out to the van," said the woman in a teal T-shirt and checkered Bermuda shorts with a terry-cloth visor on her head. She dropped a heavy shoulder bag onto the ground and rubbed her upper arm.

"Don't be ridiculous, Eileen." A chubby grandma-type sported a bag on each shoulder. She also wore Bermuda shorts, hers in a red plaid with matching red-plaid sneakers with bright-yellow laces tied in perfect bows. "It's easier to do it all in one trip, isn't it, Constantine?"

"Whatever you wish, Hilde." Constantine strained to pull the three roller bags off the elevator. He eyed the distance to the front door like he was looking for a quick escape route. The two women kept up a steady stream of suggestions.

"Riley?" Lance waved a hand to get her attention. "Looks like your lost lambs are found. Can we talk business for a minute? When can my men get to work?"

"What men?" Riley shoved her phone in the waistband of her jean shorts. "I see a man. Two if I count you." She grinned at him, taking the sting out of her words. "Can you believe the van I hired didn't show up? Caleb left a few minutes ago to rent one."

"Caleb's going to drive you all to the cruise ship?" Lance watched as two men emerged from the first-floor hallway, one tall and thin, the other short and rotund, each in sweatpants and oversize Mickey Mouse sweatshirts. They pulled one bag between them, the suitcase so large and so covered in light-reflecting tape that it could serve as an emergency float if the cruise ship went down, *Titanic*-style.

Riley's lips twitched. "That's the plan."

"What have you done to my brother?" Lance pulled her

in for a hug because truth was, the changes to Caleb were good to see. Caleb used to be so uptight, but he'd definitely loosened up since meeting Riley and her gently aging extended family at the Dorothy.

"Put him to work, that's for sure. You wouldn't believe what he's uncovered about Rainy Day's schemes." More of Riley's curls flew out of her ponytail holder when she shook her head. "We're having to report that corrupt management company to the state. It's possible we're looking at federal crimes."

Lance quirked a half smile her way. "Luckily, we Donovans have some experience with that."

She punched his arm and pulled away. "Don't talk like that. One bad apple does not ruin the bunch."

"One of your Grams' sayings? Because I think you got it wrong."

"I got it exactly right." She placed her hands on her hips and surveyed the growing pile of luggage and increased lobby occupancy, a general inspecting her troops on the battlefield. "Now, if you really want to help get things moving along, you'll volunteer all that muscle you've got packed in your too-tight T-shirt to help move luggage."

Lance plucked the T-shirt away from his chest. "It is not too tight."

"Keep telling yourself that, buddy." Riley's eyes squinted up at him, her makeup-free face radiating good humor. "Will you check on Patty? I'm worried she hasn't come down yet. Second floor, Unit 211."

"Sure thing." Lance loped off to take the stairs. He skipped the elevator ride, knowing it was being replaced in a few days. He prayed it lasted long enough to transport the second-floor residents and their luggage one last time, but he figured the less stress he put on it, the less chance of a giant catastrophe. Now, he simply had to figure out how Mendo ended up outside playing with his dog while he was turned into a bellboy. This was what happened when you let family in, he supposed. Nothing but work, work, work.

# CHAPTER 5

THE ELEVATOR CREAKED AND GROANED ITS WAY DOWN to the first floor. Lance kept a weather eye on Patty, propped against her cheery yellow walker and wearing a housedress with yellow daisies on it. She'd maxed out her cruise luggage allowance with two giant bags weighing fifty pounds each. He didn't ask what was in there. An extra walker? He didn't want to know.

They emerged into the lobby where chaos reigned. Turned out, Patty's packing was conservative compared to the ginormous suitcases littering the lobby. Mendo and Beckham were inside now, having been put to work lining the cases up inside the front doors. Mendo rolled and lifted the bags, Beckham prancing around him like a gremlin intent on tripping him. Mendo was agile, dodging the dog while adding more suitcases to the front-door lineup. It made sense now why Riley'd left LouLou in the apartment for the duration.

"I've got it." Riley's Grams' voice rose above the cacophony of the gathered residents. She pulled on the strap of a canvas bag decorated with large palm leaves, but the bag didn't move more than an inch off the ground before thumping to the floor.

"The cruise is only two weeks long." Grandpa William—who'd apparently arrived while Lance was sitting on Patty's hard-sided bags to help her latch them shut—pointed at Grams' hip-high suitcase with his silver-handled cane. "What in heaven's name could you possibly have packed?"

"A woman needs to have choices." Grams patted the suit-case affectionately and attempted to lift the palm-leaf bag again. This time, she got it hiked onto her shoulder with one mighty heave. "I've got to keep my options open."

Grandpa William harrumphed, his usual grumpy demeanor on full display. "Sometimes you have to make a choice."

Grams struggled with the handle of the silver suitcase, the palm bag swinging forward whenever she leaned in, knocking her hand off the handle every time. "This thing is supposed to roll easily. I can't imagine what's wrong with it."

"Here, Grams." Riley swooped in, snapped the handle into place, and pushed it toward the door. On her return trip, she grabbed the palm-leaf bag and rolled someone else's black suitcase behind her.

Lance didn't know how Riley did it, keeping everyone so organized. He supposed it wasn't that different from his own job, managing lots of moving parts. The difference was his people were employees or vendors, all with a vested interest in keeping the money flowing from his pockets to theirs. Riley's residents were a whole other ball game. The process of getting them to the van was an exercise in herd-ing cats. And the van wasn't even here yet.

"When does our transportation arrive?" Grandpa William clicked across the damaged terrazzo, leaning lightly on his silver-tipped cane. Lance liked to imagine that like a hero from a steampunk novel, his grandpa had a saber or some other deadly weapon custom built into the cane.

"Ask Riley." Lance shook his grandfather's hand. The ease he'd felt with Riley and joking with Patty about her body bags evaporated as he endured the familiar sensation of being scrutinized by Grandpa William. Assessed and dismissed.

Grandpa William turned his still-sharp gaze on Riley. "Shouldn't the van be here already? Check-in starts in fifteen minutes, and it will take us at least that long to load everything."

Riley looked up at the ceiling as if seeking divine intervention. So she hadn't told them that the van was a no-show. Lance hid a smile behind his hand.

"Any minute! The check-in window doesn't close until 3:00 p.m. We have plenty of time," she said brightly. Too brightly. "Do you have any other luggage we need to add to the lineup?"

Grandpa William shook his head, pulling a sad face. "Not unless I can sneak Pops in somehow. Are you sure they won't allow dogs on the cruise? I'm worried he'll think he's being abandoned again."

Riley's expression changed from barely tolerating stupid questions to stupidly empathetic. "I know, GW. But Pops is in good hands. All dogs love Danielle. They can't help themselves. She'll take good care of your fur baby."

"He's not my baby." Grandpa William huffed. "That's ridiculous. He's a good roommate, that's all."

Yeah, so that had happened. Grandpa William with a pet, a retired greyhound with arthritis no less. When he'd first heard the news, Lance had looked up in the sky, expecting to see a pig or two fly by.

"Danielle? You don't mean Danielle Morrow, do you?" A voice that Lance had only heard over the phone for far too long joined the conversation.

"Knox!" Lance pumped his older brother's hand enthusiastically, then gave in and pulled him close for a manly, backslapping half hug. Knox had been back a few weeks, but Lance still hadn't gotten used to seeing his big brother regularly. "When did you get here?"

"I dropped off Grandpa William, then it took me forever to find a parking space in this neighborhood." Knox returned the hug stiffly. "About Danielle?"

"Knox!" Riley greeted him with an enthusiastic hug. Knox didn't seem any more comfortable with Riley's affection than he had with Lance's. "You remember Danielle from high school? Her dad's been Grams' vet my whole life."

Knox's head tipped to the side, like her words were in another language and he was trying to make sense of them.

Riley tried again. "Weren't you in the same class?"

"Yeah, we graduated the same year." Knox's answer was as stiff as his military-trained body. His hand absently played with the thigh strap on the brace that supported his left leg—a visual reminder of the reason he'd had to leave the Marines. What had Knox called it? Medically separated. His only explanation since returning a few weeks ago was "IED," but Lance hoped to get the whole story out of him soon.

"Weren't you two a thing back then?" Riley dragged a clearly reluctant Knox further down memory lane. "I was only a freshman when you graduated, but I think I remember you walking around holding hands."

"Yes." Knox could be as stingy with words as he was with his smiles. His clipped tone was clearly meant to end that avenue of conversation.

Riley snapped her jaw shut and turned her attention back to directing luggage traffic.

Lance's gaze took in Knox's brace and the pain lines etched in his face that made him appear older than his thirty-two years. In every other way, he looked like a Donovan: the blond hair kept high and tight, even shorter than Caleb's artful fade, and Grandpa William's blue eyes. Years in the Marines had honed his body into a weapon, muscles bulging out from under his USMC T-shirt, a Semper Fi tattoo peeking out from under the sleeve. Lance recognized the brother he'd seen on holidays and other family gatherings, but in other ways, Knox was a stranger.

Hadn't Lance met someone named Danielle at Knox's high school graduation? The picture came back: Knox's arm around her shoulders, holding her so close to his side that her graduation cap poked his chest. She'd been a good foot shorter than Knox, her freckled face turned up to his, laughing. Two plus two equals high school sweetheart. Lance took pity on his brother. "Danielle works with a greyhound rescue organization. It's where Grandpa William got Pops. She's taking the dog back while he's on the cruise."

"And she better take good care of him." Grandpa William punctuated his sentence with a tap of his cane.

Riley placed a soothing hand in the crook of Grandpa William's arm and steered him toward the front doors. "Pops'll be fine and very glad to see you when you get back from two whole weeks of sunshine and boozing."

Grandpa William chuckled and placed his hand over hers. It was clear he had a soft spot for his soon-to-be granddaughter-in-law.

"Thank God," Lance heard Riley mutter, and her face broke into a smile so wide it could only mean one thing.

Caleb strode up the steps, a white passenger van parked illegally in front of the Dorothy. "Let's start loading them up. Daylight's burning." He joined their group in the lobby and dropped a kiss to Riley's cheek. "Lead the way, mighty cruise director."

She made a face at him. "Mom is supposed to handle all of that. She's the one who got us this deal after all."

"We both know who's going to handle everything. And it's not your mom." Caleb patted Riley's shoulder and grabbed the first two bags in the great luggage lineup. "Hey, Knox, what's up? Lance." He nodded at both his brothers. "Make yourselves useful, why don't you?"

Knox shouldered a few bags and one of Patty's oversize suitcases. Lance pulled a few pieces of luggage to haul himself. "Tell me again how you're paying for this whole thing. It's insane." Once they were outside and out of earshot, he added, "And why is Grandpa William going? He doesn't even live here."

Caleb's sigh was audible. "You know how Dad left our finances in a shambles?"

"Yours." Lance prided himself on having gotten out years before the Donovan empire fell. "I'm sitting pretty." He smirked at his brother. "Sitting pretty" might be a slight exaggeration, but his company was stable and work was steady.

"We both are." Knox's smirk mirrored Lance's. "I'll be cashing checks from the military for life."

"Yeah, yeah." Caleb grunted under the weight of Eileen Forsythe's suitcase that was so old it didn't even have rollers. "You're the brilliant ones. I had some private money, of course, but I lost the bulk when Dad went down. Grandpa

William didn't, though, and this cruise was his idea. When he offered to pay for it, Grams threw a fit. So I'm the official benefactor, but Grandpa William's the one really footing this astronomical bill."

"Didn't Riley say you got a deal?" Lance took the lead in loading suitcases onto the van. He enjoyed a good puzzle, and it would take some serious jigsaw skill to fit all the bags and all the people into this small van.

"Sure, and it turns out the cruise is significantly cheaper than putting everyone up in a hotel for a couple of weeks, if you can believe that." Caleb shoved Eileen's bag into Lance's hands with another grunt and took the three carry-ons from Knox's shoulders. "Even so, this trip isn't cheap. But Grandpa William was adamant."

"That's something else I don't understand. Why is he even involved? I thought he signed the place over to you. Us." Lance slammed the back door shut, and they headed back to the lobby for another load, Knox one limping step behind them.

"You don't know?" Caleb stopped him under a sagging palm tree. The Dorothy needed some landscape help in addition to everything else, but that would come after all the renovations.

"Know what?" Lance stretched his shoulders. Carrying the elderly residents' luggage was like lugging bricks. He pulled one arm and then the other across his chest. If he'd known he'd be roped into weight-lifting luggage, he'd have done some warm-up stretches.

"I think Grandpa William is trying to win Grams back." Caleb clapped Lance on the shoulder blade and sent a knowing wink Knox's way.

Lance was tempted to check the sky for flying pigs. "Aren't they ancient history?"

Caleb nodded to where Grandpa William sat next to Grams on the old rattan couch in the lobby, his cane planted between his knees. Grams was laughing, her head thrown back, and Grandpa William watched her like, well, like Caleb watched Riley. Bemused, a little hungry.

"Now that's the craziest thing I've heard today." Lance shook his head, bemused himself. "Imagine wanting to get back together with an ex. If it didn't work the first time, what in blazes makes him think it can work now?"

Grams placed her hand on Grandpa William's leg, right above his knee, and said something that made the old man slap his thigh and laugh.

"Maybe not so crazy." Caleb rolled his shoulders. "People do change, you know."

Lance had heard that parenting changed a person, and he couldn't help but wonder in what ways Carrie might be different now. Was he different, too? The fact that he was talking about his grandfather's love life with his formerly estranged brothers certainly indicated he wasn't the same. Would Carrie notice? Would she care? Would she let him get to know his son? She had to. He'd make sure of it.

"We should get back on luggage duty." Caleb strode toward the building. "Riley's got a schedule, and we're already behind."

"Whatever you say. You're the boss. Today." Lance shook out his arms and reminded himself that he couldn't start his renovation until these bags and residents were on their way. Hopefully, bellboy duty would be the only delay to the renovation schedule. *Yeah, right.*

Knox grabbed more bags and muscled them out to the van. Lance lagged behind. "He seem okay to you?" He nudged Caleb, watching Knox compensate for the limp with long strides and a lot of power. He and Caleb hadn't talked much about Knox since his surprising return a few weeks ago. The physical differences in their brother were observable—military fit, the damaged leg. Knox hadn't stayed in one place long enough for them to assess in what other ways he might've changed.

"We appreciate your help." Caleb handed Lance a few tote bags, not answering. Which was its own kind of answer and pretty much what Lance had been thinking, too.

"I *am* in the business of backbreaking labor and sweat." Lance added a few more bags to his other shoulder, letting Caleb change the subject because really, what could they do? It wasn't like Knox would listen to his little brothers. No, all they could do was help keep him busy, designing security for the new and improved Dorothy, while Knox sorted out things for himself. It was the Donovan way: bury yourself in work. Hey, it'd gotten Lance through his divorce, hadn't it?

"I meant we appreciate you staying with LouLou while we're away." Caleb held the door while Lance rolled a few bags through. "It's a big relief to Riley."

"No problem. I'm sure LouLou and Beckham will get along great." Lance pointed out Mendo and Beckham across the way. Mendo waved at him from a bare patch of front lawn where Beckham inspected every grain of sand with devoted interest. Apparently, Mendo and Beckham were done playing bellboy. Who could blame them?

"What?" Caleb dropped a bag in his surprise. "You got your dog back?"

"Not exactly." On the next few trips to and from the van, Lance filled in his brothers, ending with a "So congrats. You're both uncles."

Caleb stopped in his tracks. "Are you being serious right now?"

Lance nodded, hiding his unease with a smirk. What did Caleb think of him, that he'd had a son all this time and didn't even know about it?

"Congratulations?" Knox didn't look like he knew how to react. His face scrunched into an uncomfortable-looking smile. "Are you happy?"

Lance loaded up on more bags and trudged to the van, thinking. Was he happy? Truly, honestly, deeply? How did he really feel about having a son with Carrie?

"Am I happy?" He took a bag from Caleb, wedged it into the van, and turned so his brothers could see the grin taking over his entire face. "Hell, yeah."

# CHAPTER 6

LANCE STRETCHED HIS ARMS OVER THE BACK OF THE bone-shaped bench, tilting his gaze toward the cloudless sky. A faint breeze from the ocean, maybe half a mile away, stirred the humid air. Really, this dog-sitting gig was going to be a pleasure, a reason to take a break and get away from the job site for a while and get his thoughts in order. After the van finally made its way to the port, Lance had greeted the crew as they arrived. Now, Mendo had things well in hand at the Dorothy, doling out jobs to the crew and going over the week's schedule, and Lance had time to take the dogs for their first get-to-know-you outing.

As he'd suspected, LouLou and Beckham hit it off immediately, perhaps because of their shared love of running. Figure eights, laps, a few breaks to jump on his leg, then back to their game of chase. He had no doubt that both dogs would sleep well later in the day. Maybe he could convince Carrie to bring Beckham in the mornings for a good run with LouLou. Anything for the good of the dogs, right?

The mere thought of Carrie had him smiling. He knew he should be angry at her for keeping him from his son, but he'd been working through it in his mind. How many times had he said he didn't want children? Anytime a baby cried in a restaurant, he'd told her how happy he was that they'd never have that problem. In his early and midtwenties, he couldn't imagine children as anything but a burden. That was how his mom and dad had treated him growing up—a nuisance who had to be fed, clothed, and tamed into exhibiting proper Donovan behavior. How he'd rebelled against their ideas of what he should be! He'd vowed at an early age that he'd never be a father, and Carrie'd always agreed with him. Her own parents' divorce and various struggles with addiction had left their scars on her.

But now everything was different. It wasn't his choice anymore. He tried to imagine how Carrie must've felt when she realized she was pregnant. She'd had a choice at that point, too, and she'd chosen to keep it. If she was strong enough to accept a child after everything her parents had put her through, how could he do less?

Beckham jumped onto the bench next to him, tongue hanging out in obvious joy. LouLou hopped up on his other side.

"Is this the signal to go?" He petted each with one hand and stood. They raced to the gate and waited for him to hook them up. A time check assured him he had plenty of time to get Beckham to Carrie's mom by Sherry's one o'clock deadline. They settled LouLou at her place, and he fed them both a biscuit from the bag of treats he was pretty sure weighed more than LouLou herself. He refilled her bowl with fresh water.

"I'll be back in a few hours." Lance scratched LouLou under the chin. "You're getting a new roommate for the week."

She licked his hand and looked at him with her big, brown eyes. Oh, the guilt. He gave her another treat, which made Beckham jealous, so he got another biscuit, too.

"You two are double trouble, aren't you?" He clipped Beckham's leash on. "Time to get you back home, buddy."

LouLou flopped onto her belly and whimpered.

"You'll see each other again. I promise."

LouLou's tail thumped on the floor as if she understood. Beckham strained at the leash. When Lance opened the door, LouLou made a break for it. He lunged for her, dropping his hold on Beckham's leash in the process. LouLou ran to the elevator, Beckham right behind her.

"Seriously?" Lance scooped them both up and marched back to Riley and Caleb's apartment. "What have I gotten myself into?"

———————————

Carrie stood outside the front door of Volga, Dimitri Orlov's first restaurant and the one he'd decided was best for their first face-to-face meeting. She'd checked her lipstick before leaving her car, and she knew her slicked-back hair and simple pearl necklace created the professional yet feminine persona that described her design style. She wore her good-luck outfit—an olive-colored sheath dress with three-quarter sleeves and white piping at the boat neckline and waist. The hem hit precisely above her knee-cap, thanks to her mom's bit of altering. It was her favorite dress, especially when paired with her embroidered pumps.

She tucked her burgundy purse into her side and readjusted the strap on her portfolio bag. She was ready for this meeting, and standing outside until the early November heat made her sweat was not going to make things go any smoother. No, she needed to push thoughts of Lance out of her mind and concentrate on the project at hand: a three-restaurant makeover that would pay the bills for the next year.

She placed a hand on the brass handle and pulled. It wobbled in her hand, and even though she was definitely not thinking about Lance, she did wonder what he'd say about the craftsmanship. At twelve years old, Volga was a well-established Miami Beach eatery but wasn't so old that the place should be falling apart. If she were lucky enough to land this job, she'd be sure to get only the best craftsmen so the owner wouldn't have to worry about constant maintenance. Someone like Lance. Not Lance, of course. They didn't work together anymore, not since the divorce. Though someone like him—with his eye for detail, stubborn adherence to schedules, and streak of perfectionism— would be perfect.

Carrie stepped into a cavernous room with an exposed ceiling and cement floor. It didn't surprise her. Of course, she'd done her homework, visiting all three restaurants several times each on different days and during different shifts. She'd wanted to get an idea of how the space was used, what the staff and guests most needed, and how she could take what Orlov had built and make it even more remarkable.

Truth be told, she wasn't all that impressed with the restaurant's original industrial motif. The style was a perennial favorite of restaurant designers dealing with nervous new owners on tight budgets. Copper wiring, light fixtures made from hardware-store parts, reclaimed wood flooring, and steel, steel, steel everywhere. Volga and her sister restaurants all sported the same clean lines, and when no one was around, they were quite lovely. Add in a few guests, some staff, and a playlist, and the decibel level rose to unendurable heights.

On her first visit to Volga on a Friday evening, Carrie had observed how close the waitstaff had to get to guests to hear their orders, counted how many times during a dozen orders the guests had to repeat themselves, and recorded the decibel level with an app on her phone. It was a testament to the quality of the food that people returned to the restaurant. Carrie was sure it wasn't for the ambiance. It was her personal mission whenever she took on a restaurant to expertly ride the line between bustling and off-putting.

She patted her portfolio bag, loaded with bustling ambiance—soft furnishings and luxury finishes, one-of-a-kind art from a local up-and-coming artist she'd discovered at a street fair, even suggestions for upscaling the waitstaff uniforms from T-shirts to a stretchy poplin that would be as comfortable as knit but would look so much better, especially when coordinated with her river-blue theme. Oh yes, she was ready for this meeting.

"How many in your party?" A tall hostess towered over her in platforms with a bored look that said *I'd rather be modeling*. Sadly, not everyone who came to South Florida for the fashion industry made it, and a lot of them ended up in service and tourism. Of course, every one of them Carrie'd ever talked to was sure their current less-than-minimum-wage job plus tips was temporary. For the sake of future Volga customers, Carrie hoped Platforms-with-an-Attitude got her big break soon.

"Actually, I'm meeting Mr. Orlov?" Carrie hated the way her voice canted up at the end and that she'd started her sentence with the word *actually*. She'd been working on sounding more authoritative. She'd read an article that said women made less money because they used qualifying language, like *actually*, and questioning inflection to soften the blow of their demands. But it wasn't a demand to say why she was at Volga. She'd been invited. Carrie took a deep breath and tried again. "Mr. Orlov is expecting me."

Platforms-with-an-Attitude yawned and left the safety of the hostess station to walk languidly toward the back of the restaurant. Though she hadn't indicated in any way that Carrie should come, Carrie followed her winding path through a mixture of high-top tables and booths made of reclaimed wood.

"Ms. Burns?" Dimitri Orlov slid out from a booth tucked in the back corner of the restaurant and stood. He enveloped one of Carrie's hands in both of his. "How lovely to finally meet in person."

"Thank you, Mr. Orlov. It's a pleasure to meet you." Carrie wasn't sure what to do with her hand, trapped as it was in his grip. It definitely wasn't a handshake. She wasn't entirely sure what it was. *Bills paid for a year*, she reminded herself. *Weeks of research and prep.* She smiled and returned his rather frank appraisal of her person.

Dimitri Orlov was a few inches taller and a few decades older than she was. His hair was a peppery gray that came to sharp points at his temples and the center of his forehead. He was dressed expensively—bespoke if she wasn't mistaken, and the extreme fit of the coat told her she wasn't. A single, chunky gold ring adorned the middle finger of his right hand. The overhead lighting picked up a subtle stripe in the suiting material.

He let her fingers go with a smile and gestured her

toward the booth. "A woman as beautiful as you must call me Dimitri."

"Then please, call me Carrie." She slid into place, setting her purse against the wall so her portfolio was close at hand.

"Tell me, what do you think of my restaurant? You've been here before?" His eyes were a silvery blue that reminded her of a shark's skin.

She kept her smile professional. "Of course. I've been to all your restaurants. As a guest for many years and, more recently, to get a feel for how things are now."

"And how are things now?"

Ah, the tricky part. Clients wanted something new and exciting. They wanted imagination and creativity. Most importantly, they wanted what they already had except completely different. No one likes to hear their home or place of business is outdated, out of fashion, or just plain ugly. Luckily, it was easy to compliment Dimitri's restaurants.

Carrie started by naming her favorite dish. "Your dessert menu is to die for. The cherry *vareniki*? I could eat a pound of those little dumplings. I never leave Volga without a light dusting of powdered sugar all over whatever I'm wearing."

Dimitri raised an arm and snapped his fingers. A waiter appeared in seconds, a glass of water for each of them in his hand.

"Get this woman some *vareniki*, okay?"

"Right away, Mr. Orlov." He set down the waters and hurried away.

"You didn't have to—"

He chopped off the end of her sentence with a slash of his hand through the air. "Nonsense. You come to my restaurant. You should have your favorite. Would you like to order anything else before we get down to business?"

Carrie was more than ready for the getting-down-to-business part. She took a sip of her ice water. "The *vareniki* are enough for me."

"Good." He folded his hands in front of him and speared her with his sharkskin gaze. "Now that the niceties are over, tell me what you really think of my restaurants."

Carrie sucked in a gasp of air so quickly an ice cube lodged in her throat. She coughed lightly into her hand until it moved on down her throat. She took a deep breath and an even bigger risk. She told him the truth.

"I don't see anything of you in your restaurants." She kept her eyes on his face, gauging his reaction. Like a shark, he remained unemotional. No twitch of a muscle gave him away. "They look to me like something I might've done in one of my early design classes for an assignment, a sort of generic restaurant footprint, if you will. Industrial is a favorite style for new restaurants because it's inexpensive." It was risky, essentially calling him miserly, but it was part of her setup.

Now for the hard sell. She leaned forward, hands clasped earnestly in front of her. "Dimitri, I don't think your restaurants are cheap. I don't think you're cheap. Therefore, there's a mismatch between the design and the dream. Your dream."

"What do you know of my dream?" Dimitri's question was as unemotional as his face.

"You named your restaurants after beautiful rivers that flow through Russia, rivers that have supported villages, providing food, jobs, and transportation. They have flooded and receded, but they are always there for the people to rely on." She paused, gathering her next phrases. No "I think" or "I believe." She needed to bring it home in a big way. "The dream is for your restaurants to be like those Russian rivers—winding through people's everyday lives, connecting communities, and ultimately, bringing people together."

Dimitri's shark eyes gleamed. He gave a sharp nod. "Yes, that is the dream."

Carrie smiled and pulled out her portfolio. "Good, let me show it to you."

# CHAPTER 7

THE COFFEE POT SPOT WAS CROWDED IN SPITE OF ITS evident fire-hazard layout, but that was mostly to do with the location. There were coffee places aplenty in South and North Beach, but the in-between neighborhoods had been underserved for years. Any food or beverage business would do well in this location. It was a shame, really, how much more the place could be with a tad more thoughtful design. Carrie sighed. Such was her burden in life. To always see possibilities but not always be able to act on them.

The same gangly waiter as on her last visit walked up to her small table, but he clearly didn't recognize her. He must see a dozen first dates per shift. He was still friendly, introducing himself as Derek and asking her what she wanted. She ordered a hot tea.

"Aren't we celebrating?" Lance strolled up to the table, his lean form sliding easily between the overstuffed backpacks and totes that crowded the aisle. His T-shirt was different from this morning, a white cotton blend with the Excalibur Construction logo over the left breast. She felt a surge of pride. She'd helped him name and brand his company, and he was still using her ideas. Starting over would have undone years of success, so it wasn't any kind of nostalgia on his part, she knew. Still, it felt good knowing she'd created something that had served him well all these years.

"Celebrating what?" She checked that her portfolio bag

was still tucked between her feet, signed contracts neatly filed between her drawings.

"You got the new client, right?" He held his hand up for a high five.

She left him hanging for a long moment, then smiled. "I did."

He renewed the high five. "Fantastic! You were always good at reeling in new business."

She smiled at his enthusiasm but still left his high-five hand all alone up in the air. "Yes, Oliver and I will be living large now. Bills paid on time. Food in the refrigerator. It's all Candy Land from here on out."

Lance's high-five hand swiped at the back of his neck. "Has it been a struggle then? You know you could've asked me—"

"No, I'm sorry. I shouldn't have joked about our finances." She smiled up at Derek when he placed the hot tea in front of her and waited while Lance asked for an Americano. "It was tough at first, I'll admit. Leaving the firm was a hard decision to make. But my mom helped out, and we're doing fine now."

"Your mom. How is she?" Lance looked distinctly uncomfortable, and the small table leapt a bit each time his knee hit the underside. It was his I've-got-a-secret jitteriness bouncing his leg, not his usual burning off of extra energy. She could tell by how extra high the table bounced every third jitter. What could it be? She dismissed the mystery. Whatever it was, it wasn't her business.

"Mom's good. Clean and sober since the day Oliver was born. Oli changed both our lives." Carrie sipped her tea, swallowing down the small resentment she still felt that her own birth hadn't been enough to inspire her mother to get her life together. At least things were good now. She needed to stay grateful, not dwell on her crappy childhood. A change of subject was definitely in order. "But you didn't come to ask about my mom. You want to know about Oliver."

Lance leaned across the table and placed his hand over hers on the table. "I want to know everything. You owe me that much at least."

Carrie refused to acknowledge the warm thrill of his skin touching hers or the way his heat simmered up her arm and made her stomach fluttery. This was not a first date, and these were not signs of chemistry and compatibility. *Old habits, that's all.* She took a long sip of tea, lifting the cup with her free hand, and regarded him over the rim.

"You didn't want children." The best defense is a good offense, right? Her mother would be proud, even if Carrie wasn't. She'd never wanted to replicate her parents' communication style, but under stress, that was what popped out. Every time. She said things she couldn't walk back, and that was how she'd pushed Lance away. She didn't want to push him away today, but she didn't want him too close, either.

"Neither did you." He removed his hand from hers and crossed his arms over his chest. "So what happened?"

"I got pregnant. Obviously." Okay, not her most brilliant comeback, but she was busy refusing to mourn the loss of his touch. She'd always had a thing for Lance's body. All that muscle, the scrape of his stubble against her face in the morning, the rasp of his callused hands across her skin. Yeah, she'd missed him. So what? They were different people now. People who happened to share a child. She took a deep breath and another sip of tea and started over. "I made one attempt to tell you."

Lance raised a skeptical eyebrow at her. "Not very hard, apparently. What happened? You chickened out?"

"Rachelle answered the door. With a ring on her finger." She clipped out the words, angry that they still had the power to hurt her. "So yeah, I chickened out. I didn't want to ruin your new, *childless* life."

"Ouch." Lance uncrossed his arms and leaned toward her. "Sorry about that. I didn't realize until later what a mistake she was. For me, I mean. I'm sure she's making someone else very happy now, but she and I didn't last six months. Classic rebound, right?" He angled his head to the side like this was a story he told many times, waggling his eyebrows to indicate she was supposed to laugh. She didn't.

"Oh." Carrie lost the thread of her story. If only she'd tried again later, things might've been totally different. Her fingers drummed the table, a nervous outlet for the energy that urged her to reach for his hand and enfold it in hers. Her brain totally understood what was happening, but her body was simply overjoyed at his nearness. Even her feet inched toward him under the table. She crossed her ankles to put a stop to the nonsense. He was not a magnet, and she was not some abandoned paper clip drawn to his energy field. End of story. "I should've called you. Again, I mean. I'm sorry."

"I understand. It's just how you are, right?" Lance lifted his coffee with both hands and knocked back a few swallows. "Total sum game. One screwup and everything's over. No mercy."

Carrie winced. Not a flattering description of what she

considered her decisiveness and tenacity. "You're not being fair. I was pregnant, divorced, hurting. I can admit that I might not have been thinking at my clearest back then."

"And since then?" Lance's blue eyes, so deep and dark, searched her face.

She scraped her upper lip with her teeth, tasting the lipstick on her tongue, and tried to think of a good excuse for why she hadn't reached out to Lance a second time. She could think of lots of bad excuses: fear, selfishly wanting Oli to herself, pride. But a good excuse? Not a one came to mind.

"I'm sorry, Lance." Her hands, the traitors, reached across the table for his. "I really am."

His Adam's apple bobbed when he swallowed. He flipped his hands to curl his fingers with hers. "I'm sorry, too. Sorry you didn't feel like you *could* tell me. I was pretty messed up back then."

She blinked really fast, trying to hold back tears that threatened to flood her eyes. "What do you want to do? Now that you know?" She knew what she was afraid of—that he'd marshal all the Donovan wealth and influence and take her son from her. And maybe she deserved it. After all, wasn't that what she'd done to him?

"I'd like to get to know him. My son." He unclasped their hands, and Carrie again fought that sense of loss. He wasn't hers to keep. That was what divorce meant. She was grateful, though, that he didn't think like a Donovan, that his ask was so reasonable and nonthreatening.

She gave him a shaky smile. "He'd like that, I'm sure."

"And Beckham." Lance tipped his chair back on two legs. "I miss my dog."

Carrie let out a nervous laugh. "The two of them together? It's a lot. Fair warning, that's all I'm saying."

His laugh joined hers, and she dug her phone out of her bag. "Shall we set a playdate then?"

"What am I, two years old? Can we call them something besides 'playdates'?" But he got out his phone, too.

A series of bings caught both their attention. She opened the dating app and saw that she'd missed a handful of messages from potential first dates numbers fourteen and fifteen. She shook her head, knowing she should accept the meetings. She'd never find someone if she didn't *look,* after all, but the whole numbers game of it all was so depressing.

"Who is it?" Lance glanced up from his calendar app. "I've got a big job going right now, but I'm free weekends. How's this Saturday?"

Saturday? Her usual date night? Addison, the teen upstairs who usually watched Oli, had been less and less available as she got more involved with drama club at school. Had she stumbled into a perfect baby- and dog-sitting situation?

"Saturday could work." Carrie thumbed up her calendar. "I might have a date. How would you feel about hanging at my place? I could have Mom on standby in case you need anything."

"A date? You're seeing someone?" Lance was trying to look uninterested, but she could tell from the increased bounce of his knee that he was, in fact, interested in her answer.

"I've got a few possibilities. I've been doing the online dating thing."

Lance let out a long, dismissive snort. "Waste of time, if you ask me."

"Well, I didn't." Although she hadn't wanted to go on a

date very much at all, his attitude made her double down. Oh, she was going on a date alright. This Saturday. Right in front of him. And there was nothing he could do about it. She'd work out all this longing with someone else. That was the healthy way to handle the stirring Lance evoked from her. Wasn't it? It was. A few clicks and Mr. Fourteen was all lined up. *Take that, treacherous body.*

Lance gave her one of his calculating looks. When he was working on a job site, it meant a problem needed fixing and he was figuring out the best approach. Aimed at her, she wasn't sure what it meant.

His lips stretched into a forced-looking smile. "Ditch the app. I know the perfect guy for you."

Now it was her turn to snort. "Really? And you're going to set him up with me?"

His hand smacked the table. "Absolutely."

She narrowed her eyes at him. "Who is this guy? Someone you work with?"

"You could say that." Lance tucked his phone away after checking the time. "I need to get back to my site. Why don't you swing by the Dorothy tomorrow?"

"You'll introduce us?" Carrie handed her phone over for him to enter the address. "Really?"

"The man needs no introduction," Lance said grandly and typed into her phone.

She took her phone back and placed it facedown on the table. "This I've got to see."

Lance hit his forehead like he'd forgotten something. "That reminds me. This project I'm working on? We're going to need an interior designer. You should throw your hat in the ring."

"Really?" Carrie thought about how much work Dimitri's restaurants were going to be, but she wasn't so financially stable that she could bat away new leads without some consideration. Besides, back in the day, she and Lance had made a pretty great team. She was still proud of the projects they'd worked on together. In the end, it had been all bitterness and fighting over every decision—like a five-cent difference per foot in material costs would end the world—but they were both different now. He seemed much mellower than the driven-to-prove-himself Donovan black sheep, and Lord knew, motherhood had brought out a type of patience and perseverance she'd never known she possessed. Yeah, it could be different this time around. Working together, that is. "It's not a terrible idea."

"Yeah, I'm known for my not-terrible ideas." He grinned at her. "Seriously, come check it out. Luckily, you happen to know a guy who has some say in the final decision." He threw down enough money for both their drinks and a generous tip for the waiter they'd barely seen and walked away.

Man, she loved to watch Lance walk away. He had the nicest ass.

# CHAPTER 8

CARRIE ENJOYED THE SMOOTH RIDE UP THE EXPRESS elevator to Kristin Beaudry's penthouse home, the quiet glide up sixty stories, a quick trip that gave her just enough time to check her outfit in the sliver of mirror that bisected the back wall of the elevator car. The mirror was small enough that it didn't force anyone to check themselves out but large enough to allow for a nervous Nellie like herself to straighten her hemline and check her lipstick. It also reflected another mirror strip on the ceiling, a safety precaution for anyone facing the door but wondering what the people behind her might be doing.

On this ride, Carrie was alone, and she was glad for it. Although she religiously checked herself for baby barf and dog hair every time she left her condo, she still found mystery stains and errant hairs once she was out in the real world. This morning had been especially hectic. After her early run with Oliver in the stroller and Beckham bouncing along beside them, she'd been in a rush to get to Kristin's but her mother was late—construction traffic, she'd explained when she finally showed—and Carrie'd sprinted to her car, not an easy feat in four-inch heels but also not her first time doing the tiptoe prance. At least the drive to the penthouse was uneventful, and she'd splurged on valet parking, just this once.

Carrie pulled a travel-size roller from her bag and gave her chocolate pencil skirt one last go-over before the doors spread open. Stuffing the roller back in her bag, she was pleased to see only a few dark hairs caught on the sticky tape. Details were important when meeting with a client, and she'd already gotten some details wrong with Kristin.

For one, she was supposed to have checked on the bathroom's progress yesterday, but after her coffee confessions with Lance, she'd been so drained that the short drive to the downtown penthouse had felt more like a cross-country drive. So she'd called Kirk, the contractor on the project, who'd told her, yet again, that things were a bit behind schedule and that the next day would be better for her to come by. Kristin'd agreed to the change in schedule, but Carrie still felt like she'd let her client down. No matter. She'd make it up to Kristin today. She straightened the exaggerated cuffs of her button-down silk shirt and reviewed the project timeline in her head. There had to be a way to get things back on track and finish on time.

The elevator opened onto Kristin's floor, a floor she had all to herself. The front door was already ajar, and Carrie heard the buzz of a tile saw in the distance. Carrie frowned. Kirk was supposed to be done with the installation earlier today, and although generally being a few hours off schedule wasn't a big deal, the schedule had already been delayed three times due to Kirk's unexplained setbacks.

"I swear, that noise is going to drive me batty." Kristin appeared, a tall glass of lemonade in one hand, her other hand planted firmly on her hip. Kristin was a retired model who'd let herself gain an extra ten pounds since her runway days, which still made her the thinnest woman Carrie'd ever seen in real life. Tall and willowy, Kristin always reminded Carrie of one of those skinny palm trees reaching high into the sky. Her outfit, a strapless lemon shorts romper, showed off her prominent clavicle. "Promise me today is the last day I have to hear that infernal buzzing."

"That's what I'm here to check on." Carrie smiled her most reassuring smile. She liked Kristin and wanted Kristin to like her, or at least the work she did. Kristin'd moved into this apartment six months ago and was intent on a total makeover. She'd given Carrie a guest bathroom as a test. Carrie hoped to get an A+.

Kristin took a sip of her lemonade and followed Carrie down the stretch of hallway that led to one of the guest suites. Carrie pictured the bathroom in her mind—not how it was when she'd first encountered it. No, that bathroom had been an homage to all things dark and slippery—black marble and chrome accents, an oversize walk-in shower and a too-small vanity. "Too masculine," Kristin had called it. *Too depressing* was Carrie's diagnosis. She reimagined the whole thing based on something Kristin said about her new home being a "piece of heaven" all for herself. Carrie didn't do literal clouds and angels, but the gorgeous aurora marble with the pearl-glass inlays she'd picked out created a repeating abstract flower pattern, not too bold but enough to give a celestial feeling.

The tile wasn't suited for submersion in water, so the shower, which she'd made smaller to make more room for a luxurious vanity, was in durable white and silver-swirled marble. She'd brought in high-end fixtures with a champagne finish and fluffy towels in the highest thread count known to humankind.

Carrie loved the design part of her job, of course, but if pressed, she had to admit that her favorite stage was at the end when she got to dress a room. She loved to fluff towels and pillows, to light candles and unwrap scented soaps, to place the perfect accent pieces that really bring a room to life. If all went well, tomorrow she'd be back for finishing touches. And if that went well, she could send Kristin the final bill. Hallelujah.

"Kirk!" Carrie couldn't see him yet, but his sporadic texts earlier in the day indicated he was on the job. She tapped lightly on the semiclosed bathroom door and waited for him to turn off the saw.

"Come on in." Kirk pushed protective eyewear to the top of his shaved head. "Looking good, isn't it?"

Mindful that Kristin was right behind her, Carrie verbally agreed. Mentally, she was horrified. Her beautiful aurora marble was slapped to the wall, grout still oozing from the seams, in a haphazard pattern that occasionally resulted in a delicate five-petal flower. Her eyes flew around the room. Only two days ago, she'd signed off on the shower, and today she was pleased that at least her vanity looked good. Except.

She touched her finger to the top of the counter, skating it around the curve of the sink's edge. "This isn't what I ordered."

"Closest thing to it." Kirk used a dirty rag to swipe at some of the drying grout on the wall. "Your special order never arrived. Had to go with plan B."

"Plan B?" There was no plan B. Kristin's bathroom was supposed to be plan A all the way.

"Excuse me." She spun to block Kristin's view of the bathroom. "We seem to have a misunderstanding."

"We do?" Kristin arched a thin eyebrow at her.

"Kirk and I." Carrie squeezed her purse strap until her fingers turned white. "Do you mind if I have a few words with Kirk? Alone?"

Kristin's other eyebrow joined the first, a move that should have wrinkled her forehead, but it didn't. Not at all. Kristin's face was as line-free as a baby's bottom. "Be my guest."

"Thank you." Carrie backed into the bathroom and closed the door behind her. "What the hell, Kirk?" she hissed, aware that Kristin was likely still on the other side of the door but too furious not to confront Kirk right this second.

Kirk leaned a hip against the vanity. His work boots and jeans were splattered with old paint and fresh grout. His arms crossed over his chest.

"Are you still mad about the schedule? It's not my fault all your special orders took so long to come in." Kirk's lips thinned into a straight line. His gaze raked her carefully chosen outfit, quickly taking her measure and dismissing her. "Someone had to get this project back on schedule. My men don't work for free."

Carrie would've argued with him, pointed out that his job was installation, not design, but she was too horrified by the fixtures in the shower.

"Bronze?" She meant to hiss it, but her building rage pushed the words out at full volume. "What happened to my champagne finish?"

Kirk blinked at her. "I don't know what you're talking about. You signed off on the shower two days ago."

"I know what I signed off on, and it wasn't bronze fixtures. Why would you switch them out? Is that why the tiling is behind? And also, what are you doing with my tile work? It's a total disaster."

Kirk pushed off the vanity and attempted to loom over her, not difficult since he was close to six feet, but she was only five inches shorter than he was and she had on four-inch heels, so she glared right back.

"Kirk, what have you done to my bathroom?"

His silence condemned him. She knew the scam—cutting corners, switching out cheaper materials and pocketing the difference. He'd been so blatant about it. And God, her poor tiles. How was she going to salvage them?

"If you don't like my work, you'll have to fire me. But you'll still owe me for all my time." His biceps bulged like he was fighting to keep himself from reaching out to shake her, but his hands stayed firmly in his armpits.

Carrie smiled ferociously. "Oh, you're fired alright, and you're not getting a penny more out of me."

"We have a contract."

"That we do. If you'd read it, you'd know that if we part ways before the end of the job, I don't owe you a thing. It's a standard exit clause in all my contracts."

"Bitch." He stomped past her to gather up his gear. "No wonder no one wants to work with you."

That stung. It was true that she'd had difficulty finding and keeping reliable help for her remodels. Anytime she contracted out parts of a job, things never went quite right. Was Kirk correct? Was it something about her that made contractors lax? Were her standards too high?

She looked at her poor celestial wall, a confusing mess of patterns and shapes where tranquility and peace were supposed to reign. No, her standards were exactly high enough. She'd never had these problems when she'd worked with Lance. His attention to detail had equaled her own. Running her eyes around the bathroom, she realized she'd need to strip it all back down. If he'd so blatantly messed with the finishing materials, no telling what corners he'd cut behind the scenes. Thin drywall? Pipes smaller than she'd specified? She wouldn't be happy until she'd inspected every detail herself.

"Get out," she said to Kirk and waited until he stormed out with his tool kit and tile saw.

He left the door open, and Kristin poked her head in. Her eyes grew round as she looked around her guest bathroom. "Oh no, oh no, no, no."

Carrie held up a hand. "I'm going to make this right, Kristin. I just need you to be a bit more patient."

Kristin's mouth opened and closed, but all that came out was more "no, no, no."

"We're starting over." Carrie put the plan forming in her head into words. "From studs out. I have the perfect guy for the job. And it won't cost you anything, I promise. This is on me, and I swear I will make it up to you."

Kristin held out a glass of lemonade to Carrie. "It's a good thing I like you."

Carrie covered her relief by taking a long sip. She choked and had to stop a minute to catch her breath. "I didn't realize there was a secret ingredient."

"My special recipe. Half fresh-squeezed lemonade, half vodka. When I saw him carry out that lovely showerhead you chose this morning, I figured you'd need it."

"You let him walk out with it?" Carrie wasn't proud that she took another long draw of the vodka juice.

"I have enough of my own problems. I'm not taking on yours, too." Kristin raised her glass in a toast. "Better start working miracles, though. I'll give you another week, two tops, but after that, no more chances."

Carrie swallowed hard, glad for the fortifying vodka rushing through her veins. It gave her the composure to accept Kristin's ultimatum, and it gave her the courage to pick up her phone and make a humbling call.

---

Lance was surprised to see Carrie's number pop up on his phone. Sure, he'd invited her to come by the Dorothy, but after they'd parted ways yesterday, he convinced himself she wouldn't follow through. Why would she want to work with him again? That meant they had no reason to talk until Saturday, when he'd get to spend a whole evening with his son. He was both elated and slightly panicked at the thought. What did you talk about with a three-year-old? Should he bring a gift? Of course he should.

"Is everything okay?" Lance picked up on the fourth ring, once he walked out onto the front lawn where he'd have some privacy. Thanks to the large crew he'd hired for the Dorothy job, repiping the communal areas—lobby bathroom and the laundry room—was well under way, and the whole building shook as his roofers stripped the roof down to the deck.

"I need your help." Carrie's voice was so professional that he was relatively sure the problem wasn't child- or dog-related, but he checked anyway.

"Oliver and Beckham are fine?" He'd only known about

his son for a day, but already the fear that something bad might happen to him haunted the back of Lance's mind. Intellectually, he understood that Oliver's life was the same as it had been since birth. Emotion was a whole other thing. A complicated thing.

"Yes, they're with my mom today. This is a work thing."

As she explained about her renovation, he shook his head. "Kirk Robles? Never heard of him. You need a new guy?"

"I need you."

Lance was so surprised he pulled the phone away from his face to check the screen. Yep, that was Carrie alright. "I'm full out on the Dorothy project right now. I don't have any time or men to spare."

"Can you please come take a look? Tell me what you think?"

It had been a long and emotional twenty-four hours. What he needed was a beer and some serious couch time. What he should do was stay at the Dorothy and pitch in where he could. What he decided to do, however, was drive to downtown Miami. He didn't lie to himself. He was still thinking about Carrie's lips on the rim of her tea mug yesterday, that smudge of deep-red lipstick she left on every cup she used, every cheek she kissed. He was still thinking about her confident smile as she told him about her new restaurant project. He was still thinking about her. Period.

He did one last sweep of the first floor to let the guys know he expected a long day. They needed to take advantage of the empty building while they could. Once in his truck, he waited for the diesel engine to warm up and texted with Carrie, asking for pictures and some background information. That bathroom was in bad shape, but it was a small space. If Mendo kept things on track at the Dorothy, he could probably handle Carrie's bathroom himself. Did he have the time? Not really. But construction work was like that—feast or famine. It wouldn't be the first time he spread himself too thin. Since the divorce, he didn't worry about his hours. No one was waiting for him anyway.

He gunned the truck because that wasn't true. Not today. Today, Carrie was waiting for him, and he couldn't stop himself from riding to her rescue.

# CHAPTER 9

CARRIE PACED IN FRONT OF KRISTIN'S ELEVATOR DOORS, rubbing her palms together in a nervous gesture she wasn't proud of. Kristin was inside the apartment, though, so she'd never know how close her designer was to a breakdown. Kirk. She couldn't believe that guy. Carrie couldn't tell which she wanted to do more: scream in rage or ugly cry like Oliver when he was overtired. Well, minus the snot running down her face. She'd skip that part and go right into the wailing and foot pounding.

The doors finally slid open, and the breath she'd been holding whooshed out of her. *Thank God.* Somehow, having Lance here made her believe the bathroom could be salvaged. If anyone could get it back on track, it was Lance Donovan. And if he couldn't, well, she'd have to refund all of Kristin's money, dissolve her company, and start over with a new name, a new brand. So, not much at stake here. Only her whole professional life. Nothing to worry about.

"You made it."

He smiled at her, that devastating smile of his, a little crooked with the right side lifting a millimeter or two higher than the left. "I did."

They stared at each for a long moment. He looked good. He hadn't shaved today, and stubble shadowed his jaw. His untrimmed hair looked like he'd run his hands through it a dozen times. His white Excalibur Construction T-shirt pulled across that muscled chest of his, ending right below the waist of his faded work jeans. The right thigh was worn through, not quite a hole yet but starting to fray. If they were still married, she'd buy him a new pair. The thought snapped her out of her odd trance. *If they were still married.* Seeing the guy so many times in two days was messing with her mind.

"You going to show me the bathroom?" Lance's head tilted to one side, and Carrie scolded herself for finding it adorable because Oliver did the same thing whenever she told him something he didn't want to hear. Bedtime. Get out of the bathtub. No more Cheerios.

She waved Lance in and led the way to her celestial space turned hellhole. She stepped back so he could go inside.

"Who's the hottie, and why didn't you hire him in the first place? I wouldn't mind this one hanging around all day, if you know what I mean." Kristin giggled at her own joke, toasting Carrie with a fresh glass of her vodka-infused lemonade.

"He's my ex." Carrie bit out the words. She'd panicked and called him, but now that he was walking around her bathroom, the tiny room she'd had such big plans for, she was a bit humiliated for him to see how badly the job had gone. She was a professional. This didn't happen to her.

"So he *is* available." Kristin winked at her and leaned against the wall.

Available? For all their talking yesterday, Carrie didn't know if he was available or not. Was he remarried? Dating someone? Probably. How would the woman in his life feel about Lance's sudden entry into fatherhood?

"I don't know," Carrie admitted in a low voice.

"I am." Lance's back was to them, but the space was

small. Of course he could hear them. "Married to my job. That's what you always said, isn't it, Carrie?"

Not a conversation to have in front of Kristin. "What do you think? Can you do it?"

Lance joined them in the hallway. "Take it back to studs and build it to your specs? Sure."

Kristin toasted him. "Good man. When can you get started?"

Lance propped his hands on his hips. "I've got another job going right now. Any chance this could wait a few weeks?"

"I told you the timeline." Carrie didn't look at Kristin, didn't want the client to see the fear in her eyes.

"Right." He spun in place, surveying the room. "I'll have to talk to my site manager, but I think we can spare a guy or two. Give me a day to work out the details, okay?"

Elation bubbled in Carrie's chest. It was going to be okay. Lance was going to make it okay. She wouldn't have to dissolve her business and start over from scratch. She smiled at him. He smiled back.

"Sounds good." She turned to Kristin, confidence restored. "I promise you, this bathroom is going to be gorgeous."

"Within the week?"

"Hopefully." Carrie stuck out her hand to seal the vow with a shake. "Or maybe two? You did say two weeks earlier."

"I did, but really the sooner, the better." Kristin walked them to the door.

"Understood." Lance flashed his crooked smile at Kristin, his blue eyes crinkling at the corners in a way no hetero female could possibly resist. "Do you want it fast, or do you want it perfect?"

Kristin saluted him with her glass, duly charmed by his baby blues. "Perfect, of course."

"Two weeks then." He covered his heart with his hand, pledge-of-allegiance style. "I promise you won't be disappointed."

"Fine, you've got yourself a deal." Kristin sipped her drink, watching Lance from under her long, probably fake eyelashes. "I'll be glad to have tomorrow off from all the construction noise. See you Wednesday." She wiggled her fingers in goodbye and closed the door behind them.

Carrie called the elevator, nerves stretched so tight she thought she could hear them twang as she walked. That had been close, too close, and now here she was owing Lance for saving the day, for charming Kristin into extra time, for getting her business back on track. She felt unsettled by the whole thing, from her panicked call to him to his casual acceptance of the job. The Lance she knew wouldn't have been so calm, would've argued about Kristin's timeline and threatened her with all the things that could go wrong if the job was rushed. When had he learned to schmooze a client like that? When had he traded his anger for charm? For all that she'd lived with the man for five years, she found herself staring at him like she'd never seen him before.

"Come by the Dorothy tomorrow." Lance followed her into the elevator, unaware she was silently freaking out. "You could bring Oliver."

That snapped her right back into the moment. "To an active construction site?"

"Right, bad idea. I heard it as soon as it left my mouth." He smiled ruefully, a familiar expression that made him her Lance again.

"You take lunch breaks?"

He leaned broad shoulders against the back wall. "Yeah, most days."

"You can have lunch with us." She busied herself looking for something in her purse. Keys? Sure, it didn't matter. She just couldn't look at him. "If you want."

Lance waited until she looked up, and his eyes locked with hers. "Oh, I want."

Carrie stilled. Caught. Because she wanted, too. She watched him watch her, sure that want on his face was reflected on hers. He'd always read her so easily. It was one of the things she loved about being with him, how completely she felt seen. Understood. Only now she wished he wasn't quite so perceptive.

He took a step toward her. She took a step back and another until she was pressed against the elevator doors. He followed, stopping when he was close enough that the heat of his body radiated through the thin T-shirt, warming her. Melting her resistance, one particle at a time. She grasped the strap of her bag tightly with both hands. She would not reach for him.

"You want me, too." It wasn't a question, but her head bobbed in agreement. His eyes flared at the movement, pupils darkening, widening. He leaned toward her. She wobbled on her heels, knees suddenly too weak to support her. Lance shot out a hand and steadied her, using his grip to pull her closer.

He lowered his head. He was going to kiss her. She knew it, knew she should do something to stop it. Nothing good could come of kissing Lance. But he'd come and helped when she called, hadn't stayed angry at her about Oliver.

And he smelled so good, a citrusy soap and that something in the air that was simply Lance. Her Lance.

"Yes," she said even though he hadn't asked a question, and his lips crashed down on hers.

It was fierce, their first kiss since Oliver was conceived, like the years apart had left them both starving. She was starving. She let go of her bag's strap and fisted handfuls of T-shirt, hauling him closer until her breasts pressed into his chest. She moaned at the pressure. He changed the angle of their kiss, going deeper, harder. She couldn't breathe and didn't care. He was all the air she needed. God, she'd missed him. Missed this, the very *us* of them together.

The door dinged and opened, bringing fresh air against her back. She gasped and pulled away, stepping backward and over the threshold, wiping her palms down the front of her chocolate skirt. *What a mistake. What a colossal mistake.* She should say that out loud, tell him to forget it happened. She opened her mouth, but one look from his smoldering eyes silenced her. Instead, she turned and fled. She was pretty sure he'd get the message. Lance Donovan was not something she could have, and her raging hormones would simply have to calm down and get over it.

He followed her to her Blazer and leaned in the window once she'd pulled on her seat belt. "See you tomorrow?"

*Oh God, tomorrow.* She swallowed. "Yeah."

He tapped the top of her car. "Sleep well."

"I always do," she lied. Then she lied to herself all the way home about how letting Lance back into her life was only for Oliver's sake. And Beckham, of course. Yeah, it was all for them. She would put the kiss out of her mind. Old habits and all that. She was sure it meant as little to Lance as it had to her. If she never mentioned the kiss again, she doubted he'd even bring it up. It was better this way, really. She repeated that in her head until it started to sound true.

# CHAPTER 10

Lance cursed under his breath in Spanish, a habit he'd picked up from his days learning the construction business from the ground up, literally. He'd started off as a flooring laborer, learning the intricacies of tile installation, the importance of good knee pads, and how to curse a blue streak in three different languages from Mendo.

Working his way up—again, literally—from flooring to masonry to roofing, Lance learned that nothing was ever easy-peasy on a construction site. No matter how uncomplicated the plan, complications were bound to arise. He was good at complications. At least, the construction kind. He enjoyed unexpected challenges like finding mold in the walls or plumbing lines not being where they were supposed to be.

He found himself wishing the Dorothy was the exception, a smooth sail of a job, no problem solving needed. After a restless night when he couldn't get the sight of Carrie's wicked, red mouth out of his mind, he wasn't at his best, problem-solving-wise. He'd spent hours trying to remember the exact shape of her breasts against his chest. Had motherhood changed her body? Had she nursed Oliver? There were so many things he didn't know, things he had no right to ask. Bottom line? He was in trouble, and it was more than the fact that obsessively thinking about the kiss and where more kissing might lead made the fit of his jeans extremely uncomfortable. He needed to get himself under control before Mendo thought he was getting a hard-on from the disaster in front of them.

Mendo stood back from the elevator shaft, one hand on the back of his neck, hard hat tipped forward.

"Is that water?" Lance knew it was water. He could see clearly with his own two eyes that the bottom of the elevator shaft was filled with a very shallow pool of water. He supposed it could be worse. It could be a foot of water instead of the mere quarter inch he guessed the current pool to be.

"Yuh-huh."

"Where's it coming from?" Lance broke out the small flashlight he always had on him and flashed it around the bottom of the shaft. Definitely water. No clear source.

Mendo clucked his answer, shaking his head.

"At least the old car's been removed, right?" Lance looked up, double-checking that over two thousand pounds of elevator wasn't going to come smashing down on his head. Nope, coast was clear. The two-story shaft was empty. Well, except for the puddle.

It'd be stupid to step in there. Who knew where the water was coming from? Could be an old roof leak. Could be all that shivering and shaking of the roof demo had caused a cracked pipe. And if the plumbing was messed up, no telling what was going on with the electrical. Water plus electricity was never a good combination. No, he'd stay safely out here while they figured it out.

Mendo had his phone out, texting. "Got a pump on the way. Once we clear it out, maybe we can see where the leak is."

"Good news is it's not too deep. So either the leak is old or very weak. This is not a disaster." A big part of Lance's job was assuring other people that whatever setbacks and delays occurred were not, in fact, disasters but instead minor annoyances easily dispatched. Good thing the elevator project was ahead of schedule—okay, only by a few hours, but a lead was a lead, and they were about to eat up what little lead they had. He didn't want to have to tell Caleb to keep the residents away once they got back from their cruise.

The Dorothy groaned from the force of the roof crew ripping off layers above. Even if they did get behind schedule, at least the residents would have missed the worst of the roof job. He'd once seen a wineglass shimmy itself right off a rack during a roof job. He'd warned everyone to secure valuables, but he'd still do a walk-through before they returned to check for damages.

"Good to have Beckham around again, huh?" Mendo tried to sound casual, staring into the elevator shaft like there was more to learn, but Lance knew what the question was really about. Carrie. Mendo'd learned to leave the topic alone after the first few months of the divorce, but clearly he thought that door was open again. Maybe it was.

"Yeah, good to see Carrie, too." He threw Mendo the bone, figuring it would save time to cut to the chase.

"You gonna see them again?" Mendo kept the pretense of looking for the leak's origin, darting his flashlight around the shaft, but his smug smile gave him away. Mendo and his secret agendas that he wasn't very good at keeping secret.

Lance smiled fondly at the older man. "I have to. She's the mother of my son."

Mendo's flashlight splashed into the shallow pool of water. "What now? She had your kid?"

Lance opted to leaved Mendo's flashlight at the bottom

of the shaft until they knew more about where the water was coming from. "She did. Never told me."

Mendo squatted onto his haunches, looking up at Lance with shocked eyes. "You have a son? How old?"

"He'll be three next month. Oliver."

Mendo nodded and nodded, rocking a bit on his heels. Lance squatted down beside him, placing a hand on top of Mendo's shoulder. Lance knew how the man felt. Sledgehammer to the gut. It took a minute to get over a thing like that. His brothers had taken the news in stride, but then they hadn't been with him through the marriage, the divorce, the aftermath, not the way Mendo had been.

Finally, Mendo choked out a few words. "Congratulations. You'll be a great dad."

"I don't know about that." It'd been Lance's defense for years, the reason he didn't want children. With a dad like his, how could he possibly be any good at the job?

Mendo knocked him playfully on the side of the head. "You taught yourself to lay a perfectly level floor. You can teach yourself this, too. Get a book or something. You're a smart guy."

"It's a bit late for *What to Expect When You're Expecting*," Lance joked, but then suddenly he wasn't joking. Because it was too late for it all—watching Carrie grow big with his child, the birth, holding his son for the first time. He wasn't there when Oliver took his first step or said his first word. He'd missed it all, the milestones and sleepless nights, the trips to the doctor and birthday parties. Did his son have a favorite color? Favorite food? Lance didn't know any of it. He was already a terrible father, and he'd only been at it a few days. Maybe Carrie'd been right to keep him out of it. She did know him better than anyone else.

Mendo was nodding again, a regular bobblehead. "You'll figure it out, Lance. It's a great thing to be a father."

Lance nodded, the gesture apparently contagious. "Your kids are lucky to have you, Mendo."

"Ha, tell them that. Now they've all flown the coop, when do I hear from them?" He pushed himself to his feet and twisted his torso, stretching his back. "Don't worry, though. You've got ten years until the teen years hit full force. Enjoy them while you can."

"I will." Lance rose, too, with new determination. He wouldn't miss another first. He'd volunteer at Oliver's school, attend every ceremony, every game, every performance. He'd be the dad he wished he'd had. He'd be Mendo.

"What about Carrie? She say why she never told you?" Mendo returned to his study of the shaft. His flashlight had turned itself off in its shallow, watery grave. "Doesn't seem like her, not the Carrie I used to know."

"It's complicated." Lance leaned against the elevator opening. "Mendo, how do I move past her keeping my own son a secret from me?"

"That's even more complicated." Mendo clapped him on the back, hard. "But if you want to know your son, you'll have to. Consider it your first parental compromise."

Mendo was right, as usual, but he didn't know the whole story, didn't know about the kiss. Lance's emotions were as wild as an out-of-control wrecking ball, taking out walls that needed to stay standing.

"Is that water?"

Lance didn't recognize the gruff voice, but he did recognize the clean-shaven architect, Adam St. John, when he poked his head into the elevator shaft, looking first up, then down. At six feet and a bit, Lance was used to being the tall-est person around, but Adam made him feel like he could try out for a role as a Munchkin in the community theater's upcoming production of *The Wizard of Oz*. The guy was professional basketball tall, but Lance resisted asking if he'd ever played. Of course he had, and if he'd liked it, he'd still be doing it instead of designing buildings in South Florida.

"Adam." Lance shook the man's hand, marveling at the sheer size of his knuckles. Tiny basketballs, each one. Grateful for the distraction, he pumped the man's hand a little too hard. "Good to see you."

Adam's shake was perfunctory. "Looks like a disaster."

"It's definitely not a disaster." Lance gave his best client-reassuring face—a dip of the chin and a slightly furrowed brow.

And yet Adam was not reassured. Probably because he knew a thing or two about buildings. "That'll set us back a few days, I reckon."

"We're ahead of schedule, and pumps are on the way."

"Still could be a disaster." Adam stepped back from the shaft with a shake of his head. "Who knows where that water's coming from?"

Mendo cleared his throat. "Most likely it's a minor leak. Shouldn't take more than a few hours to get us back on track. I'll head out front and wait on that pump."

Adam pulled out an iPad and made some notes. "Wish I had your confidence, guys, but I'll keep my mouth shut about all the other things it could be. For now."

"Appreciate it. We construction guys like to keep it simple." Lance gave a self-deprecating smile. Like he didn't know all the awful things the leak could signal. No need to panic, though, until they had more information. That was his motto: Problem solve now, panic later. Maybe he should have it stenciled on his truck.

"Didn't mean it like that." Adam was clicking away on his iPad. "Just came to talk to you."

Lance rolled his hand. "So talk. Can't do much here until the pumps arrive anyway."

Adam clicked a few more times and spun the tablet Lance's way. The City of Miami Beach's familiar logo headed a familiar document that Lance quickly scanned.

"What?" He read the document again, this time more slowly. Still the same bad news. "Can they even do that?"

"Apparently, they can. I've been calling Caleb, but he doesn't respond."

"He warned me that they wouldn't have regular Wi-Fi for large parts of the cruise." Lance swore under his breath in Creole. "Now this is the actual disaster. If the city doesn't approve the permits, we're at a standstill."

"Not precisely. The elevator permit came though, as did the roof and plumbing ones. It's just, you know, everything else that's on hold."

"It's Commissioner Santos." Lance's mouth twisted into the same expression he'd worn earlier when the barista at the Coffee Pot Spot accidentally made his morning latte with almond milk instead of regular. An unexpected and unwanted surprise. He'd been in a rush so, wincing at the slightly burned taste, he'd sipped the thing all the way to the work site where he'd then dumped it in the nearest trash can. If only dealing with the city would be that simple and nonconfrontational. "He's wanted that parking garage at full capacity ever since Caleb dangled the possibility in front of him."

"It is the most efficient use of space." It was no secret that Adam had refused to help with Caleb and Riley's dog park. "The income alone would make it so the residents could keep renting at their current rates. It really is a win-win," Adam said, proving that contrary to Riley's theory that he hated dogs and community spaces, he really was thinking big picture.

"What do we do?" Lance rubbed the back of his neck, noting it might be time for a haircut soon. "Caleb and Riley will never agree to get rid of their dog park."

Adam tapped at his iPad some more and spun the screen toward Lance again. "But would they agree to move it?"

Lance whistled low. "Now that is something."

Adam's screen opened to a 3-D rendering of a parking garage that filled the entirety of the lot next to the Dorothy. When Caleb and Riley built their dog park, they'd used half of it for the dogs and left the other half for the parking garage. Adam's drawing obliterated the current dog park. The garage was done in the style of the Dorothy—that is, vaguely Deco-ish and painted the same color. Climbing vines covered the outside, blocking the view of the cars that would be housed inside.

"Are those palm trees on the roof?" Lance touched the screen, and the picture flickered before enlarging the upper floor of the garage. "Wait, is that *LouLou?*"

Adam tap-tapped a few more times, and the rendering gave a panoramic tour of the roof. Grass, trees, agility equipment. It was similar in layout to the current dog park, but it was twice as big and twenty-five feet in the air.

"I thought Riley would be more likely to agree if I put her poodle in the proposal. She has a soft spot for that dog."

Lance hated to admit it, but he had a soft spot for that dog, too. It was easy to imagine LouLou enjoying the fresh smells so high up in the air, running her favorite figure eights in the plush grass. And wouldn't Beckham love it, too?

"What's that?" Lance pointed to a snakelike shape running up the side of the building.

Adam zoomed in on it. "There'd have to be a dog-park-only elevator, of course, so residents or people parked in the public parking section wouldn't have to be around dogs if they have allergies or something. So that's here." He traced a finger up the side of the building. "But then I started thinking that some dogs might not like elevators and how there are so few hills here in Florida. If there were a ramp, dogs and owners could get in a bit of cardio on their way to enjoy the park. It'd be a draw for people training for marathons and the like." His fingers pinched and opened until Lance had a clear view of what was essentially a running track.

"What's the material?" The builder in Lance was intrigued. The brother in him was dreading the conversation he'd have to have with Caleb. Destroy the dog park he'd built with Riley? His younger brother was still romantic enough to put up a fight over that. But it did make sense, and if it got them the permits they needed, more income for the building, and still had the community space so important to Riley, what was the harm?

"It's a synthetic. Depending on budget, we might go with something like Tartan Track—something all weather and fairly indestructible and easy to care for." Adam rotated the view to a bird's-eye perspective.

"It's remarkable." Lance's praise wasn't even grudging. It was a pretty great solution to a sticky situation. "It'd be a draw for new tenants, too, a one-of-a-kind park on top of a guaranteed parking space?"

"Do you think Caleb and Riley will go for it?"

Adam's presentation went into slideshow mode, and with each change of angle, Lance became more sure he was doing the right thing.

"I can sign off on it."

"You can?" Adam's surprise shouldn't have nettled Lance, but it did.

"I'm not just the hired help. I'm a full partner in this venture."

Adam's eyes widened, and then he smiled. "That's excellent news. I happen to have an amended permit application ready to go."

Lance held up a hand. "Not so fast. Can you email the plans? I'd like to look at them more carefully."

Adam clicked for a moment or two. "Done. You won't take long?"

"I'll take as long as I need to." Lance wouldn't be bulldozed. Architects tended to be ambitious, and he needed to make sure the new plan wouldn't break the budget and that the plan was financially feasible. You could make a lovely drawing of a floating city in the clouds, but that didn't mean a contractor could make it a reality.

"Okay then." Adam clamped the iPad against his side and held out his hand for another shake. "Soon as you approve the plans, I'll file the paperwork."

"I can file with the city." Lance shook Adam's hand perhaps a bit too roughly.

"Sure." Adam withdrew his hand and tucked it into the front pocket of his slacks. "But you have a lot going on here, I believe." He raised an eyebrow at the elevator shaft.

Lance huffed out a long sigh. "You're telling me. Fine, I'll be in touch. If everything checks out, I think this is going to be really great."

"What will be really great?" Carrie strolled up, long legs in a skirt that grazed the tops of her knees and a short blazer that hugged the curve of her waist. Images from his long night of fantasizing about Carrie's kiss and all the delightful things that could come next crowded his brain.

Lance swallowed hard, his gaze following the line of her calf into her mile-high heels. How did she walk in those things? But she'd always insisted people respected height and that the extra inches her collection of stilettos provided were crucial to her business.

"I don't believe we've met." Adam stepped forward, blocking Lance's view of Carrie's legs so that all he could hear was the clip of her heels against the terrazzo.

Speaking of height. "Carrie, this is Adam. He's the architect on this project." He coughed into his hand to clear the huskiness out of his voice.

Carrie smiled and held out her fingers. "Nice to meet you. I'm Carrie Burns, interior designer."

"I didn't know they'd hired a designer yet." Adam took her fingers in a soft shake that made Carrie smile wider. Lance's eyes narrowed. The Carrie from his midnight imaginings would not smile at another man like that.

"They haven't." Carrie freed her hand to tuck a strand of dark hair behind her ear. "I'm here to do a walk-through, get some ideas for my proposal."

"Let me give you the tour then. I can tell you the architectural plans, a little inside scoop, if you will." Adam's eyes twinkled down at her. Freaking twinkled. Lance's cheek muscle twitched.

Carrie's smile moved from polite to delighted. "Oh, I'd love that. I don't always get to work with the architect, you know. I'd love to get your thoughts on the space."

"I'd love to give them to you." Adam produced a card from his pocket. "Here. In case you have questions later. I have to make a quick call, but if you can wait a few minutes, I'll be back for that tour."

"Wonderful!" Carrie beamed at him, and Lance felt the back of his neck heat. He rubbed it and stared into the empty elevator shaft so no one could see the emotions he felt marching across his face. He didn't know how to feel around this woman, but he'd have to figure it out fast.

Carrie moved up next to him and followed his gaze to the puddle.

"Oh my," she said. "This looks like a disaster."

"It's not a disaster," Lance ground out although he was beginning to think another disaster was in the making. Carrie's color was high, the result of Adam's *twinkling*, no doubt. Had she already forgotten about yesterday's kiss in Kristin's elevator? Or was it like the night at Grandpa William's birthday party, relegated to the Never Happened vault in her mind? He didn't like this unsettled feeling, standing next to her but not sure where he really stood with her.

She placed a hand on his arm, directly below the elbow. "I'm sure you'll fix it. You're a miracle worker with a hammer and claw."

His muscles tightened under her hand, and he found himself leaning toward her. "We'll get this under control, but a setback here means fewer available resources for your celestial bathroom."

"Oh." Her hand fell away. "I understand, of course. Do

you have anyone else you'd recommend? Or maybe Adam knows someone?"

Ask Adam? No way. He didn't like the idea of anyone else helping her out. He planted his hands on his hips, full construction-foreman style. "I didn't say I was backing out."

"But—" She gestured at the elevator shaft. Yeah, that was going to be a problem, but it could be Mendo's problem.

"Can't spare any guys here, but I'll do it." Lance hadn't fully formed the plan before it came spilling out of his mouth. "Knox can help me."

"Knox knows construction?"

Lance lifted a shoulder. "He can learn." Wasn't much for Knox to do on the security end of the Dorothy upgrades until they were further along in the project anyway. Why not drag his business partner into it? The more Lance thought about it, the more it seemed the obvious way to help Carrie. He could handle the real work, and Knox would be his assistant. With enough beer, he was sure he could bribe his big brother into it. "We'll be there bright and early tomorrow."

Carrie squealed her delight and threw herself at him in an exuberant hug. "Thank you so much. You are saving my bacon. My business. You have no idea."

His arms curved around her so naturally that he marveled that he'd ever been able to let her go. "Of course. Whatever you need."

She pulled away to smile up at him. "And thanks for introducing me to Adam. It's a great gesture on your part."

"Uh, sure."

Her smile faltered at his hesitation. "He's who you meant, right? When you said you could introduce me to someone?"

In his defense, that offer came before the smoldering elevator kiss. Also, he hadn't had anyone specific in mind. Maybe himself. But he couldn't admit that now, so all he said was, "He's a great guy. Talented."

"You really are the best. What a great way to put yesterday's slipup behind us." She patted his back and stepped away. "Don't you think the kiss was only the past sneaking up on us? All that excitement over a new job, working together again, it was all a bit overwhelming, right?"

Lance took a page from Mendo's communication stylebook and nodded.

"Who knew we'd be better off as friends than spouses?" She smiled, her gaze bobbing around, looking at everything but him. "It'll be best for Oliver if we're friends. Just friends, I mean." Finally, her eyes collided with his. "Don't you agree?"

He stared at her, the memory of yesterday's kiss blazing in his mind. Her color heightened, tinging her cheeks pink, and he knew she remembered, too. He nodded.

"Shall we?" Adam was back, elbow crooked.

Carrie took his arm, for all the world like they'd done it a million times, and walked down the hall with Adam. She didn't look back.

She wouldn't. She never looked back, always focused on the future, his Carrie. He should put the kiss out of his mind. He had enough going on that he didn't need to excavate the past to find more, and he wasn't going to spend another minute wondering what was going on in his ex-wife's head.

# CHAPTER 11

"HAVE YOU EVER SEEN SO MANY MIRRORS?" MENDO peered around the one-bedroom's small bathroom with wide eyes.

Lance took in the wall-to-wall mirrors. The edge-to-edge ceiling mirror. The mirrored cabinets mounted on the mirrored walls. It was all a bit much. He smiled, thinking what Carrie would say when she saw it. Then he tried to picture her face when he told her the owners, Kent and Marco, had left strict instructions for their bathroom to be left as is.

"Why are you smiling? It's going to be a nightmare replumbing this room without damaging all this glass." Mendo glared into the nearest mirror like it was at fault.

Lance raised one shoulder. "Clients."

"Clients." Mendo nodded sagely. "Crazy, the lot of them."

"True that." Lance took one last look at his multiple reflections. "Put your best guy on this. I like Kent and Marco."

Mendo crouched down and pulled open the mirrored cabinet under the sink. "At least there aren't mirrors in here." He rooted through some cleaning products and four types of bubble bath. "It's gonna take a long time. Easier when we can demo first."

"Sure is. But not this unit." Lance didn't know that he agreed with Caleb's decision to let the residents have some say in the remodel. Case in point, clients didn't always have the best taste. Most of the current residents, though, had been thrilled by the idea of a makeover and were especially happy with the plan to combine some of the studios and one-bedrooms to make two-bedroom units. "Lucky for us, less than half the building is occupied. It's going to be a bit of a jack-in-the-box situation, what with current residents moving into the remodeled units until we finish their units, but it'll work out if we stick to the schedule. Even more luckily, this is the only bathroom we have to restore exactly as is after the repiping."

"I know, I know." Mendo waved him away. "We respect the clients' wishes even when the clients are crazy."

"Crazy clients are our bread and butter." Lance's phone buzzed in his back pocket. He pulled it out and scanned a text from the elevator company. Now that the leak in the elevator shaft was fixed, they were full steam ahead on the installation. The elevator should be operational well before the residents returned from their cruise. Thank God.

Mendo grinned at him. "I'd rather have a steak, you know what I mean?"

Lance left the bathroom laughing and texted back that he was glad to hear the elevator was back on schedule. After sending, he saw that he'd missed a call from his stepmother. Caleb's mom, Christine. They'd never really had much to talk about, not since she'd married his dad not even two minutes after Robert had divorced Lance's mom. He'd grown up hearing from his mom what a gold digger Christine was, but when his dad was arrested, tried, and found guilty, Christine had stayed by his side. Lance guessed that said something about her character, although he wasn't sure what. She usually only called him about holiday-related things. Well, Thanksgiving was right around the corner.

He walked back toward Riley and Caleb's place, sure that LouLou would be more than ready for a trip to the dog park. He stuck in his earbuds and called Christine back.

It rang a few times while he petted the predictably over-excited LouLou, loaded up his jean pockets with doggy bags, and clipped the leash on her collar. Christine picked up after he'd locked the door behind him.

"Lance!" She sounded happy that he'd called.

He gave her a cautious, perhaps even suspicious "Hello, Christine. Did you need something?"

Her breath hitched, like he'd shocked her. She'd expected more social niceties, he supposed, but he'd left that world behind on purpose. "It's not exactly, specifically for me," she hedged, and he knew immediately what this was about. His father.

"No."

"But I haven't even—"

"No, I didn't want anything to do with him before he was in jail. I certainly am not doing him any favors now."

"Prison." She corrected him like the difference mattered. "Your father is in prison."

"Tomato, to-mah-to," he grumbled, really just because it would annoy her. She did love her brand names. He was surprised she didn't brag about his father being in the best prison facility in the State of Florida. Too much? Probably. So why hadn't he hung up yet?

She ignored his baiting. "Thanksgiving is so close. A time for family. It would mean so much to him if you boys came for a visit. Now, I'm not asking for anything big. A few minutes of your time to let him know you still care."

"I don't care." He stood on the swale while LouLou

inspected a particularly delicious-smelling coconut. "I never did."

She clicked her tongue at him, but she wasn't his mother, so she didn't get to do that.

"Goodbye, Christine," he said.

"Maybe your brothers—"

"Goodbye." He hung up and ripped the buds out of his ears, stuffing them into his front pockets, cursing the fact that Caleb was unavailable to handle Christine. Not that Lance's mother was much better in terms of parenting skills, but at least she'd had the sense to divorce Robert Donovan and wasn't overly involved in his life now. They had polite get-togethers every other holiday or so, but he wasn't one of those people who talked to his mom every day, or even every week for that matter. He'd thought he liked it that way, but now he wondered what kind of relationship Caleb and Christine had. And what about his oldest brother, Knox? Were he and his mother close? There were so many things he didn't know about his own brothers.

He texted Knox. *Wanna get your hands dirty?* And when Knox responded with a thumbs-up, Lance invited him over to the Dorothy for a beer later. Caleb had left the refrigerator fully stocked for him, and it was time to let Knox know about his up-and-coming career as construction assistant.

By the time he and LouLou returned from their stroll around the block, with only a bit of whining on her part when he bypassed the crowded dog park gate because he needed the walk as much, if not more, than the dog, Knox was already parked on the soon-to-be-history rattan lobby couch.

"Smells like mold." Knox punched the pillow next to him. "You think the cushions are older than we are?"

"Everything in this building is older than we are." Lance led the way to Caleb and Riley's apartment. LouLou jumped on Knox's braced leg. "Down, you silly mutt." Lance jerked on the leash.

"She's alright." Knox bent and picked up the poodle with both hands. "We're getting to know each other is all."

LouLou acted like they were already fast friends, licking every part of Knox's chin. At the door, Lance pulled out a key and asked, "Got much planned for the next few days?"

Knox let LouLou down to run inside. "Pricing some different systems. Why?"

"Ever wondered about life in construction?" Lance headed straight for the fridge, knowing it would be easier to sell working for free with beer in the mix. He uncapped a couple of long necks and handed one to Knox.

"Not particularly." Knox took a long draw and sat in one of Riley's mismatched dining chairs, stretching his braced leg out straight in front of him. LouLou bounced against his leg until he picked her up and set her on his lap.

Lance stayed at the pink marble breakfast bar and told Knox about the bathroom he'd promised Carrie.

"For your ex, huh?" Knox slid his beer on the dining table, rolling it in the condensation. "Is this about your kid?"

"Her income is his, you know? I couldn't say no." Yeah, that was why he'd agreed. It had nothing to do with her big, hazel eyes and those red lips he loved so much.

Knox picked up his beer and toasted in his brother's direction. "For my nephew."

"For Oliver." Lance toasted back and then grabbed another couple of beers and joined his brother at the table. He'd wait until they were on beer number three to tell him what Christine wanted.

Knox finished off a second beer in silence, sweeping his hand from LouLou's head to tail the whole time. "I've been thinking of looking up my ex."

The words were so soft, at first Lance didn't think he'd heard right. "You were married? When?"

Knox chuckled. "Naw, not me. Ex-girlfriend, from before I joined up." He tapped his USMC T-shirt.

Carrie's eyes, those red lips, the way she fit against him. Watching her walk away on Adam's arm. "Don't do it, man. Let the past stay in the past."

Knox downed half the beer in one long swallow. "You're right. What's the point?"

"We both need to meet someone new." Lance clicked his bottle against Knox's.

Knox chuckled, a gruff, unused sound. "I'll drink to that."

# CHAPTER 12

"ONE BABYSITTER-SLASH-DOG SITTER SHOWING UP FOR duty, ma'am." Lance stood on Carrie's front stoop, dressed in jeans and yet another Excalibur Construction T-shirt, this one in a faded blue that made his eyes clear as the sky behind him.

"Thank you so much. I know we said Saturday, and it's Friday. Mom was supposed to come, but she canceled like an hour ago. And Addison from upstairs has a study group or something tonight. You're a lifesaver." Carrie held open the door so he could pass through. "I'm not quite ready yet."

Lance grinned. She narrowed her eyes, knowing he was thinking of how they'd always been late because of her. Little did he know or understand how motherhood had changed everything about her grooming habits. No more soaking in the bathtub with a face mask on and mellow music blasting through the condo. Her showers were short and efficient, and her hair game was simple and no longer required curling irons or elaborate braids. Sure, a bun looked professional, but it also took only a few seconds to secure to the back of her head.

She wasn't running late tonight because of time-management issues. No, she was running late because she'd emerged from her luxuriously long shower of ten minutes—she'd used an extra five to shave her legs—to find Oliver engaged in an art project involving the back of her bedroom door and her lipstick. Her forty-five-dollar-per-tube lipstick.

"Mama!" He'd grinned up at her, his lips and teeth so red it looked like he was bleeding from a gum disease or maybe scurvy. Before moving on to mural making, he'd decorated himself first. He'd painted his front two top teeth red and drawn lines radiating from his nose out to his ears, reminding her of some kind of maniacal bunny.

"Oli, Oli, Oli." She'd held him at arm's length, not wanting to get lipstick all over the cream towel wrapped around her body. In the bathroom, she'd brushed his teeth and dunked him in a quick bath, watching her expensive lipstick swirl down the drain. "Now you won't be hungry for dinner."

"Hungry, hungry! Oli's hungry for his mac and cheese," he sang happily, splashing water all over the bathroom. She'd given up and laughed. What else could she do? Cry? She'd done plenty of that when he was younger, but she'd learned that laughing made it easier to do what needed to be done.

She'd set him in his booster seat with a plastic bowl of dry Cheerios, his favorite snack, and brought her date outfit into the kitchen so she could keep an eye on him while she got dressed.

Now, standing in front of Lance in her first-date dress, as she'd come to think of it, she wished she was more put together. More the woman he remembered. Not this disaster in a V-necked little black dress so basic that not even her fanciest pair of stilettos could make it interesting. The stilettos she was still looking for.

"It's no problem." Lance trailed after her as she flitted around the condo, picking up toys and searching under blankets. "I said I wanted to spend more time with Oli, and I meant it."

"You've been at Kristin's all day. I hope you're not too tired." She rounded on him, eyeing him from head to toe. He looked fit enough for duty. Truth be told, he looked more than fit; he looked delicious. She could gobble him up. But she wouldn't because they were friends. Just friends. That was how it was going to be. That was why she'd impulsively accepted a date from Number Fourteen. That was why she would go, even though she'd much rather order pizza and catch up on her Netflix queue.

"Knox is a big help." Lance lifted couch cushions, waving under them like she should check it out. She did find one of Beckham's chew toys, a battered Santa bear whose squeaker had been gruesomely pulled out of his throat, but no shoes. Lance let the cushions flop back in place. "We made good progress today."

"That's good to hear." She gave up on the shoes. She had fifty more pairs in her bedroom. It wasn't like it was hard to match a black dress.

"Mama?" Oli hurried after her, picking up speed until he ran smack into her legs, almost taking her down. Luckily, years of living with a Jack Russell had prepared her for such balance challenges, and she reached out a hand to brace herself on the wall. "Pick me up?" He held up his arms in a way that melted her heart and made her forget why she was rushing around like a mad woman. She swept him up and propped him on her hip.

"Oli, Lance is here to look after you. You'll be good, yes?" It was a rhetorical question. Oliver was always good, even when he was using her lipstick like a paintbrush and hiding her shoes. And her hair. What should she do with her hair?

"Leave it down." Lance's eyes were warm, and she realized she'd asked the last question aloud. The problem with living with a baby and a dog was that she'd gotten in the habit of verbally narrating her life. It kept Beckham entertained, and she'd read that the more language a child heard early in life, the more advanced his language skills would be as he matured. She didn't speak in a baby voice like her mother did with him. She talked to him like a human being. Granted, he was a short, inexperienced human, but he was her little human, and she loved him.

Carrie touched her still-damp hair. "I don't have time to dry it."

Lance lifted a shoulder. "He won't care."

Carrie ran a nervous finger over her eyebrow, smoothing the hair outward. "I have to find some heels."

Lance shooed her away with his fingers. "You go. I got this." He held out his arms, and Oliver practically leapt out of her hold. Who could blame him? The man looked like he could catch you and hold on, no matter what. Carrie tamped down the hurt feelings that Oliver didn't put up more of a fuss about leaving her and showed Lance how to adjust the height of the booster seat.

"I put things together for a living. I can figure out a chair." Lance took over, sliding the seat from its highest to lowest settings. "Relax. Put on some shoes and get out of here."

Carrie chewed the lipstick off her bottom lip. Why had she said yes to this ridiculous date? Was she really leaving her child alone with his father for the first time? Lance looked so confident standing in her kitchen that she started to believe everything was under control.

It suddenly hit her that Oliver's father or not, Lance had zero experience with children. Zero experience with *her* child. She should never have agreed to this. It was too soon to leave them alone. They'd only met twice in the past few days, when, at Lance's request, she'd brought Beckham to Fur Haven for running dates with LouLou, the adorable poodle that Beckham was clearly in love with.

Laughing at dogs and inspecting various bugs that Oliver found in the park did not mean Lance was ready to take on parenthood. Or even babysitter-hood. She pulled out her phone. "I'm going to cancel."

Lance's face fell. "You don't trust me."

She gnawed on her knuckle. "How do I agree without hurting your feelings?"

His eyes shuttered. "You don't. But you trust Sherry. After everything."

Carrie bristled. "She's clean now. Has been for almost three years."

Lance gazed at her, face rearranged into a blank canvas on which she projected all her insecurities and fear of being judged.

"You can stay." She slumped into a kitchen chair, a spindly contraption she'd bought mainly because it didn't take up much space. "I'll stay, too. We'll run through a typical evening. Next time, you can be on your own."

"You sent me a very detailed text about the good-night routine. I'm pretty sure I can handle it." He adjusted the booster seat back to its original height, and Oliver giggled when it squeaked.

She jumped on his hesitancy. "Pretty sure?"

"Very sure." He cleared his throat. "I'll even take apart

this ridiculous chair and figure out why it's making that noise. I got this, Carrie. Go on your date."

Her phone buzzed, startling Carrie out of the chair. "My shoes!" She dashed away but was back in a few minutes, hopping on one foot while she harnessed her other foot into a strappy stiletto. "Call if you need me." She hopped over and kissed Oliver on the head. "Dinner's in the fridge. Warm it up on the stove. Not in the microwave!" She hopped her way to the front door, shouting directions every step of the way.

In the entry, she checked her hair in the mirror. Still wet, but she would take Lance's advice and leave it down. Mostly because she didn't have time to do anything else and unwinding a bun at the end of the night to find the hair still damp inside was too gross. Her date was already at the bar a few streets over, waiting for her. She ordered a Lyft—even a few blocks was too far to walk in these heels—smoothed a hand down the front of her dress, grabbed her evening clutch, and closed the door behind her. She wished the click didn't sound quite so final.

---

"We got this!" Lance called out, too late. The door had already slammed shut. He looked at his son. "Well, big guy, what do you want to do tonight?"

Oliver opened his mouth and pointed, urgency in his mystery movements.

"What is it, Oliver? You're hungry?" Lance turned to the refrigerator, wondering what Carrie'd left them to eat. He didn't have the greatest memories of her cooking—mostly, they ate a lot of takeout—so was expecting to find some prepackaged kid-friendly food. Chicken fingers, maybe, or fries. He was pleasantly surprised to find stacks of plastic containers with various kinds of pasta and vegetables to choose from. He was contemplating one in red sauce versus one in white sauce when he heard Oliver coughing.

"Hang on. You okay?" Lance spun, a container of pasta in each hand. Why choose? They could eat both. "Dinner is almost ready."

Oliver was half in, half out of the kitchen and had turned at Lance's words. He opened his mouth like he was going to respond. Instead, projectile vomit that looked to be composed mostly of semidigested Cheerios flew across the kitchen. Lance's stomach roiled, and he choked back his own gag reflex.

"That's about the grossest thing I've seen in a long while." He coughed a few times and, when he no longer felt like vomiting himself, searched under the sink for cleaning supplies.

"I threw up!" Oliver announced with apparent pride. He held a hand to his stomach and wiped the back of his mouth with his hand. Barf bits clung to his skin.

"No kidding." Lance would be more worried if Oliver didn't seem so completely fine, like maybe he was even enjoying this little barf-a-palooza. Should he call Carrie? And admit he couldn't watch his own son for five minutes without her help? No way.

"I threw up a lot!" Oliver admired the trajectory his vomit had taken, ending up next to Lance in front of the stove.

"Good Lord, man, you gotta learn to hold your liquor."

Lance dumped a wad of towels on the floor and scrubbed with his foot. "No fraternity's going to want you if you can't keep it in your stomach."

Oliver's blue eyes, so much like Lance's own, rounded like he was saying something important. Lance felt proud. Fatherly advice. That was what he could offer Oliver that Carrie couldn't. He racked his brain for some child-appropriate wisdom. "And don't eat bugs." He nodded sagely, and Oliver nodded along with him.

"Give me one second." He held up a finger, which Oliver grabbed and shook up and down. Normally, Lance would be down for an elaborate handshake, but not when one person's hand was spotted with barf that rubbed off onto him. Nice. How did he extract himself without hurting Oliver's feelings?

When he noticed what looked like a bit of blood on Oliver's front tooth, Lance used his other hand to dial Sherry's number. Panic tumbled in his belly until Lance thought he might puke himself. It was only a little red, could be anything. No need to call an ambulance, right? Right? God, hopefully, Sherry would know the right thing to do.

"Lance?" She sounded congested, her voice thick and low.

"Hey, so I've got a hypothetical for you." He was pretty sure that if Oliver were really sick, he wouldn't be so high-spirited. Then again, he had maybe five minutes of Daddy training, so better safe than sorry.

When he was done describing the various colors in the vomit, Sherry laughed. "Check your texts. I can tell you exactly what happened."

A picture of Oliver with lipstick all over his face and

lipstick tube held high like the Statue of Liberty torch appeared on his phone. Swirls of lipstick decorated the door behind him.

"Carrie texted it to me less than an hour ago. Kid's an artist." Her voice grew distant, like she was covering the phone, and she coughed. "So your hypothetical situation is nothing to worry about. He must've swallowed some when he painted his teeth. If you could die from eating lipstick, thousands of women would drop dead every day."

"Women don't eat it like a lollipop." Which was kind of what Oliver looked like he was doing in the second photo she sent. That or singing into it like a microphone. Why had Carrie taken pictures instead of ripping it out of his hands? Oh, that was picture three—one very upset Oliver, crying over the loss of his paintbrush and smearing lipstick all the way up into his hair. How did he get it on his knees? And somehow Carrie had erased all evidence of the incident before he arrived? That was some ninja parenting, for sure.

"I really don't think you need to worry, but if he keeps throwing up or you see blood, call me back." *Cough, cough, cough.* "If Carrie were worried, she wouldn't have gone on her date. Believe me, Oli's swallowed worse and lived to tell the tale."

Lance's stomach muscles, ones he hadn't realized he was clenching, relaxed. "Good to know. Thanks, Sherry. I didn't want to bother Carrie."

"Anytime." She sneezed and coughed a few more times. "What Carrie doesn't know won't hurt her."

"Thanks." At first, relief swept through Lance. He'd rather Carrie didn't know that his complete unpreparedness to be a father became apparent in the first five minutes he spent alone with his son. Then he remembered Sherry handing off Beckham to him so casually. How many other secrets was Sherry keeping from her daughter? Should he be concerned? Install nanny cams in Carrie's condo? Knox would know how to do that kind of thing.

Sherry coughed again, a set of three phlegmy ones. "I'm glad you're there, Lance. Carrie will never admit it, but she needs more help than I can give. Why, that girl's whole life is dependent on her having supernatural amounts of energy."

"I remember." Lance smiled fondly. It was why they'd gotten a Jack Russell terrier. So much energy. He glanced down at Beckham who was at full terrier attention, watching Oliver's every move.

"She can't keep it up forever," Sherry prophesized darkly, the words made more sinister by a long, hacking cough. "What's Oli doing now?"

"Beckham, sit!" Oliver shook a finger at the dog. "Stay!" Beckham ignored him, shifting his glance between Lance and the containers of pasta on the floor. Lance must've dropped them when Oli started vomiting, but Lance didn't remember it happening. The white sauce had popped open, and Beckham eyed it hungrily.

"Playing with the dog. Thanks for the assist, Sherry." He listened to a few more assurances to call her any time before finally hanging up.

"You hungry, Beckham? Me, too. I'm afraid we'll both have to wait until someone gets cleaned up." Lance reached for Oliver, intending to sit him on the counter so he could wipe him down with one of the kitchen towels he was sure Carrie had stacked neatly under the sink. Before he had a firm grip on his son, Beckham licked Oliver's face, his arms, the front of his T-shirt, snarfing up every bit of vomit on the kid.

"Well, that's handy. Good boy, Beckham." It was, after all, only the second-grossest thing he'd seen today. Oliver laughed and plopped onto the floor, butt first. Beckham gave him another once-over while Lance quickly cleaned vomit off the refrigerator door and floor. Beckham moved on to the pasta container, slurping up the pasta in white sauce before Lance could decide if he should intervene or not. Well, he hadn't expected to get through the night with zero casualties, had he? It wasn't like they were going to eat the food he'd dropped on the floor, and the dog had been very helpful with cleanup duty. He deserved a treat.

Lance checked his watch. It'd been fifteen minutes since Carrie left. He settled in for a long, and likely disgusting, night.

# CHAPTER 13

BECKHAM'S EXCITED YIP STARTLED LANCE OUT OF a deep sleep. He bolted up, at first unsure of where he was. Not his place, that was for sure. The couch was far too comfortable to be his. He rubbed an appreciative palm over whatever magic fabric made it feel like he was sitting in dandelion fluff. His eyes fixed on a four-by-six photo of a laughing baby, mouth open and one foot nearly jammed all the way in. Oliver. Carrie. He should've known from the dandelion-fluff couch precisely where he was. He had to admit—he missed Carrie's eye for all the small details that made daily life more comfortable.

"How'd it go?" Carrie entered as she'd left, hopping on one foot. She snagged one sky-high heel and flicked it off, switched her weight to the other foot, and repeated the process with her second shoe. She padded toward him on bare feet, her one concession to Florida heat and humidity being that she never wore pantyhose or tights of any kind. She bent and scratched Beckham's neck with both hands before landing on the couch a safe two feet from him. "Oli's asleep? Did he give you any trouble?"

"No trouble at all," he lied, smoothly if he did say so himself. She wouldn't notice the excess of missing cleaning supplies. Probably. He'd even done a quick load of laundry, restocking the towel drawer so there was no vomit-covered evidence to incriminate him.

"Really?" She kicked her bare feet up on the tufted

ottoman, expertly avoiding the wooden tray stretched across one-third of it. "He can be a handful."

"Easy-peasy." Lance brushed his palms together like he hadn't spent the better part of an hour on his hands and knees, scrubbing her kitchen tiles.

"Then why—" She reached over and pulled something out of his hair. She held it between her thumb and forefinger for him to examine.

"Is it a pea?" He guessed based on the color. It was a green, mashed disk.

She sniffed it and nodded confirmation. Then, she lowered her hand, and Beckham quickly snarfed up the evidence of the dinner gone so horribly wrong. At least Oliver hadn't barfed that up. "You sure you don't have anything to tell me?"

"Nope." He laced his fingers behind his head and leaned back. "The peas were delicious. Just ask Beckham."

She laughed and picked another squashed pea out of his hair. "Is my son also covered in peas?"

"Absolutely not. I'm embarrassed to admit that of the two of us, I was the messy eater." Lance scrubbed a hand down the side of his face and found another pea. Son of a—

"I don't doubt it." Carrie crossed her ankles and sank back into her dandelion-fluff sofa. She let out a long sigh and closed her eyes.

"How'd it go for you?" He hated that he wanted to know. It was really none of his business. But between scrubbing various substances off every surface of the kitchen, bathing Oliver—a task that left him nearly as wet as the kid in the tub—and valiantly reading *Chicka Chicka Boom Boom* so many times he could now recite it from memory, he'd wondered where

Carrie was and what she was doing. And with whom. Had the guy walked her to the door? Had they kissed on the front step while he cluelessly napped only twenty or so feet away? Was the guy Adam? He squeezed his eyes against the images, but they were in his head, so he couldn't escape.

Carrie cracked one eye open and rolled her head in his direction. "You really want to know?"

"I do." Stupid word choice. Out of context. "Not that *I do*, obviously. I meant I do want to know."

She smiled. "I understood the first time." Her eyes drifted closed again. "It was fine. They're almost always fine. Nice guy, nice meeting place. Nice conversation."

"Sounds"—he searched for the exact right word—"nice."

Without opening her eyes, she reached out and smacked his arm. "Exhaustingly nice. Don't get me wrong. Mr. Fourteen was a big improvement over Mr. Thirteen."

Lance immediately didn't like either one of these bozos. "Why? What did Mr. Thirteen do?"

"Nothing." Her chest rose and fell in another long sigh. "They're all perfectly nice. Or fine. Or whatever word means I am so damn tired of explaining what an interior designer is that I might say yes to a second date simply not to have that conversation again."

"Wait." Lance propped his feet next to hers on the ottoman and bounced his little toe against the side of her foot. She had such long, slender feet that led to long, slender legs, and—he cut off that train of thought. What were they talking about again? Oh yeah. "You haven't been on a second date yet?"

She bopped him back, eyes still closed but smiling now. "I'm waiting to feel that zing."

"Zing?"

"You know." Her toe rubbed the side of his foot. "You remember the zing."

Lance closed his own eyes. Yeah, he remembered. He'd still been working for Carlos back then, having recently been promoted to construction manager and already planning to start his own company. The client was on-site, a private home where they'd been hired to build a guest cottage in the backyard. Mr. Ramos, the owner, was all smiles, happy with their progress and showing it off to a young woman Lance first assumed was Ramos' second or third wife. She'd been so serious, though, nodding her head and taking notes in a small flowered notebook. Also, she wasn't dressed like a trophy wife, like Lance's mother or his stepmother. She'd worn a simple leaf-green dress that turned her hazel eyes a mottled green, and when those eyes met his, he'd lost his breath for a moment.

Ramos introduced her as the interior designer, and she'd offered her hand to shake. First Carlos, then him. She'd said something polite. He'd responded, equally polite. They'd walked the site together, and by the time she climbed into her sturdy compact car, he had her number. He'd texted her as she was driving away. She'd texted him back at the first stop sign. They were married three months later.

So yeah, zing. He remembered. Sometimes, he wished he didn't, at least not so acutely. But there it was. Carrie was his zinger.

Their feet now rested against each other, and he took pleasure in sliding his toe against hers. "Zing, zing, huh? Still feel it?" He wasn't admitting that he did unless she said it first.

She dipped her head, dark hair falling to create a curtain between them. "Maybe I'm too picky. That's what Farrah—you remember her, right?—says whenever I complain to her. She says sometimes you don't know until the second or third date about chemistry."

Lance liked Farrah, Carrie's old friend from childhood. They'd often gone out with Farrah and her girlfriend. He wondered now if she and Vanessa ever married like they'd planned. Now didn't seem the time to ask about friends he'd lost in the divorce, especially if those friends were dishing questionable advice. "If you don't feel it, you don't feel it. A second or third date won't change that."

"That's what I think, too." Carrie tucked hair behind her ear and covered a yawn with her hand. "Maybe Farrah has a point, though. Maybe I should give one of them a second chance."

Lance ignored the tightening in his stomach and kept his voice light. "Why? You got one in mind?"

"No, but I do have a spreadsheet." She grabbed her phone off the ottoman and flicked it open to show him.

"Of course you do."

Once Carrie started working for that fancy design firm in Miami, she upped her game from flowered notebooks to laptops and spreadsheets.

Lance peered over her shoulder. "Show me."

Her finger trailed the side of the phone. "Name, number, where we went. First impressions."

The comments surprised a chuckle out of him. *#4: Too loud—where's his volume control? #8: Rude to waiter—if you're gonna be an ass, at least pay the ass tax and tip 25 percent. #10: Harvard? Yeah, right.*

"My love life *is* laughable these days." Carrie let the phone fall to the couch.

"I'm surprised you don't have a rating system." Lance picked up the phone and scrolled through the spreadsheet, squinting at the comments he didn't like. *#3: Nice eyes. #5: Those abs! #9: Super nice, sweet.* And then in another box directly under the comment: *but old enough for my mom.*

"What do you mean?"

"You know, from zero to zing. Here, I'll help you." He added another column to her spreadsheet. "Date number one. Give me a rating."

Carried folded her hands over her belly. "If zing is a five, then Mr. One was a zero."

Lance dutifully entered the number in the appropriate column. "That bad, huh?"

"So bad." Carrie giggled. "It took Farrah hours to talk me down. Then she said I had to get back on the horse, so to speak, and set up number two for me."

"And what's his rating?" Lance hovered his finger over the zero.

"Mmm, four?"

"Four? And you didn't go out with him again?" He typed in the four, but he wasn't happy about it.

"It was only date number two. I was still hopeful that a full zing was in my near future."

He wanted to say he knew where she could find some zing, but he clamped his lips down on the words that wanted to escape. She wasn't some girl he'd just met. She was the mother of his child, and if he wanted a relationship with Oliver, then he had to keep his relationship with her a good one. And that meant playing it cool for now, building her trust, proving he was serious about being in Oliver's life. Because he was. He'd never wanted anything as much as he wanted to be Oli's dad.

Once that was straightened out, maybe then he and Carrie could explore this zing that still electrified the air between them. Their first date would've blown her zero to zing scale to smithereens. Their first kiss? He still remembered how she'd tasted like the pink wine she'd ordered with dinner and how she'd melted against him like her body was made to be part of his.

Really, zing was too tame to describe the early days of their relationship. He smiled, remembering how happy he'd been finding a long, dark strand of her hair on his pillow after she left for the day. Man, he'd had it bad back then.

Or maybe he was the only one feeling that special something that made him super aware of every inch of her exposed skin. Carrie's deep breathing indicated she'd nodded off while he'd been strolling down memory lane, alone. He left his foot where it was and patted the space between them. Beckham jumped up, twirled in a circle a few times, ending up with his rump pushed against Carrie and his head resting on Lance's thigh. Lance stroked the Jack Russell's short, coarse hair and listened to the crackle of Oliver's baby monitor, letting time flow around him like it sometimes did. Eventually, Carrie would wake up and kick him out, but for right now, in this moment, he was precisely where he wanted to be.

# CHAPTER 14

CARRIE REPOSITIONED THE BUD IN HER RIGHT EAR AND
let the left one dangle. She liked a strong beat when running, but with Oliver in the racing-striped running stroller
and Beckham galloping along beside her, she liked to keep
one ear open for emergencies. Both boy and dog were
accustomed to the nearly daily routine, so she split her
attention between the drum solo in one ear and the swoosh
of the stroller's wheels with the other. Each time her foot
hit pavement, Carrie pushed herself harder. Even though
they'd had perfectly nice visits to Fur Haven the past few
days, she planned to skip the park today.

When she'd woken up on the couch last night, her face
cozily snuggled against Lance's firm chest, her soft cable-
knit throw pulled up to her neck, she hadn't wanted to
move. Hadn't wanted to gently wake up and send him on his
way. And that scared her. She'd been fine without Lance for
years. She didn't need to rush to the park so Beckham and
LouLou could run the fence and Oliver could hunt for bugs
to watch in the grass. She especially didn't need to see Lance
again so soon, not when the gentle feelings of last night
were still so close to the surface. No, some distance would
be good. Friend zone boundaries must be maintained, if not
for her own sake then for Oliver's.

Her morning run kept Carrie sane, a time when she
sorted through her thoughts and planned her days. It was
also crucial to help Beckham exercise some of his Jack

Russell energy. She varied the route daily, to keep it fresh for both her and the dog, and today's run had taken them down a side street filled with single-family homes built in the 1940s. She couldn't help but imagine how life would be different on a street like this—basketball hoops in the driveway, carefully tended roses climbing the trellis over the front walk, parking in the same place every night. A Shady Lady black olive tree grew in the front yard of one her favorite houses, a Mediterranean one-story with mosaic tilework at the roofline. She sighed over the For Sale sign standing proudly in the front yard of a well-maintained midcentury ranch-style home with an old sea grape tree sprawled across the lawn. A few more clients like Dimitri Orlov, and her dream of Oliver growing up with a backyard swing set would be much closer.

"Someday," she said to Oliver, who she couldn't see because she had the sunshade pulled out on the stroller but whose weight she could feel with every step of her run. He clapped his hands with such force that a Kermit cup took a flying leap to the sidewalk. Beckham picked it up, carrying it like a bone, and Carrie let him keep it. She'd have to wash the thing anyway when they got home. Might as well let the dog enjoy himself. Motherhood had taught her to choose her battles.

She pounded through the neighborhood, running numbers in her head. Down payments, mortgage and hurricane insurance, yearly taxes. Lots of variables to figure out, but no matter how she cut the pieces of her income pie, making an offer on a house simply wasn't feasible. Not yet. Rounding the corner to her street, Carrie saw her mom's silver Corolla parked by the curb. She slowed to get the stroller through the gate and maneuvered it up the front stoop to her condo door.

"My babies!" Sherry stooped down to kiss Oliver but pulled back at the last moment and merely stroked a hand down the back of his head. "I'm feeling a lot better today, but I don't want to take any chances. Germs, you know." She coughed into the crook of her elbow a few times. "Looks like you had a big walk this morning."

"Run." Carrie was a bit winded, so she bent at the waist to catch her breath. "These two should be worn out enough that you should be able to rest most of the day."

"Don't I wish." Sherry helped shepherd the stroller into the condo while Carrie unleashed the dog and headed to the kitchen to freshen his water bowl. The number of small bugs that drowned themselves in the bowl every night was a mystery. One dead bug, she understood, but shouldn't the others see the first guy and run away in fear? No, they did not. She dumped the day-old water, complete with bug corpses, into her hard-to-kill rubber plant.

"How'd the date go last night?" Sherry's voice was a bit nasally, but she otherwise seemed her usual pushy self. She pulled eggs, cheese, and milk out of the fridge, turning sideways to pass Carrie by the sink in the narrow galley-style kitchen, nearly tripping over the dog, who followed close on her heels.

In her no-children days, Carrie would've opened up the kitchen, but she'd had to choose between creating more space in the kitchen or making the junior bedroom for Oliver. Obviously, Oliver's room had to take priority on her then-tight budget, but she still dreamed of knocking out a wall, or at least a half wall, into the living room, even if it did wreak havoc with the condo's layout. She refrained, knowing how crucial a sensible room configuration was to resale value, and reminded herself daily that it wouldn't be too much longer until she had enough saved for a down payment on a real house—maybe by the time Oliver started first grade, especially if jobs kept piling up like they had this week. Adding the Dorothy as a client would definitely challenge her time-management skills, but Kristin's bathroom, Dimitri's restaurants, and the Dorothy's remodel were all on different schedules. If she juggled things right, it would work out. She hoped.

Carrie grabbed frozen strawberries out of the freezer and loaded them into the blender. After a few more trips to the fridge for pineapple, mango, and ice, she had everything she needed for her morning smoothie. She added flax and pumpkin seeds to her concoction, eyeballing the measurements.

"What's with the silent treatment? You don't want to talk about the date? Just say so." Sherry cracked eggs into the skillet while Beckham watched with rapt attention. When Sherry paused to cough, covering her mouth with the long sleeve of her shirt, she rewarded Beckham's patience with a bite of cheese.

Carrie flipped on the blender, not sure how or if she wanted to answer. Though Beckham shook with terror at the roar of the blender's motor, he bravely held his sentinel position at the stove, hoping another scrap might accidentally or intentionally fall his way. Carrie upped the speed, reliving the warm glow of the night before, but it hadn't been from the date. Oh no, Lance's citrusy scent still hung in her nostrils; the slow thump of his heart still rang in her ears. She'd fallen asleep hugging a pillow, pretending that she wasn't alone.

How did the date go? She barely remembered the date.

"Well? I know you heard me," Sherry said as soon as the blender turned off. She sniffled, and though Carrie knew it was from the virus, it still made Carrie feel guilty.

"It was fine." Carrie's standard answer. She really didn't want to talk about her love life with her mother, guilt or not. They'd never had that kind of relationship. Before Oliver, they'd barely had a relationship at all, but when in her sixth month of pregnancy, she'd told her mom about the baby, Sherry's response had surprised her. She'd joined AA that day, collecting sobriety chips a month at a time and pledging her support to her grandson.

*Surprise* was too mild a word to describe Carrie's reaction to her mother's sudden wholehearted support. After her parents' divorce when she was in kindergarten, she'd learned to raise herself. Dad's participation in her life was sporadic, and Mom would rather be out with her friends, drinking. Or home alone, drinking. Or in bed, recovering from a late night of drinking. At first Carrie'd been suspicious of her mother's change of heart, but day by day, her mother had proved her commitment was real. Carrie'd thought she could handle being a single mother, but the truth was, she'd never have been able to quit her job at the firm and start her own business if her mother hadn't been there to help with Oliver.

"Just fine?" Sherry cracked a few more eggs and adjusted the heat on the stove. "Thought it was a hot date, the way you begged me to babysit for you. Maybe even second-date material, you think?"

"Not really." Carrie gave the blender another blast, wondering why her mom was suddenly so interested. When

Carrie first told her about signing up on a dating app, her mom had predicted death by serial killer or, at the very least, some new and untreatable type of venereal disease as a result. What changed her mom's mind? She couldn't ask her mom for personal information if she was unwilling to give up details of her own.

"What? All that drama for another going-nowhere date? Honestly, Carrie, I don't understand why you're so obsessed with these online guys lately. Did you at least get home early enough for Addison to get to bed at a decent hour?" Sherry grabbed a paper towel off the roll and blew her nose. Her color darkened.

"Addison wasn't available." Carrie laid the back of her hand against her mom's forehead. Cool to the touch. "She's so busy with drama club lately."

"I'm fine." Sherry bustled away from Carrie's touch. "I wouldn't come over if I were still contagious." She searched the drawer next to the stove and pulled out the cheese grater. She created a rhythm, three shreds to the skillet, one to the floor for Beckham to eagerly lick up. The dog was such a cheese hound. "Then who stayed with Oliver? You didn't leave him alone, did you?"

Considering how much of her childhood Carrie had spent alone, she bristled at the question. "Of course not."

"You took him on the date?" Sherry shredded cheddar into the skillet, faster and faster, the flakes falling like snow, dusting the eggs, while Beckham scarfed any that fell his way. Red stained her cheeks. If not a fever, it could be exertion. She was going at the cheese pretty hard. "I can't imagine that went well."

"Mom, please. Lance watched him." Carrie considered

the other possible explanation for her mother's flush. She'd never been a good liar.

"Lance? Ooh-la-la. Tell me all about it." Sherry was definitely lying. Now that she was watching for it, Carrie noticed the signs. Forced gaiety, no eye contact, fake French, and of course, the guilt blush.

"Tell what? You already know he was here, don't you?" Carrie pointed a smoothie-dripping spatula at her mother. "Spill. What happened?"

"Nothing." Sherry flipped the omelet a bit too aggressively. "He needed a bit of advice is all, and he didn't want to bother you."

"He should've called me, not you." Carrie shook the smoothie spatula, flinging a flaxseed across the kitchen. "And you should've told me."

"I did. Just now." Sherry flipped the omelets again, whether they needed it or not. "Don't know what you're so worked up about."

Why was Carrie so worked up? Secrets, that was why. "I'm Oliver's mother. You can't keep things that impact him from me, Mom."

Sherry hugged her arms around her waist and turned red-rimmed eyes on Carrie. "Fine, I'll call you every time he falls, every time he gets a boo-boo. Every time he burps. Would that make you happy?"

"Yes." Carrie yanked the top off the smoothie and dipped her finger in for a taste. Not quite sweet enough. She added a few more strawberries. "He's my son."

"Stupid cold." Sherry wiped at her leaking eyes and blew her nose. "Look, Carrie, no one's saying you're not the one in charge. But I am his grandmother. I can handle him on my own, too."

"Because you did such a great job with me." Carrie waved her spatula.

"I'm a different person now." Sherry sniffed, long and loudly. "You said you trusted me. When I was working my steps, you said you forgave me."

"I did." Carrie's shoulders slumped, and she leaned against the counter. "I do. It's hard sometimes, seeing how you are with him. Wondering why you weren't like that for me."

"Oh, baby." Sherry wrapped her arms around Carrie, holding her in a tight hug. "I'm so sorry I wasn't the mother you deserved. I'm trying to make up for it now. Can't you tell?"

"I know." Carrie sniffed, and it wasn't because she was getting a cold. Tears filled her eyes. She swiped at them with the back of her hand. "You're doing great." She hugged her mom back with all her strength.

"Uh-oh!" Oliver's exclamation interrupted their moment. "Eggs!"

"'Uh-oh' is right." Sherry turned off the stove, but it was too late. The omelets were burned to an inedible degree. She let out a watery sigh and reassembled the ingredients from the fridge to start over.

"I'm hungry!" Oliver complained from his seat in the high chair. Usually content to wait until food was served, he fidgeted and fussed with the straps. Breakfast was taking longer than usual, but Carrie couldn't regret it. So often she danced around her feelings about her mom. It felt freeing to have said the words aloud finally.

"Sorry, Oli-Oli-oxen-free." Sherry slid the ruined omelets into Beckham's bowl. "I'm afraid the first round goes to the dog."

Beckham, that tiny trash compactor of a dog, gobbled up the omelet remains like they were an expensive delicacy.

Oliver smacked his hands on the tray. "Okay, but I'm first next, right?"

"Absolutely. You will be the second first one to eat." Sherry cracked more eggs into the skillet.

Oliver subsided, content with her answer. He liked to be first, even if he didn't fully understand the concept yet. He returned to pushing buttons on Carrie's old iPad, the one without internet access and preloaded with kid-friendly content for him to discover.

Sherry slanted a look at Carrie. "So how'd it go with Lance last night anyway? Any old sparks flying?"

"No." Carrie returned her attention to the smoothie, adding more ice to compensate for the melting that happened while she and Mom were sharing a moment.

Sherry shook her head, auburn hair brushing her jawline. "I don't believe that for a second, but I suppose you're allowed your secrets. For now."

Carrie ignored her mom's jibes and took her time testing the smoothie—consistency was as important as taste—and hit the blender for another blast. Except she'd forgotten to put the top back on, and smoothie bits immediately sprayed her in the face. She slammed the blender off but not before smoothie smacked the ceiling overhead and slid down the white cabinets in lumpy streaks.

"Careful!" Sherry spun, hand to her mouth to cover the laughter that quickly turned to a cough. "Here." She handed the dish towel that usually hung on the oven handle to Carrie. "I have one question."

"What?" Carrie hid her face behind the checkered towel, mopping smoothie off her face.

"Why all these dates?" Sherry flipped the new omelet, butter hissing. "It's not for fun because you don't seem to have fun at all."

Carrie swiped at the countertop. The cabinets and ceiling would require getting the stool out of the hallway closet, so she saved that task for last. *Scrub, scrub, rinse, scrub, scrub.*

"Come on, honey. What's the rush?" Sherry sliced the omelet in two with the spatula and plated the halves—one half on one of Carrie's bamboo-etched dinner plates and the other on a bright-orange plastic toddler plate.

"Mom, enough. Not in front of Oliver." Carrie wrung out the towel in the sink perhaps a tad too aggressively. It was one thing for Mom to help with her own grandchild, but it was too late, in Carrie's book, to act like a mother to Carrie. Sincere regret or not, that ship sailed freshman year of high school when her mom spent all of the winter break skiing with a new boyfriend in Colorado, and Carrie opened her presents alone on Christmas morning. Her mom acted surprised when Carrie cried on the phone, saying, "I thought you'd go to your father's," forgetting that Carrie's father was also out of town for the holiday. Business, he'd said. She could've gone to Farrah's house—she was always welcome there—but she hadn't wanted to admit that her own parents had forgotten her, not even to her best friend. Carrie's grip on the towel tightened even more at the memory. "Oliver doesn't need to hear this stuff."

"He's watching that ridiculous baby shark video again." Sherry placed the plastic plate on Oliver's high chair tray. "Can't you hear it?"

Carrie couldn't hear it, perhaps because it was on so much she'd learned to tune it out. She braced herself against the cabinet, back to her mother. Why had she accepted another date? What *was* the urgency that had pushed her to agree? That had her scrolling the dating app feed at long red lights and obsessing over the zing factor? Maybe she needed to say it out loud, even if her mother didn't deserve the confidence. She should say the words so she could hear what they sounded like outside her own head.

"I want a partner." She took a deep breath and turned to face her mom. "I'm so tired of being alone." Ouch, they sounded bad, those words. Needy and pathetic, two things she'd spent her entire childhood training herself not to be. But she was so tired, and it had felt good last night to come home to an adult, to sit on the couch and talk about things that mattered to her. That person couldn't be Lance, but didn't she deserve someone to build a life with?

"Oh, baby, you're not alone." Sherry held a fork over her heart. "I'm here as much as you need me."

"Except when you're not." Carrie didn't need to remind her mother about canceling on her or the distant but still painful past. It hung in the air between them. Carrie could forgive, but forgetting would take a lot longer. Besides, Oliver was Carrie's responsibility, not her mother's. Ultimately, Carrie could only truly rely on herself, and that was what motherhood was—total responsibility. Maybe her mother had always been more the grandmotherly type—coming and going as her schedule allowed. Carrie didn't doubt her mother's love for Oliver. She wished she'd had the same confidence about her own relationship with Sherry growing up. Better late than never, she supposed. "You need time for your own life, too."

"So do you." Sherry's voice softened with understanding.

Carrie felt her heart cracking, that familiar ache from childhood. She remembered that same tone when she'd come home from fourth grade, crying about no one wanting her on their softball team during PE. Her mother had made them chocolate milkshakes with extra Hershey's Syrup and signed her up for a softball camp. If Sherry had been all bad, it would be easier to hold a grudge. Sometimes, though, she knew exactly what Carrie needed, and somehow, that hurt worse than the bad times.

A glob of smoothie fell from the ceiling and splatted on the floor between them. Beckham leapt to his self-appointed cleanup task, tail wagging when he looked up at her with pink goo on his nose. Sherry laughed, but for Carrie, it was one thing too many. Tears sprung to her eyes. Really, she was going to cry over a spilt smoothie?

Her mom opened her arms, and Carrie walked into them. Yes, yes, she was going to cry over the smoothie. When she was done, she'd write a kick-ass proposal for the Dorothy, check on Kristin's apartment, and send plans to Dimitri Orlov for approval before she started ordering things for his restaurants. For now, she let her mom's soft arms wrap around her in the kind of hug she'd longed for as a child but rarely gotten. *Better late than never*. It should be their family motto.

———————

Carrie refluffed the throw pillows on her bed, propping the embroidered wildflowers against her lower back, and straightened her lap desk. One good thing about working from home was how she could stretch out while dealing with her accounts. The second good thing was that Oliver was conked out beside her, arms around his favorite stuffed animal, an orange octopus named Oink, tucked in his armpit. It was late, and she should really put Oliver in his own bed, but she couldn't bring herself to disturb the adorable picture they made.

In fact, she grabbed her phone and snapped a quick couple of pics to send to her mom. *Back to work.* Reluctantly, she opened her email.

Excalibur Construction in bold, first row. She clicked on it, butterflies in full swarm in her stomach. She'd put together a solid estimate for the Dorothy, but it'd only been a few hours since she'd sent it. And it was Saturday. She knew from experience that in cases with multiple partners on a project, rejections came more quickly than acceptances. It would take all three Donovan brothers to say yes, but only one of them needed to say no. That one was Lance, and even though she'd opened the email, she couldn't quite bring herself to read it. She hadn't expected him to look at it until Monday, hadn't expected an answer for at least a week. To get a response so quickly could not be good.

Lance, never one for lengthy texts or emails, had written ok.

Okay what? Okay, he'd received it? Okay, they were hiring her? What was she supposed to do with an okay? She hated unclear communication. Was it so hard to give actual information?

She picked up her phone and texted him: *okay what?*

Was that too demanding? Too ex-wifey of her? After the big secret she'd kept from him, did she have the right to get annoyed at him for anything? Ever again? Panicked that she'd turned an "okay, proposal received" into an "okay, I'll be telling my brothers what a demanding, unreasonable person you are so there's no way you'll get our business," she followed up with one of the pictures she'd taken of Oliver and the dog and added a smiley face for good measure.

His next text was an explosion of confetti and balloons on her screen. Congratulations! flashed in red letters. She exhaled, imagining all those swarming butterflies from her belly releasing into the air, fluttering away like living celebratory confetti. She hadn't blown it, and the only thing more fun than the idea of digging deeper into the Dorothy's past and researching the hell out of her time period was the fact that she'd get paid to do it.

*Thanks!* she texted back and held the phone against her chest. Working with Lance again, long term, was quite a commitment. She remembered the first client they'd landed together, when they were dating and Lance's construction business was less than a year old. Her boss at the swanky design firm she'd lucked into right after passing her state exam hadn't wanted such a small account—a woman with a single-proprietor law office who wanted a redesign to make space for her soon-to-graduate granddaughter to join her practice. Carrie'd been thrilled to take on the challenge of a multigenerational work space, and after speaking with the owner and researching similar practices and their layouts, had presented a design that was within budget and required moving only one wall.

Unfortunately, the big contractors her design firm worked with wouldn't take on such a small job at such a low profit margin. Luckily, she happened to be dating someone who would take on the project, if for no other reason than to please her.

"No problem," Lance had said when she'd asked him that evening over a sidewalk table outside of Pizza Rustica. He bit into his slice, cheese dripping off the side, and grinned at her.

"Are you sure?" She dabbed the sauce off her chin with a paper napkin. "It won't be weird, working for me?"

"Working *with* you." He held his slice out for her to take a bite. "It'll be a trial run, but I'm pretty sure we'll be an amazing team."

"Only pretty sure?" She rose out of her chair, balancing her hands on the metal table, and leaned into the slice. Instead of going for a bite, though, she stretched all the way across to kiss him.

"Very sure," he'd whispered as their mouths met, and he'd been right. The old wall came down, the new wall went up, the law office was decorated, and the granddaughter moved in even though she'd only be using the space to study for the bar exam. The owner loved the soft gray palette with pops of yellow for accents. She raved over the improved storage, and weeks later, she called to tell Carrie how much her clients appreciated the rocking guest chairs. Carrie remembered wishing she'd put the call on speakerphone so everyone in the cubicles around her could hear the client call her brilliant.

She wondered now if Lance was hiring her out of nostalgia or maybe pity. Surely not. They were long past the phase where he did anything with the effect on her in mind.

*Remember Brinkham & Brinkham?* She couldn't resist texting him to test the waters about how he'd come to a decision so quickly, to see if the good memories were resurfacing for him, too. For so long, she'd focused on the end of their marriage, on the big fights and the even scarier days of silence, when they couldn't exchange a civil word before heading off to their respective jobs. She'd had to hold onto the bad to get through that first year after the divorce, when Oliver growing inside her was a constant reminder that ultimately, she'd been the one to leave. The longer she didn't tell Lance about the pregnancy, the more she doubled down on those bad memories to justify her choices. Seeing Lance again, watching him press a goodbye kiss on a sleeping Oliver's forehead last night, reminded her that they'd been a lot more than those bad memories.

Can I call you?

She almost dialed him right then, as eager as she'd been in their first few months of dating to hear his voice. He'd texted pictures of the demo in Kristin's bathroom, so she hadn't driven downtown today, hadn't seen Lance at all, just his thumb where he'd managed to cut off the bottom corner of one of the pictures. Should she call? Maybe video chat? She checked on Oliver, placing her hand on his chest to feel the rise and fall of his breath. Sound asleep and she'd like him to stay that way. Not a good time.

The three dots bounced for a minute, then another, like he was typing and erasing and typing again. She waited impatiently for his response.

Good night.

She waited another moment, hoping for more. Good night, she texted back. Could exes really become friends? For Oliver's sake, she hoped the answer was yes.

# CHAPTER 15

FUR HAVEN WAS ALREADY HOPPING WHEN LANCE GOT LouLou unleashed for her morning run. She beelined for her black Lab buddy, Lady, and a small Chihuahua already running circles around the weaving poles. The dogs didn't seem to understand the poles. As Riley'd explained to him, owners were supposed to teach the dogs to go in and out of them, like lacing a shoe, but the dogs seemed to mostly enjoy sniffing and then peeing on each pole individually.

Eliza, Lady's owner, and a young woman he remembered meeting a few times before sat on one of the bone-shaped benches. Eliza lifted a hand to him, and he waved back but didn't go over. He pulled out his phone, doing some calculations with time and man power to figure out how to get the garage going before Caleb returned. He'd sent his approvals over the weekend, right after he'd told Carrie she'd gotten the interior design job. He'd been on a roll, figuring Caleb couldn't veto what was already in the works. He didn't worry about Knox. Spending the next week in close proximity while they finished up Kristin's bathroom gave him plenty of time to get Knox to see things his way. If Knox didn't? Well, there was always bribery.

"LouLou keeping you busy?" The young woman surprised him into dropping his phone. Luckily, Fur Haven's grass was soft and thick, so he wouldn't be shopping for a new device today. The Apple Store employees knew him by sight; that was how many times he wrecked a phone on the job. He picked up the cell and smiled at her.

"Sydney, right?"

"Yep, Chewy's mom." She pointed out the Chihuahua currently chasing LouLou in a loop around the A-frame.

"Right." Now he remembered seeing her at the Fur Haven grand opening with her tiny dog. "LouLou's good. We're getting along fine."

"If you need a break, let me know. Chewy and LouLou love to hang out, and I'm happy to take her for a few hours."

It was funny how much he wasn't tempted by her offer. "Naw, we've got our routines now, and it's only another week until Caleb and Riley are back."

"Right." She fiddled with the leash in her hand, clicking the snap. "How's the renovation going?"

They descended into small talk about construction stuff, a conversation he could have with only half a brain. The unoccupied half of the brain noticed when the dog park gate pinged open. Noticed when Beckham was let off his leash and dashed for LouLou. He tried not to be insulted that LouLou was Beckham's go-to and not his old pal, Lance. He tried not to notice Carrie's long legs, outlined so clearly in yoga pants with mesh panels slashed diagonally across her calves or the way her ponytail swung from side to side as she walked toward him, Oliver's small hand in her larger one.

"Lance!" Oliver let go of his mom to rush forward, slamming into Lance's leg with the force of a locomotive. Lance pretended to fall sideways, and Oliver laughed.

"Hey." Carrie looked from him to Sydney, so he introduced the two women.

Carrie was oddly formal, holding out her hand to shake.

Sydney took it, saying, "Your Jack Russell is adorable. You've been here a few times before, right?"

Carrie agreed, and they got into a discussion about the neighborhood. After a few moments, Sydney excused herself and returned to Eliza on the bench. He supposed he'd have to introduce Carrie to the older woman, too, but he selfishly wanted a few minutes with her.

"You came back." He switched his phone from one hand to the other, suddenly nervous without the buffer of another human between them. "When you didn't come by over the weekend, I thought you'd move on to new territory."

"You invited us." Carrie was still formal, still stiff. Her eyes darted to the bench and back to him again. "So what's her rating?"

"What? I don't rate women. What kind of Neanderthal do you think I am?" he huffed out in pretend indignation.

"Zero to zing?"

*Oh, that.* He shrugged a shoulder. "I wasn't thinking of her like that."

"So a zero?" Carrie visibly loosened up, her smile turning up in wattage.

Sydney was not exactly a zero, but she wasn't a zinger, either, at least not to him, so he nodded his head.

"Okay then." Carrie kept her eyes on Oliver, who was intent on catching a dog, any dog. The mutts clearly thought this little human was hysterical, letting him get close enough that he might be able to touch them before dashing off again. Beckham leaped straight into the air whenever Oli got in touching distance. Sydney and Eliza laughed at the antics. "That should tire everyone out."

"Is that your life's mission? Tire out the kid and the dog so you can get a good night's sleep?"

Carrie held up a hand to shade her eyes while she kept a lookout on Oliver. "It sounds so mercenary when you put it like that, but yes. Especially on days like today."

"What's wrong with today? Is Oliver okay?"

"Yeah, he's fine. It's just my mom. She was supposed to take them for the day, but she has a virus. A cold, maybe? She tried to tough it out yesterday, but when I got home, she was knocked out on my bed, and Oli and Beckham were neck deep in a bag of flour. An inside-out bag of flour." She handed over her phone so he could see the short video of Oliver covered in a thick layer of flour and laughing while Beckham licked his face clean. "I'm on my own."

Lance angled his body toward Carrie. "You're sure Sherry's ill?" He didn't mean to sound skeptical, and he'd certainly heard the evidence for himself when he'd placed his SOS call to her on Friday night. But back in the early days of their marriage, he'd learned the Burns' family code for hangover, and he didn't like the idea that Sherry might be slipping into her old ways.

"Yeah, she was in a bad way yesterday." Carrie blew out a sharp breath, seeming to know what he was truly worried about. "She's so proud of her stack of AA chips that I don't worry about that anymore. I'm planning to drop by her place later with some Theraflu, make sure it's not something more serious."

"That's kind of you." After all her mother had put her through, how could Carrie ever trust their son with her? Lance felt anger rising, filling his chest, and he wanted to snap at Carrie to make her understand the seriousness.

But she beat him to it. "She's so much better, you know? Like the mom I wished so hard for every time I blew out my birthday candles. But I have to keep an eagle eye on her because she will not do to Oliver what she did to me."

Carrie's fierceness surprised him. Her whole body tensed as if ready to fight. He'd always admired her ambition, her drive, her seemingly endless amounts of energy. He'd seen her pull all-nighters to impress her boss or land a new client. He'd never seen her like this, though, fierce as a mockingbird protecting its nest, bombing random cyclists who dared ride under her tree.

"I know." He wanted to reach for her, cup her cheek, and tease her about being a mama bear or, rather, bird. Not yet, he knew. Everything between them was so tentative as they figured each other out. Again. Too bad for him he was finding more to admire about her now than he had when they met eight years ago. "You're a good mother."

"Thanks, that means a lot. Considering." She turned on the bench, tucking her foot under so that her knee angled toward him. Only half an inch separated it from his thigh. He studied that distance like a superhero contemplating a rooftop jump.

Her knee bounced, a nervous habit he used to curb by entwining their legs and kissing her senseless. Which was so not an option anymore, so really, the flood of adrenaline was completely unnecessary, only serving to make him as jittery as she seemed to be.

Carrie palmed her knee, straightened her elbow, and stilled her knee. "Beckham I could leave alone for a few hours, but I'm afraid Oliver will be tagging along to work with me today."

"Client meetings?" He needed to stop looking at her leg. He didn't because that slice of mesh gave him a glimpse of the vulnerable, and he remembered, the ticklish skin of her inner knee. "No." She shook her head, and her shiny pony-tail bounced against her shoulder. "Thank God, no. Just checking in on a few ongoing projects. Kristin's included. You know how you can't let contractors make their own decorating decisions."

He laughed with her.

"Hey, while I'm here, can I take another look at the Dorothy?"

"Of course. May as well take advantage of the building being empty for this week." He laced his fingers together and stretched, knuckles popping. Carrie made a face at him, and he grinned, remembering how much she hated the sound and how it had taken her nearly two years to tell him. They'd been so careful with each other at the beginning, afraid to say anything too harsh. Maybe that was why when things finally came to a boil, it had been so bad. Years of bottled-up annoyances colored every exchange. "Sorry." He tapped his knuckles. "Forgot how that bothers you."

"No worries." She shifted, switching feet and putting more space between them. "Seems petty now, doesn't it? All the fights over stupid things. Crack your knuckles if you want. I can take it."

"Not all of it was petty." Lance's thoughts clouded with the not-so-petty words they'd flung at each other. Look at them now, still working through the weekends, dragging their kid into it. Were they really all that different than before? He cleared his throat. "Today's a good chance for you to do a walk-through of all the units. Demo on the roof is done, so it'll be quieter. Not that roof installation is silent or anything, but at least the walls won't be shaking."

She studied him through her long lashes, the ones that didn't really need makeup, they were so dark, but that she delighted in making even longer with her mascara wand. "You were serious about me getting the job, weren't you?"

"Yeah, of course. You're the best." He pushed away the memory of her fluttering those lashes along his cheeks, teasing him with light brushstrokes until he was desperate for her kiss. More desperate anyway. "Why wouldn't we want the best for our building?"

"Thanks." She smiled and checked the time on the phone she had strapped to her upper arm. "Well, I hate to cut this party short, but do you think we could do it now? I already feel like this day is so out of control."

"Sure." The day wasn't the only thing out of control. Another minute on the bench and he'd reach for her, pull her flush against him, and make her remember how good they were together. He stood, quickly, decisively. The elevator kiss could've led to more, but she'd shut it down. He had to respect that. If they got tangled up and things went south again, Oliver would be the one to suffer. Lance could enjoy Carrie's company, admire her even, but it was better for all three of them if he and Carrie kept it platonic. He imagined a black-and-white movie clapboard and someone yelling, "Lance and Carrie, take two: No one gets hurt." That was a sequel he'd pay to see for sure.

Carrie called to Oliver, and Lance called to Beckham. Both came trotting at their names, and LouLou followed out of curiosity. They walked to the Dorothy, Beckham pulling ahead like it was a race between the five of them and he was determined to win. LouLou dawdled, sniffing each palm-tree trunk they passed and stopping at particularly odorous blades of grass. When they came to a felled coconut, Beckham spun on the end of his leash and joined LouLou in a thorough inspection.

"So much for being in a hurry." Lance tugged on the leash, but LouLou dug in.

Carrie smoothed a loose strand of dark hair behind her ear. "Let them have their fun. Poor Beckham's in for a day of solitary confinement once we get home."

Lance watched as LouLou stepped aside so her buddy could get in a good sniff. When Beckham lifted his leg and peed on the coconut, it initiated a whole new round of inspections. "I could keep him."

"No, that's okay." Carrie's ponytail swung from shoulder blade to shoulder blade. "I'll only be gone a few hours."

Lance warmed to his idea. "I'll be working today, too, but at least here he'll have LouLou to keep him company. He won't get bored. She won't get bored. It's a win-win, right?"

He could tell Carrie was waffling by the way she eyed him from under her lashes. God, he had to stop thinking about what she could do with them, how she drove him wild. "I could swing by after five to get him?"

"Great!" Lance stopped and dialed back the enthusiasm. He didn't want to sound desperate. "The guys will love seeing him again."

Carrie's head snapped up. "Again?"

Oh crap. He'd forgotten about his and Sherry's little secret. He twisted the nylon leash between his fingers and confessed.

Carrie stormed ahead a few paces. "I can't believe Mom would do that without telling me. We had a deal. I thought she meant it. Every boo-boo, she said, every burp." She pulled out her phone. "I *trusted* her! And she goes and hands my dog off to, to—" She cut herself off to jab at her phone.

Lance caught up and touched her arm, stopping the call. Carrie turned to him, his fingers still in the crook of her elbow. Her workout tank top was plain black, so her eyes looked more brown than green today. She blinked up at him, and the mix of exasperation and fear in her eyes felt like a lead pipe to the abdomen.

"The important thing is that she made sure both Oliver and Beckham were cared for." Not that he was taking Sherry's side over Carrie's, never. But the two seemed to have reached a working truce, and he hated to be the wedge between them. "That's what you trust her to do, right?"

"But you're my *ex*. What was she thinking?" Carrie's words were outraged, but her tone no longer was. He'd always appreciated that about her. She might be quick to anger, but she was equally quick to cool off and consider the other side.

Oliver's loud chortle caught both their attention. He'd plopped down next to the coconut, which was roughly the size of his head, and was rolling it back and forth. He slapped the coconut with both hands. "Look at my ball!"

"That's a coconut, buddy." Lance smiled and held out his free hand. "Come on. Let's leave the coconut where you found it."

"Coconuts are yummy. Gamma puts them on cupcakes." Oliver opened his mouth wide and took a face dive toward it.

"No!" Carrie lunged for her son, and Lance was right behind her. Oliver probably wouldn't die from licking a dog-christened coconut, but it was also not something Lance wanted to see go down. Carrie was fast, but Lance's arms were longer. He scooped up Oliver, grabbing him by the stomach in a sort of Superman hold, and swung him in a circle.

Oliver was too surprised to be upset about losing his coconut. He clapped his hands and yelled, "More! More," when Lance tried to put him back on his feet.

Carrie stealthily kicked the coconut down into the street drain, a disappointed Beckham watching her with a drooping tail.

"Wait, where's LouLou?" Lance set Oliver on the sidewalk but kept hold of his hand. He must've dropped the poodle's leash when he lunged for Oliver. He looked toward the Dorothy, then back toward the dog park. No luck.

LouLou was nowhere in sight.

# CHAPTER 16

"WE'LL FIND HER." CARRIE KEPT STEP BESIDE LANCE ON yet another neighborhood side street, Oliver propped on her hip. Kid must weigh a ton, but every time he offered to take the child, Carrie shook her head.

Lance wished he had Carrie's confidence that LouLou was only a few more steps or calls away, but they'd been searching for over half an hour, and there was still no apricot poodle in sight.

"Caleb will kill me." Lance's phone burned a hole in his back pocket. He should call Caleb and Riley and let them know what happened. But what could they do from the deck of their cruise ship except worry? It'd be better if he found LouLou, and they never had to know. But if LouLou was gone, at some point, he'd have to tell them that he'd utterly failed at what should've been the fairly simple task of keeping their dog safe.

And he wanted to be a father? He couldn't even keep track of a dog for a full week without losing her. When he thought of all the things that could happen to a small child in this world, his gut tightened. He felt nauseated. God, how did parents live with this terror all the time?

They turned down yet another street, taking turns calling for LouLou. Stately black olive trees rose forty feet into the air, shading the street and sidewalks with their evergreen leaves. After Hurricane Andrew in 1992, many homeowners chopped down trees, especially ones as tall and thick as a black olive, to avoid the trunks splitting their houses in half during a future hurricane. It was rare to find a whole block of mature shade trees.

"I expect to come across a lemonade stand at any moment." Lance held Beckham's leash in one hand, trailing behind Carrie while the dog checked every crack and crevice of the old sidewalk. "It feels like we've traveled back in time here."

"This is one of my favorite neighborhoods." Carrie pointed out the For Sale sign on a midcentury ranch-style home painted blue-gray with a rather exuberant orange door. "If only, right?"

Lance whistled low. "Must have a huge yard. Look at the size of the mango trees in the back." The distinctive elliptical leaves towered far above the roofs of the one-story homes around them. "They must be at least fifty years old."

"Trees really make a street feel like home, don't they?" Carrie let Oli slide down her side, keeping a firm grip on his hand once his feet touched the ground. Oli reached up for Lance's hand, and the three moved forward, Oli's arms raised above his head.

Carrie swung her arm, lifting Oliver up a few inches between them. Lance pitched in, helping dangle Oli in the air for a moment. Oliver picked up the game, leaping into the air and jumping ahead like an excited frog-child. His squeals riled up Beckham, and the dog raced ahead before rearing back when he hit the end of the retractable leash.

"Now look what you've started," Lance chided, but he didn't really mean it. He might be freaking out inside, but in every other way, this was a nice family outing. Mother, father, son, dog. He felt weirdly patriotic about the whole thing, like they were the 1950s American dream in action. If not for the worry about LouLou, this wasn't a terrible way to spend a Monday morning. It alarmed him, really, how easy it was to settle into a rhythm with Carrie. He'd chalk it up to old patterns, but Oliver swinging between them was certainly new. It was easy to imagine a life where this was a normal day. Too easy. He let himself slide into the fantasy anyway, this vision of family life. His wife, his kid, his dog. A walk on a beautiful day, sun shining overhead, ocean breeze keeping it cool. LouLou would show up any minute. Anything less would ruin the illusion.

Lance's phone blasted out his ringtone at full volume, jarring him out of his homey thoughts. He didn't recognize the international number. Normally, he wouldn't pick up for an unknown caller, but with Caleb out of the country, he thumbed the Accept button and raised the phone to his ear.

"How's LouLou?" Riley's anxious voice sounded loudly in his ear. God, how did she know? Did she have poodle radar? Were Riley and LouLou psychically connected? He stopped walking and mouthed "Riley" at Carrie. She took the leash and showed him crossed fingers, as if luck would keep him alive after Caleb found out he'd lost his fiancée's precious poodle.

He dialed back the volume so that when he told her he was currently looking for her dog, her shrieks wouldn't deafen him. Carrie gripped his arm, squeezing tight enough to leave fingernail rings on his skin.

"What?" he said a tad too loudly.

"How's LouLou?" Riley shouted in his ear. "Can you hear me? The connection sounds fine on this end."

"I can hear you," he stalled, looking at Carrie expectantly. "Did you ask about LouLou?"

While Riley repeated her question, Carrie pointed ahead to a splash of apricot fur ducking under the thick, leathery leaves of a clusia hedge. "I'll get her. You stall," Carrie whispered, letting go of Oliver's hand before sprinting away from him, Beckham right on her heels. "Watch Oli."

Lance tilted his head and trapped the phone between ear and shoulder. Ahead of them, Carrie approached the bush and dropped to her knees. An excited LouLou emerged, some kind of stick stuck in the fur on her back, and jumped on Carrie's thighs. LouLou and Beckham took a moment to sniff a greeting before Carrie swept the poodle up, picking out the stick and dropping it to the street. She strode toward them, grinning in triumph, Beckham trotting proudly beside her as if he'd single-handedly saved the day. LouLou wriggled, but Carrie kept a firm hold on the runaway dog.

"Are you there? Can you hear me?" Riley's voice got more high-pitched with each question. "Is LouLou okay?"

"I'm here. She's here." Lance cleared his throat. No need to elaborate on how that second part was a new development. "She's good. Real good. Queen of Fur Haven and all that."

Riley audibly exhaled. "What a relief! I've been so worried about her. She's eating? Not too mopey?"

"No, no problems. And it sure is convenient to stay at your place while we start work on the Dorothy. She's not alone for more than a few hours at a time."

"I'm glad to hear it's all going well." There was some kind of tapping on the line. "What a terrible connection."

"Uh-huh." Lance felt only a tiny bit guilty at his earlier misdirection. All's well that ends well, right? "Hey, is Caleb around?"

"Sure. Tell LouLou I love her. Here's Caleb."

Lance waited a beat until his brother's voice came on. "What's up?"

"City didn't accept the parking garage plans. Santos is still pushing for a full garage."

"No way. Fur Haven is special." Caleb's immediate and firm response made Lance's gut tighten in the bad way. All this stress was going to give him abs of steel.

"I had to make an executive decision." He willed the gut knot to loosen. He'd done the right thing. Caleb would adjust. "I approved Adam's new plans. We emailed you, but I guess you were unavailable."

"For a couple of days! I haven't been able to check my email since we hit international waters. It honestly couldn't wait until we're back?"

"I keep my projects on schedule." Lance used his professional, I'm-the-expert voice. "Besides, Adam's solution is elegant. I think everyone will be happy."

"As long as Fur Haven is still there when we get back."

"It'll be here when you get back." How much longer, Lance wasn't sure. Adam wanted to break ground soon, and there was no reason they couldn't move both the garage and the Dorothy along at the same time. Remodeling and foundation building were two different skill sets. No overlap in the workers, and he trusted Mendo to be able to handle two crews.

"Everything's on track at the Dorothy? No surprises yet?"

The leak under the elevator. Galvanized steel pipes instead of the cast iron he'd been expecting. Sure, cast iron could rust and crack, but galvanized steel was trickier, often looking fine on the outside but so rusted and clogged on the inside it was like a closed-off artery that could cause a heart attack. And they were so fragile. Messing with the one under the elevator had caused cracking. All the piping would soon be replaced anyway, but galvanized steel meant more potential for leaks and drama along the way.

"We're right on schedule." Lance's own voice got too loud. "Nothing much to see yet, but the elevator passed inspections, and the roof is going on smooth as silk."

"Good, good. We'll be back in a week." Caleb paused, a muffled voice that was probably Riley in the background. "We should probably go. Others are waiting to use the landline here."

"Where are you?"

"Amber Cove."

"Nice." Lance had never been on a cruise. Maybe it was time to take a vacation himself. After the work on the Dorothy was completed, of course. Carrie held LouLou up to the phone, and she licked Lance's ear. The dog, not Carrie. He kind of wished it were the other way around, alas. "LouLou sends her love."

Caleb assured Lance that he and Riley sent their love right back to the poodle, and Lance hung up.

"Close one." Lance felt as out of breath as if he'd been the one to sprint after LouLou.

Carrie pressed her lips together like she was suppressing laughter. "Could the timing have been more perfect? It's almost like this little stinker had a plan, isn't it?"

"It wouldn't surprise me that she's smarter than she lets on." Lance stared into the poodle's dark eyes. LouLou thumped her tail at him. "Did you know it was Riley on the phone? Is that why you let us find you?" *Thump, thump* went her tail. "I think you're right, Carrie. She's diabolical this one."

"I'm so glad we found her." Carrie squeezed LouLou and kissed the top of her head.

"Me, too." Finally, Lance's stomach muscles relaxed. No more involuntary ab crunches—at least he hoped that was it for the day.

Carrie hefted the poodle in her arms. "LouLou lost her collar and leash along the way, the sneaky dog. Can you carry her?"

Carrie was all smiles, but he could see the day catching up with her, the tiredness in her eyes. "I'll take the kid."

"I've got him." Carrie smiled. "Trust me, you're getting the good end of this deal. Oli weighs like a million pounds."

"Do not!" Oliver said, very serious. "Gamma says I'm a four-hundred-pound gorilla." He held up his arms to Lance. "Pick me up, Lance! You'll see."

Lance hefted Oliver onto his hip. "I'm not sure either estimate is true, buddy."

Carrie took Oliver's defection with a rueful shake of her head. She accepted Beckham's leash and resituated LouLou under her arm. "Give it a few blocks. You'll see."

Oliver palmed Lance's cheek. "Wanna sing 'Itsy Bitsy Spider'?"

"Maybe?" Lance hadn't heard the song since he was in kindergarten. "I don't think I remember all the words."

"I can do it!" Oliver launched into a spirited performance, complete with his thumb-thumb spider interpretative dance. By the time they got to the Dorothy, Lance was singing along.

# CHAPTER 17

"I WONDER WHAT MADE THESE?" CARRIE SQUATTED down between the rattan sofa and the fake palm tree to run her finger over a series of pockmarks in the terrazzo floor of the lobby. With the dogs safely ensconced in Lance's temporary first-floor apartment and Oliver wholly occupied with stroking the stubble on Lance's jaw like Lance was one of his stuffed animals, Carrie finally had a moment to spend with her new client, the Dorothy.

"Undoubtedly a mystery lost to time."

Lance brushed Oliver's hand away from his face, but Oliver merely laughed and said, "Your face is fuzzy."

"Oli, look at me." Carrie stood eye to eye with her son held high in Lance's arms. "We leave beards alone."

Oliver nodded solemnly, dropping his hand. "And hair. And necklaces. And tails."

Lance's mouth quirked at the last addition to the list. Carrie decided not to get into it with Oli right now about the difference between people and dogs. The point of this conversation was not invading personal space, and to get distracted by semantics would derail her point.

Oliver changed his tactics from stroking to petting Lance's shoulder and saying, "Good dog," then laughing at his own joke. Still an invasion of personal space, but that was a conversation for another time. Carrie had generally found that one etiquette lesson per day was all that really stuck anyway.

Lance took his own approach, raising his hand to stroke Oliver's cheek the same way the boy had touched his and saying, "Oh, what a soft puppy you are."

Oliver threw his head back, laughing in delight. Then he grabbed both of Lance's cheeks in his hands and stared into his eyes. It was a game Oliver had invented. Carrie called it the stare down. She'd never figured out what triggered it or what the rules were. She waited to see if Lance made it to the end.

Blue eyes to blue eyes, they stared at each other. Looking at their profiles so close together made Carrie realize Oliver had his dad's chin, the sharp line and square jaw. How had she never noticed before? Probably because she'd spent much of Oliver's life pretending she didn't know anything about his father, but the truth stared her in the face. Or rather, the truths were staring each other in their faces. Father and son.

Based on rules that only Oliver understood, the game ended with Oliver double-tapping Lance's cheek and leaning forward to kiss his dad's nose. It was Carrie's favorite part of the game. She always returned the kiss, smooching his nose and cheeks and forehead until he squealed with laughter. Lance didn't, though, simply stared at his son, the kind of wonder in his gaze that Carrie remembered feeling the first few months of Oliver's life. At some point, she'd have to tell Oliver who Lance was. Would he stare back at his father with that same wonder?

She blinked back the tears gathering in her eyes. She'd done the best she could, and now she would do better. It was all she could offer, and it would have to be enough. For all of them.

"Maybe carpeting?" Carrie answered her own question from earlier, trying to get back into professional mode as quickly as possible. "Could they have carpeted the lobby at some point? What a tragedy." She inspected the perimeter of the room and sure enough, the pockmarks appeared in places where it would be logical to nail down a carpet pad. She hated when people destroyed original flooring for some fad. In the corner near the mailboxes, she found a bit of green shag caught under the floorboard. Green shag? She shuddered. At least they'd had the good sense to pull it up at some point. Too bad they hadn't had the terrazzo restored at the same time.

"Can it be fixed, or are we looking at new floors, too?" Lance switched Oliver from one hip to the other. He might be used to hauling bags of Quikrete and rock, but a wiggly kid was a whole other kind of weight.

"All in all, it's not in terrible shape. I know a guy." Carrie took a few pictures of the trouble spot. "He'll do an excellent job."

"Good as new?"

"Absolutely not." She snapped a few more pictures to entice her restorer into taking the job. He liked a challenge. "Antique terrazzo? That's a selling point all on its own. We're not going for a new Dorothy, are we? We're selling its history, and this floor has plenty of that."

"Whatever you say. You're the designer." Lance let Oliver slide down the side of his body, his small feet hitting the floor with a soft thud. Oliver reached up to take Lance's hand, and Carrie felt that tug at her heart she often felt when watching her son. She never wanted him to lose his sweetness, his trust that everyone in his world was looking out for him.

The three of them continued the tour, Carrie taking

at least a hundred photos along the way. Whenever they encountered some of the Excalibur guys, Lance stopped to introduce her and Oliver.

"Like this, Oli." Lance demonstrated how to knock knuckles with Mendo, the construction foreman Carrie remembered saving Lance's bacon more times than she could count. Lance rushed into projects, but Mendo was always a step behind him, making sure all the pieces fit into place.

Mendo knocked back, which delighted Oliver into a round of three knuckle knocks. With a smile for Carrie, Mendo said, "It's good to see you again."

"You, too." She gave him a quick hug.

"Mama!" Oliver held up his knuckles to her. She fist-bumped him, and he scurried away, accosting the nearest worker, a young man in paint-splattered jeans and a Marlins baseball cap.

"Look what you've started." Carrie's chastisement was half-hearted. She should probably worry about her son running wild on a construction site, but instead she was touched by how the men treated him, fist bumps and encouragement every step of the way. There weren't a lot of men in Oliver's life. When she stopped to count, the total number was zero. Her dad had met him once, but now that he lived in New York, they never saw him. His new family apparently took all his time.

"I've created a knuckle-bumping monster." Lance took slightly larger than normal steps to catch up with Oliver. He scooped him up from behind, swinging him around, Oliver's short legs flying out in a circle, the two of them so natural that it broke Carrie's heart.

"Again, again!" Oliver demanded when Lance set him on his feet.

"Oliver, be polite." Carrie took his hand and tugged him to her side.

"Again, please! Again, please!" Oliver wiggled away from her and ran back toward Lance.

"Since you asked so politely." Lance picked him up by the armpits and swung him around. "One more time, and then we've got to get back to work."

Oliver laughed, that maniac pitch that meant he thought he was getting away with something. Carrie laughed, too, because he most certainly was.

They continued the tour, Oliver swinging between them, and Carrie felt the old building welcoming them. It whispered to her about the families who'd come before them, the joys and sorrows the walls had witnessed, and Carrie pledged in her heart of hearts that the Dorothy would become a home again.

Lance's phone buzzed, and he let go of Oliver's hand to check the message. "Adam's downstairs."

Carrie beamed. "Wonderful! I have some ideas to run by him. And I should offer to buy him dinner."

"What? Why?" Lance stopped their progress and glared at the wall.

"He offered a lot of insight about the plans for the Dorothy. I'm sure it gave me an edge for the proposal I sent you." Carrie scrolled through some of the photos she'd just taken. "I have so many more ideas now, and I'd love to get Adam's thoughts. It'll be good if we're on the same page from the beginning."

"Same page. Sure." Lance gave a curt nod and typed his response. "You'll make a great team."

"Thanks." Carrie laid her hand on his forearm. "It means a lot to me to be working with you again. And to think, it's not one but two projects. I can never thank you enough for saving my butt with Kristin's bathroom."

He muttered something under his breath that sounded like "you could offer to buy me dinner," but she couldn't have heard him right. Things between them were so good right now. She'd made the right call, cutting off that kiss in Kristin's elevator and not following up in any kind of romantic way. They could work together and maybe even coparent, but only if they avoided their past mistakes. Sure, some of those past mistakes made for some really good memories, but she couldn't risk a repeat of the end of their marriage, not when Oliver was clearly becoming so attached to Lance. Oliver came first, always.

Carrie pulled up a few color swatches on her phone to run by Lance as possible colors for the lobby walls, and it wasn't long before the stairwell door opened. Adam greeted them with a "Lovely day, isn't it? And who's this? Little young to be put to work at a construction site, aren't you?"

Oliver dashed for Adam, offering his knuckles. Adam chuckled and fist-bumped him with a "My man," which made Oliver giggle.

"My son." Carrie introduced them. "Oliver. Oliver, Adam."

Oliver offered his knuckles for another bump, and Adam obliged. It was adorable to see Adam stoop from his great height to Oliver's small one.

"I have a few questions. Do you have a minute?" Carrie swiped away the paint colors and opened up her notes. "There are a few points where architecture and interior

design overlap, and I don't want to start making plans until
I run it by you."

"I have a meeting very soon." Adam checked his phone
for the time. "But I wanted to give Lance the news in
person—parking-garage permit approved. In record time,
I might admit. It's almost like someone behind the scenes
is pulling strings."

"Excellent." Lance's verbal response was positive, but
his body language—hand to the back of his neck, twitchy
cheek muscle—showed he was worried about something.

Adam, though, was all sunshine. "Isn't it? Thought you'd
want to know so you can get working on that schedule."

"I'm on it."

Adam offered his phone to Carrie. "If you'll put your
number in, I can call you later to set up a meeting?"

"Sure." Carrie punched her numbers.

"Maybe Saturday night?" Adam saved her contact with a
series of taps. "Over dinner?"

"Oh!" Carrie's pulse fluttered. "I was going to ask you."
She'd mostly been joking, telling Lance she owed Adam
dinner. Sure, she'd flirted with Adam at their first meeting,
but honestly, she hadn't thought about him at all since then.
He was tall, handsome, smart, and most importantly, not
Lance. Lance was the past, and she needed to think about
the future. "This works, too, though. I'd love to have dinner
with you."

"Great. We'll talk details later." He offered them all a
wave and Oliver one last fist bump before he was on his way.

Lance scowled after him.

"Feel like babysitting again?" Carrie leaned a shoulder
against the hallway wall, a little weak-kneed at how quickly

it had all gone. In front of Lance, no less. That showed how far they'd come. Next thing you know, she'd be setting him up with one of her friends. Except Farrah and Vanessa were really the only friends she had, and they were unavailable in several ways—like being in love with each other and living in North Carolina because Vanessa'd gotten a really good teaching job there. Well, she'd find some way to pay Lance back for introducing her to Adam. Then they could double date. Yeah, that would be great. Totally fun. Hooray for modern divorce.

Lance turned his scowl on her. "Of course I'll babysit. Text me the time."

Oliver clapped his hands. At least one person in this hallway was completely happy. Carrie wondered why it wasn't her.

# CHAPTER 18

CARRIE BREEZED DOWN HER SHORT HALLWAY AND stopped in Oliver's room for a good-night kiss. He sat on top of his sailor-blue coverlet with his orange octopus Oink tucked in his armpit. He turned the pages of his favorite book, *The Snowy Day*.

"Snow!" He pointed to the swath of white on the page. "I like snow."

"I know." Carrie'd been through this a few thousand times. "You want to see snow. Maybe this winter, we'll go find some."

"Oink likes snow." Oliver used one of Oink's plush tentacles to point out more snow. One thing the picture book had going for it was plenty of snow.

Carrie didn't want to get into a biology lesson about why Oink would not like snow. Adam would be here any minute. She needed to hurry the bedtime routine along.

"Did you brush your teeth?" She lifted her own front lip, and Oliver giggled, pointing at her teeth. She ran her tongue around the front of her bite and tasted lipstick. "Good catch, Oli. Now let me see yours."

He bared his teeth in a ferocious grin, growling like Beckham.

That was all the invitation Beckham needed to hop onto the bed. He nosed his way under Oliver's other arm and licked Oliver's cheek. Oliver squealed, which was the opposite of the calming bedtime ritual Carrie was trying to create.

"Beckham, down." She pointed at the floor. He pretended not to hear her and gave Oliver all his attention, licking his chin and neck and even one of Oink's tentacles.

"Beckham, down." Lance's much deeper voice commanded the dog's attention. Beckham slunk off the bed and sidled up to Lance. She'd left the front door open for Lance, but it still surprised her to hear his voice.

"Good dog." Lance smoothed the hair on top of the dog's head, making Beckham's tail beat a few times against the hardwood floor. "Knox and I put in a few hours at Kristin's today. Should be able to finish up as early as next Tuesday."

"Thanks." Carrie didn't look at Lance to offer her gratitude. She didn't actually feel grateful. She felt annoyed and yes, a little hurt that her Jack Russell obeyed a man he hadn't seen in years over her. Sure, she'd jogged with Oliver and Beckham to Fur Haven every day this week. Sure, that meant Lance roughhoused with the dog and spent a lot of time identifying bugs with Oliver. Beckham and LouLou ran circles and figure eights while Carrie watched, bemused by the normalcy of it all. She'd even chatted a few times with Sydney and Eliza and was starting to feel like one of the neighborhood regulars. Perhaps they, dog included, were all a little too comfortable with how easily Lance fit into their lives.

Maybe it was a bad idea to leave Lance on baby- and dog-sitting duty. Beckham might get the wrong idea about who the real alpha was around here. She should text Adam and call the whole thing off. Then she could kick off her uncomfortable shoes and curl up next to Oliver for more *Snowy Day* action while she planned some sort of vacation for them that would allow Oliver to experience the joy of snow for himself. If she also imagined Lance as part of that snuggle sandwich and as the person who taught Oliver how to make snowballs, well, no one needed to know that but her. Yes, canceling was an excellent idea.

Except Adam was also an architect. And architects worked with the same clients as interior designers. It could mean a lot to her business if he recommended her work. Besides, she owed Adam, and she could definitely use a night out, a night away from the temptation of Lance's deep-blue eyes and deeper voice. A night dedicated to possibilities, to the future. She pulled out her phone and ordered a car. Adam could be the answer. Lucky date number fifteen.

---

Adam walked her to her door. Of course he did. He'd been nothing but an ideal date all night, smiling at the right times, really listening when she talked about her work and Oliver. Plenty of women did a double take walking by their table at the Thai restaurant where they'd eaten drunken noodles and red curry, family-style. There was no denying he was a handsome man. A tall, handsome man. She tilted her chin up and up and up to say good night.

"Thank you for dinner. It was lovely."

Adam cupped a large hand around the back of her neck. "You're the one who is lovely." He swooped down and lightly brushed her lips with his, a gentle back-and-forth motion that she had to admit felt…nice. She turned her head slightly, redirecting his lips to her cheek before he got any ideas about deepening it. Nice was not zing.

"I'd like to see you again." Their foreheads touched, and his breath smelled like lime and basil.

"Text me." She reached behind her and braced against the door. Nice wasn't zing, but maybe it was second-date material. Keeping her options open seemed wise. Who was she going to find better than Adam? A picture of Lance flashed through her mind, but she shoved it aside. Lance was in the rearview, romantically speaking. Yeah, a second date with Adam might be exactly what she needed to focus on the road ahead instead of behind her.

He straightened to his full height and smiled. "Count on it."

She watched him walk away, the tight pull of the trousers against his trim butt. What did an architect do that made him so muscled in all the right places? They'd talked about a lot tonight, but now she realized she'd done most of the revealing. On his side of the table, it had been observational humor about living in Miami and a few references to his college days. What college? He'd never said. Yet he'd made her feel interesting, how he'd leaned on his elbow and watched her while she gestured with her chopsticks about something silly Oliver had said earlier in the day.

Next time, she'd make sure to get him to open up. She touched a finger to her bottom lip, wishing she'd felt more zing. *Maybe next time.* She smiled while she opened the door, remembering playing chopstick tug-of-war with him over a baby corn. She took a breath and pushed into the condo, ready for whatever chaos Oliver and Beckham might have created with only an inexperienced Lance to keep things under control.

Carrie didn't know what she'd expected, but it wasn't this.

The TV cycled through its various screen savers. Mountain-scape. Beach-scape. River-scape. A brightly colored parrot. A pile of three raccoons. And Oliver's favorite: polar bear.

Oliver was zonked out, nestled between the back of the couch and Lance's chest, a line of drool dripping from the corner of his mouth and stringing down to Lance's T-shirt. Beckham sprawled across Lance's belly, frog-leg form, and Oliver's hand rested on the scruff of his neck. Lance's head was propped on the couch arm, his neck at an uncomfortable-looking angle, and a light snore escaped his open mouth.

Carrie clicked the front door closed behind her as softly as she could. Man nor boy nor dog stirred. What on earth had gone on here this evening that Beckham was too tired to notice the door opening or her stealthy entrance? The perpetually hyper dog only slept this deeply after multimile hikes through state parks or hours of fetch.

*Let sleeping dogs lie.* She would take advantage of not having to take the dog out immediately or resettle Oliver in his bed with a bit of indulgence. She crept past the pile of sleepers and helped herself to a few bites of the Häagen-Dazs strawberry ice cream she kept on hand for late-night treats. Not even the opening or closing of the freezer door alerted Beckham. She took another few bites, spoon scraping cardboard side, before squirreling the ice cream into the depths of the freezer shelves, out of the sightline of a certain small child and hidden behind a giant bag of mixed vegetables so her mother wouldn't find it.

She leaned against the kitchen arch and watched Beckham and Oliver rise and fall with each breath Lance took. She held a hand to her chest, calming the wild pound of her heart.

*My boys.* All three of them.

She slid down the wall and rested her chin on her knees. *My boys.*

She should stop kidding herself. There wouldn't be another date with Adam St. John. Everything she'd ever wanted was right here in her very own condo. Too bad she couldn't have it.

# CHAPTER 19

Lance buried his fingers in the curls around LouLou's neck, giving her a good rub that made her back foot slap against his thigh like a metronome. "Park?"

She shot off the couch and threw herself against the front door as if he hadn't taken her out to the front to pee on the palm trees less than two hours ago. She scratch-scratched at the threshold like she'd dig her way out if he didn't hurry.

"I'm coming; I'm coming," he said in response to her high-pitched whine. She spun in delight, and he had to laugh. Hanging out with dogs, a guy couldn't help but feel more optimistic about the world. Like maybe Carrie would bring Beckham to Fur Haven for a morning run with his poodle pal, and Lance could get some quality bug-hunting time with his son. Right, he wanted to spend his Sunday morning with palmetto bugs, beetles, and fire ants.

Lance took a quick moment to fill a thermos with coffee from Riley's Keurig, then made LouLou's dreams come true by taking the leash off its hook on the wall. He let her lead the way, the poodle a heat-seeking missile on course for maximum destruction. He sipped his too hot beverage, not so casually scanning the street for signs of Carrie's Blazer. Just because he didn't see it didn't mean she wasn't already there or on her way. Sometimes she came to Fur Haven as part of her morning run; on busy days, though, she drove. Either way, she'd probably be here soon. Strangely, there weren't any dogs in the park this morning, but several owners and their pooches milled outside the gate.

"What's going on?" He slid into the small crowd next to Eliza. Lady dropped her large head to greet LouLou, their two tails beating back and forth in the same rhythm.

Eliza pointed to an official-looking sign posted to the gate. "We're locked out. They're closing the park."

"They who?" Lance wished his coffee were of the Irish variety. His slow Sunday putting finishing touches on the lobby bathroom and laundry room before the residents returned from the cruise on Tuesday was off to a rocky start. Caleb would absolutely kill him if he came home and Fur Haven was already gone.

At her accusing look, he held up his hands. "It's not me, I swear." He took a step closer and read the sign. "Wait, I'm sorry. It *is* me."

"What?" A woman holding a chubby pug in her arms stepped into his personal space. Way into his personal space. "You're closing down the park? It hasn't even been open a month. This is ridiculous."

"Calm down, Kiki." Eliza scratched the pug's wrinkled neck. "I'm sure Mr. Donovan here has a very good explanation. Don't you?"

Lance's cheek twitched. Santos had really outdone himself with the sign, declaring the park closed indefinitely with no explanation as to why. And on a Sunday, no less. Why was the city commissioner so hell-bent on pushing the parking garage forward at lightning speed? Whatever the reason, he'd doubled down on the sign by chaining the gate closed with a large padlock. Which, Lance seethed, he had no right to do. The park was technically private property, and while their deal did include the city getting a piece of the garage for public parking, there was no parking garage yet. He had half a mind to call Santos and blast him at—he checked the time on his phone—seven in the morning.

"Well?" Eliza swung a full plastic bag in a threatening manner. The stench wafted his way, but he bravely held his ground. He was reasonably sure she wouldn't throw it at him.

Lance cleared his throat. "The good news is that we're building a bigger, better park for the neighborhood."

"And the bad news is that it's in Kendall?" If Kiki's glare were weaponized, he'd be dead. Other dog park goers nodded, turning to him for answers. He really wished he had some, or at least better ones. Ones vetted by his brothers and already in motion instead of ones he was making up right now while a handful of suspicious people and their dogs looked on.

"No. Right here." Lance raised his coffee thermos high, pointing to the sky. "And up a few stories."

Eliza dropped the plastic bag in surprise. It's wet slurp as it hit the ground made Lance glad she hadn't hurled that thing at him. "What are you talking about?"

"Yeah, what's going on?" Sydney crowded past a family with a Lab that had taken one look at the gate and turned around to return home. Chewy rode high in a sleek, silver bag, his tiny nose poking out over the zipper.

"Give me a second." Lance dropped LouLou's leash and stepped on it, then thumbed through emails until he found some back-and-forths with Adam that included a few of his drawings. He flipped his phone around. "See? It's going to be amazing."

"Hmmph." Eliza rested her hand on Lady's head. "How long are we talking about?"

"Based on the city's, er, enthusiasm for the project, it should be less than a year until the new dog park is ready to go. Trust me, it'll be worth the wait." Lance brandished the drawing again, like it would somehow convince everyone that it wasn't a huge inconvenience.

"A year?" Sydney echoed. "What're we supposed to do in the meantime?"

"Yeah, Lance *Donovan*. Does Caleb even know about this ridiculous plan? I can't believe he agreed." Eliza had a point he didn't want to acknowledge. Theoretically, Caleb was okay with the changes, but Lance had expected a few more weeks before they'd have to face the reality of logistics and community relations.

"Of course they have a plan."

Lance's head snapped up at the sound of Carrie's low, sure voice cutting through the crowd. Dressed in her running gear, coordinated leggings and tank, with gold-laced running shoes, she shoved the three-wheeled stroller through the thick grass like a sailboat cutting through waves. Oliver waved at him from his spot under the sunshade, and Beckham strained at the leash, doing his best to get to LouLou despite his leash being a few feet too short for that plan to be feasible. But dogs were hopeful creatures; Lance was just surprised that Carrie was, too.

Carrie pulled a bud out of one ear and looped the wire around the back of her neck. "The amazing thing about the new park is that once it's built, it's going to bring in income for the Dorothy that will help keep rents down. You know how long some of those folks have lived here.

The Donovan brothers are doing what's best for their residents, but it's also going to be a showcase, drawing people to the neighborhood. Good for the surrounding property values for sure."

Kiki nodded her head, clearly trusting Carrie's confidence more than Lance's fumbling of the issue. If he'd had time to prepare, he could've said what Carrie was spouting off the cuff. He was a work-with-his-hands guy, though, not a smooth talker like his brother Caleb. Why couldn't Santos have waited a few more days so that this PR nightmare could be Caleb's and not his?

"So?" Eliza wasn't as convinced as Kiki. "What is this grand plan?"

Lance sent a desperate look at Carrie. He had no plan, and the coffee hadn't kicked in yet. Clearly, he needed more. He chugged a good half the thermos while racking his brain for a solution.

"You know how they're going to re-landscape at the Dorothy?" Carrie stepped close to his side, laying her hand on his arm inches below the elbow. His muscles tensed, then relaxed at her touch. "That's the very last step in the remodeling plans. Adam, the architect, told me it's going to take two to three months per unit to finish the remodel, so that's well over a year until the Dorothy's complete. In the meantime, we'll be fencing in the front area for use as a temporary dog park. It should only take a day or two to move all the equipment and benches."

The dog owners seemed satisfied with her answer, moving away and on with their day with only a few comments among themselves and a few pointed ones aimed at Lance. He nodded and smiled and agreed to pretty much whatever they asked, all the while amazed that Carrie stood by his side, hand still resting on his arm, saying things like *we* and generally saving his ass. *We.* No denying he liked the sound of that. He put his arm around her shoulders, pulling her against his side, listening while she reassured the last few stragglers that a little patience would pay off big time.

When it was just the two of them, two dogs, and Oliver, Carrie's forehead dropped against his chest, and she let out a shaky laugh.

"Did I make things worse?"

He shifted so he could wrap his arms all the way around her in a loose hug. "No, the opposite. I was scrambling. Thanks for saving the day."

"I have no idea how much it's going to cost to do all the things I promised. Or how much time. Have I overcommitted you?" Her arms snaked around his waist, and she rested her weight against him.

Lance tightened his hold. "We would eventually have come to the same conclusion, I'm sure. Caleb and Riley would never leave the neighborhood without a dog park. You simply hurried the process along."

"It was a spatial problem, right?" Carrie stepped out of his embrace, fussing with the sunshade over Oliver's head. He'd dozed off sometime during the long, boring adult conversations, and she was careful not to wake him as she adjusted the angle of the shade. "Factor in available square footage plus desired function plus timeline. It was a pretty simple equation. I still think Caleb and Riley are going to hate me."

*But I love you.* The words almost escaped him, but he caught them just in time. Only a squeak emerged, which he covered by clearing his throat and taking the last sip of coffee from his thermos. He squatted down to pick up LouLou's leash and ended up with a lap full of Jack Russell. He roughed up Beckham's coat, lavishing the overwhelming affection he felt on the dog.

"Can I buy you breakfast?" He stood, poodle under one arm, Beckham under the other.

Carrie checked on the sleeping Oli and then consulted the phone strapped to her upper arm.

She seemed undecided, so he made her an offer he knew she couldn't, or at least wouldn't, refuse. "There will be mimosas."

A slow smile broke over her face. "When you put it like that."

"Balans?" He named a perennial Lincoln Road favorite, a place where they'd spent many a Sunday brunch and that he hadn't frequented since their divorce because he couldn't look at the menu without remembering all her favorite dishes.

"Enough. I said yes. No need for heavy artillery." She shoved the stroller back onto the sidewalk. "Meet you there?"

"Meet you there." He didn't sprint to the Dorothy, but LouLou did get to stretch her legs a bit. The guys could get started without him. He'd be back in plenty of time to make sure the laundry room was fully functional and all the toilets in the lobby bathroom flushed properly. A quick change of clothes later, he ordered a Lyft. The usual challenge of finding parking on South Beach was always compounded by the size of his work truck. Besides, mimosas. Maybe it hadn't only been Carrie who enjoyed them.

# CHAPTER 20

CARRIE WALKED UP TO THE BALANS' HOSTESS STATION with a bundle of nerves in her stomach so large she wasn't sure there would be room for any food. She smoothed a hand down the sides of her short, flared skirt, wondering if she should've chosen something more business appropriate. After changing outfits three times, though, she'd made herself leave the condo in what she was wearing, primarily because Addison had given the skirt two thumbs up.

"Is it a second date?" Addison had sat cross-legged on Carrie's bed, Oliver in her lap, while Carrie modeled her choices.

"Something like that." Carrie was not going to get into it with a fifteen-year-old, but her face flushed all the same.

"You like him!" Addison smiled wide, showing off a mouthful of metal and rubber bands. "Don't rush home, if you know what I mean." She waggled her eyebrows. "I could use an influx of cash this week. I'm saving up for a special effects makeup kit."

It was easy to distract Addison from her love life by asking about drama club and Addison's new fascination with stage makeup. The time passed quickly, and before she knew it, Carrie was running late. She threw her phone at Addison and asked her to call a ride while Carrie applied some light makeup and strapped on some very strappy, very high-heeled sandals.

"How do you walk in those things?" Addison handed

her phone back. The app announced the car was two minutes away.

"Practice." Carrie kissed Oliver's head and Addison's
cheek. "Be good, you two."

Addison laughed and fell back on the bed, tickling
Oliver. "Always!"

Carrie left, the sound of Oliver's laughter in her ears,
and flagged down the Honda Accord before the driver got
frustrated and left without her, a situation that had, to her
shame, happened a few too many times.

Now, she stood still while tourists streamed around her
and waiters bustled by, trays weighted down with plates of
bang bang chicken, avocado toast, and fresh fruit salads.
When the hostess asked her how many in her party, Carrie
stammered out, "I'm meeting someone?" like she was a
fifteen-year-old out on her first date. She inhaled deeply and
tried again. "I'm meeting a friend."

"Is that him?" The bored hostess nodded toward an outdoor table where Lance sat, a pitcher of mimosas already
gathering condensation in front of him. He saluted her with
a glass, and her pulse fluttered at the sight of his smile.

Not good. She'd agreed because Lance was helping her
with Kristin and had hired her for the Dorothy. They were
in business together again, and he was getting to know
Oliver, and that was all. She recited "That's all" to herself
under her breath while she slid into the seat across the small
table from him. Maybe she wouldn't ever go on a second
date with Adam, but this thing with Lance wasn't a date,
either. She needed to put the brakes on these backsliding
feelings before she said or did something really stupid. *Keep
it friendly.* Anything else would only lead to them hurting

each other again, and that meant hurting Oliver, which was absolutely not an option.

"Where's Oliver?" Lance looked around as if their son would come toddling along on his own at any moment.

Of course. Carrie flushed at her mistake. The invitation had been an excuse to spend more time with his son. Carrie was glad Lance couldn't see her hands wringing in her lap under the table. "He's not a big fan of mimosas. At least not yet."

Lance chuckled. "Probably for the best. We haven't really had a chance to catch up, have we?"

The bundle of nerves in her stomach immediately lodged itself in her throat. Catch up? On what? All the times she could've told him he was a father but didn't? She gave him a smile that trembled. "Tell me everything then."

He surprised her by leaning back in his chair, long legs stretching out in front of him, sipping from his mimosa, and telling her the full tale of how Caleb convinced him to get involved in the Dorothy. The story took them through ordering, a few refills of her glass, and the arrival of the entrees.

Lifting a bite of quesadilla to his lips, he paused. "Your turn."

The champagne had dissolved that troublesome nerve bundle, and his ease made her feel, well, easier. "It's a tale best told in pictures, I think." She got out her phone and gave him access to a few of her photo albums. Oliver's first year, each of his birthdays, a few of her design projects she was especially proud of.

Lance ate with one hand and thumbed through the photos with the other. When he hit a picture he especially liked, his eyes would light up and he'd say, "Tell me about this one." Slowly, picture by picture, she filled him in on the highlights. When the check arrived, she was shocked to find that a full two hours had passed.

Lance held up the empty pitcher. "I'd order another one, but I do need to get to work. Caleb and crew return tomorrow."

"Of course." Carrie plunked her credit card on the table. "My treat. It's been quite a week, Lance."

Lance frowned at the card, and she could see the thoughts cross his face. He wanted to fight her for the check. "Let me get it."

"My treat means my treat." She covered the check with her hand. If he paid, it was a date. If she did, it was a thank-you for bringing her in on the Dorothy. She wasn't so tipsy that she didn't realize how relaxed the mimosas made them, how blurry the friend zone boundaries looked through the bottom of a champagne glass.

"Fine." He leaned back, arms crossed over his chest. "I'll consider it payment for the work at Kristin's."

"I was planning to pay you. With money." Her fingers played with the stem of the champagne flute. She left the last few sips at the bottom of the glass. She'd clearly had enough.

"No need. If you take a hit on the job, it impacts Oliver, right?" Lance's posture relaxed, hands dropping to the table to fiddle with his napkin. "Knox and I both volunteer our time. For Oliver."

"That's so nice." Against her better judgment and probably because of the mimosas, she reached across the table for his hand. "Thank you, Lance. For the work. For being so understanding. I'm really glad you're in Oliver's life now."

Lance stared at their entwined fingers as if mesmerized, then turned his slightly tipsy gaze to hers. "You should've told me."

Carrie's teeth ground down on her lower lip. "I know."

"I want to be his dad." His fingers tightened around hers, almost painful now.

"You are." She tugged her hand free. "He already talks about you all the time."

If anything, her words made Lance fiercer. "You have to tell him, Carrie. Tell him I'm his father."

The number of times Oliver asked why he didn't have a father were few and far between, and he always accepted her explanations. At some point, though, he'd make friends his own age and learn that divorce didn't mean daddies moved away even though they loved their sons very much. It wasn't really a lie she'd been telling Oliver all these years, but it wasn't exactly the truth, either.

She forced a smile for the waiter who came to collect her credit card and hardened her mimosa-softened heart. "When it's the right time, but not until then. I don't want to upset Oliver's whole world."

"But you had no trouble ripping holes through mine." Lance's eyes turned glacially blue, ice spears pinning her in place.

Whether he referred to her leaving him or her keeping Oliver a secret, or both, didn't matter. He was right. Every step of the way, it had been her decision. She nodded, sucking on her bottom lip so hard she tasted blood.

"Jesus." Lance ran a hand along the stubble on his chin. "You're not even sorry."

Carrie was. She was so sorry, and she'd said so. She

wasn't going to spend the rest of their lives apologizing for her mistakes. She straightened her spine, leaning forward to tell her arrogant ex-husband a thing or two when the waiter returned. She tipped generously—it wasn't the waiter's fault her fruit salad sat rock hard in her stomach. She signed the check and stood, her indignation giving her perfect posture.

"I hope this doesn't affect our work together." She clipped out the words, hating that she felt the need to say them, but a lot of her pending income was dependent on him. She couldn't believe that once again, she'd let herself become dependent on Lance Donovan. It was a mistake she wouldn't make again.

"I'm not the one who backs out of commitments." He snorted. "And I'm perfectly capable of keeping the personal and professional separate. But make no mistake. If you don't tell Oliver who his father is, I will."

She swung her purse onto her shoulder, so agitated that she put too much muscle into it and bashed the person sitting behind her on the head. After a quick apology to the young man she'd surprise purse-bombed, she turned her ire on Lance. "You won't talk to my son unless I say you can."

Lance launched to his feet, shoving back his chair with enough force to rock their table. "You don't get to make those decisions by yourself anymore. I want custody."

And there it was. The ugly C-word, the word she'd been so afraid of, thrown up between them, thick as a load-bearing wall and just as immovable. She was suddenly and stunningly sober. Oh, her eyes were opened alright.

"That's what this was all about." She swept her arm over the table, taking in the dishes that still hadn't been cleared, the treacherous mimosa pitcher. "I should've known. I see right through your stupid Donovan power play." For all that he claimed to have left behind everything related to his father, blood will tell, as her mother would say. The connection she'd felt growing between them, their sweet little catch-up session, the babysitting, hell, even that kiss in Kristin's elevator that she was stupid enough to replay every night as she fell asleep—all of it calculated on his part to wear her down, make her forget all the bad between them so she'd soften and hand over custody of her son. She'd had nightmares about this since Oliver was born, and she'd decided long ago when Lance could have custody. Never.

She clenched the long strap of her bag until her knuckles whitened. "Nice try, but I'm onto you now."

"What is that supposed to mean?" Lance took a step toward her, his face contorted in innocent confusion she knew was fake.

"You want to fight over Oliver like your parents fought over you?" She lowered her voice, conscious of their very public setting. If he wanted it spelled out, she was only too happy to oblige. "Dragged back and forth between two households, neither one of them every truly a home? I won't have it."

"At least my parents cared enough to fight for me." Lance steadied himself on the back of his chair, fingers clutching at the top rung like a lifeline. If he'd ever been tipsy, he was dead sober now. "My dad didn't give up on me like yours did on you. At least my father wants a relationship with me."

Carrie blanched, literally felt all the blood drain from her face and straight to knuckles that wanted to punch Lance in his smug mouth. "At least my father's not a criminal."

"No, just criminally neglectful." He smirked. Smirked!

"Get him, girl," the man she'd bonked on the head with her purse earlier stage-whispered at her, and Carrie's blood reversed its retreat, flooding her face until her cheeks felt sunburned from the heat. A quick glance over her shoulder showed their avid audience, two of whom were openly filming the scene.

Carrie licked her lips, breathing as deeply as she'd been taught in her birthing classes. "This is why we broke up." She folded forward a bit, the heaviness of her words weighing her down. "You can't hide who you really are forever, not in a real relationship. And deep down, you and me, Lance? We're terrible people."

"Ouch." The man behind her whistled. "You tell him." His friends offered similar encouraging remarks, but they only made her feel worse.

Although their audience was clearly rooting for another round, Carrie didn't stick around for act two. That was what divorce meant. She didn't have to listen to his accusations or justifications. She ran as fast her heels allowed, purse bouncing against her side, and cut down Michigan Avenue so no one had to see the tears streaming down her face.

---

"Sir? Don't forget your card." The waiter stacked the dirty plates on a tray, making it abundantly clear that Lance should get going. He lurched away, unsteady on his feet even though his anger had burned off his mimosa buzz. He ignored Carrie's fans, the ones trying to wave him down from the next table for details. He might've just enacted a scene from a reality show, but he had no desire to be recognized for it. His hasty exit took him to the meandering koi pond in front of the movie theater, and he stood for a moment studying the orange-and-white fish before taking a seat on the rock ledge.

Lance held Carrie's abandoned credit card in his hand, staring at the letters that spelled out her name like they were in a foreign language. He wasn't completely sure what had just happened; all he knew was it felt an awful lot like the last few months of their marriage—flash-in-the-pan arguments that escalated so quickly he almost never remembered what he'd said, although it was usually whatever he knew would hurt her the most. Not that she ever held back either. They were excellent at destroying each other. One such argument, one he barely recalled the content of, was the reason he'd ultimately agreed to the divorce. Why live with someone who could eviscerate you with a few well-chosen words? Maybe Carrie was right about them being terrible people. Lord knows, he certainly felt terrible right now.

He'd made a dick move, bringing up custody. It'd been on his mind, of course, since the day he found out about Oliver. But he knew he wasn't ready for full- or even part-time fatherhood. He'd thought he'd have time to ease into it. Hell, in his most idiotic moments, he'd even imagined getting back together with Carrie, creating their own little perfect nuclear family. She'd made him so mad, not wanting to tell Oliver who he was when every time he was with his son, it became harder and harder not to tell him. He wanted to introduce Oliver to his brothers, hell, even his grandfather. He wanted Oliver to be part of his life.

And now he'd blown it. No way would Carrie let him

anywhere near Oliver without a court order. So be it. That was the risk she took with keeping her secret. He'd get a lawyer, take the legal route, let a judge decide what he and Carrie so clearly couldn't decide for themselves. Right now, though, he needed to get to work. He shoved Carrie's credit card in his pocket, figuring walking a few blocks before calling for a ride would help blow off some steam.

It didn't. Luckily, a text from Mendo alerted him that all hell had broken loose with the Dorothy's plumbing. Lance rubbed his hands together, thankful that the distraction was both huge and ill-timed. He'd handle these runaway emotions his favorite way: not at all.

# CHAPTER 21

"*Idiota!*" Mendo smacked Lance on the back of his head, mumbling more unflattering things under his breath. They stood outside the Dorothy, shoes sinking into the mud created when they'd dug up the main drainage line. Lance was reattaching the sections, restoring water to the building.

"Hey, I found the clog. Nothing idiotic about that." Lance rubbed his hair and winced for dramatic effect. Mendo's slaps were more attention-getting than painful. They'd spent the past two hours snaking the main drain out to the street line, trying to solve the mystery of why all the first-floor bathtubs had a couple of inches of brown back-flow in them. It finally paid off when they fished out a mop head with hundreds of used condoms stuck to it.

The discovery left Lance with many questions. Who flushed a mop head down the toilet? Like, how did that even work? Secondly, wasn't this a fifty-five-plus building? Because that was a lot of condoms for a building full of people who couldn't get pregnant anymore. It must've taken years for the mop to capture so many condoms, enough to block all drainage to the city sewer line.

"I'm talking about you getting a lawyer." Mendo shook his head, winding the drain snake back onto its coil. "Nothing good will come from that. You need to apologize to Carrie. Work it out between the two of you."

Lance cleaned his hands on his jeans, leaving long

streaks of mud down his thighs. "Not gonna happen. I don't think she'll ever talk to me again."

Mendo placed a fatherly hand on Lance's shoulder. How Lance wished Mendo really were his father, instead of the crappy one the genetics lottery had landed him. Whatever Mendo was about to say, he would listen. He would do it, no matter how crazy the advice, because Mendo was a good man, and if Mendo had raised him, maybe Lance would be a good man, too. He'd start right now, this minute. Whatever he said.

"What should I do?" Lance knocked one work boot against the other, shaking dirt loose, afraid to look at Mendo and see disappointment in his eyes.

"Grovel." Mendo shook Lance's shoulder, emphasizing his point. "I'm talking on your knees, flowers and candy, hire a skywriter, organize a flash mob kind of groveling. It's your best shot."

Lance stiffened. "She said awful things, too. Why do I have to be the one to grovel?"

Mendo clapped him on the back. "Because you have the most to lose."

*Dammit.* "Couldn't I start with something easier? Like a text?"

"Don't be such an *idiota*. Go now." Mendo gave him a shove in the direction of his truck.

Right now. Whatever Mendo said, Lance had to do it because he was trying to be a better man than he was raised to be. He got out his keys and checked the balance on his bank app. He had a feeling groveling wouldn't be cheap.

Carrie took one last swipe at her smeared mascara before putting on a big smile. "I'm home!" she called, dropping her bag onto the couch and slipping out of her heels. The sooner she could take off her stupidly optimistic flared skirt, the better. Beckham skittered to her side, the nails on all four of his feet painted with green glitter.

"How was it?" Addison hurried into the living room, her hair in an intricate braid with a zigzag part. Oliver burst into the room a second later, his nails also painted with green glitter.

"Beauty day, I see." She hugged Oliver, perhaps a bit too tightly. He squirmed out of her grasp.

"We're matching!" He held up his hands for her inspection. "First Addison, then Beckham, then me."

"Lovely. You all look gorgeous." Carrie collapsed onto the couch, and Beckham jumped up beside her.

"You look…" Addison cupped her hands over Oliver's ears. Sure enough, her nails sparkled with glitter, too. "…like you did not have a good time."

"It was fine." Standard answer. She was not getting into it with Addison.

Addison pursed her lips. "Oli? Do you want to draw your mom a picture?"

Oli jumped in place, fist pumping in the air. "Yes!" He streaked to his room. "I'll give you glitter nails, too, Mama!"

"Wonderful." Carrie propped her feet on the ottoman and took out her wallet. "Let me give you a bit extra for being available so last minute." She pulled out some cash, noticing the blank spot where her credit card should be. "Oh shit."

Addison giggled. "You don't have to give me extra if you don't have it."

"No, not that. You earned this." She handed over the cash. "I must've left my credit card at the restaurant."

"What happened?" Addison sat on the floor and drew her knees to her chest. "Was he mean to you?"

"You know what?" Carrie felt around in her purse for her phone. "He was. He was really mean."

"And that's why you were crying and left your credit card behind?" Addison nodded, like she could picture the whole thing in her mind. Maybe she didn't have to imagine. Maybe the whole thing was on YouTube now, thanks to their overly interested table neighbors.

Carrie called the restaurant, and they tracked down her waiter, who assured everyone that the gentleman had the credit card. Carrie hung up, frustrated. She'd have to talk to Lance again if she wanted it back. Maybe she didn't. She had other cards. She could live without it.

"At least you don't have to cancel your card." Addison tended to see the bright side of things, a trait many people said Carrie possessed as well. Today, though, it was all dark skies, gloomy clouds, and thunder in the distance. Not a rainbow in sight.

"It'd be easier if that were my biggest problem." Carrie shoved the wallet back in her purse, tears starting up again in her eyes. She tried to blink them back, but she wasn't fast enough. A few escaped.

"What happened?" Addison rocked in place, obviously upset that Carrie was upset. "Was it bad?"

Carrie couldn't believe she was confiding in a fifteen-year-old, but the story came pouring out.

"Oh no!" Addison moved to the couch and put her arm around Carrie's shoulder. "Oli talked about Lance a lot today. He loves that guy."

"I know. I've made such a mess of things." Carrie leaned into Addison's sideways hug. "Lawyers are so expensive."

"You don't need a lawyer." Addison soothed a hand down Carrie's arm. "You need to apologize."

Carrie stiffened in shock. "What? He said he wanted *custody*. Of course I need a lawyer."

Addison turned to sit cross-legged on the couch. "Look, he's not wrong. Not completely. He is Oli's dad. You did keep them apart for Oli's entire life. He has a right to be a little paranoid, don't you think?"

Carrie did not want to think about Lance's side of the story. "I apologized. He said he understood."

"Still." Addison fidgeted with the end of her braid. "It sounds like you were saying he couldn't be Oli's dad, and maybe he got scared that you'd keep them apart again."

Carrie stilled. The fifteen-year-old had a point. If Carrie hadn't been so scared herself, maybe she would've understood that Lance was scared, too. She had cut him out of Oliver's life; it made sense that he'd worry she'd do it again. Maybe getting legal custody was the only remedy he could think of to make sure he was always connected to his son. When she thought about it like that, their whole argument took on new dimensions.

"You're pretty smart, you know that?" Carrie leaned over to hug Addison. "I do owe him an apology. Thanks for listening."

Addison grinned. "No problem. I love Oli, too, you know."

Carrie's eyes welled with tears for the third time that day, but these were the good kind. "I do know."

Oliver stood in the hallway holding up a large white

paper. "Look, I put everyone in the picture." He pointed to various squiggles and configurations of lines and circles. "Here's Beckham." The shortest circle. "And Mama. Gamma. Addison." All the circles had green hair. He pointed to the tallest one. "Lance! And that's me next to him."

"Everyone, huh?" Carrie walked over to admire the drawing close up.

He handed it over with a big smile. "Yep, everyone in the whole world."

Addison laughed. "Oli, Oli. There are more than five people in the world."

"Right." Oliver nodded solemnly, bangs sliding forward to cover his eyebrows. "I meant all the important people."

Carrie held the drawing to her heart. "It's perfect. Let's hang it on the refrigerator, shall we?"

"Yes!" Oli ran ahead of her to the kitchen.

"I've got trig homework waiting for me." Addison slipped on the polka-dot flip-flops she'd left near the front door. "You should really call him."

"I am." Carrie held up her phone. "Right now." It buzzed. "Or right after this text."

Addison left with a wave, and Carrie checked her messages. A picture of her credit card and the words peace offering?

Shaking, she typed back *please come over*. Before, after a fight, Carrie and Lance would pretend that it never happened, try to go back to how they were. A pattern for disaster, she now realized, but still frightening to deliberately break. But if she wanted the future to be different from the past, she had to be willing to try. *And you're not a terrible person*, she typed, getting a small part of the apology out of the way before she had to look him in the eye.

The three dots bounced. Neither are you.

She smiled.

# CHAPTER 22

CARRIE STOOD FROM HER SEAT ON OLIVER'S BED, tucking his nautical blue-and-white-striped bedspread around his shoulders. She leaned down, unable to resist one last good-night kiss to the forehead. He was already sound asleep, arms wrapped around Oink the orange octopus, long eyelashes curled against his cheeks like a little angel. Her little angel. She couldn't help how mushy she felt sometimes. It was as much a part of motherhood as the sleepless nights of nursing and the near-constant laundry duty. Would she always feel this visceral tug on her heartstrings every time she saw his sleeping face? She hoped so.

In the living room, the father of that precious face was also fast asleep. Knocked out on the couch, one arm flung over his head and the other clasping an embroidered throw pillow to his chest. The same dark lashes she'd admired on Oliver swept Lance's cheeks, a contrast to his light-blond hair that had always fascinated her. Like with Oliver, she was tempted to bend down and kiss Lance, but unlike with Oliver, she didn't plan on aiming for the forehead.

*Stop it.* They were divorced for good reason. And just because she couldn't exactly in this exact moment remember the exact reason didn't mean it wasn't a darn good one. Their marathon talk this evening reverberated through her. The things they'd admitted to each other, the fear they both had of losing Oli, negotiating a way forward that didn't require lawyers or courts. She was proud of them. They were adultier adults now, able to calmly and rationally hash out their misunderstanding.

When she'd opened the door earlier, he'd handed her an elaborately wrapped box with an enormous sparkle bow. "For Oli?" she'd asked, taking it from him.

"For you." He stood on the welcome mat, jeans stained with mud and a shyness about him she'd never seen before.

She opened the door wider, wordlessly inviting him. He ducked his head and entered, asking, "Where's Oli?"

"Upstairs with Addison." At the last moment, Carrie'd panicked. What if Lance came over and they got into another argument? She didn't want Oliver's childhood memories to be like hers, listening to her parents fight through the wall. Pretending she hadn't heard anything when inside, her stomach was all topsy-turvy, and even something as simple as a glass of orange juice made her throw up. No, better to get him out of hearing range. Addison had been so happy to earn a few more bucks today, she'd thrown in dogsitting for free.

Carrie perched on the couch, and Lance watched while she unwrapped the gift, tearing through the wrapping and layers of tissue paper until she found the gift. Her credit card.

Her laugh was a nervous one. "That's a lot of pomp and circumstance."

"I wanted it to be a moment." He loomed across the ottoman from her, ignoring her patted suggestion for him to sit with her.

"It certainly was. Any particular reason?" She'd run her finger along the edge of the card, thinking about how she'd never use it again without thinking of him.

A loud thump drew her attention to him. Lance knelt on one knee. Kind of like… No, he couldn't be, could he? Her hands flew to her cheeks. His other knee dropped to the floor, his face contorted in an uncomfortable expression she didn't know how to read. "I'm here to grovel."

The words were so angry that at first she'd missed their meaning. "Grovel?"

"Yeah, Mendo said I should. I'm sorry I threatened you about custody. It was stupid of me." He stayed on his knees, head down. Slowly, inch by inch, his chin rose until his wild blue eyes crashed with hers. "Is that enough?"

"Enough groveling?" She was still having trouble processing this gesture. Lance's apologies were usually no more than a light, half-hearted "sorry," barely a blip on a communications radar.

"It's not." He rubbed his hands together like he was warming them over a fire. "Okay, I've got more ready to go. I'm also sorry—"

She'd rushed him then, circling the ottoman, grabbing both his hands in hers, and pulling him to his feet. "Stop, Lance. Please, stop."

"So it was enough?"

The hands that held his shook with the power of her emotions. "I appreciate the apology. I was really scared." Whether she made the conscious decision or her legs simply gave out, she wasn't sure. But the next thing she knew, she was on her knees. "I should be the one asking for forgiveness. I was awful to you. Back then. And now. I'm sorry."

She'd looked up then, and the astonishment on his face was almost worth the humiliation she felt about her own behavior. He cupped a finger under her chin and pulled her up until they were standing face-to-face, hands still clasped.

"Let me finish." Lance launched into a clearly somewhat rehearsed speech about how learning about Oli had made him feel and his fear of being cut off again. Carrie's knees stayed wobbly, but she stood her ground, really listening. When he was done, she'd told him she was afraid of losing Oli, too, and that led to more confessions of things they were both afraid of. Now. And then.

When it was all over, they were on the couch, companionably close, Carrie's feet propped on the ottoman and Lance's work boots planted firmly on the floor.

"I can't believe Mendo was right. There really is something to this groveling thing." Lance yawned. "Takes it out of you, though, doesn't it?"

"It helps that you opened with the perfect gift." She crinkled the wrapping paper shreds next to her. "You really took me by surprise."

"He said flowers or candy, but I didn't want to feel like I'd bought your forgiveness, you know? Returning something you lost while we were together? Seemed right." Another yawn stretched his face into comical lines.

"Symbolic, really." She folded the discarded wrapping into small squares and stacked them on the side table, keeping herself busy to distract herself from thinking of some of the words they'd said. Coparenting. Shared holidays. It was all getting so real. "Why don't you take off your boots, make yourself comfortable? I'll run upstairs and get Oliver and Beckham."

"Sure, I'd love to tuck him in before I hit the road, if you don't mind." He'd covered a yawn with his fist. "Sydney took

LouLou for the night because I wasn't sure how long this would take, but if I leave now, it's not too late to pick her up, is it?"

Carrie checked the small clock with big numbers hung over the TV. "It's nearly midnight. You should probably leave LouLou where she is."

"You're right." Lance stifled another yawn. "How about I wait here for you to get back with Oliver?"

She'd smiled. "Sounds perfect." A perfect opportunity to let Oliver know Lance was his father. It was time. She felt it in her bones.

When she'd returned fifteen minutes later with Oliver and Beckham in tow, it was Lance who got the tucking in. He was fast asleep, head propped on a fluffy throw pillow, and not even the slam of the door or the pitter-patter of little feet on hardwood floors woke him. Oliver gathered up the chenille throw she kept on the back of the couch and stretched it over Lance's long frame.

Oliver made a production of tucking the cover around Lance's broad shoulders. "Sleep tight, Lance. We'll look for bugs tomorrow!" Oliver's whisper was as loud as his normal voice, but Carrie found it sweet that he tried. So sweet that she didn't have the heart to tell him Lance wouldn't be here in the morning. Lance sighed and shifted in his sleep but didn't waken, not even when Oliver pecked him on the cheek.

Now Oliver was as deeply asleep as his father, and Carrie envied them both. She couldn't wait to climb between her bamboo sheets and scheme a perfect way to let Oliver know about his relationship to Lance. Maybe she could think of something as simple and meaningful as Lance's gesture this evening.

First, though, she had one more of her boys to settle for the night. Beckham bounced against her leg for attention.

"One last outing for the day, huh, big guy?" She walked toward the front door, Beckham excitedly clicking behind her. When she grabbed his leash off the hanger near the door, he jumped as high as her hip, executing a small flip before crashing to the floor.

"Hey." Lance's sleepy voice carried to the entryway, which wasn't all that far. He sat up and rubbed the top of his head, hair flying in all directions. "What'd I miss?"

"Oli's down for the night." She clipped the leash onto Beckham's collar and stuffed plastic bags in the pockets of linen pants. "Just taking the dog out one last time before I call it a night myself."

"I'll do it." Lance lumbered to his feet, work boots hitting the floor with a *thump*.

"It's fine. You probably want to get going." She added another bag to her pocket. Hey, you never knew how many it would take.

"Not particularly." He pried the leash from her hands, and their fingers brushed, a gentle graze that fluttered her heartbeat. "We can walk him together, like when he was a puppy."

Carrie wasn't sure revisiting the early days of their marriage was a good idea considering how raw she felt. She studied Lance's grip on the nylon lead. His callused hands, the short fingernails, the squareness of his knuckles. She swallowed a half-hearted protest. She didn't want him to leave. Why pretend otherwise?

She jerked her head in an awkward nod. "Give me a second to grab the baby monitor. We'll keep it short, to the corner and back."

Lance waited until she reappeared with the monitor in hand. "You think of everything."

"I try." She gave the monitor to Lance, and he tucked it into his back pocket. "This thing's got a range of two thousand feet, and the stop sign's about seven hundred feet away, so we'll be fine."

She held the door open. Beckham lunged through, hitting the end of the leash and the bottom of the stoop at the same time.

"Where does all the energy come from?" Lance hopped down the four front steps. "Didn't everyone say he'd calm down as he aged?"

"So they say." Carrie followed them, hand on the smooth rail she'd recently painted herself because she couldn't stand to look at the flaking paint for another day. "He's not always this hyper. Just mostly. Addison probably gave him some treats. You know how that ramps him up."

"What's your secret, buddy?" Lance waited while Beckham sniffed the same plants he sniffed multiple times per day. "How do I feel so much older, but you're still energetic as a puppy?"

"Between Oli and this one, I feel a hundred years old some days." The confession was out before Carrie could edit it. Why not? It had been one long day of confessions, hadn't it? What was one more?

Lance held open the front gate for her, winking at her as she passed through. "You don't look a day over eighty-nine."

"Thanks a lot." She smacked his arm, then waited while Lance untangled the leash from around his leg. It was easy to lose track of Beckham, whirling dervish that he was. Once freed of Lance's leg tangle, Beckham lunged ahead, straining on the lead enough to show how anxious he was to get going but not so hard that he choked himself.

"You got a hot date or something?" Lance said to the dog, letting him decide the direction. To the right. Carrie wasn't surprised. There was a particular crepe myrtle that was especially snifferific. At least Beckham seemed to think so.

"He's got a tight schedule." Carrie lagged behind, enjoying not being the one dragged along for a change. "Places to go, people to smell."

Lance chuckled at her lame joke. "Where do you usually go on a night walk? If Oli's with you, I mean."

"This time of night? We usually do a lap through the alley."

"You walk through alleys late at night?" Lance tugged on the leash to slow Beckham down, the bulge of bicep keeping the dog in check and riveting Carrie's attention. "That's not safe."

Carrie's jaw tightened. Just because he was good at controlling her uncontrollable dog didn't mean he got to control anything else about her life. They'd agreed to talk things out, not issue dictates to each other. "It's fine. This is a nice neighborhood."

"Bad things still happen in good neighborhoods." So he was going to talk it out.

She sighed. "I don't need you tell me how to be safe. I can take care of myself."

Lance clamped his mouth shut, and not one second too soon, as far as Carrie was concerned. She had enough worries on her mind without adding fear of her own alley to the list. There were streetlights. She never took them out this late. Who was he to tell her what was safe or not in her own neighborhood?

She jumped at Lance's touch on her arm.

"I'm sorry." His hand warmed her skin. "I didn't mean to offend you."

"It's fine. Though I could get used to this apology thing." She should pull away. She didn't. Instead, she compounded the problem by placing her hand over his. "We've been on our own a long time. You don't need to worry about us." Her fingers danced up his arm like they had a will of their own.

They'd stopped under a streetlight while Beckham thoroughly inspected the pole, leaving his mark for future dogs to ponder. Lance's hand tightened on her arm. She took a step closer, those dancing fingers now caressing his shoulder. Her breath staggered in and out of her lungs. What was she doing?

"Do you want to be alone?" Lance's question rumbled out of his chest. He used his grip on her arm to draw her closer.

Carrie tried to be honest with herself. As a single mother, she couldn't afford delusion. She understood his question, could feel the familiar pull of him, like her very cells couldn't stand to be separated from him for another moment. She wanted to blame muscle memory, her string of bad dates, that she was ovulating—something besides her own desire to press against Lance's hard body and kiss him until they were both breathless.

"Do you?" she countered, not willing to put into words the feelings pounding through her. As much as they'd shared earlier, this wanting made her vulnerable, and that made her hesitate.

"No," Lance rasped, placing a hand on her hip to draw her closer, erasing her hesitation with his touch.

"Me neither." She closed the last bit of distance on a quick exhale, lifting her face to his.

She thought he would kiss her then, would pull her in for a kiss as hot and all-consuming as the one in the elevator, the one she'd replayed a hundred times in her mind. He didn't. Instead, he cupped her head in his hands, his rough thumbs tracing her cheekbones with exquisite tenderness. Slowly, he smiled, right side hitching up that extra millimeter.

"Hi," he whispered.

"Hi," she whispered back, smiling. She stood on her tiptoes and reached up, lacing her fingers behind his head.

"I'm going to kiss you." The smile tipped further to the right.

"I wish you'd get to it already."

Lance's eyes flashed, hungry and wild. The smile disappeared, and finally, finally, he kissed her. And she kissed him. Her laced fingers pulled his head down. He held her jaw in one hand while the other plowed through her hair. She leaned into him, forgetting they were on the street, illuminated by the streetlight. Forgetting Beckham, engrossed in the scents of the lamppost. Forgetting all the reasons why she and Lance would never work. She kissed him, and he kissed her back, and Carrie hadn't felt anything this right in a very long time.

Her legs trembled from standing on tiptoe so long. Keeping her hold on Lance's head, she pulled him toward her, keeping the kiss going as she lowered her heels. Then she felt something else, something squishy. They both smelled it, and Carrie broke the kiss with a grimace.

"Let me see." Lance took a step back and twirled his finger for her to turn.

She lifted her foot. "Guess Beckham got tired of waiting for us."

"In good news, we can head back to your place now. Right?"

She scraped her shoe on the edge of the sidewalk. "Right."

"You are going to invite me in, right?" Lance scooped up the remains of Beckham's gift with a bag from his own pocket.

It was such a bad idea. Carrie scraped and scraped. Life with a dog was often messy and kind of gross. Or maybe that was simply life. "Right."

Lance smiled. Carrie smiled. Beckham pulled them all the way home.

# CHAPTER 23

LANCE DIDN'T MIND BECKHAM NEARLY PULLING HIS arm out of the socket. No matter how much of a hurry the little Jack Russell was in, Lance was even more so. His need for Carrie thrummed through his veins, as steady as his own heartbeat. The gate, the stoop, the front door. In the entryway, he spun and hauled her against him, picking up the kiss where they'd been so rudely interrupted.

She laughed and pushed on his chest, extricating herself in order to settle the dog. Even though the baby monitor was stuffed in his pocket and they hadn't gone more than a thousand feet from her front door, she still tiptoed in to check on their sleeping son. If Lance wasn't so anxious that she would change her mind, he might find it adorable.

But he was anxious. She'd said yes on the street, but now they were in her condo, on her turf, the signs of her life with Oliver everywhere he looked. The throw rug between the TV and coffee table was tactile, a multicolored kind of rag-knot, that he was sure she'd chosen purely for the texture. He remembered doing a nursery renovation with her in their second year of marriage. She'd done so much research on baby rooms and created a design that would help a growing child learn colors, shapes, and textures. In her own condo, she'd extended the idea in small touches around the home. The baseboard, he noted, was a scratchy rattan, perfect for a crawling baby to feel with his tiny hands.

Her life was all about Oliver. He saw it in the tiny rain-coat hanging by the door, the stuffed animals stuck in the crack of the easy-to-clean leather armchair, and the toys in the basket under the TV. There were also signs of Carrie herself—scuffs on the wooden floor from her many pairs of high heels, touches of green in the throw pillows and on the walls. The condo was cozy and comfortable, so much so that he became uncomfortable. There wasn't room for him in this space. He didn't belong here.

*You're a builder*, he reminded himself. *You can make your own space.* Although he couldn't imagine it now, the thought gave him hope. He quietly made his way to Oliver's room and observed Carrie as she swooped down to kiss his forehead. She tucked the covers in around his legs and repositioned the big orange octopus so it wasn't covering his mouth. She must've felt Lance watching because she looked over her shoulder at him and smiled.

Lance's abdomen tightened like he'd taken a swinging wooden beam to the gut. When he and Carrie split, this was what he'd given up. And suddenly he didn't simply want Carrie for tonight, he wanted her back. He wanted Oliver and Beckham and space for his work boots in the closet. What he wanted, really wanted, was his wife.

Carrie turned her head, sending him a smile over her shoulder, and his heart sped. Maybe, just maybe, his wife wanted him back, too. He waited in the hallway while she tiptoed her way to him. A guy could hope, couldn't he? Lance framed Carrie's face in his palms and kissed her with all the longing he'd spent years burying. He'd built some pretty firm walls after the divorce, but the way she kissed him back was a wrecking ball, leaving him in rubble at her feet. He backed her toward the bedroom, one step at a time, because if he was going down tonight, he wasn't going alone.

———————————

Carrie landed on the mattress with a *thump*, the jade comforter soft on her exposed back. Between the hallway and the edge of the bed, she'd lost her silk top and linen pants, but her ivory bra and bikini set were still in place. Lance, too, was topless, and she worked his belt buckle as quickly as she could without letting go of their kiss.

The kiss. This kiss. She'd never been anywhere else, done anything else. The kiss was the beginning and end of time, and even as she felt her lungs burning from lack of oxygen, she couldn't break away, couldn't be the reason they reentered reality. No, she was riding this kiss as long as she could, hands shoving down Lance's jeans while his fingers unsnapped her front hook bra. She gasped at the touch of air on her breasts, gasping again when his warm palms replaced her bra, lifting and holding her, the pressure enough to make her moan.

Lance changed the angle of their kiss, and she sucked in a lungful of air. Their lips crashed into each other, tongues exploring, breath mingling. He moved the kiss to the side of her mouth, down her neck, and it was okay, because it was still the kiss. Their kiss. Her back arched, jaw lifting, as the kiss moved down her body, suckling one breast and then the other before moving to her navel. Then lower and lower still.

Carrie looked down the length of her torso, mesmerized as the kiss moved to the very core of her, Lance's blond head between her thighs. Her knees fell open, and he growled his pleasure, cupping her buttocks and bringing her right. To. His. Mouth.

Her fingers tangled in the longish strands of his hair, curling and uncurling with each lick of his tongue. Her hips rose, spine arched, and she couldn't watch anymore, the bob of his head, the smooth expanse of his muscled back between her legs. She threw her head back, clutched clumps of the comforter beside her, panting because she couldn't scream, not with Oliver asleep down the hall, but oh, how she wanted to.

Lance's hands moved from her butt, parting her, a finger, then two, finding its way inside her. The kiss didn't let up, their kiss that started and ended everything. The kiss that was her whole world. He kissed her, stretched her, and she came apart, turning her head to bite the pillow as her whole body trembled its pleasure.

And still the kiss didn't stop, though it did gentle, moving back up her body to glide across her belly, dip into her navel, reverently revisit each breast, her collarbone, the column of her neck. Until finally, finally, he was back at her lips. She could taste herself on him, and it drove her even wilder. She lashed him with her tongue, his punishment for leaving her alone up here, but he didn't seem to mind.

The kiss stole more time, stretching minutes into hours and hours into eons. She pushed her hips against his, restless now that her trembling was done. She felt his smile against her lips, his hand parting her thighs.

"Condom?" he whispered.

Her head thrashed to the side. "IUD."

"Thank God."

Finally, he was inside her. And it was better even than the kiss. His lips sipped at hers, stealing what little breath she had. Her hands roamed his ropy back, following the lines and contours of muscles to his butt, where she squeezed.

He reared back, breaking the kiss, but it didn't matter because he was inside her, and they were moving together. His gaze bored into hers, a connection closer than any kiss. The blue of his eyes had always been her sky, her world, and she felt broken pieces of herself fitting back together. Until they were together, one breath, one heartbeat, one eternal moment when together, holding tight, they rode to the edge of time. And leapt.

# CHAPTER 24

LANCE'S INTERNAL ALARM USUALLY WOKE HIM UP WELL before dawn and long before his alarm, which he always set for the last possible moment, rang. This morning, though, he woke to his old life—Carrie snuggled beside him, one possessive arm thrown across his chest, and Beckham on the bed, nose lifting Lance's hand in a bid for attention.

"Hey, buddy, need a little lovin', huh?" Lance scratched the top of Beckham's chin. "Guess we both are hearing nature's call."

It felt so normal to stealthily peel Carrie's arm away and slide out on his side of the bed, pulling on boxers and his jeans in one swift move. Beckham leapt to the floor, jumping straight up and turning midair in joy at the prospect of going out. Lance held his finger to his lips, like that would keep the dog from skittering on the hardwood floor, and padded out to the hallway.

A light at the bathroom entrance let him know he wasn't the first awake this morning. The door stood wide open, and Oliver was positioned in front of the toilet, red fire-engine pajama pants pooled around his ankles, peeing directly on the floor. And indirectly on his pajama bottoms.

"Morning, Oliver." In the old days, the eternal dilemma was: who needed to pee more, him or Beckham? With Oliver in the mix, option three: bathroom cleanup, kid cleanup, and a lesson on how to use the step conveniently placed near the toilet. Would Beckham wait that long? How did Carrie do it? He was tempted to wake her up. One of them could handle Oli, and the other could take the dog.

The way she'd smiled at him last night as they drifted to sleep, her chin propped on his chest so she could stare into his eyes...

"Thank you," she'd said, then yawned and turned her cheek against his pecs. His heart had beat harder in his chest, like it was trying to reach her through bone and skin.

"My pleasure." He'd stroked his hand down the silky length of her hair, listening to her breathing even out, and sometime in the waiting, he'd fallen asleep, too.

Wake her from that lovely memory to deal with multispecies urine? Not exactly a romantic start to the morning. If Carrie could handle these two on her own, surely he could figure it out.

"How about a shower, big guy?" You don't leave a child standing around in his own pee. That seemed pretty obvious. Oli obligingly climbed the rest of the way out of his pajamas and into the tub.

Beckham whined, pacing in and out of the bathroom. Lance looked from child to dog, dog to child.

"You know how to take a shower?" he asked his son. He couldn't remember how old he was when he'd learned to shower, but since he didn't remember baths, he figured it must've been pretty young. Like, probably close to Oliver's age, right?

"Yes!" Oliver clapped his hands together.

Lance looked at his son skeptically. He seemed a bit short to operate the faucets and handheld showerhead. "Let me get the water started, and you can take it from there."

"Bath time!" Oliver grabbed a bar of soap in one hand

and rubbed it on his arm. Demonstrating mastery of the basics, Lance supposed. Good enough for him.

Lance turned knobs until the temperature was a safe lukewarm and handed Oliver the showerhead. "Back in two minutes, got it?"

"Got it!" Oliver directed the spray at the spot on his arm where he'd rubbed soap. Excellent. Part one of Lance's two-part plan was a success. Even though Oli didn't look like he needed any help, Lance knew better than to leave a three-year-old alone in the bathtub, which was why part two involved a quick dash to the entryway. As soon as he let Beckham out the front door into the condo garden, which was, he knew, likely against condo rules, he'd be right back in the bathroom to monitor his son's bathing ritual. The front door could stand open for the few minutes it would take to towel off the boy and get the dog back inside, all before anyone in the building could complain about a loose dog in the garden or Carrie woke up. Lance snapped for Beckham, pleased with the incredible efficiency of his plan.

Fresh-brewed coffee or breakfast in bed might be thoughtful morning-after gestures, but he'd knock it out of the park with his handling of her morning responsibilities. How surprised Carrie'd be when she woke up and there was nothing to do. He couldn't wait to see her face when she woke up to a clean bathroom, a dressed-and-ready-for-the-day son, and the smell of that light-roast coffee she liked brewing in the kitchen.

Oh yeah, he was killing the morning after, no doubt about it. Beckham bounded down the stairs just as an early-morning jogger opened the front gate to the building. Beckham yipped with excitement and shot off toward the opening.

"Son of a—" Shirtless, Lance took off after him, jumping the front stoop and landing on the sidewalk with a *thump*.

The jogger didn't notice the dog streak by, but her eyes widened at the sight of Lance barreling toward her. She held up her hands like he was going to mug her or something.

"Catch him!" He pointed at his Jack Russell, gleefully streaking toward the street. The jogger and Lance raced after him.

---

"Mama!"

Oliver's high-pitched and urgent call catapulted Carrie out of bed. Naked. Taking a moment to pull on her short cherry-blossom wrap, Carrie rushed toward the sound of her son's voice. Funny, Beckham served as her incredibly reliable alarm clock—6:23 a.m. on the dot every day, except for when the time changed and they had a week or so of adjustment when he was all over the map and she resorted to using an actual alarm. She wasn't tripping over the dog, and he wasn't at the front door waiting to go out. Maybe he was in the kitchen, waiting for the first treat of the day?

"Mama, help!"

"What is it?" Carrie followed Oliver's voice to the bathroom, hurrying but not too worried. Last week, he screamed her name, and she'd come running only to discover he was upset that there was too much toothpaste on his toothbrush.

She stopped dead in her tracks, like Beckham when he spotted a squirrel in the garden. Then, also like her dog, she sprang into action.

"Give me that!" She got a face full of water from the showerhead before she wrestled it out of Oliver's grip and turned off the water. Her son was naked in the bathtub, his pajamas soaked in water in front of the toilet, and every surface of the bathroom was sprayed with water. Droplets dribbled down the medicine cabinet's mirror. The framed birds-of-paradise photos on the wall had water leaking inside the glass frames, darkening the edges of the mounting boards. The shower curtain, an oversize bird-of-paradise print, hung heavy on the rings, drenched like a washcloth. The toilet was filled to the brim, and every towel on every bar was soaking wet.

Oliver held his hands over his head. "I showered!"

"Yes, you sure did." She looked down at her feet and realized it wasn't only shower water wetting the floor. Her threshold for grossness had certainly changed since becoming Oliver's mother, so she didn't panic. She hopped into the bathtub with Oliver and gave her feet a quick soap, scrub, and rinse. Oliver nodded, as if approving her technique. She placed the showerhead back on its hook, well out of Oliver's reach, and tried to figure out how to cross the bathroom without stepping in the watered-down yellow puddle that stretched from the toilet base to the wall.

The front door opened, and Beckham's nails skittered on the floor. Heavy work boots stomped her way. Carrie glanced down at Oliver, still as naked as the day he was born, and herself with her satin robe clinging to her, the cream background turning translucent where it was wet. Which was everywhere, thanks to the initial face blast from Oliver.

"You're up early!" Lance poked his head in the door, eyes making a circuit of the room, smile slowly fading as he took in the extent of the damage. His cheek muscle twitched. "I was going to surprise you."

"I'm definitely surprised." She crossed her hands over her chest, hiding the way her nipples puckered. She was sure it was the chill from the AC hitting her wet gown, not the way Lance's gaze ran approvingly over her, lingering on all the particularly damp places. "Your idea? Giving the two-year-old a hose?"

"He's nearly three. And he said he knew how to shower."

Lance's defensive tone brought back memories, and not the good kind. Lance saying he'd had to stay at the job site after hours to meet their contract goals, or that he'd meant to pick up her prescription on the way home but forgot, or how he was too tired to attend her office's holiday party with her.

Carrie found herself shutting down, like she had back then. She didn't want to fight with Lance. She never had. It was a cycle they'd been unable to break, and here they were only a few hours from some pretty earth-shattering sex, back at it again. They'd had such a breakthrough yesterday. Surely, they couldn't be regressing already.

She swallowed the words she would've said back then, attempting to keep it neutral. "Could you fetch us some dry towels from the closet at the end of the hall?" It was only a few steps away, but space—any space—between them felt like a good idea right now.

"Absolutely." Lance disappeared, his voice getting louder as he walked away. "I'm really sorry, Carrie. I had no idea one small person could do so much damage in such a short period of time. I was only going to be gone half a minute, but then someone left the gate open, and Beckham got out. It was a whole thing."

Lance apologized? That's not at all how their fights went. Had he forgotten his lines? He was supposed to blame her for some aspect of the debacle, so she'd get defensive and angry, too. Instead, she found herself smiling. They weren't regressing at all. New territory opened up before them, ready to explore.

"He is a small destruction machine."

"Not unlike Beckham's puppyhood. Tell me, has Oliver eaten any of your shoes? Chewed through a dining chair leg? Mangled any electrical cords?" Lance appeared with an armload of towels. He spread two out on the floor, soaking up the puddles, and gave one to her. The last one, he held open, and Oliver stepped into it. Lance wrapped the towel around him and lifted him out of the tub.

"Shh." Carrie stifled a laugh. "Don't give him more ideas. He has plenty of his own."

"I can dress myself!" Oliver laughed his maniacal laugh and ran to his bedroom.

Lance raised an eyebrow. "Is it true? Or does he habitually overstate his abilities?"

"Sure, as long as there are no buttons." Carrie stepped out of the tub, squeezing past Lance in the close bathroom. "He's mastered Velcro and zippers, though he sometimes decides he'd rather leave them undone."

Lance clasped her hips with both hands, arresting her progress toward her bedroom and dry clothing. "I think we forgot something."

She tilted her head. "Yeah?"

He tipped his chin and brushed her lips with his. "Good morning, beautiful."

Carrie felt the heat rise from her chest, no doubt coloring her neck and cheeks. "Morning, yourself."

"I'll start the coffee." A gentle push on her back sent her out the door. "You do what you need to do. I'll take care of the bathroom."

Carrie was tempted to turn and gape at him. Who was this guy? Her Lance had been fun; he'd been spontaneous and romantic. And so, so hot. But he'd never been very thoughtful or all that willing to clean. She kept walking forward, across the hall and into her room, planning the day ahead. No more looking back; she didn't have to look into the past to see Lance anymore. His broad chest and long, chiseled legs were filling up the present and, she dared to hope, her future.

# CHAPTER 25

LANCE HAD NEVER MET A COFFEE MAKER HE COULDN'T figure out, but he had to admit that Carrie's was particularly challenging. She'd clearly bought it for its interesting lines and shiny knobs rather than functionality, a hazard of her profession—appearance over substance. It had driven him crazy during their marriage, how she seemed to believe that if things looked right, then they were right. He'd felt them growing apart long before she'd acknowledged it. Perhaps because he worried about how things were constructed, was an expert at taking things apart and putting them back together, he'd spotted the fractures in their relationship, the cracks in the foundation that eventually led to the total demolition of their marriage.

Carrie'd pulled the trigger, but he'd seen it coming, and like any cash-challenged homeowner facing an overwhelming expense, had ignored the signs until it was too late. Not again, he promised himself. This time around, he'd be vigilant for any cracks, proactive with his newly discovered superpower of groveling. After all, he wasn't just protecting himself anymore. He was protecting Oliver, too. Carrie would have to get on board with the new plan. He was back in their lives. For good, he hoped.

He located Carrie's stash of coffee beans, the grinder, her eco-friendly strainers. Slammed two oversize coffee mugs on the cabinet, recognizing that he was pissed off but not sure why. Because he'd had to look the coffee maker up on his phone to figure out how to use it? Because his totally efficient morning plan had been thwarted by his own son? Because he was starting to realize how much he'd missed by not being in Oliver's life? None of those felt right, but they all added fuel to the fire building inside him.

Oliver trundled into the room, dressed in orange cargo shorts and a red T-shirt with a cartoon *T. rex* on the chest. His shorts' zipper was up, but the button was undone.

"You certainly can dress yourself. Want some help with that last button?" Lance flipped the knob he hoped would start the coffee brewing. It did.

"No, thank you." At least Oliver had excellent manners. He stuck his finger in his own belly button and made a whooshing sound, like a balloon letting out air. He grinned up at Lance.

Lance grinned back, the growing anger inside him diffused by Oli's gap-toothed smile and the way his blue eyes crinkled at the edges, exactly like his great-grandpa William's.

Apparently appreciating Lance's reaction, Oli repeated the action, this time collapsing in slow motion to the floor. Lance couldn't help himself. He laughed out loud.

"What's so funny?" Carrie entered the kitchen, a two-person space at most. She placed her bare foot on Oliver's tummy. "Is this a new rug? It's so squishy and soft."

Oliver giggled, and Carrie curled her toes, tickling him. He rolled to his side, laughing.

"What a strange rug, rolling all over the place. I guess I'll have to nail it down. Lance, do you have a hammer handy?" She held out her hand. He pretended to pull something out of his back pocket and handed the imaginary hammer to her. She knelt down and pretended to pound on Oliver's shoulder. Beckham helped out by licking the kid's nose. "There. That should hold it."

Oliver jumped to his feet. "Mama, it's me! Oliver!"

Carrie slapped a hand to her chest and staggered backward, bumping into Lance. He steadied her with a hand to her hip. "Oliver? Where did you come from?"

Lance's arm slid around Carrie, pulling her back against him. Oliver launched himself at his mother, hugging her legs. Lance reached down to pat his son's head, surprised at how nice it felt to stand in the kitchen, the smell of coffee in the air, his family in his arms.

His family. The anger burst back. How many mornings had Carrie had moments like these? Hundreds? And he had one, this one. His arms tightened around them while he acknowledged that although he'd said he understood why Carrie had done what she did, the truth was far more complicated. Yeah, he understood, but no, that didn't make it okay. It didn't give him back years with his son, years with her, years of the three of them being a family.

As a little boy, Lance and his mother didn't have the kind of relationship Carrie and Oliver enjoyed. He should've known Carrie'd be a great mom. They'd talked about how their terrible parents made them confident they shouldn't be parents themselves, but they'd been wrong. Carrie knew what it was to feel invisible, an unimportant player in her parents' drama, and she clearly went out of her way to make sure Oliver never felt the same. Lance was so grateful to her and so angry at the same time.

He didn't know what to do with these messed-up emotions. He needed a real hammer and something to bang. He needed to get to work, first at the Dorothy, then to Kristin's to finish up the tile work. He needed to get out of this kitchen. He stepped away from Carrie and busied himself pouring two cups of coffee.

"Anybody home?" Sherry's voice carried to the kitchen. "I hope some of that coffee's for me." She entered the definitely-too-small-for-this-many-people kitchen, stopping in surprise. "Oh, hi, Lance."

"Gamma!" Oliver flung himself at his grandmother, who scooped him up to rain kisses on his cheeks. Beckham bounced off her thigh.

"I was leaving." Lance handed her what he'd thought would be his cup of coffee. He grabbed his keys from where he'd dropped them by the TV last night, hearing Sherry's "What was that about?" as he strode to the door.

"I don't know." Carrie's voice followed him out, as did Beckham.

"Not now, Beck." He squatted to give the dog a good scrub behind the ears. Beckham tilted his head and watched Lance walk away.

---

"Hello, handsome." Kristin lounged in the entrance to her apartment, still in what looked like a nightgown even though it was nearly lunchtime. Lance forced himself to smile. Everything had been going so well at the Dorothy that when he'd checked in with Mendo earlier, he'd learned they were waiting for the roof inspector to show up. He'd done a walk-through of the residents' places to make sure nothing had been damaged during the shimmying and shaking of roof replacement, but it hadn't provided the hammer-swinging, bang-something-until-it-was-nothing-but-dust therapy he needed.

"Good to see you. My brother's already here?" Lance shifted from one foot to the other, eager to get to the bathroom and hopefully some mind-numbing work.

Kristin stepped back. "Tall, hot, and silent's hard at work. Unfortunately. That man does not relax, does he?"

Lance didn't know enough about his brother to agree or disagree, but he nodded because when in doubt, the client was always right. When not in doubt, the client was right, too. If you wanted to get paid anyway.

Kristin wandered away, diaphanous wrap billowing around her. He could see why Carrie got the idea for a heaven-inspired bathroom. Kristin possessed an otherworldliness that drew the eye and held it.

Knox knelt on the cement floor, wiping the extra grout off Carrie's accent wall of pearl-inlaid tiles. Now that the pattern was complete, it was lovely. Swirling, soothing, just a bit shiny. He could imagine standing under the hot shower spray and getting lost in the flow. Whatever he personally felt about Carrie might roller-coaster from moment to moment, but there was no arguing she was good at her job.

"Looks good."

Knox started at the sound of Lance's voice but didn't pause in his cleaning duties. "Does that mean we're down to the last part? The floor?" Knox wiped the last bit of grout off the wall and pushed to his feet, braced leg held out straight while he powered up with his other leg. Lance had learned not to offer help. Knox preferred to handle things himself.

Lance pulled out his razor-blade knife and cut away the

plastic wrap around the floor tiles piled neatly in the hallway. "This small a space shouldn't take more than a few hours, as long as we prep the subfloor well."

"Prep?"

"The cement's in good condition, so we'll lay out a tile membrane and a layer of thinset. Once that dries, we'll mark out the pattern and get started." Lance inspected the cement flooring one more time to be extra sure there weren't any cracks. "We can use some fans to speed the drying along. I know Kristin's in a hurry to get her bathroom done, and we don't want to keep the lady waiting." He also knew Kristin was standing right behind him. He grinned at Knox, then spun around in exaggerated surprise. "Kristin! We were just talking about you."

"Mmm-hmm." Still in her pearly-white wrap, she held out two glasses. "Thought you might need some water."

"Thanks." Lance took one glass and, when Knox didn't react to her offer, took his, too. "We'll prep the floor today, set up fans overnight, and lay out the tiles tomorrow. Once that dries, my lady, you will have a new bathroom."

"Fantastic." She flounced away in a cloud of her own making, material flapping and with a scent Lance couldn't quite place. Probably some kind of flower.

Lance and Knox worked together for a few hours, measuring out the tile membrane that would allow the floor to expand and contract without cracking the tiles, and then remeasuring and measuring yet again before carefully cutting into the material. Once it was laid, Lance mixed up some quick-set mortar and demonstrated how to spread it with the flat side of the tile trowel.

"No, keep all the strokes in one direction. Like this."

Lance took the trowel from Knox and smoothed out the swirls he'd made in the quick-set before they, well, set quickly.

Knox reclaimed the trowel with a rare smile. "I can see it now."

"Yeah, it's not hard. Just tedious." Lance picked up his own tool. Twice the number of hands, half the work time.

"Not the technique, the teacher." Knox stretched out along the floor, smoothing the quick-set in an extended straight line. "You're patient. Good at explaining things. I see how you'd make a good father."

Lance dropped his trowel, creating a small crater he immediately smoothed out. "You think so?"

"Yeah." Knox fished another scoop of mortar out of the five-gallon bucket and slopped it onto the floor. "Neither one of us had the best role model, but we turned out okay. No thanks to *him*. Imagine what an advantage your kid has with you in his corner."

"Thanks, man." Lance swallowed hard and kept up a steady smoothing motion with his trowel.

Now that he'd had his say, Knox returned to his silent, intense focus on his work. Lance lost himself in the repetitive motion, imagining Oliver in another ten years, crammed into this small bathroom with them. He'd be all elbows and knees at that age, maybe even annoyed that he'd been dragged to a work site again. But Lance would stay patient and ask for his help to finish up early so they could surprise his mom with some Chinese takeout for dinner. Oli would reluctantly agree, but once he got the hang of the trowel, he'd be all focus. Maybe his tongue would stick out the side of his mouth. It was easy to imagine big, silent Knox still there, too, conferring silent approval on his nephew. A family business.

It hit Lance then, how this must be what his father felt back when he and Knox were teens. Lance remembered his first day on the job, how his father had proudly introduced him to everyone on-site. Knox had already left for the Marines by then, and Lance remembered the tremendous responsibility he felt, being the boss's son.

Lance remembered, too, the look on his father's face the day he'd quit. He'd seen one too many shady dealings go down to be comfortable working for his father anymore, and even though he didn't have a fully formed plan about what he'd do instead of inherit the family business, he'd thrown his resignation in his father's face with the full superiority of all his nineteen years.

How would Lance feel if Oli ever hated him the way he'd hated his own father? His fingers curled thinking of it. It would be awful. And if he had two sons who left him? Three? For the first time, Lance felt a glimmer of sympathy for his father. All alone now, except for wife number three, humiliated, broke, incarcerated. At the very least, he owed Christine a phone call and an apology.

# CHAPTER 26

CARRIE BALANCED TWO LARGE SHOPPING BAGS ON EACH shoulder and double-checked the bungee holding the boxes on her rolling cart before stepping off the elevator onto Kristin's floor. Today was D-Day. Actually, it was a Wednesday, but it was also her favorite part of any project: final touches. Her personal D-Day—decorating—was enough reason for the excitement rising like champagne bubbles in her chest. It never got old, the final transformation where her imagined vision became reality. The fact that Lance was still on-site was no reason to check the tiny buttons on her sleeveless silk tank top or the hemline on her moss-green pencil skirt, but she did.

They'd exchanged a few rather terse texts since the morning. She knew he wasn't the most enthusiastic texter, so she told herself she had nothing to worry about. Lance hadn't stormed out of her condo on Monday; he'd left when her mother arrived in a very natural flow of events. That they hadn't seen each other yesterday was also nothing to worry about. Their night together held a lot of ramifications. It was smart, very adulty of them to take a breath and let things settle. At least, that was what she'd been telling herself to keep from freaking out.

Sleeping together one time didn't mean he owed her any explanation. She wished for an explanation anyway. What were they now? His few texts made it clear they were working together, but though she'd reread each update on

Kristin's bathroom multiple times, she hadn't been able to find a trace of affection or humor. Or any acknowledgment that he was thinking about their night together as obsessively as she was. If she was honest with herself, and she always tried to be, she wasn't sure what to do next when it came to the mystery of Lance Donovan.

Business first. She knocked on Kristin's door, smile on her face. Lance and Knox had met the deadline, texting her around noon that they were done, and she was here for the final walk-through and to sign off on their work.

"Carrie!" Kristin swung the door open and greeted her with a kiss to each cheek. "I'm so impressed with these boys of yours. Gotta say, I'm sad to see those two beefcakes go. I may have to hire you again, if only so I can get my daily dose of eye candy."

Carrie's fake smile turned real. Kristin was happy; she was talking about hiring her for the rest of the apartment. It was everything she'd hoped for, and she hadn't even added the cloud-soft towels she'd sourced from the same supplier who made the Ritz Carlton's linens. She couldn't wait to turn that bathroom into a showpiece.

"Hi, Carrie." Knox stood outside the bathroom, propped languidly against the hallway wall. He rubbed the muscle above the leg brace. "Lance is quadruple checking things in there. I had no idea my brother was such a perfectionist."

"Says the best crew member a guy could have." Lance joined them in the hallway, wiping damp hands on his jeans. "Knox, you really came through. Wouldn't have made this deadline without you."

"Enough with the self-congratulations. Let's see it!" Carrie placed her bags on the carpeted floor, noting to herself that given free rein, the cream low-pile would soon be replaced. Parquet? Tile? So many options. She poked her head in the door.

"Oh, Lance." Her hand covered her mouth. "It's gorgeous." The accent wall with the pearl-inlay tile swirled in its flower patterns. The champagne-finish fixtures gleamed in the glow from the cut crystal light fixture. She stepped inside, checking corners, joints, turning every faucet, even flushing the new toilet.

"You're pleased?" Lance's voice was so close behind her that she spun and almost bumped into him. The aqua of his Excalibur Construction T-shirt lightened his eyes to a swimming-pool blue. She gazed into their depths, nodding.

"I want to see." Kristin pushed her way in, and Carrie stepped into the walk-in shower so Kristin wouldn't feel crowded. Kristin ran a finger along the pearl-inlay wall, turned a full circle, and switched the light on and off.

"Well?" Carrie couldn't wait another second.

"It's"—Kristin braced her hands on the vanity, and her eyes met Carrie's in the mirror—"heavenly."

Carrie held both hands to her chest. "Wonderful. Now get out. I need to get to work."

Kristin laughed and exited, saying something to Knox out in the hallway.

Carrie stepped out of the shower, and Lance handed her one of the bags. "Magic time, huh?"

She smiled, pleased he'd remembered her phrase for the final-touches stage of any interior design project. "It should only take a few minutes, if you want to stick around for the final reveal."

"Send me some pics." He took two steps backward.

"Everyone gets back from the cruise today. Caleb has me on bellboy standby."

Carrie tried to hide her disappointment, but those champagne bubbles popped, one by one, leaving her deflated. "Okay. Thanks again."

He pointed finger guns at her. "Anytime. I'll bill you later this week."

Finger guns? Carrie buried her hands in the sculpted-cotton bath rug she'd picked for its architectural elements—high loft, white garland on a linen background—and of course for its luxurious softness. She rubbed the looped pile, trying to recapture the feeling she'd had when she found it, that mixture of triumph and satisfaction that let her know when she'd found the perfect product for a job. Instead, all she felt was Lance's absence. He wasn't the warm, affec-tionate man from early Monday morning. Something had changed, made him chilly, maybe even downright cold. The finger guns said it all. Their night together had been a relapse, one he clearly regretted. All those amazing feelings she'd felt? He hadn't.

Too bad. She wouldn't mind coming home to orgasms like that every night. But she couldn't linger on the loss; she had a job to do. Whatever happened between them, it was clearly over now. As a child, she'd perfected the art of anticipation, that hopeful gaze into the future. She relied on it now. No sense dwelling on mistakes made. She should probably call Adam after all for that second date. He seemed like the kind of guy who'd appreciate a perfectly placed sea-glass soap dish.

Lance rubbed his sore shoulder. Lugging a few hundred pounds of other people's stuff would do that to a guy. It didn't seem possible, but he was pretty sure the Dorothy's residents had returned with more luggage than they'd left with. After marveling over the new elevator—it didn't shake! Or groan! And the numbers on the panel were so big!—the residents were finally settled, and as far as he was concerned, he was long overdue for a beer. He grabbed one from Riley's fridge, popped it open, and downed half of it in one long swallow.

"Who's the very best dog in the whole world?" Riley scooped up LouLou and squeezed the dog to her chest, pressing kisses on the top of her fuzzy head. "Is it you? Yes, it is."

"She doesn't like LouLou to worry about who the good girl is," Caleb explained with a fond smile at his fiancée. "She tries not to let rhetorical questions dangle too long for fear of hurting LouLou's self-esteem."

Lance snorted. "LouLou's self-esteem is just fine."

"No kidding." Caleb clapped a hand on Lance's sore shoulder. Lance manfully held back his wince. "Thanks for taking care of her."

"No problem." It was Lance's hope that Caleb and Riley never learned of the afternoon LouLou ran through the neighborhood, but he figured someone was bound to tell them. His plan was to avoid that conversation as long as possible by not bringing it up himself. "It was convenient to be on-site for the beginning of the project."

"Can't believe the elevator's already done. And the roof? You're a miracle worker."

Lance smiled. "That I am. Plumbing in the lobby

bathroom is finished, too. Laundry room is once again fully functional."

"Incredible!" Caleb tugged Riley toward him. "When do I get a little poodle time?"

Riley smiled and handed over the dog. Caleb rubbed LouLou's ears. "Did you take good care of Lance for us? Yes, you did!"

Lance noted that Riley was not the only one concerned about leaving LouLou in doubt as to her greatness and central importance. Lance had to admit it, though. He was going to miss the fuzzy fur ball.

"She and Beckham became good friends while you were away."

"I bet you did." Riley held LouLou's face between her palms.

Caleb set LouLou on the floor, and she promptly jumped on his leg, asking to be picked up again. "Wait, I thought Beckham lived with your ex."

"He does." Lance cleared his throat. "They've been coming by."

"Really? With your son?" Caleb gave in to the poodle's demands, slinging her up and over his shoulder in a clearly practiced move. LouLou curled around Caleb's neck like an old-fashioned fur wrap.

Lance smiled at the ridiculous sight. "Yeah."

Caleb waved one of LouLou's paws at Lance. "And how's that going?"

How could he explain to Caleb what he couldn't explain to himself? Lance decided to stick with the brief, work-focused version. Because as long as he kept it about business, he didn't have to think about Carrie's disappointed face when he walked out of Kristin's bathroom. "I hired Carrie to be our interior designer, and she's been bringing Oliver and Beckham to Fur Haven and also sometimes with her to work."

"You hired someone without asking me?" Caleb handed the poodle back to Riley.

"Your son?" Riley held LouLou under her arm like a football. "How come I didn't know you had a son but Caleb did?" Her accusatory glare scraped both brothers.

"Wasn't my secret to tell." Caleb shoved his hands in his back pockets and rocked on his heels.

Lance looked up at the ceiling. "We're going to need more beer."

"A lot of it."

"I'm calling Knox." Riley set LouLou on the floor and picked up her phone. "Enough with you brothers and your secrets."

---

Crammed in Riley's less-than-spacious living room was not what he'd meant when he asked Knox to have a beer with him sometime soon, but apparently their older brother had a soft spot for Caleb's fiancée and answered her messages much faster than he ever answered Lance's.

Lance stretched his legs out and crossed his ankles, beer resting on the flat plane of his belly. "So I hired her. She really is the best. You guys won't be disappointed."

Caleb grumbled something, and Knox saluted him with his own half-empty bottle of beer.

"I'm good with it." Knox took another swig of beer and

petted the poodle who'd parked herself on his lap. "I like her."

"I had some people lined up." Caleb picked at the label on his bottle, some weird Belgian ale that Riley kept stocked for him. "There were going to be interviews."

"You're welcome." Lance grinned. "Look at all the work I saved you."

Caleb growled.

Lance stood. "Maybe you all can day-drink the afternoon away, but I have work to do."

"We're not done here. What happened with the permits?"

They were so done here. He wasn't ready to spring the whole new dog park plan on them, not yet. He needed this emotional roller coaster of a day to end. Tomorrow was soon enough for Caleb and Riley to learn the fate of their beloved dog park.

Lance gave Riley a little wave. "Catch you all later. Maybe you should schedule some business meetings or something, Caleb. Get us all on the same page."

"Oh, I will schedule a meeting. A mandatory meeting." Caleb was already tapping away at his phone. "There will be shared calendars and quarterly reports. You have no idea what you've unleashed here."

Knox shook his head and downed the rest of his beer.

"Another one?" Riley popped out of her seat on the couch next to Caleb.

Always a man of few words, Knox merely smiled his agreement. Lance took the opportunity to sneak out.

"I see you." Riley held a bottle of Caleb's ale in one hand and a long neck for Knox in the other. "You totally have more secrets. Trust me, you should come clean now. We're going to find out eventually."

"I know." Lance saluted her. "See you eventually." He let the door close behind him. Just because he had a son now didn't mean he was any better at family than he used to be.

———————————

Carrie kicked off her heels as soon as she crossed the threshold into her condo. She really should put a shoe rack by the door. If only she had more square feet, she would. A shoe rack in this entryway would be a fire hazard, which was what the shoes would also be if she left them there. With a sigh for the never-ending concerns that dictated her every waking moment, she hooked the shoes with two fingers and headed for her bedroom.

"Carrie!" Sherry emerged from the kitchen, the same something smeared across her cheek also splattered on her white polka-dot blouse. "We were making you some dinner."

"I've told you, you don't have to do that." Another sigh escaped Carrie. She loved her mother; she really did. But she could be exhausting. And outside of omelets, she was a terrible cook. Carrie had been looking forward to putting her feet up and ordering some Chinese food. Mmm, Chinese food. Vegetable dumplings. The way she was feeling, she'd been planning one of everything from the menu.

Instead, she accepted a lumpy bowl of mac and cheese that looked as dejected as she felt.

"How did it go with that fancy bathroom?" Sherry

brought her a glass of pink wine, obviously picking up on the crap-day signals Carrie was throwing out.

"Fine." Carrie chugged the wine first. It would make the mac-n-cheese easier to swallow. "Kristin loved her bathroom."

"And I suppose everything is fine with Lance, too, and that's why you look like your best friend died." Sherry's wineglass was filled with apple juice. She liked to keep it classy.

"Farrah is not dead." Carrie choked down a bite of not-warm-enough-but-not-cold-enough-to-complain pasta. Or so she assumed. They hadn't talked in forever. At this point, BFF was more an honorary title than a description of their actual relationship. "Everything is fine."

"Uh-huh." Sherry watched Carrie over the rim of her glass. "Why don't you take a bubble bath tonight? I'll stay and watch Oliver."

Carrie smiled grimly. "Sure. That sounds"—she searched for the right word—"fine."

"Well, as long as everything is fine, no need to worry, is there?" Sherry flounced into the kitchen.

Carrie held Beckham on her lap, stroking his wiry fur and shoring up her courage. She wouldn't mope around about Lance like she had after the divorce. He'd moved on quickly back then, and she'd take a page from his book. They could be perfectly civilized adults when it came to Oliver, but she wouldn't let her heart get broken. Not again.

While Sherry kept Oliver busy in the kitchen, Carrie found Adam's number on her phone and sent a text: *Dinner soon?*

His response was immediate: Thai or Indian?

They worked out the details for the next night, but it wasn't Adam she was thinking about as she fell asleep after her long bubble bath and an even longer session of reading *Chicka Chicka Boom Boom* to Oliver. Instead, she tossed and turned in the bed she'd shared with Lance until she couldn't take it anymore and finally got up to change the sheets. Clinging to the idea that she could still smell him on her pillow wasn't helping anything. She'd considered calling Farrah and asking for advice, but she didn't want to be that friend who only called when having romantic problems. No, it might take a minute or two to find a new normal on her own, but she'd do it. If not for her own sake, then for Oliver.

# CHAPTER 27

"THANK YOU SO MUCH FOR MAKING TIME FOR ME THIS morning, Ms. Carson." Carrie followed Riley into Grams' second-floor apartment. First stop on the road to normal: work. Now that Kristin's bathroom was completed, she could throw herself wholeheartedly into her plans for the Dorothy. She loved going into research mode, immersing herself in time periods and styles, hunting for the perfect inspiration for her client. When she'd called Riley about getting some background on the building, Riley suggested calling her grandmother. Luckily, Grams invited her right over, enticing Carrie with promises of thousands of photographs.

"Please, call me Grams. Everyone does." Grams' décor was so perfectly 1985 that Carrie wanted to take some photos for inspiration. Burgundy carpet, mauve sofa, teal throw pillows. Carrie couldn't help but imagine a new color scheme and a few updates for the living room, but she wisely kept her ideas to herself.

"We're happy to talk with you." Riley sat on the overly stuffed sofa. An equally overly stuffed cat jumped onto her lap. Riley stroked her hand along its back. "Anything we can do to help."

"You mentioned you have photos of the building from its early days?" Carrie got comfortable in a Queen Anne mahogany wing-back chair upholstered in a large floral print with a celery-green background—a horrible thing to do to such a lovely piece. She placed her portfolio bag on the floor beside her, and the cat hopped down to sniff it. "I'm pulling together some ideas for the redesign, and I'd love to see the building's original décor."

"No problem." Riley popped off the sofa, calling to her grandmother, "Did you find them yet?"

"Here we go." Grams bustled in with an armful of photo albums. Dressed in mauve pants and a flowing top in a lighter shade, Grams cut a dramatic figure with her upswept hair and rhinestone-adorned sandals. She sat on the couch, her pants blending into the upholstery, and laid the albums on the coffee table, an oblong top on Queen Anne legs that matched the wing-back chair.

Carrie scooted in closer. "Wonderful." She sat on her hands to keep from reaching for the albums. "I can't wait."

"We had some good times back then." Grams flipped the top album open to pictures of a holiday party. Grams figured prominently in every photo in a red satin dress with a plunging neckline and a slash up the thigh that from certain angles showed a Christmas bow peeping out.

"That dress!" Riley laughed. "Grams, I can't believe you."

"You know what I always say. If you got it, flaunt it. And baby, I've always got it." Grams shimmied her shoulders to an inaudible beat. "Come on, girls. You've got it, too."

Riley groaned, but Carrie was game.

"Like this?" She shook her shoulders and found it lifted her spirits. Perhaps shimmying regularly would be part of her new normal.

"You got it now." Grams hummed a jazz tune, shaking-shaking along with Carrie until Riley finally relented and joined in. Grams sat back with a satisfied grin. "That's more like it. Now you'll understand the Dorothy better. She's a bit of a party girl, I have to say."

Carrie sent Riley a questioning look, but Riley merely shimmied back at her with a grin.

Grams turned the page in the album, and the season changed. Grams wore a floppy straw hat, large sunglasses, and a bathing suit coverup that slid off one shoulder to reveal the black strap of a bikini top. A few women in similar outfits gathered around her, and they raised what looked to be piña coladas toward the camera in a toast. Behind them, the Dorothy sparkled in the sun, its bright-pink exterior newly painted and the palm trees flanking the front walkway still held up by support planks.

"The place looks amazing." Carrie scooted the chair forward a few inches to get a closer look. "I'm really interested in interior shots. Can we go back to the holiday party?"

"Sure, sure." Grams flicked back a few pages, eyeing Carrie with a gleam in her eye. "You know I don't show just anyone these photos."

"Yes, yes you do." Riley pulled a photo album from the bottom of the pile and leaned back on the sofa, flipping through it on her own. "You love to show off all your crazy outfits."

Grams' lips thinned. "As I was saying, these photos are special. For special people. Like family. But I hear you're practically family. Isn't your son going to be Riley's nephew once she and Caleb finally get married?"

"Finally?" Riley glared at Grams. "We met in August. It's November. Exactly how fast do you want us to go?"

Grams flipped her hand. "Changing the date, changing the venue. People are starting to talk."

Riley huffed in exasperation. "Translation: You're talking to people about it."

Grams ignored her. "And what they're saying is that maybe you're not going to get married before Christmas after all. And then poor Patty will lose her bet. Is that what you want to have happen?"

Riley dropped the photo album back on the coffee table with a loud *thump*. "I will personally pay Patty whatever she would've won from the stupid bet."

"Ha! So you are changing the date." Grams shoved an album at Carrie so she could turn her full attention to Riley. "I don't know why you don't tell me these things."

"I can't imagine why not," Riley grumbled, sounding so much like Oliver when he was upset that she wouldn't let him eat dirt from the garden that Carrie had to smile. She covered it with her hand and flipped open the album.

Jackpot. Page after page of photos taken inside the Dorothy. The lobby back when the rattan furniture was new and the terrazzo shone from frequent buffings. Pictures inside various units, showcasing the older cabinetry and Art Deco tile work in the kitchen and bathrooms.

"Do you mind?" Carrie pulled out her phone and held it up. "I'd like to take some shots for reference."

"Knock yourself out." Grams opened a third album and flipped through the pages. "You are about to be family after all. Eventually." She gave Riley the side-eye.

Riley rolled her neck like she was trying to get rid of tension. "Grams, you know how crazy it's been. Wedding planning has taken a back seat, but we'll get to it. Soon. I promise."

Carrie flipped a page to a wedding shot, Grams and a

handsome man made less attractive by some truly egregious 1970s sideburns. Grams wore a bohemian-style wedding dress with bell sleeves and a tie around the waist that looked to be made of fresh flowers. The collection of albums brought home to Carrie how fleeting style is, and while interior design lasted longer than, say, a runway look, there was a lot of variation from year to year, album to album, in the look of the Dorothy's interior.

"Seems to me a woman's wedding should be a priority." The cat jumped onto Grams' lap, and she stopped perusing the albums to pet him. He kneaded her thighs for a few moments before settling into a large, purring lump. "That's all I'm saying. A priority."

"You would know," Riley grumbled. "Three weddings and counting."

"Counting what?" Carrie flipped and snapped, figuring better to have too much source material than not enough.

"I believe there was a bit of a shipboard romance." Riley's tone was light and teasing, but Grams stiffened like she was offended.

"That's no one's business but mine."

"Shipboard romance, huh? Sounds romantic." Carrie decided to help Riley with the topic switch. Grams was clearly used to always having things her way, so a bit of table turning seemed in order. Besides, she liked Riley. If things had worked out differently, they would've been sisters-in-law.

"Yep, Grams and Caleb's grandfather were seen taking quite a few moonlight strolls on the upper deck."

Grams harrumphed and petted her cat.

"Grandpa William?" Carrie was surprised enough to stop flipping pages in the album. "That grandfather?"

"I keep forgetting you know them." Riley laughed lightly. "The Donovans, I mean. All of them. I should probably ask you what it's like, marrying into a family like that."

"You probably don't want to ask me." Carrie closed the album in front of her and put away her phone. She had plenty of shots to work from. "I'm not exactly the poster child for how to work things out with the Donovans."

Riley reached across the coffee table to cover Carrie's hand with her own. "I'm so sorry it didn't work out. Lance is a great guy, and you seem really great, too. It's sad when people split up, isn't it?"

A lump rose in Carrie's throat, catching her unaware. The prick of tears stung her eyes. She flipped her hand over to squeeze Riley's. "Yes, it is. But you and Caleb seem like a good team. I wish you every happiness."

Riley squeezed back. "Thank you. I hope you'll come to the wedding."

"Whenever they deign to have it." Grams stacked her albums, action that disgruntled the cat. He leapt to the back of the sofa with a disapproving glare.

"Oh, that's not necessary." Watch Lance all dressed up in a tux, relive their wedding as Riley's played out before her? No thank you.

"We're not going to leave Caleb's nephew off the guest list. Three years old is probably a bit young to attend a wedding by oneself, so perhaps you'll consider being his plus-one?"

A smile tugged at Carrie's lips. "Okay, that sounds fine."

"Perfect." Riley released her hand and stood. "Do you have everything you need?"

"Yes, thank you so much. This has been really helpful."

Carrie gathered her bag and purse. "If you need any help converting the front lawn into the new dog park, let me know. It was my big mouth that promised everyone it'd be done this week. Least I can do is pitch in with the conversion."

Riley's mouth opened, then closed. She raised her hand, then dropped it. "What now?" she finally squeaked out.

Oh crap, she didn't know. "The, uh, dog park's been closed."

"Fur Haven is *closed*?" Each word screeched up the frequency ladder until Carrie suspected only dogs would've heard anything else she said.

"But Lance and I talked to everyone, uh, last Sunday." God, it seemed like months ago now. "We promised to move the park over here. Fence in the front, bring over the equipment and benches. That's why I, uh, offered my help?"

"Fur Haven is *closed*?" Riley hadn't moved past it. "Closed?"

Grams brought over an afghan and wrapped it around Riley's shoulders. "Maybe you should call Caleb."

"I will." Riley burrowed into the blanket, drawing it tight around her, and headed for a back room. "Right now. All I'm saying is he better not already know." She disappeared down the hallway, muttering under her breath about Donovans and their stupid, secretive natures.

Grams folded Carrie into a hug. "Bring my grandnephew by some day. We're all dying to meet him."

Carrie had to swallow down that stupid lump in her throat again. For so long, her family had been small. Carrie, Oliver, and Gamma with occasional help from Addison. She'd focused for years on what would happen when Lance found out, what kind of dad he might be, if he'd fight for custody or simply want nothing to do with them. She'd never thought beyond him—to his brothers, his parents, Grandpa William. All the relatives Oliver had never met. What would her son think, meeting them all? She knew she'd deprived Oli of his father, but she'd never thought that she'd also been depriving him of extended family.

Carrie forced a smile. "I'm sure he'd love it."

"Good." Grams walked Carrie to the door. "I'll be in touch."

Then Carrie was standing in the hallway, studying the battered loops of twenty-year-old carpeting, wondering yet again how things would've been different if she'd told Lance the truth years ago. Would she ever be able to stop circling the past like a dog that couldn't decide where to lie down? No wonder Lance iced her out yesterday. If she could barely live with what she'd done, how could he?

# CHAPTER 28

CARRIE EYED THE DISTANCE FROM THE COUCH TO THE door like it was a vast tundra and she was an underprepared Arctic adventurer, out of food and water but still determined to complete the trek. Beckham's escalating barks cheered her on. All she had to do was shift Oliver off her lap and stand. No problem. She stood all the time. Standing was no big deal.

Whoever it was knocked again, dashing her hopes that it was a delivery, a ring and drop that she could deal with later. Much later. Like after her brain no longer felt like it was composed entirely of snot and goo, floating so loosely in her skull that the slightest pressure sent it sliding out her nose.

She'd been absolutely fine this morning when she'd left for Grams', but by the time lunch rolled around, she'd been inordinately tired. She'd stopped at home to find that Oliver was running a fever, so she sent her mom home and rushed to the doctor's office, for all the good it did. Nothing to do for a virus except wait it out on over-the-counter medications.

The trip had exhausted them both, and Oliver slept through the doorbell, the knocking, and now her inelegant struggle to get him off her lap and on the couch. Yeah, she'd given him the nighttime stuff during the day. They both needed sleep because by the time they'd made it home, Carrie's own temperature was rising, and every muscle in her body ached.

She laid a hand against Oliver's heated skin. Still too warm, but not as bad as earlier. She fought her way to her feet, belting her cherry-blossom robe more tightly around her waist, and one step at a time, made it to the door. She looked through the keyhole, hoping it was her mother here for sickroom duty backup.

"Lance?" She croaked and unbolted the door. Of course it wasn't her mother. She was still dealing with the remnants of the virus herself. But Lance? Had she missed a meeting or something? She racked her mildly fevered brain and found nothing. It'd be at least a week before she could get started on the Dorothy's décor. In the meantime, she could handle everything from home—sourcing products, negotiating contracts, arranging delivery dates in such a way that everything arrived when she needed it.

"You can't blow me off when I have time scheduled with Oliver." Lance barged in as soon as the last lock clicked open. "It's not fair to him. Or me."

"What?" Carrie held a hand to the wall, steadying herself. Lance's energy was a burst of force pushing against her.

"I know things are weird between us, but Oli is still my son. You promised we could spend time together, and you don't get to change your mind whenever it's convenient for you." Lance crowded her personal space until her back was pressed against the wall. He held his phone in front of her face. The letters swam. "Tonight canceled? No explanation? No apology? What is wrong with you, Carrie?"

She slid in slow motion down the wall until her butt hit the floor. She vaguely remembered sending a text while they were in the waiting room at the pediatrician's office. She'd been proud of her thoughtfulness, letting him know well in advance that the evening's plans were kaput. She'd copied the same message to Adam, adding some sick-face emojis. She should've sent the emojis to Lance, too. More information, less spelling involved.

"Sorry?" She looked up. He loomed over her, a ubiquitous Excalibur Construction T-shirt dusted with what looked like plaster, a slash of dried paint across the thigh of his jeans. He looked good, and truth be told, she was glad to see him. Even as awful as she felt, her pulse did an energetic jig at his nearness.

He squatted across from her. "Seriously, what's wrong with you?"

"Virus. Oliver, too." She offered him a wobbly smile. "Surprised you don't have it. You know, after the other night."

He ignored the reference, holding out a hand to help her up and guiding her to the couch. "Oli looks knocked out."

"Children's Nyquil." She plopped onto a cushion and checked her son's temperature with the back of her hand again. "Fever's dropping, so that's a good sign."

"You should've told me." Lance sat on the other side of Oliver, laying a hand on the boy's ankle.

"I thought I did."

Lance shook his phone at her. "This is not an explanation. You should've called."

Carrie nodded, properly chastised. She simply wasn't used to thinking of anyone else when it came to Oliver.

"You look bad." His gaze made her already fever-flushed face burn. Her hair felt lank, and any makeup she'd started the day with had long ago worn off. No bra. Overdue for a manicure. Definitely not how she liked to present herself. Definitely not how she wanted Lance to see her.

"You don't have to stay." She crossed her legs, a bare knee peeking out from her robe. As far as she was concerned, he'd barged in; he could barge out. "Doctor said it's a virus. Should pass in a day or two."

Lance watched their son sleep, a look on his face she'd never seen before—a mix of fierceness and helplessness. "I'm not going anywhere."

The relief sweeping through her surprised Carrie. She'd told herself she had things well in hand. She'd stocked up at CVS on the way home from the pediatrician. They'd eaten soup for lunch. The only thing left to do was lie around and get better. No help needed. So why the warm sense of comfort at Lance's declaration?

"Thanks," she said after a too long, too awkward silence. She should argue with him, but she didn't have the energy. Or the will.

"What can I do?"

She propped her feet on the coffee table and toed the remote his way. "It's broken."

He pushed the power button, and nothing happened on the TV. Like she'd said, broken. Then he smacked the remote a few times, and the screen lit up. He scrolled to Netflix. "Any requests?"

"He loves *Doc McStuffins*." She liked it, too, all one hundred twenty-five episodes that she'd already seen a few times each. But if Oliver wanted to watch a little girl play doctor with stuffed animals that came to life, she was all in. She wouldn't mind if her son became a real doctor someday, although she understood it was much too early to be predicting these things.

Lance found *Doc McStuffins* in the Watch Again queue

and hit Play. The familiar music filled the room, and before the opening credits were even done, Carrie felt herself drifting into a semi-medicated and hazy sleep. She struggled to keep her eyes open a little longer, watching as Lance rearranged Oliver onto his lap, head snugged under Lance's chin.

Oliver blinked his eyes open and smiled at her. She let her eyes finish closing, no longer on high alert for any sign of change in Oliver's condition. Lance would wake her if needed. In the meantime, she let her medications take over while the Doc counseled one of her patients on the TV, saying, "It's very brave to ask for help."

---

Lance hated to admit that he found *Doc McStuffins* dangerously addictive and quite soothing to all the agitation he'd brought with him but now had nowhere to direct. He'd been so sure Carrie was blowing him off, and he'd been wrong. He should've known such a short, terse text was out of character for her and that something was off. He'd let his fear of losing touch with his son take over. He and Carrie might have had a civilized agreement about visitations and how to handle future disagreements, but on the drive over, stoking his anger into a raging wildfire hot enough to burn through the entirety of the Everglades, he'd realized that he wasn't going to be happy with any arrangement that didn't include letting Oliver know Lance was his father. Nonnegotiable. That was what he'd been practicing, stomping up her walkway, banging on her door. Nonnegotiable, and if she were going to be stubborn about it, he would call one of Grandpa

William's lawyers. He knew he was backsliding, letting the anger make decisions he'd later regret. Still, he drove to Carrie's. He couldn't seem to stay away.

He'd driven away on Monday with mixed feelings. Yeah, the sex had been great. Phenomenal even. But he couldn't shake the sense of loss, all those years separated from Oliver. He wanted Oliver, wanted Carrie, too, but how could it possibly work out if he couldn't get over what she'd done? It'd been cowardly, hiding behind work the past few days. Sitting now with Oliver on his lap and Carrie napping beside him, that sense of rightness slid over him again.

Oliver shifted in his sleep, digging a heel into the soft tissue above Lance's knee. Lance changed their position on the couch with a few adjustments, stroking Oliver's hair. Beckham tucked himself against Lance's hip, and *Doc McStuffins* sang a song about bubbles. Lance stared at Carrie, a few physical feet but a thousand emotional miles away from him. Why hadn't she told him they were sick? Why didn't she ask for help? It was frustrating, how much she kept to herself. It reminded him too sharply of the last year of their marriage, when there seemed such a mismatch between the words they said to each other and what was really going on. He should be honest with her about what he was feeling, both the good and the bad. Maybe if they came to an agreement about what their future looked like, it would be easier to let go of the painful past.

Her phone, face up on the coffee table, buzzed. Sherry. He knew he shouldn't, but he reached over and picked it up.

"Sherry, it's Lance. These two are sick as dogs."

Beckham's tail beat against the back of the couch at the mention of dogs.

"Oh no, I was afraid they'd gotten my virus." Sherry coughed. Great, another symptom to look forward to. "What're you doing there?"

"Helping." Not much, but he did feel proud he'd gotten the cranky remote control to work, and Oliver seemed to enjoy using him as a mattress.

"Gamma?" Oliver slapped his hand on the phone. "Gamma, I'm sick."

"Poor baby," Sherry cooed. "Is Mr. Lance taking good care of you?"

"Yes!" Oliver sat up, driving a foot into Lance's knee hard enough to make him grunt. "*Doc McStuffins* says 'Just take a deep breath and calm down.'"

"She always knows the right thing to say, doesn't she?" Sherry cough-laughed into the phone. "Can I talk to Mr. Lance again?"

"Sure." Oliver handed the phone back to Lance, repositioning himself on the couch for a better view of the TV.

"Do they need anything? I can be there in fifteen minutes." Sherry coughed again. He didn't need three sick people to take care of.

"No, I've got this. Decongestants, fever reducers, and fluids." He was about to hang up, but Sherry's voice stopped him.

"It's good you're there, Lance. She's missed you."

Lance didn't answer.

"Hard to tell with her. She plays things close, doesn't she? But a mother knows. Don't give up this time, Lance. She needs you."

"I'm not the one who gave up." He hung up the phone, the Everglades-burning rage flaring up again. He squeezed his eyes shut, and when he opened them again, Carrie was awake.

"What?" She patted her hair. So typical. Always worried about appearances. Not that he didn't appreciate her appearance. Even sick and unkempt, she was still the most beautiful woman he'd ever met. But that wasn't the most important part of her. Didn't she know that? For the first time since he'd met her, he wondered if maybe she didn't. She had, after all, built an entire career around keeping up appearances.

"Why'd you give up?" The words were out before he had a chance to police them.

"I'm sick." She tucked strands of hair behind her ear and fussed with the hem of her robe. "It's not exactly a red-lipstick kind of day."

"You look great." He meant it. She always looked good to him. "I meant about us. Why did you give up on us?"

Carrie grabbed a tissue from the small table beside the couch. "I didn't. You're the one freezing me out. I don't even know what I did wrong."

Lance ran a hand over Oliver's silky hair. He was sound asleep again, the congestion making him sound like an old man snoring. "Not this time. When you filed for divorce."

She blinked her big hazel eyes at him. "You were so unhappy. You deserved—deserve—to be happy."

"I wanted to be happy with you."

"But you weren't." She held his gaze, even though tears popped up without falling, her eyes turned wet and vulnerable.

"I was an idiot."

His words surprised a laugh out of her. "Hard to argue with that."

"And you were too scared."

"Fair." She grabbed more tissues from the box but didn't use them. "Things changed between us. I wanted to end it before we truly hated each other."

"I could never hate you."

Carrie flipped a hand at him. "Easy to say now. I saved us. It's why we can be friends."

Lance felt the growl building in his throat. "We can never be friends."

Her big eyes got bigger. She held the tissues to her chest like she was stanching blood from a shot to the heart. "Ouch. I thought, at least for Oliver's sake, you'd be willing to try."

Lance reached across the three feet of space, the length of Oliver's body, and a wiggling Beckham to grab Carrie's hand. "You misunderstand."

Carrie licked her lips. "I do?"

Lance nodded, lifting himself from the couch and pulling her to her feet. They stood wedged between the couch and the coffee table, between their son and *Doc McStuffins*.

"It's true we can never be friends." He tilted her beautiful face toward his with a finger under her chin. "Because I love you. I've never stopped loving you."

From out in the cold straight into the heart of an inferno. Carrie visibly swallowed. He waited for her to say the words back. Instead, she wrapped her arms around him, burying her face in his chest.

"Now you say it? God, three days ago, I would have…" Her whole body shook. He held her tight, but that seemed to make it worse. Sobs racked her body. He pulled away to see her face. Swollen, red eyes. Swollen, red nose. Tears soaked the collar of her robe and his T-shirt. "I can't believe you."

"I didn't mean to make you cry." He knew he'd been running hot and cold the past few days, but he didn't think he'd totally blown his shot with her. Of course he had, though. Carrie didn't wallow, didn't wait around for things to settle. Didn't wait for him.

She sniffled, loudly, wetly. "I think you should go."

She wasn't going to say the words back. She didn't love him. The other night hadn't meant what he thought it had, or else he'd killed it by being such an ass the next day. She'd slipped away from him, yet again, but the panic he felt was sharpened by the child sleeping on the couch. *Remember the groveling. No lawyer threats.* He took a deep breath and put his heart on the line for the second time.

"I want to tell Oliver the truth."

"Fine. I'd planned to tell him the day after we, you know, but then you were all, you know—" She waved her hand around like it meant something. He just couldn't figure out what. "Not today, though, okay? When he's feeling better."

"Okay." He searched her face, trying to figure out what was going on with her. As always, she slammed her composure on like a mask.

He couldn't look at her another moment. He stalked to the kitchen and poured two glasses of water and brought them back to the living room.

"Hydrate." He shoved one into her hands and left the sippy cup on the coffee table for Oliver.

The door closed behind him, and it felt worse than signing divorce papers. Worse than the time he'd dropped a wheelbarrow full of demolition debris and broken three bones in his foot. He didn't know what to do next. He sank onto the front stoop and stared at that freakishly large staghorn fern. What do you do when the only person you've ever wanted doesn't want you back?

# CHAPTER 29

"WE'RE NOT GOING TO BURN THEM?" ADAM'S FACE scrunched up in adorable confusion. His architect's iPad tucked under one arm and dressed in slacks and a button-down, Adam looked ready for a meeting. Was the meeting with her? She had requested to speak to him, but she hadn't meant it in such a formal way. She'd just figured out a way to preserve a bit of the building's history, and she was excited to get him on board.

Looking at the ratty rattan sofa, love seat, and chair of the Dorothy's lobby, it was easy to see why he was dubious of her plans. However, she was the designer, and furnishings were her domain, not his.

"I did a bit of research. This set is early Florence Knoll. Florence Knoll!" Carrie fanned herself, still hardly able to believe that she'd almost trashed a piece of midcentury history because it hadn't been properly cared for. She took a tissue out of the pocket of her dark slacks to discreetly wipe at her still drippy nose. It'd been four days since the virus' onset, and while she felt mostly better, a few of the symptoms lingered.

"And?" Adam rolled his hand for an explanation.

"Properly restored, the sofa alone is worth eight to ten grand." She watched the words settle on him.

"For that?" He pointed at the sagging cushions, the beat-up legs.

"And for a complete lounge set? Let me put it this way. I

couldn't even find a complete lounge set to get a comp. This set is a treasure, and I'm restoring it." She smoothed a hand along the back of the chair. Someone, probably thirty or so years ago, had recovered the cushions in a loud floral pattern. "Not only am I restoring it, I'm going to upcycle it into Hollywood Regency style. Black rattan, bright leafy-green pillows. It's going to be the inspiration for the whole lobby."

Adam held up a hand. "Hang on. The building is classic Art Deco. Why not stick to geometric shapes and seating a bit less"—he searched the ceiling—"vintage?"

Carrie tapped her Ferragamo-clad toe on the terrazzo floor. She might not be one hundred percent back on her feet, but you wouldn't be able to tell by looking at her. Concealer could hide a lot—dark under-eye circles from sleepless nights, a sickly complexion, a battered heart. She still couldn't believe Lance declared himself when her temperature was over a hundred and *Doc McStuffins* played in the background. Had it all been a fever dream? Only his daily text asking if Oli felt well enough to be told the truth yet convinced her it had really happened.

"Look around. See the detailing above the door? And here"—she drew him to the wall and a small section where she'd excavated fifty-plus years of paint jobs—"look at this fuchsia. Classic Hollywood Regency. Trust me, Adam. I know what I'm doing, and this lobby was once an ode to glamour."

"All of that"—Adam swept his arm, indicating the intricate detailing near the ceiling—"is coming off. We're going clean, geometric, Deco."

"No! Not my detailing." She stomped her foot. "That's a huge mistake. Why destroy the building's interesting architectural history?"

"People understand Deco. They don't understand hybrids."

"We'll make them understand."

Adam shook his head. "It's not going to happen. I'm sorry if you've wasted time on this direction, but you should get your head back in the Deco game."

Carrie's mouth snapped shut. Had he just told her how to do her job? Her mouth open and closed once, twice, and then she blew out a breath. "You don't tell me how to do my job."

"And you don't tell me how to do mine."

Standoff. When Oliver threw down, a bit of tickling usually brought him around. She was tempted to do the same to Adam, but she was a professional. She did not tickle her colleagues.

"Let me mock up my lobby plan. Maybe we can compromise." There, that was a perfectly professional solution. Of course, by compromise, she meant that he would change his mind and go along with her plans.

"I can't stop you from wasting your time, but I do encourage you to have a backup. Now that Caleb's back, we'll be finalizing the common area details." Adam eyed the Knoll love seat skeptically, forehead furrowed. He clearly didn't see what she saw when she looked at the set: a classic beauty, a bit of design history, a potential showpiece. All it needed was a bit of love and styling.

"You make your plans; I'll make mine." She could do standoff, too. She pulled a sketch pad out of her portfolio bag and plopped onto the admittedly ugly sofa. Just because she knew what it could be didn't mean she didn't see what a wreck it was now.

"We're still on for tonight, right?" Adam's smile was shy, like it was only now hitting him how he'd antagonized his dinner date.

"Of course." Work had nothing to do with her private life. She was professional. If that were true, why did she have to keep reminding herself of the fact? She dabbed at her nose with the tissue.

Adam caught the gesture and tilted his head in sympathy. "You're sure you're feeling up to it?"

"Absolutely." One thing a woman with a small child and her own business didn't have time for was being ill. She'd let herself have a full twenty-four hours of rest and recovery, but that was all she could really afford. Back to work on Friday, research through the weekend. Besides, she was looking forward to this date. She was counting on Adam to stop her mind from circling back to that night with Lance, over and over again. Hot sex one night, cold treatment the next day. Confession of love or not, she couldn't get back on that merry-go-round with Lance again. Even if her heart could take it, it wouldn't be fair to Oliver. It was going to be confusing enough when he found out Lance was his dad.

Adam smiled. "Great, shall we say eight?"

"For what?" Lance's work boots clumped up to them.

"Dinner." Adam folded his arms across his chest.

"We have some things to discuss. We're at an artistic impasse, I'm afraid." So much for separating personal and professional lives. Apparently, she wasn't letting it go. "He thinks we should dump the building's history and peel everything back to the basics."

"There is nothing basic about Deco," Adam grunted.

"All I'm suggesting is dumping this sad set of lobby furniture and getting something fresh. A modern take on Deco, something geometric maybe?"

"Florence Knoll." Carrie rolled her eyes, ignoring the slight ache in her head. "Architect. Businesswoman. Icon."

"If you're right—"

Carrie choked at Adam's implication, but he soldiered on. "—we could sell the set for a pretty penny. It'd pay for some really nice furniture that the residents could enjoy."

Carrie threw up her hands. "Why would we sell such a valuable set when we could use it?"

"Because it's disgusting?" Adam wrinkled his nose at the many stains on the chair.

Carrie turned on Lance. "Am I the designer or not? Do I even have to listen to this guy?"

Lance slumped into the chair in question, kicking his legs out in front of him. "Ideally, the two of you would work together. I'm no designer or architect, but it seems like they shouldn't be at odds, right? You wouldn't put country farmhouse in a Colonial Revival, would you?"

"Lord no." Adam sounded truly horrified.

Carrie let her Ferragamo tapping speak for her.

"So I'm sure you two will work it out." Lance looked from one to the other. "Apparently over dinner tonight."

Carrie's Ferragamos stopped their tap dance, and she nodded.

"Need a babysitter? Someone to wear out the dog?" Lance flashed her a smile. She hated that smile. Why wasn't he as wounded as she felt inside?

She lifted a careless shoulder. "Sure. Mom could use the break."

"Shoot me the details." Lance stood and left her alone with Adam.

Her blood was up. No denying it. She wanted to fight. Instead, she pulled out a charcoal pencil and started sketching. She'd learned early on that words didn't change anything. If she wanted Adam to agree with her, she just needed to work harder. Work was always the solution.

———————————

It wasn't ideal, watching Carrie prep for a date, so Lance focused on his son. Oliver rubbed his eyes, clearly tired and still a bit sniffly, and squeezed that weird orange octopus to his chest. Beckham levered himself between Oliver's hip and Lance's thigh, chin resting on his paws in a thoughtful pose.

"Again." Oliver yawned big enough that Lance could see his back teeth.

Lance opened *Chicka Chicka Boom Boom* to page one. "Do you think there will be enough room for all the alphabet in one small space?" He pointed to the palm tree where, for reasons that were inexplicable to Lance, all the letters wanted to gather.

"No!" Oliver laughed. "They all fall out. Boom, boom, boom."

"Yeah, buddy, that's how it goes." Lance read page one, waiting while Oliver inspected the illustration for the millionth time. Somewhere on the page six-seven spread, Oliver fell asleep. Lance stayed where he was, watching the slow rise and fall of his son's chest. Everything about him was so small—his straight nose, the slightness of his frame under the light blanket, the tiny toes that stuck out from under his covers.

"You're a saint." Carrie stood in the doorway with what Lance could only describe as a mushy look on her face. "I am so sick of that book, it makes me want to scream. Scream and throw it."

"Why do the letters even want to climb a tree? It's mysterious." He rose carefully, giving Beckham a final pat.

"Right?" Carrie turned sideways so he could pass. "Thanks again for covering tonight."

"Not a problem. I like spending time with him."

Carrie's eyes got mushier, so mushy he thought for a second she was about to cry. A knock on the door caught her by surprise.

"He's here! Where are my shoes?" She wandered off to her bedroom, a very un-Carrie-like lack of focus in her gait.

"You look great!" Lance called after her, wondering how she got her hair to twist up in that pattern. He used some of his nervous energy to cross the condo and opened the door.

Adam stood on the stoop with a goofy grin on his face, arms full of yellow dahlias as big as dinner plates. "Thanks for the tip, man. I would've guessed roses."

Roses? For Carrie? Adam didn't know her at all. Not that there was anything wrong with roses. Carrie liked them fine, but if you wanted to make her smile, it had to be dahlias. The petal patterns pleased her, their pointy tips in a soft circle. She claimed that the yellow ones were like holding a small piece of the sun.

Predictably, Carrie was overjoyed when she saw the flowers. "How on earth did you know?" She took the flowers and buried her face in them, taking a long sniff. "Oh, they're delicious. Hold on a moment while I put them in some water."

Carrie was still a bit congested and, in his opinion, shouldn't be going out tonight. Lance knew he should fade away. He didn't.

"So, uh, thanks again." Adam ducked his head to enter the condo. "You watching Oliver tonight?"

"Yep, he's already asleep, so I'll be getting some paperwork done. Setting up inspections. That kind of thing." He didn't have to explain himself to Adam, but he had to say something standing awkwardly in Carrie's hallway with her date.

"You run a tight ship." Adam slid both hands into the pockets of his dark trousers. "I like that. When do you think we can break ground on the garage?"

"Soon. Waiting on a few more details to fall into place."

"It's all about the details, isn't it?"

The click of Carrie's heels on the floor announced her arrival. "Ready?" She smiled brightly at Adam. Adam crooked his arm. Lance closed the door behind them.

Beckham stared at him with begging eyes.

"I know, B. We could both use a treat. Let's see what's in the fridge, shall we?"

Beckham wagged his agreement and led the way to the kitchen. They split a slice of leftover pizza—Lance got the toppings, Beckham enjoyed the crust. After a few moments of watching Oliver sleep, Lance set himself up on the couch and cracked open the laptop. A night of paperwork awaited him.

It was almost two hours later when a cry from Oliver's room jolted Lance awake. He'd fallen asleep, slumped over on a fuzzy pillow, laptop caught between the couch cushions.

At the sound of Oliver's distress, Lance jumped to his feet and, Beckham leading the way, raced to Oliver's side.

A quick scan of the room showed Oliver sitting upright in bed, holding his knees to his chest and rocking. Dark shadows lingered in the corners, and a sliver of moon shone through the small window above Oliver's bed. When he saw Lance, Oliver thumped his head on his knees and cried.

"What is it?" The twin bed sagged under Lance's weight. Beckham hopped up and circled to Oliver's other side, snuggling in between the wall and Oliver's small body.

Oliver sniffled. "I'm a big boy."

Lance soothed a hand down Oliver's back. "I know you are. What's the problem, big boy?"

"Big boys stay in their beds all night." Oliver's pronouncement was heavy with sadness. "Every night. Because they aren't afraid of the dark."

Aha. "Did something scare you?"

"Maybe." Oliver's voice squeaked on the word, and he coughed into his elbow. "I'm not a baby. I'm a big boy."

"You are a big boy." Lance kept his hand moving up and down Oliver's back, the motion soothing him as much as it did his son. "Nothing can make you into a baby again."

"You sure?" Oliver's head turned so that his cheek rested on his knees. Fat tears hung on the ends of his long eyelashes.

Lance's heart contracted at the sight of his son holding back his emotions. How many times had his father told Lance that Donovans don't cry? That he wasn't sad? Or scared? How many nights had he hid in his room, watching the night crawl by endless hour after endless hour, wishing he were stronger, braver, more like his father? Would things

be different with Carrie if after they'd had the most amazing sex of his life, he'd admitted that he loved her and asked
to be part of her life again instead of icing her out over old
resentments? Was he no better than a soon-to-be three-
year-old, afraid of being judged for his emotions? That nonsense stopped tonight.

He curled an arm around Oliver's slight shoulders so
that they sat side by side. "Although there's no reason to be
afraid *of* the dark, big boys, hey, even grown-ups, get scared
*in* the dark. It's perfectly normal. We can't see in the dark,
and our eyes can make shadows seem like they are hiding
something. When we don't know what's hiding, we get
scared."

"Really?" Oliver used the sleeve of his *T. rex* pajama shirt
to wipe his nose. "Even grown-ups? Even you?"

"Especially me." Lance gave Oliver's shoulders a squeeze.
"You know what I do?"

"What?" Oliver blinked his big, wet eyes up at Lance.

Lance stood and walked to the wall switch. "I turn on a
light, so I can see exactly what's going on."

"But big boys stay in their beds all night."

Lance was starting to hate this particular quote. How
could Carrie do this to her son? "Who told you that?"

"Gamma."

Well, then, at least Carrie wasn't spewing nonsense at
their son. Still, Lance didn't like thinking of Oliver, sitting
alone in his bed at night, too scared to sleep, too concerned
with his big-boy status to ask for help. No little boy should
feel alone in the dark.

"Let's see what's hiding in the dark." Lance flipped on
the overhead light.

"It's not a monster!" Oliver pointed at a red bundle huddled in the far corner. A thermos poked out of the unzipped front pouch. "It's my backpack!"

Lance crossed the room and picked it up. "First, do you really think Beckham would let a monster into your room?" Beckham picked up his head and panted at the sound of his name.

Oliver petted the dog's neck. "No way!"

"That's right. If Beckham's not worried, you shouldn't be, either." Lance raised the backpack off the floor. "Where is this supposed to be?"

"In my closet!"

Predictably, Carrie'd set up the closet so that everything had a place. Each nook had a laminated label with a picture of what went inside. Large black letters spelled out the objects' names under each photo. He smiled, visualizing Carrie taking the time to so painstakingly set up a system that Oliver could both understand and grow into. Although Lance had gotten in trouble plenty of times for his messy room, he couldn't recall his mother ever taking the time to show him how to put his things away properly. He still tended toward chaos when left on his own except for the whirlwind of stuffing things in closets before his monthly cleaning service arrived. His son might choose messiness someday, but it wouldn't be because he didn't know better.

Lance tucked the bag into the appropriately labeled cubby and rolled the door shut. "Anything else you need to check out?"

Oliver hopped out of bed, bare feet slapping the floor. "Can I have a glass of water?"

Lance was pretty sure that in the extremely long text Carrie sent about the bedtime routine, late-night drinks and snacks were prohibited. But Oliver had been crying. Clearly, he should rehydrate.

Lance held out his hand. Oliver grabbed it and pulled him toward the kitchen. Beckham danced behind them, also clearly aware this was a forbidden activity and, in true dog fashion, enjoying the novelty.

A glass of water for Oliver, half a dog treat for Beckham, and they were just getting into a bag of tortilla chips when the sound of the front door froze the three of them in place. Very, very carefully, Lance did his best to silently feed one chip to Oli and one to the dog. With equal stealth, he rolled the top of the bag and resealed it with the monkey-face chip clip.

"What's going on in here?" Carrie leaned against the kitchen entrance, arms folded over her chest. Her bare feet crossed at the ankles, showcasing a mighty fine calf under the hem of her black dress.

Oliver opened his mouth, and a crumb fell onto the floor. Beckham snarfed it up. "Mama!" Oli lunged and wrapped his arms around her legs. "You're home!"

"And you're not in bed." She rumpled his hair until it stood out in all directions. "Bad dream?"

Oli shook his head against her thigh. "I saw a monster. It was my book bag."

"It certainly is scary when we don't put our things away, isn't it?" She patted his head, restyling the crazy strands into place, and Lance bit back a smile. Leave it to Carrie to use monsters as a motivation for organization. "Let's get you back to bed, shall we?"

"Lance will do it." He turned his sharp face up at her, for all the world like a puppy begging for a treat.

"Okay. Sure." Carrie raised a palm at Lance like, *Would you mind?* He placed the chip bag on the counter and spread his arms like, *At your service*.

"Come on, kiddo." He rounded up boy and dog and herded them to Oli's small room. Beckham jumped on the bed, twirling in circles until he found the right spot at the foot of the bed. Oli climbed in slowly and pulled the pale-blue sheet to his chin.

"What if I get scared *in* the dark again?" Oliver's lower lip wobbled.

Lance tucked the covers around Oli's slim shoulders. "You call for me."

"But you don't live here."

Lance knew Oliver hadn't really stabbed him in the chest; it just felt that way. Carrie's gasp indicated she'd felt the knife, too. His eyes crashed into hers, observing them from the doorway. Could she see how much he wanted to be here every night, reassuring his son that he was safe? How much he wanted the *click-clack* of Beckham's nails on the floorboards behind him as he locked the door and checked that all the windows were closed? How much he wanted to slip into bed beside a sleeping Carrie, knowing he was right where he belonged—with his family? If she did, she didn't let on, staring at him with unblinking eyes, irises wide in the low light.

"I'll get you a flashlight." Lance retucked Oliver's covers and stayed by his side, the light rasp of Oli's breath as he drew close to sleep the sweetest music Lance ever heard. At the foot of the bed, Beckham snored, snout resting on his outstretched front paws.

Lance felt the push of tears in his eyes, but he was a big boy. He blinked them back. He'd told Carrie he loved her, but she didn't feel the same. That was what divorce meant. They weren't a family. He thought he'd dealt with all those emotions, back when he was with Rachelle. But he hadn't known about Oliver then. Who was he kidding? Even if she had told him about the pregnancy, he would've been angry. They'd agreed: no kids. He would've accused her of manipulating him.

As much as it hurt to admit, he was starting to think things really did work out the way they were supposed to. At least this way, he'd never been a dick to her and his unborn child. At least this way, he was getting to know his son. If this was the best he could ask for, he'd take it. But he couldn't seem to stop himself from wanting more.

"Nice night?" He shut Oliver's door gently behind him, knowing his son was almost asleep and not wanting to startle him into full wakefulness.

"Still no score for the zing-a-meter." Carrie sighed. "Probably my fault. I thought I was feeling fine, but sometime after that first glass of wine, it hit me. All I wanted was a slug of Nyquil and my bed."

Lance shouldn't be glad. He should want Carrie to find happiness. "Too bad."

"Yeah."

They stood in the hallway, facing each other. The overhead bulb wasn't kind to Carrie, showing the smudge of mascara under her eyes, the tiredness in the way she held her shoulders. She was still beautiful.

Lance reached out a knuckle and stroked her cheek. "Is this how it is then? I babysit while you go out hunting for Oliver's stepdad?"

Carrie inhaled quickly, and she closed her eyes. "That's not what I'm doing."

"Isn't it?" Lance forced himself to walk away before he did something stupid like kiss her again. He paused at the front door, one hand flat on the wood. He didn't turn to face her, but he knew she'd hear every word, could feel her warm presence at his back. "If you don't tell Oliver who I am, I will."

"Not tonight." Her words were soft and resigned.

"Soon." He opened the door, but her next words stopped him in his tracks.

"Fine. If he's awake, let's do it together."

He tripped over his own big feet, spinning so quickly in place. "You're serious."

Her eyes were wide and wet, and her voice shook as it carried through the condo. "Oli? You still awake?"

"What, Mama?" Oli appeared, rubbing his eyes with one hand and Beckham's ears with the other.

"Come here." She perched on the edge of the couch, patting the cushion next to her. Beckham took the invitation first, lying out along the length of her thigh. Lance positioned himself in front of the TV, legs spread wide like he was expecting a blow. "We have something to tell you."

Oli launched himself onto the couch, crawling over the dog to snuggle into his mother's lap. "Am I getting a little brother? Because that's what I want for my birthday, okay?"

Carrie's mouth opened, then snapped shut. Her eyes flew to Lance's, and it was all he could do to keep the smile off his face. That kid, never a dull moment.

Carrie took a deep breath and wrapped her arms around

Oli's waist. "We're not talking about your birthday, but this *is* about family. You know how I told you I was divorced, and that's why your daddy wasn't here?"

Oli bounced in her lap. "But if he knew me, he would love me because I'm a special guy."

Lance covered his laugh with a cough. He could tell Carrie wasn't fooled. She glared at him. "It turns out he does know you. Lance is my ex-husband. And your father."

Oli's mouth dropped open as dramatically as a shocked cartoon character. "For real?" His head swung from his mother to Lance and back again. "For reals, real?"

"For reals real. Right, Lance?"

Sure, he'd been amused at Carrie fumbling through the conversation, but now that she shifted the burden of coming up with words to him, he found himself at a loss. What did you say to a son you didn't know for all two years and eleven months he'd been alive and then babysat a handful of times without telling him the truth? Would Oliver forgive him for not being around? For not telling him the truth as soon as he found out? Would he think they'd lied to him all these weeks?

"Uh." Lance wet his lips and tried again. "It is true."

Oliver streaked from Carrie's lap and threw himself at Lance. Lance saw him coming and scooped him up so he sat on his hip. Oli held Lance's face between his palms. "You have blue eyes like me."

It was the other way around, but Lance didn't correct him. "True."

"Will I be as tall as you?"

"Uh." Of all the questions Oli could ask, Lance wasn't prepared for a genetics lesson. "Maybe?"

"If you eat healthy, you'll be as tall as you're meant to be." Carrie's answer was clearly more practiced.

Oli nodded happily. "I'm going to call you Lance-Daddy. Because first you were Lance, and then Daddy."

Again, slightly backward. Or was it? Lance's head spun. He'd wanted Oliver to know, but the kid seemed to be handling it a lot better than either him or Carrie. "Okay."

"Lance is enough." Carrie's voice sounded as mommish as he'd ever heard.

"Or Dad," he found himself saying, maybe to spite her. Maybe because it's a word he'd like to hear coming out of his son's mouth.

"Silly Lance-Daddy." Oliver patted his cheeks. "You already have a name."

"Guess that settles it then, Oliver-Son." Lance exchanged a look with Carrie. She seemed amused; the corner of her mouth twitched like she was holding back a smile.

Oliver squealed. "I already have a name!"

Lance was learning a lot about toddler logic quickly, so he didn't point out that he'd already had a name, too. Instead, he nodded solemnly and said, "Oliver, isn't it long past your bedtime?"

Oliver looked at his mom, then leaned in to whisper in Lance's ear, except his whisper was as loud as his regular voice, so Lance was sure Carrie heard every word. "You can tuck me in, okay? Not her. She makes the covers too tight."

"What?" Carrie sputtered.

Lance shook his head and carried his son to bed. They repeated the bedtime ritual they'd already been through once tonight—one reading of *Chicka Chicka Boom Boom* that still left Lance puzzled as to why all the letters wanted to be in one small palm tree, good-night pets for Beckham, and firm, but not too firm, tucking of the covers around Oli's shoulders.

"Good night, Oliver." Lance kissed his son's forehead.

Oliver smiled with closed eyes. "Good night, Lance-Daddy. Will you make me pancakes in the morning?"

"He won't be here in the morning." Carrie spoke from the doorway, her words strangely husky.

"Silly Mama." Oliver rolled onto his side. "Daddies live with their families. That's how it works."

Carrie choked, and Lance moved to her side, ready to slap her back if needed. She held up a hand. "We'll talk in the morning, okay, Oli?"

He didn't answer because he was already asleep. Carrie closed the door and leaned against it, facing Lance in the hallway.

"That went well." Lance smiled cautiously.

Carrie thumped her head against the door. "I suppose."

He was close enough that when she exhaled, he could smell the pink wine she must've had with her dinner. Her tastes were sophisticated in so many ways, but man did she love her pink wine. The scent took him back to their first kiss, the way she'd looked up at him, eyes shining with a joy he'd found contagious.

Like that first night, she raised a hand to his chest. His heart stuttered at the touch. He felt pulled toward her, lowering his head the smallest fraction of an inch. She strained toward him, and their lips brushed for the briefest moment.

The hand on his chest pushed, and he immediately stepped back.

"We can't do this." She whispered the words, but he

heard her loud and clear. He didn't wait around for an explanation. He slammed out of the condo. Furious at his seesawing emotions. If he'd finally gotten what he wanted, why did he feel so crappy?

# CHAPTER 30

CARRIE GAVE THE REUPHOLSTERED COUCH CUSHION A final pat and stepped back to admire her work. The palm-leaf pattern, so big it was almost abstract, was in keeping with her early-midcentury, Hollywood Regency vibe. The rattan looked better than new with its black lacquer finish, and a bit of work with nails and screws ensured a safe seat for all who plopped down on the firm cushions. The restored rattan set was the design centerpiece of the Dorothy's new lobby, and Carrie had to admit that replacing the old 1970s mailboxes with a more period-appropriate style made the room more dignified. Add in the fresh, crisp paint, and Carrie was quite pleased with the overall result. Welcoming, with a bit of flash in the gold accents, the lobby captured the spirit of the Dorothy's early days while still feeling fresh and modern.

Monday evening's date with Adam might not have been a romantic success, but she'd at least persuaded him to let her have a go at the lobby without his interference. He'd liked her drawings, he'd said, but she knew it was more about not wanting to be at odds with her. Whatever it took, she thought with a shrug. She'd spent a full three days restoring the furniture set, and Mendo made sure the rest of the lobby work got done. Next week was Thanksgiving, and Carrie really wanted to have the place finished before the holiday.

She repositioned the lobby furniture layout so that

while sitting on the sofa, residents had a nice view of the front garden, or rather, temporary Fur Haven dog park. Fur Haven wouldn't always be a chain-link-fenced lawn, separated in two by the front walkway. Small dogs to the right, big dogs to the left. Caleb had made quick work of moving the benches, agility equipment, and if she wasn't mistaken, a few of the trees over. Even now, two Labs enjoyed the large-dog side, rolling in the fresh plugs of grass, feet comically batting the air.

"A facelift was absolutely what she needed." Grams glided off the elevator, taking in all the details with a long, studied gaze.

Carrie beamed. "I'm glad you're pleased. Your pictures helped tremendously. I felt like I really got to know the Dorothy."

"It's good to see the old girl shine again. If only all the other renovations were as quick as yours." Grams tested out the recovered rattan chair, bouncing a bit like a kid on a new mattress.

"The lobby was structurally sound. Once we enhanced the architectural features"—Carrie pointed out the fine details over the front door and hallway entrances that she'd highlighted in a subtle gold—"the rest was cosmetic. Of course, we have to wait to restore the terrazzo floor until after the rest of the reconstruction is done. I don't want workers tracking who knows what all over my diamond-polish finish."

"I do love cosmetics, and I can't wait to see this old floor restored to its former shine." Grams winked at Carrie. "I've been thinking of the old days ever since you came by. I believe it's time to have a party."

"Riley's planning something once the reno is complete, I'm sure." Carrie's open-toed heels were starting to pinch at the back. She relaxed onto the love seat, stretching her arm out over the back. Very nice, if she did say so herself. It'd been worth it, pushing so hard to get it done by the weekend.

Grams huffed. "I don't want to wait that long. It could be months. You know what's not months away? Thanksgiving." A loud ring, like an old-fashioned car horn, blared from Grams' purse. She pulled out her phone and stabbed at some buttons. "Wouldn't it be something to have Thanksgiving right here in the lobby? What a treat!"

Carrie could easily see it. Grams' photo albums had been filled with pictures taken during various lobby parties. Carrie hadn't changed much about the layout, just the location of the mailboxes to a more convenient spot at the back, so there was still plenty of open space for tables and chairs. Perhaps that was why she'd been in such a rush to finish before the holiday; the Dorothy wanted a party. "That would be something."

A small, apricot poodle jumped onto the love seat. "Hey, LouLou." Carrie petted her head. "Did you run away again?"

"Again? What do you mean again?" Riley arrived, slightly out of breath, her ever-present ponytail in disarray. Caleb and Lance trailed after her, apparently deep in conversation, but Lance must've caught the gist of Riley's inquiry. He sent Carrie a pleading look.

"She loves to run. That's all." Carrie wasn't going to tattle on Lance. "I've been bringing my Jack Russell to the dog park sometimes. The two of them tear it up out there."

Riley laughed. "Sounds like my LouLou alright. So what's this emergency, Grams?"

"Thanksgiving. Here." Grams swept her arms wide. "The whole family. Everyone from the Dorothy. Invite your dog park friends."

Riley looked around the lobby as if seeing it for the first time. "Oh wow, Carrie, it looks fantastic."

"Thanks." It was nice to be appreciated, and if she wished Lance would do a bit of that appreciating, well, he didn't need to know.

"Primo spot for a party once again." Grams smacked her hands together. "Let's do it. Maybe your mom will even be in town."

Riley searched the ceiling, newly painted a fresh white, as if seeking guidance. "I was thinking something small for Thanksgiving. Maybe at a restaurant?"

Grams gasped and clutched her stomach like she'd been shot. "A restaurant on Thanksgiving? Riley, how could you suggest such a thing?"

"If you'll excuse me." Carrie attempted to extract herself from what was clearly a family matter. Thanksgiving at a restaurant sounded perfectly normal to her. It was how she and her mother had always celebrated—lunch at a diner somewhere they could load up on side dishes to take home for later.

Grams threw out her arms. "Not you, young lady. This concerns that son of yours. He's a Donovan, too, isn't he? Don't you want him to be around family for the holiday?"

"He has family." Carrie didn't mean to snap, but really, Grams was kind of insulting. She and Oliver were a family, and Sherry spent every holiday with him. Her son was not neglected.

"Of course, of course." Grams waved her hand, like

erasing a whiteboard. "He could meet his uncles. His great-grandfather."

"Aha!" Riley snapped her fingers. "That's what it's really about. You want to invite GW over. You don't have to plan an elaborate party, Grams. Just ask him out already."

Grams' cheeks flamed with color. "This is about family, Riley Carson. Family you're about to join. Come on. Part of you is already making a list, right?"

Riley leaned back, laughing. "You got me. Carrie, what do you say? Thanksgiving at the Dorothy?"

Carrie hadn't been invited to a Thanksgiving celebration. Ever. Not even to Farrah's. "I can bring my mom?"

"Bring whoever you want." Grams clapped her hands together. "It's going to be huge. We need to go to Costco."

"You are dangerous with that Costco card. Can you be trusted?" Riley pulled out her phone and started making a list.

Carrie settled back on the love seat, small poodle in her lap, and helped sketch out a plan for the big day. She fluffed LouLou's ears and scratched along her spine. She watched Riley and Grams bat ideas back and forth, Caleb agreeing with whatever the women wanted when consulted. She knew she should get going, but somehow, her trip to the design district to look for inspiration for Dimitri Orlov's restaurants seemed less pressing.

"Potluck!" Grams' enthusiasm grew by the moment, and she gestured so dramatically that LouLou jumped down and sought refuge between Lance's firmly planted boots. He bent down and scooped her up, whispering something in her floppy ears that Carrie couldn't hear.

Grams and Riley started a list of who could bring what.

After assigning various side dishes and desserts, Grams pinned Carrie with a speculative look. "And you, young lady? What's your potluck specialty?"

Lance chuckled, and Carrie glared at him. While it was true that during their marriage, they'd eaten a lot of takeout because neither one of them was particularly good in the kitchen, things had changed when Oliver came on the scene. You can't feed a growing boy Szechuan vegetables and rice. At least not every day. She made a mean baked potato, and she'd perfected the cheese sandwich, cut into four triangles precisely how Oliver liked it. Neither of her famous, at least to her son, dishes sounded right for Thanksgiving celebration. What did?

"Mashed potatoes." How hard could they be? Buy some potatoes. Smash them. At Lance's snort, she upped her game. "Garlic mashed potatoes."

"One vat of garlic mashed potatoes." Riley marked it on her list.

First, Carrie'd have to get a vat. Then she'd have to learn to make mashed potatoes. No problem. It should be precisely like baked potatoes, only more violent. She could still feel Lance's gaze on her; as with the sun, she might not look directly at him, but she always felt his warmth when he was near her.

"What're you bringing?"

"I'm no dummy." Lance set LouLou on the floor. "I'll bring napkins."

"Napkins? That's it?" She was going to make mashed potatoes, and he was getting away with napkins? Not fair. Why hadn't she thought of it? Stupid competitive streak.

"A lot of napkins. A ton of napkins. More napkins than

you've ever seen in one place before." His competitive streak kicked in, which made Carrie feel better.

"They better be fancy, too." Riley marked down his contribution on her list. "I'll text you once we have a color scheme."

"Color scheme?" Lance echoed, and Caleb cracked up.

Carrie's phone buzzed against her leg.

You wanted to discuss restaurant plans?

She looked up at Lance. He hadn't answered her when she'd texted him yesterday about working on Orlov's restaurants with her, but he wanted to talk now? It wasn't a huge job—mostly booth installation and a bit of rewiring. The challenge, though, was in her pièce de résistance: an indoor water feature meant to evoke the feeling of Russian rivers. The artist she'd commissioned would create the piece, but plumbing and installation were on her. Or, she hoped, Lance. Her phone buzzed again. Praying hands emoji. Oh, he needed an escape from napkins and color schemes? So did she.

"Please excuse me." Carrie stood. LouLou pawed at her thigh as if there were a huge mistake. She patted the dog. "I do have some work today."

"With Lance, no doubt." Grams winked at her. "I believe he was heading out, too, hmm?"

"Now that you mention it—" Lance gave the group a jaunty wave.

Carrie stuffed her phone in her bag. "It's a consultation."

Grams waved a hand. "Consult away, my dear. We'll be in touch about the party."

"Please do." Carrie hated how formal she was with them after they'd been so nice to her, including Oliver and her in their holiday plans.

Coffee Pot Spot?

Even though they were both standing in her beautiful, mostly finished lobby and the building was filled with suitable places for a quick consult, she couldn't deny that caffeine and sugar would brighten her day.

*Meet you there*, she typed. Next up, she opened a browser and typed in garlic mashed potatoes. Research, shopping, practice rounds. She had a lot to do before Thanksgiving.

# CHAPTER 31

THE COFFEE POT SPOT WAS AS CROWDED AND DIFFICULT to navigate as usual. Carrie made her way to a small table but was waylaid by a friendly voice calling her name.

"Addison!" She stopped at the table where Addison sat with two other girls about her age. "How are you?"

"Good, good. Did you ever apologize? You never told me." Addison leaned forward, and so did her clearly in-the-know friends.

Carrie bobbed her head quickly, embarrassed now that she'd taken relationship advice from a sophomore in high school.

"Is that him?" the girl to Addison's right asked, pushing back her black hoodie for a better view.

Sure enough, Lance strode into the coffee shop, eyes scanning the place for her.

"Yes, that's Oliver's father." She pulled her bag in tight as another patron attempted to pass her in the aisle.

"He's hot," the girl hissed under her breath. The third girl's braids bounced up and down in agreement.

"Told you." Addison smirked. "Is this a date?"

Carrie did not want her life to be the equivalent of a day-time soap, so she put on her sternest face. "Business."

"Right. Business." Addison gave her an exaggerated wink, and her friends giggled.

Carrie took a deep breath. Someday, Oliver would be a teenager. This was practice. "I've got to go, but it's good to see you. Want to babysit this weekend?"

"Do you have a date?" Addison drew out the last word. "With Lance?"

"Please, Addison, leave it alone."

Something in her tone got through. Addison dropped the smirk and said, "Of course. Text when you need me, and I'll work it out with my mom."

"Thanks." Carrie took another deep breath. "Nice to meet you all." Then she walked across the shop to the empty table farthest from the girls.

"Fan club?" Lance was quick to join her in the Siberia of tables, conveniently situated by both the kitchen door and the bathroom.

"Something like that." Carrie rustled through her purse like she was looking for something. Maybe she was, and she'd know when she found it. Maybe she was simply stalling. It was unsettling being around Lance, how she longed to pull him close but felt compelled to push him away all at the same time. She hauled out a flowered notebook and pen.

"About the restaurants." She flipped to a clean page.

"Of course. Business." He folded his hands on the table.

She nodded crisply. "To business."

They talked for half an hour, but when she got home, she couldn't read a word of what she'd written in her notebook. It was all scribbles and swoopy hearts, and down low at the very bottom, she'd written Carrie Donovan. Clearly, it was the fifteen-year-olds' influence.

"See you at Thanksgiving," Lance had said after paying their check. "Looking forward to those mashed potatoes." He'd grinned, and there was no other way to say this: she'd fled. Snapped her notebook closed and ran. How was she supposed to keep it just business when he smiled at her like that? The fifteen-year-olds giggled when she passed their table, but she didn't slow down. She was a grown woman with grown-woman stuff to do. She did, however briefly, wonder what Addison's advice would be this time. She was beginning to fear it would never be just business with Lance.

---

Carrie tightened her hold on the vat of mashed potatoes and took a steadying breath. Into the fray, as it were. She pushed on the glass double doors, holding them open for Oliver and her mom to pass through.

"Is that him? Is that my great-grandson?" Grandpa William's voice carried down the long table set up in the Dorothy's lobby.

Lance visibly cringed and rose to greet Carrie, Oliver, Sherry, and one very excited Jack Russell in the entry. "Sorry about that. He only found out yesterday."

The fray was already fraying her nerves. Carrie only nodded in response and searched the room for a friendly face. Lots of faces, for sure, but no one she knew well enough to get her out of following Lance to the table.

"Shh." Grams smacked Grandpa William on the arm. "You'll scare the poor thing. You know little Oliver doesn't have any family."

Carrie was glad she'd transported the potatoes in a metal pot. A glass container would surely have shattered in her grip by now. She tightened her hold and shot an accusatory look at Lance.

"I am really, really sorry." Lance ducked his head and

held up his hands like she was about to shoot. "I think they think you can't hear them?"

"Here." Carrie shoved the heavy pot of potatoes at him. She didn't need to be judged, not by anyone, but especially not by her ex-relatives. "Maybe we should drop these off and leave."

"No, no. Please stay. I'll get them to behave. Or at least I'll talk to my grandfather." Lance sniffed the pot like he was suspicious, but the only odors emanating from her cooking triumph were butter and garlic. Lots of garlic. "I don't think anyone can get Grams to behave."

"I heard you!" Grams called, waving at the group of them. "And you're absolutely right! Now bring those mashed potatoes over to the buffet table, will you?" She pushed out of her metal folding chair and glided toward them.

"Grams?" Oliver tugged on the sleeve of Carrie's burnt-orange button-down that she'd paired with a goldenrod pencil-skirt. "Is that like a Gamma? Is she Lance-Daddy's Gamma?"

"Almost but not quite. Or at least not yet." Lance squatted down, balancing the mashed potato vat on his knees. Beckham came over to inspect the spot. So did LouLou, appearing from under the table in a burst of curls and wiggles. Lady, the black Lab from the park, came sniffing, too.

"I heard that!" Grandpa William yelled, keeping a hand on his greyhound's head to keep Pops from joining the growing pack sniffing the mashed potatoes.

"How many dogs are at this party?" Carrie surveyed the crowd and spotted one more furry friend in the mix—Sydney's Chihuahua, Chewy, who sprinted toward them as fast as his little legs could move.

A laughing Sydney joined them at the door. "Ain't no party like a dog park party, huh?"

"That's where all the people are from?" Aside from the main table stretching the length of the lobby, satellite tables were scattered around the edges, and even her refinished rattan set was full of folks. Some she recognized from the dog park, some from the Dorothy, and some she'd never seen before.

Sydney took the pot from Lance with a smile. "Neighborhood color, that's what we'll call it. Come on. Riley and Caleb saved you all some seats, but you'll want to load up at the buffet table first."

Carrie followed, an unusually subdued Oliver stuck close to her side. Sherry chatted with Lance a bit, something about street parking being such a nightmare these days and how back in the old days, one could drive right up to Ocean Drive and find a spot but now the valet businesses had ruined everything. Carrie tuned out the tirade—she'd heard it before—and focused on getting to the buffet table. Sydney stopped a few times along the way, chatting up neighbors and introducing Carrie to them. Carrie smiled and said polite things, she was sure she did, but it was all starting to blur together.

It was too much. She was used to it being just Oliver, Beckham, and her mom. The cornucopia on the table, the small rubber ducks at each place setting dressed as pilgrims, Native Americans, and turkeys, the table runner that looked as if it were made entirely of leaves—it was all too much. How she'd longed for a holiday like this when she was little, but she was grown now and had made peace with the fact that her family simply didn't do holidays.

But Lance's sure did. Even Knox sat at the end of the long table, braced leg stretched out of the way of folks lining up at the buffet. Oliver tugged on her hand, and she looked down. His eyes were wide, and his smile was wider. "It's like a movie," he whispered, and because his whisper was exactly as loud as his normal voice, the people near them heard and laughed.

"It's only Thanksgiving." Carrie didn't mean to sound dismissive, but his clear infatuation with the whole scene made her defensive. It wasn't like he'd never had a Thanksgiving meal before. *Sheesh.*

Lance settled a hand in the middle of her back, directly below the strap on the bra she probably shouldn't have worn today. Black and lacy, it matched her panties, and together, the set was the sexiest thing she owned. She'd felt the need to arm herself, like coming to this Thanksgiving dinner would turn into a battle, but now, with Lance's hand warming her skin, all she could think about was his hand inching up and unsnapping the hooks. Not in front of everyone, of course. They'd sneak off, maybe to one of the unoccupied units she'd staged yesterday. She could attest to the springiness of the cushions on the couches she'd chosen. Lance's hand slid down to her waist, leaving a prickly trail of heat in its wake. Carrie stepped away from him. It was too dangerous to be near him. He made her forget that she was only here for Oliver's sake.

They finally made it to the buffet line, and Carrie helped Oliver choose small helpings of basically everything. Oliver filled his plate with her mashed potatoes, bites of cranberry sauce, corn salad, and of course, the mandatory turkey.

At the table, she and Oliver were seated directly across

from Grandpa William and Grams, with Riley and Caleb to their right and Sherry to the left. Lance sat beside his grandfather.

"Well, are you going to introduce us?" Grandpa William's cranky words were belied by his smile.

Lance took on the challenge. "Oliver, this is my Grandpa William. That makes him your great-grandfather."

Oliver looked skeptical at the news. "I already have a grandpa."

"You can have more than one." Carrie set her fork down. Eating would have to wait until this field of social land mines was successfully traversed. "Besides, a great-grandfather is different from a grandfather."

"How?" Oliver jabbed at the mashed potatoes on his plate.

"Because we're great, that's how." Grandpa William petted Pops with one hand while swirling his mashed potatoes and sweet potatoes together on his plate. "Better than regular grandpas, that's for sure."

Oliver chewed thoughtfully. "Okay. Show me."

Grandpa William blinked his sharp blue eyes. "Show you what?"

"Be great." Oliver put down his fork and watched Grandpa William expectantly.

Grams' laugh tinkled up the musical scale, and she covered her mouth with a gold paper napkin. Carrie stifled her own laugh. She could step in, she supposed, and mediate this standoff between great-grandfather and great-grandson, but she didn't. Pride filled her. Her son knew how to stand up for himself.

As if reading her mind, Lance sent her an approving

nod across the table. "What's your play, Grandpa William? Oliver's waiting."

"I'll take you out on my boat." Grandpa William leaned back, smug in his response. "I'll teach you to fish."

Oliver stood up, hopped onto his chair, and leaned across the table, hand outstretched. "Deal."

Grandpa William looked confused at first, like he wasn't sure what to do. Then he stretched out his own hand and shook on it. "Deal."

"Call my mama." Oliver sat back down. "She'll tell you when."

Carrie's phone vibrated in her purse. She pulled it out. Did our son just tell my grandfather to call his people? Is he like some little Godfather-in-the-making?

Carrie grinned, proud that all her hours of talking to Oliver, exposing him to language, encouraging him to tell her all his thoughts, was paying off in such a satisfying way. *I'll make you an offer you can't refuse.*

Lance's response was quick. How could I refuse you anything?

Definitely not business. Carrie dropped her phone in her lap and looked across the table at Lance. Sure enough, he was staring at her. His lips quirked in that way that meant he was holding back a smile. Their relationship was like standing on shifting sand, and she was unable to find her balance. She fought the urge to text him to meet her in one of the empty units. Old habits and all that. One more time wouldn't change anything. They could be a family without being together. Somehow, some way, she'd figure it out.

"Now that's settled." Grandpa William stood and pinged his knife against his glass. Since the knife was metal colored but not really metal, not much happened. Grams stuck two fingers in her mouth and whistled loud enough to crack an eardrum or two. The lobby crowd hushed, and all eyes turned toward Grandpa William.

"Today is a day for family." Grandpa William raised his glass of iced tea into the air. "I'm blessed to be here with my three grandsons." Here he paused and tipped his glass toward Oliver. "And my great-grandson."

There were some calls of "hear, hear" and raising of glasses, but Grandpa William wasn't done. "A long time ago, I had a beautiful wife, the beginning of a beautiful family. I betrayed her and lost her." His eyes sought out Grams.

"What can I say? You were an idiot." She flashed the crowd a grin and held up a hand to him, limp at the wrist. "A womanizing, short-sighted, unappreciative idiot."

"You know me so well." He took her fingers in his and lifted her knuckles to his lips. "It is my greatest regret that I hurt you, Gloria."

Grams looked at him. "We've settled this, Billy. There's no reason to drag it all up again. Especially not in front of all these fine folks."

"These fine folks don't mind a bit!" Eliza called from her seat at the far end of the table. Lady sat at her side, eyes fixed on the plate of turkey in front of her. "In fact, some of us wish you'd speak a little louder, William. I'm not sure I caught that last bit."

"I was saying—" Grandpa William stopped to clear his throat, running a finger around the collar of his button-down shirt. Sweat popped on his forehead.

"Yes, dear?" Grams projected across the room, loud enough that beachgoers half a mile away could probably hear her. "Do you want to explain more about your bad choices as a young man?"

Grandpa William took a long sip of iced tea and set his glass back on the table. "No, I was trying to move on from that."

"Louder!" Eliza called, and the guests around her laughed.

Patty, who sat next to Eliza on her walker-turned-seat in a housedress decorated with falling leaves, leaned forward and yelled, "Five bucks says he's about to—"

"Miss Patty, I'll thank you to stop right there." Grandpa William cleared his throat and tried to take another sip of iced tea, but his glass was empty.

"Let her finish. Patty's usually right, you know." Grams tugged at her hand, attempting to get it back, but he held firm. "You shouldn't go around shushing women just because they're saying things you don't want to hear. Why, I imagine it would do you some good to—"

"Gloria, please." Grandpa William squeezed her hand to get her attention, meeting her eyes with his. She must've seen something there because she clamped her lips shut and rolled her free hand, signaling *Go on*.

"Truth is, I'm trying to… Gosh darn it all to hell…" Grandpa William reached into the pocket of his gray slacks. He pulled out a small, black box. "You are the single most difficult woman…" Slowly, painfully, Grandpa William used his cane and the seat of the chair to lower himself to one knee.

Grams inhaled sharply, scooting her chair back so fast she rammed into Riley.

"Gloria." He opened the box and held it up to her. "I was

indeed an idiotic young man, but I hope that I am at least a little bit wiser now. Wise enough to know that I can't let you get away a second time."

Grams' eyes filled with tears, and for once, she didn't have a witty comeback. She reached for the box. "Billy, it's too much."

"Nothing is too much for the love of my life." He placed both hands on his knee. "What do you say? Will you marry me?"

Grams leaned forward and pulled Grandpa William off his knee. When they were both standing, she wrapped her arms around his neck and stood on her tiptoes. "I thought you'd never ask."

She kissed him. He kissed her back. For a long time.

Eliza started the cheering, and Patty started taking bets on when the wedding bells would ring. Soon everyone at the long table was whooping it up, wolf whistles and all. The dogs got all riled up, and LouLou started a game of chase around the buffet table that even Grandpa William's elderly greyhound joined. Still, the kiss went on. And on.

It was, um, awkward. Carrie worried what Oliver would think, but he was tucked into his mashed potatoes, downing them in large gulps. Carrie checked on her mother. Sherry watched the now-engaged couple with damp eyes. Carrie guessed it was kind of romantic. A bit too public for her taste, but then, it wasn't about her. Grams clearly adored the attention.

When the kiss finally ended, both Grams and Grandpa William were short of breath. Grams turned to Riley and grabbed both her hands. "Riley, we can have a double wedding!"

"I am so happy for you. For both of you." Riley stood and hugged her grandmother. "But no. Absolutely not."

Grams' face cycled through expressions quickly— shock, hurt, outrage, amusement.

Riley squeezed Grams' hands. "You deserve your own special day. I would never dream of stealing any bit of your spotlight."

Grams' face settled on pleased. "You're right, darling."

Caleb raised his glass of tea. "Congratulations!" The sentiment echoed around the table, and the engaged couple was toasted. Not that they noticed. They were too busy looking at each other.

Carrie looked at Lance, and Lance looked back. There was no denying the romance of the moment, a divorced couple reuniting after years apart. Grams and Grandpa William made it seem possible that two people could move on from their past, break the old habits that drove them apart, hope for a new future together. Carrie couldn't deny that a part of her—okay, a large part of her—wanted that with Lance.

But the smaller, more practical part of her thanked God she had another date with Adam this weekend. It might feel more like a chore than a chance at romance, but she'd had to try something after the awkward coffee meeting with Lance. And she'd been right. Look at her mooning after Lance with their family members crammed in all around them.

She'd remember forever the look in his eyes when he said he'd always loved her, but she couldn't let herself forget how fast he was to freeze her out. He might think he loved her, and maybe he still did, but he'd never truly forgive her for keeping Oliver from him. He might've mastered the art of groveling, but if she knew one thing about Lance, it was that he held on tight to his grudges. Look how he'd cut his father out of his life. She didn't think she could survive it if he did the same to her. It was better for everyone if she moved on.

"Sorry I'm late." A petite woman approached the table, a large cake plate balanced on one hand. She placed the other hand on Lance's shoulder and leaned in to kiss his cheek. "Thank you for inviting me."

"Mom?" Caleb's mouth dropped open, showing that at least he was enjoying Carrie's garlic mashed potatoes. "What're you doing here?"

Lance stood and pulled a chair over for the woman. "I invited Christine."

"Why would you do that?" Caleb clamped his mouth shut and swallowed. "She doesn't do potlucks."

Christine pushed the cake plate toward Caleb. "Now I do. Doesn't it look delicious? It's your favorite, Caleb, a red velvet from Chez Bon Bon."

"How sweet of you." Riley placed her hand over Caleb's on the table. "Thank you for bringing it, Christine. Why don't I help you get it set up on the dessert table?" Riley rose and guided Christine away.

"What the hell, Lance?" Caleb pointed an accusatory fork in Lance's direction.

"I didn't think she'd actually come." Lance leaned back, stretching his long legs under the table until his foot tapped Carrie's. She tapped him back, and they stayed that way under the table, the pointed toe of her high heel resting on top of his cowboy boot.

"Why would you invite her at all?" Caleb jabbed the fork

at Lance again. "This is just like the dog park, making decisions without consulting me. You're out of line, Lance. Again."

"Somebody had to do it." Lance glared across the table at his brother. "Both times. If that makes me the bad guy, well, isn't that who I am in the family? The black sheep?"

"Here we go again." Caleb rolled his eyes. "For the last time, you weren't forced out of the family. You left, as I recall, as soon and as fast as you could."

"Louder!" Eliza shouted down the table. "Are you boys arguing?"

"We're not arguing," Caleb muttered through clenched teeth. "We're discussing Lance's habit of making decisions he has no business making."

"Like you were ever going to sign off on moving the dog park." Lance shoved back his chair, the metal squeaking in protest. "But if we didn't move it, we'd lose the permits, and who knows what else one of those corrupt commissioners would cook up to stall our project? I had to do what was best for our business."

"You don't think I can make sound business decisions?" Caleb's hands clenched in fists in front of him. The plastic fork snapped under the pressure.

Lance sucked in a long breath. Carrie admired his restraint. In the past, Lance would've given as good as he got, if not more. He loved to win a fight. Now, though, he gathered his composure before speaking. "The point is, Caleb, it would've been difficult for you, given your history with Riley. I made the call so you wouldn't have to."

Lance's words visibly deflated Caleb. He picked up one half of the broken fork, toying with it between his fingers. "It was the right call. I just wish I'd been consulted first."

"Noted." Lance watched Caleb carefully, like he was afraid of being stabbed with the plastic fork. "I should've asked about your mom, too. It's just that I felt sorry for her." Lance raised his eyebrows, one cocking higher than the other. "She doesn't have anyone else."

"You're right." Caleb slumped in his chair. "I'm sorry. She's always on me to visit our father."

Lance drummed his fingers on his thigh. "Would that be so bad? He doesn't have anyone else, either."

"Absolutely not." Caleb glared across the table. "Knox, back me up here."

"I'm not getting in the middle." Knox stood. "Think I'll get myself some cake. Haven't had Chez Bon Bon in over a decade." He limped away as Christine and Riley returned.

Riley took in the tense situation with a quick glance at the mangled fork. "What'd I miss?"

"The boys made up!" Eliza crowed from her end of the table. "It was touch and go for a minute, but they've decided to share the business decisions from now on."

Riley looked to Caleb, who looked to Lance.

Lance raised a shoulder. "What she said."

"That's all good then." Christine held up her crystal-encrusted phone case. "Anyone mind if I take a few photos to share with my husband?"

Lance stared at Caleb, hard.

"Fine." Caleb shoved more mashed potatoes in his mouth. "But I'm not smiling."

"Is she another Gamma?" Oli asked loudly. The whole table laughed, but no one answered him. "Well, is she?"

"We'll talk later," Carrie whispered to her son. "For now, let's eat."

Oli had no trouble shifting gears, shoveling turkey into his mouth with apparent pleasure. Carrie took a bite of her own potatoes. *Not bad.* She watched Christine make the rounds, taking photos and short videos, her face nervous but pleased.

Carrie tapped Lance's foot with hers and sent him a quick text. *You did a good thing.*

He read the message and smiled. Carrie knew it was dangerous, but she left her foot on top of his. If Lance could forgive his father, maybe there was hope for her after all.

# CHAPTER 32

IT WASN'T SPYING, NOT IN THE TECHNICAL SENSE. JUST because he knew Adam planned to take Carrie down to South Pointe and just because he'd packed Oliver and Beckham into his truck—a surprisingly involved process what with the special seats and bags of accessories—to head down to South Pointe Park didn't mean they'd run into each other. If he didn't see them, it wasn't spying. If he did? Maybe, technically, one could argue stalking. What was the likelihood that Carrie would see them? Slim, he assured himself. Slim to none.

He was lucky to pull into the small public parking lot right as someone else pulled out. He snagged the spot and paid on his phone app for parking before unloading boy, dog, and enough equipment for a short camping trip. It hadn't surprised him that Carrie's closet was filled with bags labeled for various excursions—park, beach, shopping, Gamma's. It did surprise him how heavy the park bags were. Knowing Carrie, though, he'd be glad of something in the bag before the evening ended.

"Hold on, guys." Lance clipped on Beckham's leash before the bundle of pure energy launched himself out of the truck. Then he set himself to Oliver's safety-seat hooks and buttons, a job that would've been much easier if Oliver hadn't helped, tangling his chubby fingers in the straps and laughing at Lance's muttered curses.

Finally, they were ready to go. He slung the flowered

backpack over one shoulder and the dog-paw-covered shoulder bag over the other. Joggers swerved around them as they slowly ambled toward the playground, passing by the popular steakhouse, Smith & Wollensky. The outdoor seating sprawled toward the channel that connected the Port of Miami to the Atlantic Ocean, breaking for the width of the paved walkway, then picking up with more tables and chairs on the grassy shoulder that bordered the rocky seawall.

It was perfectly normal to scan the restaurant patrons. It was called people watching, definitely not spying. People watching was a favorite pastime in Miami Beach. Why, at this moment, a young teen posed in a puffy yellow dress near a low sea-grape shrub. Probably a quinceañera photo shoot, judging by the tiara on her head and the assorted light reflectors a few feet from her. Sure enough, a photographer shouted directions to her, telling her to turn to the left, to lift her chin, to take a step sideways, then back, then forward. A black cat, one of the many strays in the area, watched haughtily from its perch on a rock that jutted out over the grass.

Swiveling his head side to side, trying to appear like a normal people-watching guy with a kid and a dog out for an evening stroll, Lance spotted her. Or rather, them. Carrie and Adam were seated on the outdoor porch, a space elevated one step above the outdoor seating. Carrie leaned across the table, covering Adam's hand with her own, and they smiled at each other. Adam was such a serious guy usually; it was weird to see him throw back his head with laughter. Lance jerked his gaze away, worried that the longer he watched, the more likely they were to see him. He took longer strides, leaving the restaurant behind in a few paces. Beckham wagged his tail at the change in pace, charging ahead. Lance steered them left, toward the playground.

Oliver picked up speed when he saw the slide, Beckham leaping along beside him, one hop for every three of Oliver's steps. The playground was crowded with kids ranging in age from younger than Oli to preteen, their screams filling the air. Why did children scream so much? Lance scowled in their general direction. Maybe his crankiness came from wanting to scream himself. Yes, spending time with Oli was the highlight of his day. Knowing that Carrie was on the hunt for a stepdaddy for Oliver, though, sucked some of the joy out of their outing.

Yesterday's Thanksgiving celebration weighed on his mind. It'd been right to have her and Oli there, even Sherry. Hadn't she felt the same sense of family? He'd thought so, the way she wanted to play footsie under the table, but as soon as the meal was over, she'd made the rounds of good-byes, stopping at Christine's place to admire some of the pictures she'd taken, and taken off. He'd only heard from her when Addison fell through as a babysitter. Which was fine. He'd asked for opportunities to spend more time with his son. He simply wished that time also included his son's mother.

Lance helped Oli into a swing, the kind that was a small plastic seat with holes for the legs to pop through, and gave him a push. Of course Adam and Carrie would work out. Both were obsessed with design, and in complementary ways. Much like when he and Carrie had started out, they'd be assets to each other's businesses. Perhaps they'd merge their professional as well as personal lives. Of course they would. He pushed Oli higher and higher. Beckham leaped at Oli's feet every time they swung by him.

"Higher!" Oliver called after his next push sent him skyward. He kicked his legs. "Higher, higher!"

"Excuse me?" A woman's voice caused Lance to miss a push.

"Yes?" He turned to the young mother. She held a baby, maybe six months old, on her hip, and a toddler clung to her hand. "Can I help you?"

"My daughter is afraid of dogs." She took a step that put her little girl slightly behind her leg.

"Beckham loves kids." Lance tugged on Beckham's leash, encouraging him closer. "She's welcome to pet him."

"Dogs aren't allowed on the playground. You need to remove him." Her voice was frosty, and the baby fussed in her hold.

"He's not doing anything wrong." No Dogs Allowed signs were common on the Beach, but most people ignored them. As long as your dog was well behaved and leashed, no one much cared.

"Don't make me call the cops."

"Call the cops? On a dog?" Lance scooped up Beckham and held him under his arm. "Are you kidding me?"

"He shouldn't be on the playground." The woman's sloppy bun listed to one side. She kept a protective hand on her daughter's head.

"Fine." Lance snapped. Technically, she was right. Technically was a big thing today. He grabbed Oli on his next swing, slowing the momentum until he could wrangle him out of the seat—no easy task while maintaining his hold on Beckham. "Come on, Oli."

Oliver didn't notice the adult tension. He grabbed Lance's hand and tugged him toward the slide. "Next, please," he said with a charming smile, clearly remembering the manners his mother tried to drill into him.

"Sure thing, kiddo." Lance watched Oli climb the short ladder, figuring that if he were holding Beckham, then Beckham wasn't *technically* on the playground. What, they were going to give him a ticket for taking up air space with his pet? He ignored the woman's glare and watched Oli's slow descent on the slide. When he hit the bottom, he hopped off and ran for the ladder. Rinse and repeat indefinitely. It took about fifteen turns on the slide before Oliver was ready for something new. By then, the no-dog woman had wandered away, apparently deciding the dog was controlled enough that she didn't need to call the authorities. Beckham wiggled in his grip, but Lance kept a firm hold.

Oliver eyed the rope net that some older children clambered on with interest and turned a hopeful face toward him.

"Sorry, kiddo." The openings between ropes were twice the length of Oliver. "Wanna climb the hill?"

South Pointe Park boasted a small hill, man-made of course, as all elevations in South Florida were. The trail, popular with walkers and cyclists, wound around the side. Some folks parked beach chairs on the hill and watched the cruise ships sail through the channel and out to sea. Another trail cut through the middle of the hill, a shortcut to the beach path on the other side.

They passed the kid fountain, water spurting from wiggly poles in unpredictable bursts. From toddlers in diapers to children who looked much too old for this kind of game, children ran through them like sprinklers. Parents overflowed the benches, for the most part absorbed in their phones. Some took pictures, and others sipped from cold drinks bought at the small concession stand.

"What do you say, guys?" It was a hot evening, the air thick with humidity.

"Yes, yes!" Oliver's legs pumped faster. Beckham hit the end of his leash and looked back at Lance with accusation in his eyes. Lance picked up his pace, too, and they raced through the fountain area together, Oliver screaming his delight.

"Again!" Oliver spun around, unfazed by his wet shirt and shorts or the way his shoes squeaked when he took a step. He took off before Lance could say yes or no. Beckham raced after him. Lance resigned himself to a thorough soak.

"One more," Lance cautioned, following Oliver as he made his third dash. When Oliver spun for a fourth turn, Lance placed a calming hand on his shoulder. "Hold on. Let's see if your mom predicted this."

Sure enough, the flowered backpack contained a towel. First he wrapped Oliver up like a mummy and hustled him under the hill and through to the other side, where hopefully, with the fountain out of sight, it would also be out of mind. He toweled his own head dry, and then, for good measure, roughed up Beckham's coat. Should he stuff the towel back in the bag? Wouldn't that get everything in there wet? Maybe he should stuff it in an outer pocket. When he unzipped the side pouch, he found a plastic bag perfect for a small, wet towel. Perhaps if he'd been parenting for almost three years, he'd think of everything, too. No. This level of preparedness was all Carrie.

In the shoulder bag, he found a thin sheet perfect for spreading out on the grass. He led Oliver and Beckham up the hill, and when they got to the top, he spread the sheet out. Beckham spun a few times, lay down, stood up, spun a few more times, sniffed the grass at the edge of the sheet, then dove into the grass, nose first, for a roll. Legs in the air, he wiggled, tongue hanging out the side of his mouth like a total goof.

Oliver laughed and copied him, rolling in the grass, arms and legs like a dead bug in the air. Could they be more adorable? Lance suddenly wanted so badly to share this moment with someone else. With Carrie. He pulled out his phone, a poor substitute, and filmed a few seconds of the back-rolling duo. His finger hovered over the button that would send it to Carrie, but at the last second, he stopped himself. The cruise ship's horn in the background was a dead give-away of their location. He sent it to Caleb. He didn't know why. He could've shown it to Carrie later, but the urge to share was too great.

Oh my God. He was one of those fathers. Next thing you know, he'd be posting pics of Oliver's every move-ment to his various social media platforms, the ones that previously he'd primarily used to keep up a presence for Excalibur Construction. He'd always scrolled quickly past baby photos. God, it was worse than posting pictures of every meal. Maybe all parents felt this urge to document. Had Carrie?

Why hadn't he thought of it before? Maybe Oliver's first step, first word, first swim were all documented on Facebook. But when he looked her up, her profile didn't mention Oliver at all. No pictures, even when he went through her photo albums. Everything about her social media was professional, nothing too personal, nothing family oriented. No Oliver. Why?

Because she'd been hiding Oliver from him. It hit Lance then, how much more involved her lie had been than simply neglecting to tell him. She'd avoided social media, must've avoided anyone they both knew, stopped going to places they might run into each other. For all that Miami Beach was an international destination, it could be a surprisingly small town when you'd lived here your whole life. He'd never thought much about how completely she disappeared from his life after the divorce. Considering that he sometimes ran into his third-grade teacher at the movie theater and got together with his high school friends every few months, it should've occurred to him earlier how deliberate her absence was. Never see her on Lincoln Road? Never run into her at the Sunday farmers market, one of her favorite weekend activities?

Only now did he admit to himself that maybe he'd been looking for her at their old haunts, that he'd somehow thought they'd run into each other again. That was some fancy footwork on her part. Watching Oliver roll onto his side, planting his face square on Beckham's exposed belly, Lance felt a sweeping loss, followed quickly by that now-familiar rage. Yeah, he'd said he understood, even forgave her for keeping Oliver a secret. Didn't mean he wasn't still angry and cheated and—if he was honest with himself, which he was desperately trying to be—sad. Sad at the loss of all that time with Oliver and sad over how he couldn't seem to get his conflicted feelings about Carrie under control. She was the moon to his tide, and even he couldn't keep up with the constant push-pull of their relationship.

As if his anger conjured her, he spotted Carrie on the wide path that ran alongside the channel, ending at the southernmost tip of South Beach. Her long hair trailed down her back, and her face was upturned, laughing. Adam pointed out a sailboat on the horizon. In his other hand, a doggy bag hung from Adam's fingers. Carrie'd always loved the enormous slices of coconut layer cake but could never finish one. He'd bet that was what they were taking home, maybe to share over coffee later.

He didn't think about what he was doing as he packed up the sheet and corralled Oliver and Beckham into sliding down the front side of the hill with him. Oliver laughed, thinking it was a game, and Beckham leapt ahead, sure it was a game. They slid to the bottom a few moments after Carrie and Adam passed their location, and Lance took up a casual pace, trailing them.

Not spying. Not stalking. He was walking his dog. Spending time with his son. If they turned and saw him, he would act surprised. What a coincidence!

But they didn't turn around, strolling toward the South Pointe pier. When they got to the end of the walkway, they paused to kick off their shoes. Carrie turned her head, and Lance spun in place, tangling Beckham's leash around his legs in his hurry to act like he was walking in the opposite direction.

Lance stepped over and through Beckham's leash, somehow getting even more tangled than he'd been in the first place. Beckham bounced in place, higher and higher with each jump, until he was clearing Lance's hip. People gave them a wide berth, passing without much of a second glance. He attempted to step over the leash at the same time the dog let out a yip, inspiring Oliver to plop onto the ground and give Beckham a hug. The leash moved; Lance misjudged the step, and the next thing he knew, he was on his knees, blinking up at the darkening sky.

"Lance?" Carrie's voice sounded as surprised as he was planning to act. "Oli? Is that you?"

"Mama!" Oliver took off at a run, and Carrie squatted down to catch him when he threw himself at her. Lance pushed to his feet, his right knee twinging from taking most of his weight when he went down. He brushed at his jeans impatiently, wishing that the fall had rolled him into the channel so he could swim anonymously away, knowing Oli and Beckham were safe with Carrie. Then, he'd never have to admit to trailing after her like a lovesick but angry puppy.

"Need some help?" Adam held out a hand for the leash. "I can take him for a bit."

"I've got it." Somehow, he was already tangled up again. The dog was a whirling dervish of excitement. Lance studied the leash's pattern around his leg and, with a few strategic twists, finally freed himself. "How are you?"

"Good." Adam's long toes poked out from the hem of his tan pants. His loafers rested between his wide-set feet.

"Nice evening for a walk on the beach, isn't it?" Lance shielded his eyes, playing it casual, like he was only here for the beach, too.

"It sure is. Funny seeing you here." Adam's gaze was knowing. He clearly remembered disclosing the location of his plans to Lance when they'd both been on-site earlier today. He was not going to buy the coincidence theory.

Beckham switched from his high bounce to a lunge, pulling against the leash in his desperation to get to Carrie and Oli. Lance let the retractable leash out a bit more so he could reach them.

"These two needed to blow off some steam." Blaming a dog and a child. Shameful but better than admitting to spying. Or stalking. Neither of which he was doing because neither involved this excruciatingly awkward conversation. "Well, you two should get back to it. We were heading over to the dog park. Beckham could use a good run."

"In these clothes?" Carrie coached Oliver to raise his hands overhead. "What have you been up to? Why are they both wet to the skin?"

"The fountain." Lance jerked his head in the direction of the hill.

Carrie reached for the shoulder bag, ripping it down his arm like removing a Band-Aid—quickly, efficiently, no concern for the pain it might cause. She rooted around in the main compartment, emerging with a clean T-shirt.

Oliver stuck out his lower lip. "I don't like that one. It's for babies."

"Too bad." Carrie shook out the navy cotton, a wrinkled Peppa Pig smiling from the center of the chest. "You can't run around in wet clothes."

"Lance-Daddy said I could."

Lance gaped at the son who had just stone cold thrown him under the blame bus. "I didn't actually say—"

"Lance-Daddy doesn't get a vote." Carrie pulled the shirt over Oliver's head.

He squirmed, head stuck in the neck hole. "It's too small, Mama. I don't fit anymore."

"The shorts are probably too small as well. It's only been a month since I changed out the spare outfits, but you are growing like a weed." Carrie blew out a frustrated breath and pulled the shirt off Oli. "He can't run around in wet clothes."

"He'll be fine." There were plenty of times on summer job sites when he'd stood under a hose, soaking himself to the skin, and then gone right back to work. Evaporation cooled the skin. "A little water never hurt anyone."

"You know he was just sick. Are you trying to cause a relapse?" Carrie glared up at Lance. "Plus, he has sensitive skin. He'll get a rash wherever the cloth rubs." Her tone implied he'd failed a test.

Well, hell. He supposed it was true. Oli'd been so cheerful and active; the virus seemed a distant memory. He really hadn't thought about it. And sensitive skin? He certainly didn't know about that, would never have even thought to worry about it. What else didn't he know about his own son? He swiveled his head, looking up and down the walkway like a fresh change of clothes might suddenly appear. "I'll take him right home."

"I'll take him." Carrie stood, wiping her hands on her black skirt. Apparently, once you fail a test, you don't get a second chance. "You don't mind, do you, Adam?"

Adam slipped his loafers back on. "Of course not. Whatever you need."

Lance felt a surge of triumph. The date was ending, and rather badly, too. Then he saw the look Adam gave Carrie, a sort of good-natured resignation, and the triumph turned to guilt. He wanted Carrie to be happy. She'd been enjoying herself before he'd stumbled into their date. She deserved a couple of carefree hours.

"No, no." Lance shouldered the bag once again. "I've got

him. Adam, you don't have safety seats, do you? My truck's all set up."

"It is? Since when?" Carrie tugged the wet T-shirt back over Oliver's head. He wiggled in protest but obligingly stuck his arms through the holes.

"Since your mom texted me photos of what I needed, and Amazon took care of the rest." He flashed her some pictures of the kid-friendly adjustments to his ride because he could tell by her wrinkled nose that she wasn't sure if she believed him.

Carrie tugged one last time on Oliver's shirt, smoothing it over his belly. "I suppose that's best then." Small victories.

"We'll go straight to the condo. He'll be dry in no time flat." Lance reeled in Beckham's leash, bringing him close. The dog immediately wound himself around Lance's legs, necessitating more twists and turns to untangle himself. He bent his sore knees and picked up the still-damp dog. Easier to carry him than take another tumble. Who said he didn't learn from his mistakes?

"Good idea. Make sure Oli gets a warm bath." Carrie kissed the top of her son's head, giving him a gentle push toward Lance. "See you at home?"

"We'll be there." Lance swallowed the lump in his throat, the one full of words he wanted to say but knew Carrie didn't want to hear.

"Do you mind?" Adam dangled the doggy bag at Lance, but Beckham lunged at it as if it were a treat meant for him. Only Lance's firm grip on the dog kept him from taking flight. "If you could take that home for her?"

"Uh, sure." Lance opened up the shoulder bag and dropped the smaller bag inside, out of the dog's sight. What was one more thing to lug?

"Thanks." Carrie and Adam resumed their walk, Carrie's high-heeled sandals swinging from her fingertips, her hair a silky curtain bouncing with each step.

Lance couldn't watch. He herded Oli and Beckham in the opposite direction, pretty sure Mendo would say it was time to grovel again. This time, Lance didn't disagree.

# CHAPTER 33

CARRIE STARED OUT OVER THE TUMBLING WAVES, ARMS wrapped around her waist as if she were chilled. She wasn't. Her stomach churned more than the incoming tide as it hit the shore, bubbling up and creating tiny air pockets in the sand. Small seabirds hurried to peck at the bubbles, no doubt disappointed when they came away with only air instead of the tasty crustacean treat they'd hoped for. Out on the water, a few people bobbed in place, determined to stay in the ocean until the last ray of light was gone. Carrie and Adam strolled by families packing up coolers, shaking out towels, and folding up tents. Ahead at the orange-and-yellow Third Street tower, a lifeguard stood on the wooden deck, arms resting on the railing and a red flotation device at his feet.

"I'm so sorry," Carrie finally mumbled, then repeated loudly and more clearly. "Really sorry. I don't know what that was all about." She'd thought they could get the date back on track after the Lance interruption, but it all felt wrong now. She felt wrong.

"Don't you?" Adam slowed his walk to let her catch up. With his long legs, he kept getting ahead of her. She scurried to reach him, then reached out to grab his hand. Holding it in hers, she stopped their walk. As mixed up as her emotions were, she couldn't imagine what he must be thinking.

"It was crazy what Lance did, following us tonight. What else can I do but apologize?" She held Adam in place with her grip and her gaze, craning her neck at a sharp angle to look up into his face. She wasn't responsible for her ex's actions, but maybe Adam didn't see it that way. Maybe his long silence since Lance's departure was him blaming her or simply plotting how to get away from her with as little drama as possible. She figured they were full up on drama for one night already. Sticking around was probably simple politeness on his part. "I *am* sorry."

"You don't need to apologize." He smiled down at her, but sadness shaded his eyes. Behind his head, the sky streaked pink and blue. "You need to decide what you want."

A nosy seagull wandered over, probably hoping for a french fry. It hopped off when all they did was continue to look at each other. The hope she'd felt earlier at dinner when Adam laughed at her jokes and seemed genuinely impressed that Oliver could write his name and only drew the *r* backward half the time departed as well.

"I didn't ask him to come tonight." Carrie wasn't sure why she felt so defensive. She wasn't the one who'd ruined the date. She stopped herself, recognizing her mother's voice in her head, justifying her actions, blaming someone else for what went wrong. Yes, Lance's actions were not her fault, but his spying only brought to the surface what had been brewing underneath. For all that Adam was so handsome other women slowed their walk as they passed him just to get a better look, and no matter how well she and he worked together or how much she admired his building designs, she'd wished more than once this evening that Lance sat across the table from her. That they'd brought Oli and taken a table out on the grass so Beckham could sit under her chair and shred napkins while they shared her coconut layer cake.

Adam dropped her hand and resumed their walk, angling them away from the ocean and toward the dunes. "Did you know Lance told me yellow dahlias are your favorite?" He guided her through the roped path, sea grass on either side swaying in the light breeze, to perch on the low coral wall that separated the dunes from the pedestrian walkway. "He also suggested I take you for dessert at Smith & Wollensky. Said you loved their cake selection."

"No." Carrie flattened her palms against the uneven top of the wall, scooting her butt until she was comfortable. She could believe Lance tanking her date; she couldn't imagine him trying to improve it. "Why would he do that?"

"He wants you to be happy. That's what he told me." Adam sat, too, and even with his legs out of the height equation, he was still a foot taller than she was. "Even if it's with someone else. He loves you."

Carrie's head shook so fast that she got a mouthful of her own hair. "It's over. I told you that."

"I don't think it is. I saw him look at you." Adam tilted his head, smiling that sad smile at her again. "And the thing is, Carrie, I saw you looking back."

Carrie swallowed, her wave-tumbled stomach doing its best to flip the cake she'd already eaten upside down. She didn't like that he was right. "It's just looking."

"Is it? I like you, Carrie. A lot. But I don't want to be with someone who'd rather be with someone else." Adam climbed to his feet, towering above her like one of the palms that lined the walkway. "Take some time. Let me know what you decide."

Carrie slipped her sandals on in slow motion and followed him back to the restaurant valet. Adam drove her home but didn't walk her to the door. She kissed his cheek before climbing out of his Range Rover. There was something final about the way he said, "Good night."

"Thank you." Carrie left it at that. The sky darkened to a moonless night.

---

Carrie ignored Lance's long, lean body stretched out on the floor, stepping over a denim-clad leg in her five-inch heels to reach Oliver's bedside. He slept soundly, plush octopus under one arm, Beckham next to his hip. His hair was dry, and he smelled of freshly laundered pajamas. She smoothed back his bangs—he needed a trim—and kissed his forehead. He smiled in his sleep, and that somehow made the whole night better.

Skirting around Lance, she headed to the kitchen for a glass of water. Or maybe pink wine. She'd decide when she got there. Her limbs hung heavy off her body, like the time she'd completed a Pilates boot-camp workout and had been too sore to take off her own shoes that night.

Her frosted-glass cake plate sat next to the sink with an envelope taped to it. Intrigued, she opened it and read Lance's scrawled words: *Consider this my groveling for the night. More to come.* She lifted the lid and found her coconut layer cake cut into small cubes. That he remembered how she prepped her leftover cake for binge-watching TV into the wee hours settled her uncertain stomach enough that she popped a piece in her mouth and reread the note.

She flipped it over and wrote on the back: *Please don't be here when I wake up.* She read her message over and found it to be an honest plea for what she could handle but a tad colder than she wanted. She added one more line: *and please eat some cake.*

The next morning when she entered the kitchen to turn on her coffee maker, she was disappointed to find that the cubes of her cake under the frosted dome remained untouched. He'd done as she'd asked, disappearing in the night, so she had only herself to blame for missing him.

---

Fur Haven Park was not the same, squashed onto the front garden area of the Dorothy. It wasn't doing much for the curb appeal of the building, either, with the five-foot chain-link fence and motley crew of mutts crowding the area. Beckham didn't care about any of that. As soon as Carrie turned the stroller onto the Dorothy's street, his tail started wagging a hundred beats per second.

Once she opened the gate and unhooked him, he dashed toward his buddies. LouLou, Lady, and Chewy enjoyed a good round of sniffing with him before tearing off to run the perimeter in quick laps.

"The big-dog, small-dog separation doesn't seem to be taking." Carrie pushed the stroller up to where Riley, Eliza, and Sydney stood behind one of the bone-shaped benches.

They greeted her with smiles and exclamations over Oliver's cuteness. Nothing put him into a deeper sleep than a long ride in the jogging stroller, so he didn't wake up. Carrie adjusted the sunshade to better shield him and joined in the conversation about best dog beaches in the area.

"We should have a website." Sydney grabbed Riley's arm

in her excitement, the exaggerated bell sleeve of her cropped denim top flapping at the sudden movement. "Think about it. We could archive lots of dog info—best beaches, parks, events. It'd be like an old-fashioned community bulletin board, but online."

Eliza patted the sweat off her hairline with a tissue. "Or we could make an old-fashioned bulletin board. Weatherproof, of course. Something sturdier than that." She nodded at a notice posted on the gate, encased in plastic that was already fraying at the edges.

Carrie inspected it. "What a great idea, letting everyone know the plans for the new Fur Haven."

"Caleb thought of it." Riley joined her at the gate. "I'll admit to being super sad that the park Caleb and I built was short-lived, but Adam's been working with us on the new design, and it's going to be beautiful."

Carrie studied the drawing. It'd become more detailed than the last version she'd seen, more landscaping and dog equipment. The neighborhood was filled in around it, and the projected view of the ocean from the top of the garage looked spectacular. "People are going to come just to watch the sunrise."

"I know!" Sydney spun toward the building so quickly the stack of silver bracelets on her arm jingled. "The website could have an activities calendar. We could make the Howling Halloween party an annual event. Add in other festivals. Think, Riley, this could get more people into the Dorothy. Fill up those empty units you're so worried about."

A speculative light dawned in Riley's eyes. "Sydney, would you call the new Fur Haven a venue?"

Sydney clapped her hands together, the bell sleeves of

her crop top swaying like actual bells. "Yes, a unique venue. For unique events."

"Like weddings?" Riley smiled.

"Oh my God." Sydney flung her arms around in her in a hug. "Perfect! Getting married in the space that brought you together? What could be more romantic?"

Carrie felt like an outsider, watching the two women fall into planning together like they did it all the time. Maybe they did. Carrie wouldn't know. This wasn't her neighborhood or her building, even if there were times in the last few weeks when it had started to feel like it was.

"Hey, can I talk to you?"

Carrie startled at the unexpected voice behind her. Lance leaned on the fence, work boots scuffing the already abused lawn.

"We've got the kid. And the dog." Riley pushed her out the gate. "Go. You two *really* need to talk."

Oli slept on; Beckham wouldn't even notice she was gone. "Okay, thanks."

"Anything for my soon-to-be nephew." Riley gave Carrie a sideways, one-armed hug. "I'm serious."

Carrie returned the hug, feeling less left out than a few minutes ago, and made her way to Lance.

"Coffee Spot?" He gestured toward his truck, but she shook her head.

"I've only got a few minutes. Orlov's suddenly on fire to get Volga's redecorating done for a big New Year's Eve party he wants to have."

"Let me know when you need me and my guys." Lance led her to the side of the Dorothy. They could still see Oliver's stroller but were well out of earshot of the others.

"I appreciate it." Carrie took a breath, digging deep for the words she'd practiced in the shower this morning. "I think we make a good team, professionally. I hope we can keep working together."

Lance's face shuttered, as battened down as a home before a hurricane hits. "Of course. We'll be ready to start the Dorothy's interior in the next few weeks when the first remodeled unit gets finished up."

"I know. I'm looking forward to all of that." She twisted her fingers together in front of her, then freed them one by one. "About last night."

"Sorry I fell asleep before you got home." He scratched at the stubble on his chin, clearly gathering his words. "You didn't get the full force of the groveling I'd planned. I shouldn't have gone to South Pointe last night. I'm sorry."

"Thank you for that." She untwisted her fingers, only to find them twisted again. "We're confusing Oliver."

Lance's eyebrows shot up. "Oliver's confused?"

"Yes. We tell him you're his dad. You come over and stay with him. He wants to know why you don't live with us." She skirted the issue, centering the confusion on Oliver. But she and Lance were adults; they should handle their own stuff. It was her job to protect Oliver, to make sure he didn't have more than he could handle on his emotional plate. "We need boundaries. Professional boundaries."

Lance's cheek muscle twitched, never a good sign. "What kind of boundaries?"

"I don't think you should babysit for me anymore." She held up a hand, cutting off his protests. "Not at my home anyway. The time you spend with Oliver should be on your turf. So he can understand that we have two different lives."

"Even if we don't want to have two different lives?"

Carrie gave up on her fingers and shoved them through her hair. Only her hair was in a bun, and it came tumbling down at the rough handling. She took a minute to reposition it and gather her own thoughts. She couldn't let the back-and-forth with Lance impact her decision. Oliver's needs came first. Her own didn't matter.

"We do want that. Work together, parent Oli together, live separately. That's how it has to work."

"Because you said so."

His words were sharp enough to cut her. She did feel like she was bleeding a little bit, but better a little now than a lot later. She nodded. Adam was right. She did need to decide what she wanted, and she'd never be able to do that in their current unstable situation.

"Fine." He took her favorite word, and that was how she knew it wasn't fine at all. But it'd have to be.

"Fine." She stuck out her hand to shake on it.

He looked at her outstretched fingers for a full minute before spinning on his heel and walking away.

# CHAPTER 34

CARRIE WALKED INTO VOLGA AND CRINGED. CHAOS WAS an important part of the redesign process. You couldn't install the new without taking out the old first, but she didn't love that part of it. Lance did, though, and she wished for a brief, fierce moment that he was there with her, working on the restaurant project hand in hand with her instead of simply swooping in at the last minute for the water-feature installation. She shook her head as if to dislodge the thought. Just because things were going well with them, professionally and parenting-wise, didn't mean she should wish for more.

It'd been almost a month since they'd struck their deal, and Oliver now spent several days a week with Lance. When Grams called to invite her and Oliver to a Christmas Eve party at the Dorothy, she'd declined for herself but let Oliver go with Lance. Her son had a blast, coming home with tales of a visit from Santa and a sack full of toys clearly from his extended Donovan family and not a mythical elf.

She didn't begrudge Oliver the extra attention from his newly discovered family, but she did miss when it was just the two of them. A few times, he'd spent the night at Lance's, a perfect opportunity for her to reactivate her dating apps and dive back in, but she didn't. Like Adam pointed out, she needed to know what she wanted. Problem was, she was pretty sure what she wanted would end in disaster. Again.

Instead, she'd spent long evenings on the phone with

Farrah, catching up and making plans to see each other as soon as Farrah could get away from work for a long weekend. She'd also taken to hanging out at the temporary Fur Haven park and often grabbed coffee with Riley or Sydney afterward. Sydney's website was coming along nicely, and so was the parking garage. With Lance taking Oliver so frequently, even her mother was getting a break from so much babysitting and had joined a gym and a book club. Really, all the changes were for the better. She should be happy, and she was. Mostly.

"I'm not sure this is better." Dimitri emerged from the kitchen's swinging doors, both hands held out to her.

She took them and gave them a squeeze, then dropped her hands to her sides before the gesture became anything more than friendly. She'd seen the look in his eyes a few times from other clients, and she stayed firm in her resolve never to get involved with someone who owed her money. It could be hard enough to collect final payments when things went well. Add in disappointed romantic entanglements, and she'd never be able to pay her mortgage.

"You shouldn't be here for this part. Can't you wait until the big reveal like a normal client?" She got out her camera to shoot some pictures. She liked to document the process. She also liked to keep her hands busy so Dimitri didn't grab them again.

"Stay away from my dream? How could you be so cruel?" His smile belied his words.

"Please." She gestured for him to follow her. "Let's take a tour of the destruction, and I'll fill your head with the glory of what's to come."

Twenty minutes later, she sent a pleased Dimitri on his

way. She was deep in conversation with one of the Excalibur guys about how many more days they'd need the construction dumpster. Lance might not be hands-on this whole project, but she wasn't going to hire anyone else to work with her, either. His crew was easy to deal with, competent and quick. They were a full day ahead of her original schedule.

She spotted Lance out of the corner of her eye, entering through the front door with rolled plans under one arm. She finished up with the hard hat and hurried away.

"Carrie?"

She heard him calling but ducked through the kitchen and out the back door into the alley as if she hadn't. The door thunked closed behind her, and she leaned against it, breathless.

"You gonna decorate the alley next?" Knox lifted a bag of debris into the dumpster pushed against the restaurant's wall. It landed with a loud *thunk*.

"No." Carrie's laugh was jittery, too high-pitched. "Just needed a minute."

"Saw Lance, huh? Guess he's right that you've been avoiding him." Knox hurled the second of three large bags into the dumpster.

"No, that's not true. I see him all the time." Carrie shifted so all her weight was in the heels of her shoes. It wasn't great for her Jimmy Choos, but it did relieve pressure off her toes.

Knox halted, midswing of the third bag, giving her blank face until she cracked.

"Okay, maybe a bit." There was that jittery laugh again.

"Oli's a good kid." Knox finished with the bags and slammed the dumpster closed with another loud bang. "Lance adores him. The whole family does."

Talking about how amazing her son was? Carrie could do that all day. She relaxed against the door. "I know. I'm glad Oli has all of you."

Knox walked to her, not quite limping but not smoothly, either. He rubbed the muscle above his brace, stopping a few feet from her. "I was deployed back when you and Lance got married. And divorced. But I did recently spend nearly two weeks in a very small bathroom with the guy."

"Thank you again for that. Kristin's already asked me to do her kitchen."

"That's great." Knox pulled the work gloves off his hands and stuffed them in his back pocket. "Not my point, though. Two weeks, small bathroom, toxic chemicals. A guy talks. At least Lance sure did. And it was all about you."

Carrie's hand flew to the tiny pearl on her necklace. "He did? You must hate me, after what I did to him."

"I should." Knox looked her up and down, assessing. "So should he. But he doesn't, so I don't, either. He's angry, yeah, but mostly he talked about how talented you are, what a great mom. Blah-Blah-amazing-Carrie-blah-blah. There was a lot of sawing. Sometimes I didn't hear everything."

Carrie's mouth dried out. "Must've drowned out all the bad. Knox, there's a reason we got divorced."

"And you've got really good reasons to get back together."

"I know, Oliver. He loves Lance."

"Lord, no." Knox shuffled his feet. "The kid's fine. I meant that you love each other."

"You don't know me." The defense was sharp and automatic, but it slid off Knox like she hadn't said anything.

"What're you afraid of, Carrie?" His face was stoic as ever, but his Donovan blues bored into her.

"Nothing." Carrie's lip trembled at the lie. Her pulse raced in full-on fight-or-flight mode. She didn't have to answer Knox. She should walk away.

She didn't. She swallowed, closed her eyes, and then forced them open again. "Knox, I've been terrible to him. No matter what we may or may not feel for each other, the truth is, deep down, I don't deserve another chance with Lance."

Knox snorted. "God save us all from what we deserve." His words were joking, but his eyes darkened with memories. "Besides, it's not up to you, is it? Only Lance knows if it's worth the risk."

"I kept his son from him." Her fingers danced nervously on the pearl at her dry throat. She tried to swallow, but her tongue stuck at the back of her throat. "How can he ever forgive me? When I think about all the what-ifs, like what if we hadn't run into each other? How much longer would I have waited?" She inhaled shakily. "Honestly, if the roles were reversed? I don't know that I could forgive him. What kind of life could we have with that always between us?"

Knox let her sniffle for a moment, then took a few steps toward her and laid a comforting hand on her shoulder. "That's the thing about forgiveness. It's not up to you. If you're truly sorry, tell him."

"I have, but he's still angry. I can see it in him some-times." She sniffed back more tears and leaned her cheek against Knox's hand. "And I don't blame him. I ruined us; before I even knew about Oliver, I walked away."

"From what Lance has told me, he was kind of an asshole back then. He's grown up, though. He's certainly not the jerk I left behind when I enlisted." Knox shook her shoulder a little until she looked up at him. "The way I see it, if you're both trying for a better future, what will the past matter?"

Carrie knuckled away a few runaway tears, knowing Knox spoke the truth. Lance was different, and so was she. "I guess at the end of the day, I'm scared. What if we try and it doesn't work? How will that make Oli feel?"

"Everybody's scared, Carrie. Why should you be any different?" Knox chucked her chin with his finger and stepped away. "Look, it's simple. Don't be an asshole, and everything will work out."

Carrie bit her lip and stood aside so Knox could reenter the restaurant. She stayed by the dumpster for a long time, waiting for the tears to dry up. It took a while, but she finally sniffled her last sniffle. Determined, she blew her nose and freshened her makeup. Deserving or not, scared or not, she knew what she wanted. And she knew what she had to do. *Don't be an asshole.* It was surprisingly good advice.

---

Inside Volga, chaos still reigned. She ducked a couple of guys carrying out an old table, searching for Lance's tall form amid the clutter and rubble. Spotting him at the front, she inhaled deeply and marched forward. Knox gave her a thumbs-up when she passed him, but she didn't slow down. Once you decide to do a thing, you want the thing to be done as quickly as possible.

"Lance?" She tucked a strand of hair behind her ear. She'd started out with a braid, but it had spent the day slowly unraveling. She should've taken a minute in the alley to check more than her makeup, but it was too late now. If he was going to say yes, he'd have to take her as she was, imperfections and all.

"Hey." Lance smiled with a caution that broke her heart. She'd done that to him. Suddenly, the thing she had to do was too scary. She backpedaled into some small talk. The thing could wait. Maybe later, like next week or next month.

"Everything okay?" She clutched her iPad to her chest. "Oli's fine?"

"Grams and Grandpa William took him fishing today. My guess is he's better than fine."

"You told them to use a lot of sunscreen, right? He's very fair." She couldn't help but worry. Intellectually, she understood that other family members loved her son. Emotionally, it was hard to believe anyone would take care of him like she did.

"And his skin is sensitive." Lance pulled out a phone to show her a picture of Oliver on Grandpa William's boat. His wide-brimmed hat took up most of the frame. "We covered all the bases."

"Sorry." She flinched at the sound of something crashing in the background. Nothing to worry about on a demo day, but still startling. "I worry."

"I know." He reached forward, tucking another wayward strand of hair behind her ear. "Me, too. How's Adam?"

Carrie's eyes knitted together in confusion. "Fine, I guess. Don't you see him more than I do these days?"

"No more dates? He didn't tell me."

"What's to tell? We were never together anyway." A drill started up in the background, forcing Carrie to step closer to Lance in order to hear him.

"And you're not dating anyone else?"

"No, deactivated my online dating accounts." She shook her head, the final straw for her poorly constructed braid. Hair tumbled over her shoulder. Lance reached for it as if mesmerized, then dropped his hand.

"What about you?" Carrie leaned in to be heard over the demolition noise. When he didn't answer, she took another step closer. "Are you seeing anyone?"

"What? No." He canted his head down, and they were so close she could feel his breath on her cheek. Her breath hitched in her lungs. She placed a hand to the center of his chest, and his heart beat wildly against it. "What're you doing, Carrie?"

His words broke the spell, and she swallowed hard, lowering her hand. "Do you want to see someone?"

He watched her, wariness in his blue eyes. "I have someone in mind."

"So do I." She was doing it. She was doing the thing! Her blood pumped louder than the construction around her.

"For me?" Wariness turned to curiosity, then back to wariness. "You're setting me up?"

"I think you'll like her." Carrie smiled, really smiled. It felt good to know what she wanted, but this was not the place. Noise and sawdust, a lot of curious eyes. She had a better idea. "Come by my place tonight. I'll introduce you."

Lance took a moment, scanning their surroundings, before his eyes came back to her. "I'm not sure what's going on here, Carrie. I don't want to play games."

She placed her hand back on his chest. His heart still beat a crazy rhythm. "I'm not playing. Come over."

He covered her hand with his own, flattening her palm against the warm plane of his chest under the thin T-shirt. "See you tonight."

# CHAPTER 35

"THANKS, AGAIN." CARRIE FIDDLED WITH THE ROPE BELT at the waist of her floral maxi dress. It wasn't her usual style, but she was tired of her usual self. Her usual self made a lot of bad decisions. Tonight, she needed to be someone different, someone braver. Someone who wasn't an asshole.

"Believe me, it's my pleasure." Riley sat on Carrie's couch, a lapful of poodle and Jack Russell jockeying for her attention. Although she petted each dog with a separate hand, each eyed the other hand enviously. "I'll take good care of your boys."

Carrie slipped on the espadrilles she'd bought with the dress. She hadn't quite been able to let go of her stiletto obsession, but the braided espadrilles provided a stable platform. She could walk for days. It was a different kind of powerful.

"I'm so nervous." Carrie and Riley's friendship was still new, but the words burst out anyway.

Riley scratched both dogs under their respective chins. "You don't need to be. He's crazy about you."

"You think?" Carrie alighted on the sofa's arm, then quickly stood again, so much energy coursing through her that she didn't know what to do with herself. She double-checked the contents of her evening purse—phone, money, ID, lip gloss, keys. Then she tripled-checked, like her purse might've accidentally emptied itself in the three seconds since her last inspection.

"I know." Riley kicked off her flip-flops and folded her legs onto the couch, crisscross applesauce style.

Carrie jumped at the knock on the door. "Do I look okay?"

"You are one gorgeous woman, and you know it. Go open the door already." Riley shooed her away. "We've got hours of Animal Planet to watch."

"I love Animal Planet," Oliver yelled from his room, his words arriving a few seconds before he did. Dressed in his fire engine pajamas, he padded barefoot to the couch and lifted himself to a seat beside Riley.

"Everyone loves Animal Planet." Riley clicked on the TV. "*Meerkat Manor*. Aren't we lucky?"

Oliver clapped his hands. "I love meerkats."

Riley transplanted Beckham from her lap to his. "Who doesn't?"

Carrie took a deep breath. Oli was in excellent hands. She should relax. She rolled her shoulders and opened the door. The moment of truth. She'd practiced what to say all day. She couldn't remember any of the words now. "Hi."

Lance cocked his head. "Hi."

She looked at him, specifically the center of his chest where muscle pushed against the athletic-fit blue T-shirt. Her hand raised and placed itself there, palm between his pecs, measuring the beat of his heart. It sped up, and her own heart did the same.

"Carrie? Is everything okay?"

She wrenched her eyes up to meet his and nodded. "Can we go outside?"

"Sure." He stepped back, making room for her on the front stoop. "You're worrying me. Is Oli okay?"

She nodded.

"Beckham?"

She swallowed. She really needed some words. She could see the panic rising in his eyes. "Everything's fine. Everyone's fine."

"Did the mystery date not show?" He was still looking for problems.

Carrie clasped her hands in front of her before they did anything else without her consent. "I've decided to start dating again."

Lance's face fell. This wasn't going at all how she'd imagined it. He was supposed to realize where she was going with this.

She tried again. "Someone special, someone I have a lot of history with."

Were her hints not clear enough? This was his chance to declare himself again. To ask her out. It would be so much easier if he would take the lead. He didn't. Because she was being an asshole, putting it all on him.

Lance let out a disappointed sigh. "You said this wasn't a game." The telltale muscle in his cheek twitched. "But I am definitely feeling played."

"Oh, uh." Wow, what happened to all her people skills? She'd never felt so tongue-tied in her life. She needed to do the thing, but she was so scared her legs trembled.

"Carrie, what the hell is going on?" Lance took a step back, crossing protective arms over his chest. His biceps bulged under the thin sleeves.

She tore her gaze away from his body, choosing to study the overhead light on her patio instead. Lots of dead bugs in there. She'd need to clean it soon. Enough distraction. She took a long, deep breath.

"You're freaking me out." Lance drummed nervous fingers on the railing. "Just say it."

She wrung her hands, like some kind of damsel in distress from an old movie. "I'm sorry. I'm doing this badly."

"Yes." He snorted. "Whatever this is."

"Lance?" She dropped her hands to her side. Open body language, open heart. "Will you go out with me tonight?"

"What?" He was so startled he took another step back, which took him off the stoop and down the first step. Once he slipped the one step, he kept on going, arms flailing, until he caught the railing. At the bottom, he righted himself, staring up the four steps at her. "What did you say?"

"Let's go on a date. Tonight." Her hands clasped her skirt. She knew she was wrinkling the fabric, but she couldn't care about that. Not now, when her whole future seemed to hinge on the next word out of his mouth.

"Say yes!" Riley stood by the front window, glass cranked open, huge grin across her face. "You know you want to."

"Riley?" Lance's confusion had him leaning against the railing like he couldn't stand on his own. "What're you doing here?"

"Babysitting, what else?" Riley stuck out her tongue at him. "If you'd say yes already."

"Say yes!" Oliver's face appeared in the window and disappeared. "Yes, yes, yes!" He jumped up and down until Riley finally caught him and held him in place.

Lance shook his head, hair flipping back and forth, like he was trying to clear an Etch A Sketch. "Why should I say yes?"

Carrie sent a desperate look Riley's way. Riley nodded and pulled Oliver out of the window, giving them some privacy. Carrie took a step down, then another. She stopped on the step above Lance, so they were the same height for once.

"Say yes so we can start over. Say yes so we can go on a date. A real date. An intentional date. You and me."

"Why?" His voice was hoarse, his hands fisted at his sides.

He was going to make her say it, say it right now, and that was fair. He'd put it all out there for her, and she'd sent him away. Why should he make it easy for her now?

"Because I love you. I've always loved you." Her voice trembled as the words, so raw and broken, escaped her in a rush. She waited for them to land, to see what he would do. If he rejected her, it was no more than she deserved after all she'd put him through. She held her breath, held it until she felt she would explode.

Then his mouth was on her's, filling her lungs with his own breath. She drank him up, pressing herself as close as she could get. He held her so tight, her feet lifted off the stair like she was levitating.

"Do you mean it?" He pulled away, just far enough to ask the question.

"Yes. Oli loves you, too." She rained light kisses on his lips. "Lance, let's be a family."

"Yes." He picked her up and spun her around before kissing her again. "Yes, please."

Riley and Oliver cheered from the window, but Lance didn't seem to notice. He was too busy spiriting her to his truck. She turned and blew Oliver a kiss.

"Where are we going?" Carrie asked as Lance hoisted her into the passenger's seat.

He kissed her while buckling her in. "Does it matter?"

"No." She laughed, holding his precious face in her hands. "I'll go anywhere with you."

"Even back to the altar?"

"Even that."

# EPILOGUE

Lance swallowed hard, inspecting the judge's chamber one more time before the ceremony. He knew Carrie waited on the other side of that thick wooden door, and he wanted to be sure that all the details were precisely right. Dahlias everywhere a dahlia could be put? Check. Paperwork signed, guests assembled, soft music playing in the background? Check, check, check.

"Second time's a charm." This time, instead of Caleb sitting in the back row of a florally exploded church, he stood at the front of the makeshift aisle, dressed to the nines in an expensive suit, Lance's and Carrie's rings tucked into his right trouser pocket.

"I hope so." Beside him, Lance fidgeted more than his son, Oliver, who he held by the hand. They wore matching blue suits, white shirts open at the throat, and brown shoes so shiny they glinted in the light.

"Still can't believe you're getting married before me." Caleb nudged Lance with his shoulder, but Lance didn't budge.

He cracked a forced smile. "You're here. Riley's here. Why not jump in? I'm sure the judge will give us a two-for-one special, right, Your Honor?"

Judge Connor chuckled but didn't look up from inspecting the paperwork on his desk.

"Grams would kill us." Across the makeshift aisle, Riley stood, a pink swirl of a dress wrapped around her as tightly as Beckham's leash was tied around her wrist.

"I would." Grams agreed from her seat next to Grandpa William. "And think of poor Patty. She's so been looking forward to your wedding."

Grandpa William patted Grams' hand where it rested on the arm of the office chair. It was a good thing that, in addition to the wedding party, they only had the five guests, because four chairs were exactly how many the judge had in his chamber. Mendo sat in one, thrilled at the turn of events and the success of his groveling advice. Christine sat next to him, already taking photos to share with Robert when she visited him later that week. The last seat remained empty, awaiting Sherry's arrival.

Knox stood on Lance's other side in his Marine dress blues. He even had a matching brace for his leg.

"I'm only marrying people with actual marriage licenses today. But feel free to come back anytime with your own." Judge Connors smiled as he circled the desk, taking his spot between them in his black robes. He held a small book in front of him and gazed expectantly at the door.

Lance and Carrie might have opted for a small wedding, but Carrie had insisted on a bit of ceremony. The judge's chamber door swung open slowly, and Carrie stood outlined in light.

Lance couldn't look away. At their first wedding, Carrie'd worn an elaborate, beaded gown with a veil that had obscured her face. Today, she wore a simple white summer dress with her signature gravity-defying heels. Her hair streamed around her, a few flowers pinned into the dark tresses. She was, in a word, stunning. He certainly felt stunned. His breath caught in his throat, and he couldn't breathe again until, gripping her mother's arm tightly, she completed the handful of steps to the judge.

Sherry transferred Carrie's smooth hand to his sweaty one. She smiled up at him, and his lungs started functioning again.

"You okay?" Carrie smiled up at him, too, her hazel eyes filled with love and concern.

"I'm perfect." He knew it was too soon in the ceremony, but he couldn't help himself. He dropped a soft kiss to her lips. "You're perfect."

Her lips clung to his, and he suddenly wished it were all over. The judge and the vows and the fancy lunch Dimitri Orlov insisted on providing at Volga. Lance wanted to start his life with Carrie right now.

He'd trembled at their first wedding, jitters about what he was getting himself into. Was he doing the right thing? He trembled today, too, but from excitement. There was no doubt in his mind that Carrie was the woman for him. Reluctantly, he pulled away from her. "Are we getting married, or what?"

The judge said a few words of greeting and launched into the words that would bind Lance and Carrie together forever. Lance knew they were important, that he should pay attention, but all he could see was Carrie's glowing face. All he could hear was the pounding of his own heart.

Caleb bumped his arm, and Lance was forced to let go of Carrie's hand. Oliver held his hands out flat, like they'd practiced, one ring in each palm.

"Good job," Carrie whispered to him, picking up Lance's ring.

They must've exchanged rings at their first wedding, but it hadn't felt like this, he was sure. When Carrie slipped the ring onto his finger with a softly spoken "With this ring, I thee wed," Lance felt everything click into place. His wife, his son, his life.

He placed the ring on her finger, the judge said a few more words, and finally, they kissed. His brothers patted him on the back. Oliver jumped up and down, clapping, and even Beckham seemed to understand the importance of the moment, spinning in place, twirling the leash into a Twizzler stick.

"Good luck to you both." The judge dismissed them with a smile.

"We don't need luck." Lance squeezed Carrie's hand. "We've got each other."

Carrie's color was high, and she laughed, as giddy as if she'd downed a pitcher of mimosas all on her own.

Grandpa William had rented a limo. The wedding party loaded in, an excited Oliver hopping in and immediately finding buttons to push. Windows went up and down.

"I got this." Caleb dove in, scooping up his nephew, distracting him with tickles.

"After you." Grandpa William waved Carrie into the limo, but Lance put out a hand to stop her.

"We'll catch up." He exchanged a long look with his grandfather, and Grandpa William gave him a sharp nod.

"See you there." He escorted Grams into the dark interior, and the driver closed the door behind him.

"What's going on?" Carrie turned happy but puzzled eyes to him.

A BMW, in a blue so dark it looked navy, pulled up. The driver stepped out of the car, adjusted his dark suit coat, and opened the back door.

"This is us." Lance gestured for her to enter first.

"What a mystery." Carrie climbed in, holding out her hand for Lance to join her. He didn't need to tell the driver where to go, since it was all prearranged. He sank back into the cushioned leather seat and stretched out his legs, one ankle crossed over the other.

Carrie leaned her head against his shoulder. "I should probably be more suspicious, but I'm just so relieved."

"You don't want to go to the after-party, huh?"

"No, the reception will be fun." Her head rolled against his bicep. "I'm relieved to be married to you again. Until the judge finally said the words, I kept thinking something would happen. But it didn't. And now we're married."

"No escaping this time." He kissed the top of her head.

"Thank God." She snuggled into his side, one of the flowers tickling his chin. "I never want to go on another first date again."

He laughed, shifting so his arm was around her shoulders. He held her close to his side as the streets grew more tree-lined and condo buildings gave way to single-family residences.

"Aren't we near the Dorothy?" Carrie watched the passing scenery with a contended smile.

"One block over."

The BMW rolled to a stop in front of a midcentury gem, one of Carrie's favorites, he knew, with its butterfly roofline. A large sea-grape tree dominated the front yard, and a horizontal wood-slat fence circled the lawn. At the corner of the property, the wall zigzagged around a towering sabal palm. Carrie'd told him on one of their many exhaust-the-dog walks that she found it charming that the owners had built a wall around the tree rather than chopping it down.

"I've always wondered what it's like inside." Carrie's wistful voice made Lance smile.

He reached into his pocket and pulled out a set of keys. "Why don't you find out?" He dangled them in front of her.

"Why do you have the keys?" Her eyes widened, then widened some more. "Lance, what did you do?"

"It's my wedding gift for you. Do you like it?" He grinned. He knew she did.

She smacked his hand, hard, and snatched the keys. "Are you serious right now?"

He opened his door and pulled her through. "Let's take a tour. If you hate it, we can find another place."

She shook her head, the bright flowers jogging loose until one fell to the sidewalk. "It's perfect."

"We haven't even gone inside."

"Location, location, location." She checked off three fingers, then raised a fourth. "Great bones. Anything else? We can fix."

"We *are* a good team." He pulled her against him, unable to stand the few inches of distance between them for another minute.

Her hands flattened against his chest. "The perfect team."

Every kiss with Carrie was special, but he knew he'd remember this one for the rest of their lives. The heat was there, the love, but this time, there was something different. New. It felt like the future opening around them.

She stepped back, her eyes knowing, like she'd felt it, too. "Let's go see what our future looks like."

Hand in hand, they walked to the front door. His initial walk-through right before the closing had revealed there'd be repairs to make, details to restore, and God knew what they'd find if they peeled up the flooring in the kitchen. But it didn't really matter what surprises the house had in store for them. As long as they were together, they could handle anything.

Carrie took the lead, trying a few keys before finding the one that unlocked the door. She looked over her shoulder at him and smiled. He followed her inside.

"Oh my." She held her hands to her cheeks, taking in the original tile work, perfectly restored, the high ceilings, and the way light streamed through the large windows. "It's beautiful."

"You're beautiful." He stepped close, wrapping his arms around her waist from behind.

She leaned against him with a contented sigh. "It's the perfect place to raise a family."

His heart thudded in his chest. "Our family."

She turned in his arms, twining her arms around his neck. "'Til death do us part."

"No take-backs this time." He lowered his face to hers. She laughed, but he didn't. His gaze bored into her. "I mean it."

"I know." She cupped his face in her hands, holding his eyes with hers. Steady. Unblinking. "So do I."

His forehead dropped to hers, breath shuddering out of his lungs. The BMW's horn broke the moment. He'd only hired it for an hour. Time was ticking, but he didn't care. Let them charge him double for the second hour.

"Guess we need to get back to the family. Oli will be wondering where we are." Carrie didn't move, though, staying in his arms like she never wanted to leave.

"We'll catch up later. Right now, we have a future to start. Wait 'til you see the master bedroom."

"Show me everything, Lance."

"That's a tall order."

"You're a tall guy." She giggled and stepped back. "Quick tour and then to the restaurant?"

He quieted his impatience and led her down a short hallway to the master suite. The bedroom was large with French doors that led to a private deck. Carrie was suitably appreciative, stepping outside and exclaiming when she discovered the small hot tub tucked in the corner of the patio.

"Keep looking."

She spun in place and noticed the envelope on the wrought-iron bistro set. She picked it up, pulling out two tickets.

"Greece?" She turned shining eyes to him.

He nodded, suddenly worried. What if Greece wasn't her dream destination anymore? Why hadn't he asked her?

She flung herself at him, Oli-style, and he caught her up in a kiss.

"Just when I thought today couldn't get more perfect." She kissed every inch of his face, then moved onto his neck.

He'd thought the honeymoon would start tonight, but they were in their new home. They were married. They were alone. He pulled out his phone and sent the BMW on its way.

He scooped her up and strode back into the bedroom. Their bedroom. He was tired of waiting. He wanted his future to start right now. He backed her against the wall, growling into her neck. "Do you mind being late to your own wedding celebration?"

"Please," she panted into his ear. "Please make us late."

He grinned. "Whatever makes my wife happy."

She smiled up at him. "You make me happy."

His lips slammed into hers, fiercer than he'd ever felt before. She kissed him back, equally fierce. They might never make it to the restaurant, and he didn't care. His whole life was right here, in his arms. He kissed her neck, right below her ear.

She leaned her head back, giving him more access to the sensitive skin of her neck. The movement pushed her breasts into his chest. He moaned at the sensation.

Her eyes fluttered open. "Lance?"

"Hmm?" His lips trailed toward her collarbone.

"I love you." She caught his face in her hands, forcing his eyes to hers. "I'm sorry I was such an idiot before."

His heart kicked in his chest, an unmanned jackhammer. He mimicked her gesture, palms to her cheeks, staring into her hazel depths. He was drowning, and he never wanted to come up for air. Carrie's chest rose and fell in an uneven rhythm. He trailed one hand down and laid it against the beat of her heart.

His lips stretched into a slow smile. "What matters is we're here now."

"In our home."

"You're my home."

"Well, then, Lance Donovan. Welcome home."

There's more love to be found at the park!
Don't miss the first book in Mara Wells's
heartwarming Fur Haven Dog Park series.

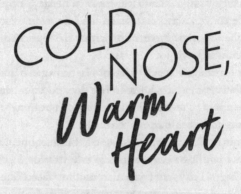

# CHAPTER 1

RILEY CARSON'S BUTT BUZZED. SHE PRETENDED NOT TO
feel her phone's vibration through the denim of her cutoff
jean shorts and lifted her face to the morning sun, sucking
in a lungful of humid air.

"Ah, nothing like late summer in South Florida." She kept
an eye on her toy poodle, LouLou, who galloped around
the patchy grass of the neighborhood dog park alongside
her best dog park pal, a black Labrador ten times her size.
Well, it wasn't really a dog park, more an empty lot that the
good dog folk of the surrounding area had commandeered
as their own. And Lady wasn't really a Lab, more a mix of
large breeds with a Lab head and soulful eyes.

"If only there were more mosquitoes." Eliza, Lady's

owner, batted half-heartedly at a few early-afternoon pests. "And more humidity so one hundred percent of my clothing can stick to my skin instead of the usual eighty percent."

Recently retired from her legal practice, Eliza was a dog park fixture, bringing Lady from their home across the street multiple times a day. She'd been the one to find LouLou, abandoned in a cardboard box with holes punched in the top, just outside the lot's entrance.

Riley crinkled the ever-present plastic bag in her pocket, remembering meeting Eliza on her door-to-door search to find the poodle's owner. "I can't believe it's been over a year since you brought LouLou into my life."

"Love at first sight, wasn't it?" Eliza dabbed at her steel-gray hairline with a tissue. White streaks at her temples defied gravity and frizzed around her face. "She was a pathetic thing, wasn't she? So dirty and with the worms."

"Nothing a body shave and a trip to the vet couldn't fix." Riley didn't like remembering those days. LouLou had been skeletally thin, her apricot coat sparse and matted. She'd been weak, her survival touch and go, especially given her advanced age. Now, she was the picture of health, clearly finding joy in herding her giant friend around the perimeter of the chain-link-enclosed lot.

"They're quite an unlikely pair, aren't they?" Eliza tracked the dogs' progress while they ran the fence. Clods of dirt flew from under Lady's paws, and LouLou chased after them as if they were toys. The fact that the clods crumbled in her mouth didn't stop her from chasing the next one, but it did remind Riley that she needed to bust out the dog toothbrush. Poodles had notoriously bad teeth, and Riley figured there was nothing wrong with a bit of prevention.

Luckily, LouLou liked both the vanilla-mint flavored tooth-paste and the extra attention.

"Opposites attract, I guess. I'm glad they're such good friends." That Riley was also grateful for Eliza's friendship went unspoken. Morning, afternoon, and evening, the two met up to let the dogs run, and somehow that had turned into long hours of conversation, day after day, that left Riley hoping when she reached Eliza's age, she'd have half as many funny stories to tell about her life as Eliza did. Right now, though, her life was the opposite of exciting—work, work, and more work.

Riley's butt buzzed again. She winced and pulled out her phone. She texted a quick reply and added another item to her to-do list. Although she wasn't technically always on call, in practice, it certainly seemed that way. "I'm sorry. I know the dogs both love a good run, but we have to cut it short today."

"Butt problems?" A smile was never far from Eliza's lips, and they stretched into a grin at Riley's sigh. Eliza patted the tissue behind her ears and down her neck before stashing it under her bra strap, hidden by the neckline of her floral blouse. Riley had seen her pull a key and a driver's license out of her blouse. She wondered what else Eliza stashed in there.

"Mr. Cardoza problems." Riley thumbed through a few more messages, turning the screen so Eliza could see her to-do list of the day. "Duty calls."

"You're good to them, those pesky residents of yours at the Dorothy. Sure keep you on your toes, don't they?" Eliza patted Riley's arm and called Lady. The big dog slid to a stop a mere inch from crashing into Eliza, head lolling to the side with a doggy grin. Such a large dog for such a small woman seemed incongruous at first, but Riley had quickly learned that they shared an irreverent sense of humor and a great love of pâté.

"You know it. But after the disaster at my last job, I'm grateful for the work. See you this evening?"

LouLou came running, too, now that Lady was leaving, and Riley bent down to clip on her leash.

"Wouldn't miss it." Eliza threaded Lady's leash through her fingers. "Kiki and Paula got back from Italy yesterday. They'll bring Princess Pugsley, which will be a nice treat for Lady, and I for one can't wait to hear about every moment of their trip."

"And see every picture, right?" Riley smiled at Eliza's enthusiastic nod.

"You know, they met right here at the park. Kiki had that old Maltese, God rest her cranky soul, and Paula started bringing Princess Pugsley when she was a puppy. Gosh, that must be five years ago now."

"A real doggy love match." Riley pulled her hair back into a sloppy ponytail and secured it with a band from her wrist, following Eliza through the gap in the fence they used as the dog park entrance. Two poles, meant to hold the chain-link upright, tilted away from each other, creating a slot large enough for humans and dogs to slide through.

"But it sure wasn't love at first sight. Those dogs hated each other. Kiki and Paula on the other hand..." Eliza winked. "Just you wait, Riley. Maybe the dog park will bring someone special your way, too."

"Thanks to you, I have my someone special." Riley squatted to give her poodle a good scratch behind the ears. "I don't need anyone else. Come on, LouLou. Maybe Mr. Cardoza has some treats for you."

"You're skeptical," Eliza called to Riley's retreating back, "but I'm usually right. You'll see. I have an excellent sense for these things."

"No romance for me, thank you very much. Work your matchmaking wiles on some other sucker." Riley waved but didn't turn around. Getting into it with Eliza about her failed engagement was a topic for another day. And the name of that day was Neverday.

Riley'd shared a lot with Eliza about growing up in the area, how her mom's job working for a cruise line had her out of the country for weeks, sometimes months, at a time, leaving Riley's grandmother to mostly raise her. She hadn't shared much about her love life, though—neither her disaster of an engagement nor how she sometimes fantasized about the cute UPS driver with the sexy accent who delivered Eileen Forsythe's medications on the first Tuesday of every month. No, for now, her job, her poodle, and her Grams were enough commitments in her life. Who had time for anything more?

LouLou followed Riley along the sidewalk that led back to the Dorothy, the Art Deco apartment building where Riley spent her days—and quite a few nights—trouble-shooting maintenance problems for the residents. Another failure. Her gig at the Dorothy was a long way down from her position as an assistant manager at the luxurious Donovan Resort in downtown Miami, but when the whole chain was sold off due to a series of political and financial scandals that ended up with the CEO in prison, she got laid off, and she didn't have a choice. It was the job at the Dorothy or no job at all.

Really, she was grateful for the strings her Grams had pulled to get her hired. It meant she was an elevator ride away from her favorite relative, the woman who'd provided the only stability in her young life, and she was certainly learning a lot of new skills. Skills she'd never thought she'd needed, but who wouldn't want to add handywoman to their résumé?

Sure, she missed her Donovan Resort team, the inside jokes, and the after-shift drinks at the bar. She missed greeting returning guests and welcoming new ones for their first stays. She missed her not-too-shabby paycheck and how putting on the Donovan Resort's requisite black blazer and pulling back her hair instantly made her feel like a kick-ass professional.

She did not miss being unemployed, though, and after wrestling with plumbing and electrical problems, single-handedly regrouting the lobby bathroom, and negotiating lower rates from the cable company, she didn't need a blazer to make her feel kick-ass. Her Dorothy uniform of cutoff jeans and thrift-store T-shirts was more comfortable anyway. Oh, who was she kidding? She did miss that blazer. Who would've noticed if she'd never returned it? The Donovan Resort, and every one of its sister properties, would likely never open for business again.

Riley and her poodle circled around to the front of the building, and as always, Riley admired its graceful lines. Although a bit faded in places, the cheerful pink façade never failed to lift her mood. She'd loved coming to Grams' as a child, imagining the building had been painted her favorite color just for her. When her mom popped into town, they'd lived in a series of one-bedroom apartments in neighborhoods near the port—not always the most kid-friendly places in Miami. It was a relief to be dropped off at Grams' when Mom's job took her away for long stretches, and Riley cried every time Mom picked her up when the cruise finished. "You'll be back soon enough," Grams said each time they said goodbye, and she'd been right.

Mom moved up at the cruise line, assigned to lengthier charters and adventure cruises until it wasn't uncommon for her to be gone for six or eight weeks at a time. Grams and the other residents at the Dorothy welcomed Riley and made her feel like part of a large, loving family. Now the Dorothy was Riley's home, too, and her job was to make sure that all those who'd helped her through her childhood and rocky teens were safe and happy. Really, she was simply returning the favor.

Inside, LouLou panted with excitement as they neared the elevator. Riley wished there was something in her life she loved as much as her poodle loved a ride on the elevator. The car shook on its slow ascent; a lesser dog might be afraid of the movement, the noise. Not LouLou. Her tail never stopped wagging. As soon as the doors rumbled open, LouLou dashed inside, tugging Riley along. The building was only a two-story, but the elevator took its job seriously, stretching out the ride so that it felt as if more than a mere one floor of distance had been covered.

At the ding, LouLou was as excited to exit the elevator as she'd been to enter it. Dogs. Riley knew she should be taking life lessons from her pooch about the importance of living in the moment, but it was hard to shake off the feeling that she should be doing something different. Something more. She just didn't know what. Or how on Earth she'd ever make time for more, whatever that might be.

"Ah, my favorite girls are here!" Mr. Cardoza opened his door before Riley had a chance to knock. A proud "eighty-five and still alive," as he liked to say, Mr. Cardoza cut a dapper figure in his tailored chinos and navy suspenders. His thick head of gray hair and status as a longtime widower made him the most sought-after of the silver foxes in the building. His refrigerator was always stuffed with offerings from the female residents of the Dorothy—casseroles and lasagnas, homemade pies and mango preserves. He should be thirty pounds overweight, but his strict regimen of daily walks and trips to his senior-friendly gym kept him fit.

"What can we do for you today?" Riley kissed both his cheeks with genuine affection. When she was fourteen and going to her first high school dance, he'd driven her in his old Saab and explained in excruciating and embarrassing—at least back then—detail how a young man should act around her. And exactly what she should not allow, on or off the dance floor. Thanks to his thoroughness, she'd been perfectly happy to dance with a group of her girlfriends and sit out the slow dances.

Riley cocked her head at the familiar grinding sound coming from his kitchen. "Is it that new garbage disposal? I told you to stop jamming chicken bones down there."

"The ad said it could grind anything." He tucked her hand into his elbow and escorted her to the kitchen, LouLou trotting behind them, her fluffy ears brushing Riley's calves. "Anything."

"Anything but chicken bones. As we've discussed. Many times." Riley unclipped the leash, and LouLou promptly nosed around the kitchen, finding bits of who-knew-what in the hard-to-clean space between the floor and cabinet lip. "Alright, Mr. Cardoza, let's take a look, and if it's chicken bones again, I'm leaving you to fend for yourself. Also as we've discussed. Many times."

Mr. Cardoza nodded solemnly and slipped LouLou a sliver of chicken from a plate of already precut-to-poodle-size bites. "You won't leave before you let me make you my famous café solo?"

So it was chicken bones. Again. But pass up his hand-ground dark-roast coffee? Riley placed a hand to her chest. "Never!"

She opened the cabinet under the sink and pulled out the flashlight and pliers she'd bought especially for Mr. Cardoza's apartment. It was both her nature and her Donovan hotel training to anticipate guests' needs, and she'd known from the first call from Mr. Cardoza about his unauthorized garbage disposal that she'd be back again and again. Easier to keep supplies here than to haul them back and forth on the daily. She looked over to where Mr. Cardoza sat, LouLou in his lap taking bites of chicken from his fingers. *The things I do for caffeine. And chicken. And Mr. Cardoza.*

Riley's butt buzzed again, and she grabbed the phone. Grams' Google wouldn't Google. Riley shoved the phone back in her pocket and flipped off the power to the garbage disposal. It was going to be a long day, but what else was new?

At least the long hours of her job kept her from thinking too much about her life, but sometimes in the wee hours of the morning, with antiseptic and Band-Aids freshly applied to whatever scrapes and cuts she'd acquired during the day's maintenance challenges, she did worry. Was her blazerless status at the Dorothy her whole future? Would she be patching stucco and unclogging drains for decades to come?

When she thought of her careful plans so carelessly

destroyed, she could cry. Did cry. But crying never changed anything. She firmed her chin, got hold of a semicrushed chicken bone, and yanked it out of the drain. The bone popped out with a slurp and a cheer from Mr. Cardoza. Riley turned to give him a thumbs-up before diving in for the next one. For now, it was enough to be needed.

# CHAPTER 2

"You've got to be kidding me." Caleb Donovan checked his phone for the address, hoping it was a mistake. This couldn't be the property Grandpa William thought was the answer to their problems. But no, 1651 was definitely it. The Art Deco façade, once painted in a Miami Beach palette of pastel pinks and oranges, had long since faded. Latex strips hung like old palm fronds in need of trimming. Sagging gutters promised roof problems, and the overgrown crown-of-thorns shrubs flanking the entrance threatened to jab someone in the eye with their spiky branches.

Grandpa William had said "quaint." He'd said "charming." He'd said "original period details." Caleb should've known real estate code for *money pit* when Grandpa William first said "fresh start," something Caleb could really use after the chaotic, life-altering disappointments of the last two years but seriously doubted this old apartment complex could provide.

But he was here. Might as well take a look, even if Grandpa William's plan was half-baked and, well, surprisingly sentimental. The surprise wasn't that Grandpa William wanted to rebuild the family business but that his plan apparently also included rebuilding the family. Or at least the part of the family currently not serving time for fraud, embezzlement, and a slew of other state and federal crimes.

Caleb slammed the door of his carmine Porsche Boxster, then immediately patted the door handle apologetically. In the left-behind neighborhood not far enough south to be part of the upscale South Beach scene but not north enough to technically be part of North Beach, either, the Boxster was distinctly out of place on a block full of aged Volvos and family-oriented SUVs.

A coconut fell from a curbside palm tree, bouncing off the Porsche's front bumper with a loud *thump*.

"Son of a—" Caleb kicked the coconut into the street and inspected the bumper and front grill. No visual damage. No chipped paint. He ran a hand over the area to be double sure then glared up at the offending palms when he felt the slightest indentation above the bumper. A half-dozen lawsuits-waiting-to-happen hung high above the sidewalk, ready to attack a vehicle or a litigious neighbor out for a power walk.

Wasn't there supposed to be some kind of manager on-site? Someone making sure the coco palms were trimmed regularly so that innocent bystanders weren't thunked on the head by coconut bombs? Of course, it'd be terrible if someone were hurt—he'd read somewhere that falling coconuts killed more people than sharks—but at the very least, the manager should make sure the building wasn't liable for injuries and damages.

Caleb thumbed through the notes on his phone until he found the name. Riley Carson. Hired a year and a half ago. His trained-from-the-cradle real estate developer's eye took in the three boarded-over windows on the front of the old apartment complex, two stories high, and the peeling paint on the portico's stepped columns. So far, not so good.

This Carson guy might think he could get away with collecting a paycheck from Grandpa William for doing nothing, but Caleb wouldn't let anyone take advantage of his grandfather, not on his watch, and especially not now that he feared Grandpa William was growing soft—definitely in the emotions, but maybe it was impacting his business sense, too. With Caleb's parents on frequent, prolonged business trips and his two older brothers striking out on their own, cutting ties with their father before Caleb was even in high school, Grandpa William was the one person he could count on.

Although the past two years had made Caleb question a lot of things about what it meant to be a Donovan, his love for his grandfather never wavered. The very least Caleb could do while scoping out Grandpa William's claim that the crumbling apartment complex had "unlimited potential" as a condo conversion was to put the fear of God—or at least a fear of the Donovans—into this do-nothing building manager.

Caleb strode toward the double front doors, cutting across the front lawn that was more sand than grass. Okay, he admitted to seeing some potential. Install a bit of lush landscaping—a bougainvillea or two and a handful of traveler's palms—and the curb appeal would improve one thousand percent. Above the arched front door, the name Dorothy stood out in relief, a pale reminder of how many buildings from the era were named after women. Original details, indeed.

"Well, Dorothy, I can't say it's a pleasure to meet you." Caleb stopped at the call box that was easily as old as he was and punched in the code Grandpa William'd given him. The box wheezed and the door locks clicked, but when he pulled on the handle, it didn't open.

Fantastic. Not only did the place need a serious make-over, but the technology was both outdated and inoperable. He knew from viewing dozens of foreclosed properties that the possibilities for disaster were endless. But this wasn't a foreclosure. It was Grandpa William's secret weapon, a property his grandfather had separated from the company holdings before the authorities confiscated all of Donovan Real Estate Group's assets.

*"One property at a time,"* Grandpa William had said last night over drinks on his deck overlooking the Intracoastal Waterway. *"That's how you build a solid business."* Caleb had bought into the fantasy that he'd somehow restore the family name and bank accounts.

Now, Caleb wondered if he was being naive. He'd only done one thing in his life—follow in his father's business footsteps. For good or for bad, real estate development, especially in the hospitality industry, was his specialty. Hotels, casinos, time-shares—that was the world he knew, and the one his father so carelessly lost with his less-than-legal approach to dealing with city officials and the IRS. Residential real estate wasn't Caleb's thing.

But things could change, even his things. They had to. Since the trial and his father's subsequent conviction, he couldn't rely on his father's example anymore. Robert Donovan wasn't the respected and powerful businessman he'd portrayed himself to be. He was a criminal. Caleb hadn't believed it at first, not at the indictment, not at the beginning of the trial. Seeing was believing, though, and as the prosecution slowly and methodically convinced the jury of Robert's guilt, Caleb became convinced, too, and he'd lain awake many nights after, cursing himself for his gullibility. His blind faith.

He should've seen the fall coming, should've listened to his brothers' numerous warnings over the years. But he hadn't, and he'd lost the business right along with his father. Caleb fingered the metal key chain in the pocket of his pressed trousers, the keys his grandfather had tenderly handed over.

*"Lots of good memories in that building."* Grandpa William wasn't usually nostalgic, but he had a distinct gleam of tears in his sharp blue eyes. *"Never could part with it. Figured I'd go back someday and make something of it. Now it's your turn, Caleb. Rebuild. Make the family whole again."*

Grandpa William's plan included Caleb's half brothers and Caleb convincing them to work on this project with him for the good of the family. The family they'd wanted so little to do with that Knox joined the Marine Corps as soon as he was legally old enough to sign the paperwork himself, and Lance started his own construction company, refusing any jobs their father tried to send his way.

Somehow, though, Grandpa William had faith in Caleb, that he could do this. Rehab a building, reel his brothers back in, take the nightmare of the past few years, and turn it into some kind of American Dream fairy tale. It was unrealistic; Caleb had thought so when Grandpa William spelled out his terms, but now, looking at the run-down Dorothy, he wondered if it was downright delusional.

When Caleb's father had argued that Caleb didn't need college, that he could learn everything he needed on the job, it was Grandpa William who'd paid Caleb's college expenses. Grandpa William who showed up at parents' weekend, helped him deck out his dorm room, and was the only family member at his graduation. At the very least, Caleb owed him a walk-through.

He used the key to open the front door and stepped into the lobby. Original terrazzo floors, pockmarked and stained, would need to be restored. Rattan furniture circa 1970-something would have to be replaced and, judging by the mold growing on the cushions, possibly torched. He checked his phone again. The manager's apartment number was 101. Mr. Carson was about to get an earful, for sure. Or maybe Caleb would simply fire him with no explanation. Florida was an at-will employment state, after all, and Mr. Carson shouldn't need to be told that he was seriously derelict in his duties.

Caleb was about to take the right hallway, following the placard's directions that apartments 101 to 108 were to the east, when straight ahead, a single elevator dinged. An older woman, white-haired and thin, pushed herself forward on a cheery yellow walker. She angled her path toward the five-foot-high bank of mailboxes against the lobby's south wall. She wobbled as she walked, and when she held out the mailbox key, her hand wobbled, too. Wobbled so much the key shook right out of her hand and hit the floor. He rushed to her side, bending to pick up the key.

"Here you go, ma'am." Caleb pressed it into her palm, glad that Grandpa William, though well into his seventies, was in good health. There'd been a scare a few years ago, right at the start of the legal troubles, but he'd pulled through. He walked with a cane—an intimidating hand-carved contraption with a silver handle specially molded to his hand and engraved with his initials—but he was still as headstrong and opinionated as ever. "Slippery things, those keys."

The woman exhaled a labored breath, and for the first

time, he saw the clear tubes snaking from her nose to a small oxygen tank mounted on her walker. "Aren't you the gallant one? Thank you, young man."

"No problem. You take care now." It didn't surprise him that a woman of her age lived in such a run-down building. It was a sad truth that those on limited retirement incomes often couldn't afford any better. A rush of gratitude flooded him. Thank goodness Grandpa William separated his personal holdings from the Donovan business when he did so he could keep the home he'd custom-built over twenty years ago.

A high-pitched yip brought Caleb's attention back to the elevator—not a cute Deco-style box with brass trim that would make a great selling point but a clunky 1970s-era contraption that, no surprise, clearly needed updating. A tiny dog, some color between orange and pink, dashed out of the ancient elevator before the doors stuttered to a close. The fuzz ball, no taller than eleven or twelve inches, turned dark eyes up to him and let out a soft woof.

"Ma'am?" Caleb called, and when the woman didn't turn around, he tried again, louder. "Ma'am? Your dog?"

"That's not my dog." She angled her walker back toward the elevator, a few envelopes in her left hand. Her shoulders sloped dramatically in her faded housedress, and she leaned more heavily on the right side than the left. "Never had a dog. I'm a cat person myself. How about you, young man?" Even her smile was a bit crooked.

"I don't have any pets." Caleb slid his hands into his dark trouser pockets and rocked on his heels. "Never have. At least, not of my own."

"Isn't that a shame." She shuffled a few steps forward

before resting again. "Everyone needs a little unconditional love in their lives, don't you think?"

Caleb straightened, her words hitting him almost as hard as Grandpa William's *"You owe it to your family to try."* He cleared his throat before saying, "I thought cats were too independent for that kind of sentiment."

She blinked rheumy eyes at him. "No one loves more fiercely than an independent creature. It's too bad you don't know that yet."

Caleb didn't know what to say so he stuck with a safe "Yes, ma'am," and she made a humming sound of agreement before continuing her slow progress toward the elevator.

Something soft and damp nuzzled against the tips of his fingers. He looked down and found the fluff ball gazing up at him with a clear—though to him, unreadable—plea. Guessing, he scratched behind her soft ears. She stood on her hind legs, placed her front paws on his thighs, and bounced. Mr. Pom-Pom—hey, he didn't name his mother's Pomeranian—used a similar move when he wanted to be picked up, so Caleb crouched down and scooped up the poodle. Her little heart beat fast against his hand, and her soft, springy fur curled around his fingers.

"LouLou!"

Caleb heard the frantic voice seconds before the stairwell door slammed open, and a young woman emerged, blond ponytail collapsing, sending wild curls springing every which way. She was tall, leggy, and long, with brown eyes that dominated her round face.

"Patty, have you seen my LouLou?" Barefoot, the blond rushed toward the woman with the walker. "I was just leaving Grams' when the elevator dinged. You know how she is about the elevator."

Patty smiled her crooked smile, scrunching up the wrinkles around her eyes. "She rode down with me. Such a sweet girl. You know I always enjoy her company, but right now, she's enjoying someone else's."

"What do you—" The blond's eyes caught on Caleb's dark-brown Gucci loafers and traveled up his legs until they landed on her dog. Her brows pulled together, and she angled her face up, one hand to the base of her throat. "What're you doing?"

Caleb wasn't sure if the question was for him or the dog. Patty shuffled back to the elevator, leaving him alone with the poodle and her short-shorts-wearing owner. Suntanned legs and delicate bare feet with hot-pink nail polish. He'd never considered himself the type to have a foot fetish, but the flip-flop tan across the top of her foot was definitely turning him on—making him wonder what other tan lines she might have. But he was here for business, and he never let anything get in the way of business. Time to hand over the dog and be on his way to find and fire Mr. Carson.

He hesitated, though, strangely reluctant to let go of the dog or the view of that flip-flop tan line. LouLou's warm body grew heavy, so he shifted the poodle into a more comfortable position and scratched under her chin. "LouLou's a cute name. How old is she?"

"She's a rescue so we're not completely sure. The vet guessed around eight or nine years old." Riley's back pocket buzzed. She pulled out her phone, frowned at it, swiped, and tucked it away again. "Should've named her FloJo, though."

"Is that a rapper name or something?" Caleb continued

to pet LouLou, but apparently he wasn't doing it exactly right. The poodle maneuvered her head so he could get behind her jaw.

"FloJo? Florence Griffith Joyner, the fastest woman of all time?" The woman laughed, a light and airy sound that hit him like a shot of his favorite sipping rum—straight to the gut. "My girl here loves to run. A bit too much, I'm afraid."

"She's a getaway artist, huh?" He didn't usually chat up residents of buildings he was scoping out, but he was curious about her and her dog. When was the last time he'd been curious about anything? Anyone? When the judge's gavel came down and his father's sentence was announced, Caleb's whole world had turned upside down. He'd been scrambling for so long to put things to rights that he'd forgotten what it was like to simply be, to have a conversation with a stranger for no other reason than she and her little dog interested him. The gentle smile he'd given the woman with the walker spread to a full-out grin. "An escapee? A dog dodger?"

She laughed again. "Indeed she is. Luckily, everyone in the building knows her. She rarely gets far."

"This building?" Caleb didn't care for the sound of that. Pets could do a lot of damage in a small space, especially in a situation where all the units were rentals. Owners fixed up their places before selling, but renters moved on. "I thought no pets were allowed."

The blond flushed, turning almost as pink as the polish on her nails. "That's what the lease says, for sure, but you can, you know, get special permission from the manager. In special circumstances. That are, you know, special."

So pet damages were another thing Carson would have

to answer for. The list of grievances grew by the second, and Caleb felt even more justified in his decision to fire the guy as soon as possible. But none of it was this woman's fault.

"She seems like a special dog." A special dog who didn't live here. The woman was visiting; she'd said as much. Maybe her Grams had a cat or something. That was why she'd been flustered. Didn't want to rat out her own Grams. He roughed the poodle's fur and widened his smile.

She smiled back, and it did weird things to him, narrowing his focus until all he could see was her. The wide lips, the way her eyes tilted at the corners, the color still staining her cheeks. Would she say yes if he suggested a coffee date? Drinks? Dinner? Her left hand darted up to tuck one of those wild curls behind her ear. No ring. What was her name? That was what he should ask first. *Say something, say something.* But nothing came out, and the silence grew longer and more difficult to break.

She licked her lips, drew in a deep breath. Maybe she'd ask his name. Ask him out. The dog squirmed in his arms as if even she knew someone needed to break the awkwardness.

"Come on, LouLou. Let's go." The woman reached for her dog.

Caleb knew he should hand her over, but then LouLou turned her head so he could dig in behind her ears, which he did. She grunted a doggy sigh of satisfaction and angled her head, encouraging him to scratch the other side.

"I'm sorry." The woman sighed, too, so forcefully that a curl bounced on her cheek. "It's a bit embarrassing how shameless she is. Her first owner must've been very affectionate. She's sweet and well socialized. I can't imagine anyone giving her up. But they did. In the cruelest way. People are terrible sometimes, you know?"

"They certainly are." Caleb flashed to his last visit with his dad, separated by a pane of glass, surrounded by other inmates and vigilant guards. "Even people you think you know."

Her surprised eyes locked with his. "Isn't that the truth? Luckily, dogs are good through and through. All the way to the bone, you could say."

Her optimistic words washed over him, soothing the tightness in his neck that never quite went away. The lilt of her accent sounded local but more musical than that of a typical South Floridian. She settled a hand on the dog's back, just below the hot-pink collar. Their hands were an inch apart, then half an inch when she slipped her fingers under the band to give a good scratch. The poodle's fluffy tail thumped double time against his arm.

What would it be like if he moved his hand that small distance to touch her? Although he kept up the steady pressure under LouLou's ear, his mind wandered to how the woman's skin would feel. As warm and soft as it looked? He was holding his hand very, very still, careful of her space, careful not to spook her, when Riley's finger slipped from under the pink collar and brushed against his.

*Contact.* Pinkie finger to pinkie finger. Accidental? Or had she wondered, too, what it would feel like? It was like he'd imagined, only better. Warmer. Softer. Both of them stopped petting the dog. He stared at their fingers. She stared at their fingers.

He wanted to slide his hand until it covered hers, but

that wasn't like him. He didn't touch women he just met, no matter how soft the skin or how good they smelled. Was it strawberries? Something fruity filled his nostrils, and he inhaled deeply, reminding himself that he didn't do random hookups like his father. He was sensible in his romantic life, dating women with similar interests and incomes so they were always on a level playing field. But he also couldn't move his hand.

She didn't move either, not toward him or away. Then her fingers curled in LouLou's hair, and when they uncurled, she'd put a few breaths of space between them. He itched to close the gap and feel her skin again. *Inappropriate*, he scolded himself. *You're not some kind of caveman who can't control his urges.* But he felt like one.

Then he felt something else. The frantic wiggle of a dog with a mission. He'd been around Mr. Pom-Pom enough to recognize the signs, so he crouched down to let LouLou go off to do her doggy business. She didn't go far, though, before copping a squat.

"Oh no! Oh my gosh." The woman pulled at his arm, and he let her drag him away from the scene of the dog crime. "Oh, I'm sorry. Really, really sorry. No wonder she beelined for the elevator before I could get her leash on. Hang on, I'll be right back."

She dashed next to the elevator where, like many Miami Beach buildings that boasted a common-area lobby, a door displayed the stick figures universally signaling a public restroom.

Soon, she was back, miles of paper towels heaped in her hands and trailing behind her. "The lobby restroom's mostly used during the holiday party in December and sometimes by the mail carrier. Oh, and that time Rhonda in 202 forced some questionable sausage on the cutie-pie UPS guy when he delivered her new shower seat. It's usually not a high traffic area, but I will definitely need to restock the paper products after today."

She tore off a few feet of paper towels and handed them to him, then stooped to drop some on the floor, still chattering in what was apparently a nervous habit. He found himself leaning toward her, the sound of her voice, waiting for the next syllable to fall from those berry lips. About a public restroom. Good Lord, what was wrong with him, waiting to hear more about delivery folks with intestinal distress and paper-restocking protocols?

"She's really a very good dog." The woman gave him another wad of towels, although he wasn't sure what she expected him to do with them. She swiped more around on the floor with her bare feet. "We were at Grams' longer than usual, and we were on our way back to the dog park when she ran for that stupid elevator." Swipe, swipe. She pressed more towels, and more words, on him. "And she is getting older. It's hard to find homes for older dogs, you know? I couldn't take her to a shelter, not knowing what might happen. That's how I ended up with her."

"I'm sorry I waylaid her." He finally found his voice, although it didn't sound much like him. Rusty, croaky. He cleared his throat and tried again. "It's okay. These things happen."

She nodded so vigorously that more hair flipped out of her ponytail to wave wildly around her face. "Sadly, they happen pretty often with her. At home, she has her pads and the patio, but there are still accidents." She stopped wiping the floor for a moment to inspect him from head to toe. "Sorry about the shoes."

Shoes? He looked down. Sure enough, they'd taken a bit of spray.

Her bottom lip shifted back and forth as though she were chewing on the inside of it. "I can have them cleaned for you? Do dry cleaners even take shoes? I'm not sure. Maybe it's easier to give you money for a new pair? What do you prefer?"

Prefer? He'd prefer that she stop throwing paper towels at him and look him in the eye. Her raggedy cutoffs, her Grams living in this old building. She didn't need the extra expense of designer shoes.

He didn't have to force his smile. "I said it's okay. It was an accident."

She fluttered her hands at him, up and down. "There must be something I can do."

"Have dinner with me."

He got his wish. Her eyes flew to his and locked there. Shocked.

She squashed the last clean paper towel in a tight ball and let it fall. From the waist up, she was motionless, but her toes tap-tapped a nervous beat. "You don't even know my name. I don't know yours."

"That's easy to fix. What's your name?"

She shot out a hand to shake his. "I'm Riley, Riley Carson. And you are?"

He didn't take her hand. He couldn't. "I'm here to fire you."

# ACKNOWLEDGMENTS

A heartfelt thank you to my husband, Michael Crumpton, who puts up with a lot so I can do this thing. Thank you for the love and support.

For help with research, I am indebted to Damian Carlin, Ben Cook, and Amanda Thibodeau. Any mistakes are mine, but I swear I was listening.

I am grateful to my beta readers, Jenny Luper and Joyce Sweeney, super stars who keep me on my toes!

Thank you to my writing friends who take the time to listen, advise, and understand: Kait Ballenger, Laurie Calkhoven, Alex Flinn, Stacie Ramey, and Katy Yocom.

Alison Morris, thank you for helping me figure it out. I wouldn't have gotten this far without you.

Nicole Resciniti, agent extraordinaire, I am so grateful for all you do.

Again, I must thank Kay Rico Coffee for the neighborhood vibe, tasty treats, the couch, and the support. To Brian Acebo, who introduced me to the drink that has become my writing staple, and to Alesandi Sanchez, who keeps the dirty chais with oatmilk coming—you are baristas without compare. Thank you to Dan, Tim, Liz, and JR for the best launch party ever!

And of course, it's all possible because of the Sourcebooks Team, especially my editor Deb Werksman, and the amazing folks behind the scenes who make everything happen: Dawn Adams, Sabrina Baskey, Susie Benton, Diane Dannenfeldt, Rachel Gilmer, Stefani Sloma, Jessica Smith, Sierra Stovall, Katie Stutz, Jocelyn Travis, and Cari Zwolinski. Thank you!

# ABOUT THE AUTHOR

© Michael Crumpton

Mara Wells loves stories, especially stories with kissing. She lives in Hollywood, Florida, with her family and two rescue dogs: a poodle mix named Houdini Beauregarde and Sheba Reba Rita Peanut, a Chihuahua mix. To find out more, you can sign up for her newsletter at marawellsauthor.com.